GETAWAY DEATH

LILY ROCK MYSTERY BOOK ONE

BONNIE HARDY

PROLOGUE

Overheard in Lily Rock

"I love the town of Lily Rock. Their lies are so authentic."

Fog rolled over the mountain road. Despite the poor visibility, the woman drove as if her life depended upon it.

A sharp curve to the right—her squealing tires issued a warning.

Tentatively removing one hand from the steering wheel, she kept her eyes on the road, her fingers reaching down for her windshield wipers. *Swish.* The blade on the glass moved to the left, then the right. Her gaze remained fixed on the road in front of her. Reaching over the steering wheel, she swiped with her hand at the thick condensation blocking her view from inside the car.

Veering into the next curve, she felt her stomach lurch. Brakes squealed again as the car catapulted into an unexpected second hairpin turn. Her head lolled to the right. As she came out of the curve, she pushed the button on the foggy driver's side door and rolled down the window, revealing clouds of fog.

1

Another vehicle rumbled behind her car, close to her bumper.

"I guess somebody's in a big hurry," she snapped to the empty car.

The window slid shut as she looked out of the front windshield to the right, then the left. No turnout lane yet. Tightness stiffened her neck as her hands began to shake on the wheel. *Stop tailgating me. Please.*

She felt the tires slip on the road, the car floating for a moment. As she slammed on the brakes, her body heaved against the seat belt, her neck and head rocking forward then back. Her stomach came up to her throat.

As her car skidded toward the cliff, she only had one thought:

I finally know how I will die.

CHAPTER ONE

Overheard in Lily Rock

"I'm not going to talk to anyone. I didn't come here to make friends."

"You sound like a girl on The Bachelor.*"*

Her eyes fluttered open. "Ouch." She touched her palm to her forehead. The deployed airbag held her body snugly against the seat, though her arms felt sore where she'd shielded her face at the time of the crash.

Reaching to release her seat belt, she noticed she couldn't get out on her side; the door was crushed inward, almost touching her. She stared out of the passenger window. Her heart beat wildly. From where she sat, there was a steep cliff on the other side of the door, but there was no other way to escape. Was that ... had she just felt the car move a little? *I'd better get out of this car right away!* Nervously jerking her body around she froze. *Better move slowly. I may pass out.*

She hit the side of the passenger door with her fist. Placing both hands against the paneling she shoved, and as the door gradually opened she froze again. *My purse. Where is my—* She touched the strap over her shoulder. Her small bag still clung to her body, having survived the crash intact.

Bracing herself with a hand on the side of the car, she wedged her body to the outside, where a small amount of ground waited to catch her. The area might have been big enough to hold a few people, but it was far too small for her liking. A wave of nausea overtook her. Bending over she nearly vomited but stopped suddenly, hearing rustling overhead. She looked up toward the main road.

A tall man with dark hair peered down at her. He hollered, "Are you okay?"

She blinked away her fuzzy vision, as her knees trembled. Standing up from her crouched position she rocked back and forth on both feet until her stomach stopped lurching.

Unable to talk, she watched the man scramble down the berm, his boots slipping on the dirt and rocks. He came to a halt in front of her with a concerned look in his eyes. He offered her a hand.

"I thought you were dead," he explained, pulling her a few steps farther away from the car. "You went over the cliff right in front of my eyes." Seeing her confused face, he put both hands on her shoulders. "Your pupils are dilated. Are you feeling dizzy?"

She steadied herself by locking both knees to stop them from shaking. "The last thing I remember is the car free-falling."

"You most likely thought you'd end up at the bottom of the canyon. From the road, no one can see the shelf under the bank. It looks like a steep drop-off, but it's just a couple of feet over the edge. You were very lucky."

"If you say so." Her tone was soft and pained.

His voice lowered. "I don't think your car fared as well. You didn't answer me. Are you feeling dizzy?"

"I am kind of wobbly and I have a headache," she admitted, holding her palm against the bump on her forehead.

The man's voice turned all business. "We'll have to call a towing service. It can take time for them to get to this neck of the woods."

His eyes looked back toward her Ford Focus, taking in the smashed windshield and crushed driver's side door, where she'd hit a tree on the way over the berm.

As he inspected her face more closely, his chin jutted forward. "If I knew you better I'd lecture you on driving mountain roads in the fog. Do you have your vehicle registration? The tow guys will want to see that, along with your proof of insurance."

She pointed toward her car. "The registration is in my glove box, but you shouldn't go in there either, unless you want the ride of a lifetime down the cliff." She shrugged out of his grasp, testing her wobbly knees.

"My name is Olivia, Olivia Greer," she said, taking a closer look at her rescuer. He stood over six feet tall, a worn plaid shirt hugging his strong arms, tapering to his jeans.

He smiled. "Nice to meet you, Olivia Greer."

Before she could ask his name, a sharp pain stabbed her head, accompanied by another round of dizziness.

Unable to speak, she felt her chin droop toward her chest. He lunged forward to take her elbow before she fell to the dirt. "Let me help you," he suggested.

Olivia shook her head. "I've got this. I'm fine now. The first responders will be here soon. You did call them, right?"

"How about I help you find a safe place to sit down over by my truck." His firm voice made arguing impossible. She only needed to glance back at her car to realize she needed to get to higher ground. *I could have died. One more inch ...*

He reached into his back pocket. "Before we hike up the

5

cliff, here's your cell phone. It must have fallen out of your pocket. Do you want to make the phone calls?"

Instead of taking the phone, she rubbed her forehead to clear her disconnected thinking.

"Since you know my name, could I ask yours?"

She felt his hand on her shoulder. "I think you may have a concussion. Do you feel kind of fuzzy?" Dark eyes stared into her face.

"So you're not going to tell me your name?"

"It's Michael—Mike. You'll be okay."

Shoving past her initial distrust of strangers, she remembered her better manners. "Thanks, Michael. I can't imagine what I would have done without you." How close she'd come to death ... Her eyes filled with tears.

"Take my hand. We're going to head up this cliff toward my truck so that I can give you a place to sit. At least you'll be safe." Without waiting for her permission, Michael took Olivia's arm. "One step at a time," he cautioned, as if speaking to a child.

He half-dragged and half-lifted Olivia up the steep berm. As she swayed from foot to foot, he placed his hands on her shoulders. "Don't close your eyes," he warned. "You'll find your balance. I've got you."

"You said you have a truck?" Olivia asked as her head cleared again.

"Right over there," he pointed.

Olivia's eyes narrowed when she saw his vehicle. "You're the one," she muttered. "You were the guy tailgating me up the hill!"

"If you mean I'm the one who saved you from death, then yes, I am the one."

"You didn't save me. You pushed me over the cliff. The

closer you got to my bumper, the more anxious I felt. I tried to drive slower so that you'd back off. You nearly killed me."

Michael ducked his head. "I guess you could see it that way. I was concerned about you, that's all. Your driving was erratic for this road, in these conditions. I wanted to help you out if you needed it, not make you afraid."

Olivia swallowed her anger. "I don't need any more of your help. Thanks a lot." She looked back over her shoulder. "The towing service can get my vehicle registration. I can handle things from here."

At the sound of a honk, Olivia looked down the main road. Traffic had lined up bumper-to-bumper as drivers gawked at the tall man and the small woman arguing with each other.

A green Chevy pickup executed a quick left turn, gravel spraying behind the wheels. A man stuck his head out of the window. "Need any help?" he hollered. "You got things covered, Mike?"

Olivia responded first. "I do need help. Would you take me into town? Ouch," she cried, rubbing her hand against her head again.

"I can take you to the doc in town," Michael offered.

She stood on wobbly legs, determined to stand on her own. Turning her around to face him, he said, "I am going to lift you into the cab of my truck and I don't want any back talk. You can thank me later."

With effortless strength, he hoisted her over his body like a sack of potatoes. A few long strides later, he placed her in the front seat. He waited until a faint smile came to her lips.

"Very noble of you, I must say," Olivia muttered. Feeling self-conscious, she ran her fingers through close-cut brown hair. One long strand hung over her right eye, and she pushed it aside.

He smiled gently. "I would call 911, but in Lily Rock we rarely get assistance from the police unless there's a dead body involved—too small a town. So I'd appreciate it if I could drive you. Since it's all my fault, I'd like to make a police report and take you to the doctor to have you checked out. Would you let me do that?"

The hopeful look on his face brought a gentle smile to her lips. She dismissed the possibility that he'd deliberately driven her off the road to steal her car or her money or her person. She didn't trust him, but she was in no position to refuse his offer.

"Do you need any more help?" hollered the man again from the green pickup. He'd watched the entire interaction between Michael and Olivia.

Olivia felt Michael move closer to the passenger side door in a protective way. He waited for Olivia to make up her mind.

Looking from one man to the other, she considered her options. *I can let the Mike guy drive me, but I'm not sure I trust him.* She touched her head, quickly deciding.

Raising her voice to be heard over the traffic, she shouted to the man in the green pickup. "Thanks, but I'll drive with Michael. Appreciate your offer."

He leaned farther out of the window. "I'm Arlo. Just ask around. Everybody in town knows me. Come on in for a beer on the house when you're feeling better." He steered his truck onto the highway, merging with the slower traffic.

Olivia watched him drive away. "Beer?" She turned to Mike.

"He's the owner and manager of our local brew pub. He's used to pretty women paying attention to him. Just so you know? Never cross the local bartender. Words of wisdom from my father."

The words sounded familiar, like an old television western she used to watch with her mother when she was very small.

Michael shrugged. She realized he was a man of short sentences, which implied deeper meaning. Since she did not ask about his father, he stepped toward his truck to close the passenger door.

"We'd better get going. No one is showing up to help you out. Things must be busy in town, what with the fog and the tourists. I think some ice applied to your head may stop the swelling."

He shut her door and hopped in on his side. As Michael eased into oncoming traffic, she leaned against the passenger window to place her throbbing forehead on the cold glass. Her eyes drooped shut.

The turn signal clicked. Then his voice said, "Fog's lifted. We'll be in town just short of twenty minutes."

Her head swirled as the truck picked up speed.

"How long—"

"It's only fifteen minutes more. We're ahead of the worst congestion." Michael navigated the sharp curve in the road, as Olivia's stomach tightened.

"You live up here?" she asked. "You seem to know the roads."

He answered her question with another question. "You are just visiting?"

"I am visiting for the first time—a friend." She wondered why she bothered to answer his questions—him a stranger and all. *As usual I'm being too friendly.* She clamped her jaw shut.

"A friend?" He waited for her to fill in more information. When she failed to add details, he pointed to a sign stretching across the street. "We're here. Welcome to Lily Rock."

"I saw the sign," she said. "*Welcome to Lily Rock.* Some

9

welcome. I almost get killed being shoved off a cliff. I may turn around and go home today."

"You mean," he corrected, "you almost got killed due to the fact that you didn't know how to drive in the mountains in the fog. You had your headlights on."

"Of course I had my headlights on. I couldn't see!" Olivia kept her eyes closed as she huddled into the passenger-side door. "Where are you taking me?"

"Instead of driving to the emergency care down the hill, which is a longer distance, I can take you to our local guy who provides health care in the village. I think he can take care of your head. He's an MD."

"I guess that works. What happened to the cops, anyway?"

Mike sighed. "This is a small town. Most of our responders are volunteer. It takes the sheriff at least twenty minutes to pick up a call and then another hour to find someone up here to show up. You've probably never lived in a small town."

Against her better judgment, Olivia corrected his assumption. "I have lived in a small town. Playa del Rey."

He nodded. "Oh, I know Playa. But honey, it is not small. It's a suburb of Los Angeles and has five times the population of Lily Rock. You may think it's small, but compared to what?"

"Since I am the one who lives there, I can call Playa small. Instead of correcting me, why don't you just drop me off at the doctor's?"

Rich laughter filled the truck cab. Michael shook his head.

Once in town he found an empty parking space. "Here we are. I'll walk you in."

"That will not be necessary." She unlocked the passenger-side door, sliding both legs over the running board to the pavement beneath. Her body followed, crumpling to the ground.

Michael sprinted around the back of the truck. He didn't catch her this time, but he did hover over her limp frame. Before he could lift her to her feet, a voice interrupted.

"Who do you have there, Michael?"

"I found her in a ditch on Route 63. She may have a concussion." Bending over Olivia's body, he touched her wrist for a pulse. Then he reached to brush the strand of hair from her face. Her eyes popped open.

"Oh no, you don't," she mumbled. "I've got this. You do not need to carry me again."

He lowered his voice to whisper in her ear. "You may not remember this later, but I'm just telling you, it is my absolute pleasure to carry you anywhere." Standing at his full height, he looked over to the woman who glanced at them from the sidewalk.

Michael said, "Skye, help me out here. I'll call the doc if you will stay with Olivia."

"Olivia? You're on a first-name basis?" Skye smirked.

"She's dangerously close to passing out again," he added impatiently.

Skye stepped from the wooden walkway to look down at Olivia. "She's very pretty, if you like skinny girls."

"I can hear you, and I'm not skinny. I have an athletic build. Do we have to talk about this now? My head hurts!"

Skye and Michael both laughed. Skye shoved Michael's shoulder. "Okay, Boy Scout, you can go now. I'll make sure Olivia gets the care she needs. Is she visiting for the weekend?"

Mike looked down at Olivia and then back to Skye. "I'll let her tell you why she's here. She's done talking to me—at least for now."

Skye reached out with both hands to Olivia. "Grab on, honey. We'll get you inside. Don't blame you for cutting him off. He's very nosey and too opinionated, if you ask anyone in town."

Olivia grasped both of the woman's outstretched hands. Pushing with her legs, she rose to a standing position, her head spinning with the effort. The tall woman's arm reached around her shoulders.

"I've got you. Let's walk right into that door over there, and I'll summon the doc. We'll have you fixed up in a jiffy."

The two women hobbled away.

CHAPTER TWO

Overheard in Lily Rock
"You need to learn to relax."
*"I'm not sure I can relax—it's the tension that keeps me
together."*

Gray eyebrows lifted as a man stared into her pupils.

Olivia blinked. "Where am I?"

"You are currently in the doctor's office in Lily Rock. I'm
Callahan May." He used one finger to painfully explore the
open wound on her forehead. "Who are you?"

Olivia dipped her chin as he pulled back his hand. When
she didn't answer his question, he repeated, "Would you mind
telling me who you are?"

She closed her eyes, willing her thoughts to make words.
Finally she replied, "I am Olivia Greer."

"Don't stop there. Tell me more. How old are you? Where
are you coming from? What brings you all the way up the hill
to Lily Rock?"

The doctor's warm voice felt inviting, like a father would
sound—if only she had one of her own. Olivia began telling

the doctor her story. "I'm thirty-four years old, and I live in Playa del Rey. I am here to visit my friend Marla Osbourne—"

The doctor reached for a pad of paper and a pencil. "Marla's your friend? Did she invite you to visit, or are you just dropping in?"

"Of course she invited me! I don't make it a habit to surprise people by arriving unannounced on their doorstep."

The doctor smiled. "Well, let me beg to differ. You sure did drop in on me unannounced. I only wondered if that is your habit with other people."

Olivia chuckled. "Well, Doc, I guess you are right. I did drop in on you."

The old man's face softened. He placed the pad of paper on the edge of his desk, then turned to continue his examination. First he listened to her heart with his stethoscope before he looked deeply into her eyes again.

"Olivia, I think you may have a concussion, and I'd like to check that out, with your permission. Do you have any health insurance that I can bill?"

Her smile faded. "I do not have a policy. I'm in between companies right now."

"Do you want to say more about that?" inquired the doctor with a gruff voice.

"No, I don't. I'll get a new policy. I have to wait for an enrollment period."

In an instant—and completely unwelcome—Olivia remembered that conversation with her ex.

"You can't afford anything without me. You don't even have health insurance. Stuck with me, right, baby? To the bitter end."

She wished she could forget.

The doctor shrugged. "Frankly, I don't think you will need the insurance. Just take it easy and stop in tomorrow. I'll be able to assess your symptoms and let you know then. You seem like a strong, healthy young woman to me. I think a couple of stitches on your head now and some rest may be all that's necessary."

Olivia ran her hand through her short hair. "But I've been going in and out of consciousness. I don't remember how I got to your office, for example."

"We can talk about that later." He turned on his heel, leaving the room, closing the door behind him.

Olivia sighed. She liked how carefully he paid attention to her. The only male attention she'd had growing up was from her mother's friends. She had imagined a father of her own, gruff and smart, how he might have been, had he not died before she was born.

As she glanced around the consulting room, her focus stopped on a photo of a large dog. Curly chocolate-brown fur covered the face and body of the dog, who smiled at the camera. Under the photo a sign read, *Mayor Maguire*.

"Hey there, doggy," Olivia said aloud. A knock on the door and a vaguely familiar woman bustled into the room.

"Hello, dear. I'm here to get something for the doctor. He will be back shortly."

Olivia admired the white nurse's cap perched on top of the woman's head. Her starched blouse crackled as she lifted her arm to push aside a stray hair, which had escaped from the bun at the back of her neck. Pinning the curl next to her scalp with a bobby pin, she looked across the room.

The woman's white Oxford shoes squished across the linoleum floor as she came closer to Olivia.

"Do I know you?" Olivia asked.

"Oh yes, dear. When Michael brought you to us, you were a bit confused. My name is Skye Jones. I work for Dr. May. I'm his receptionist and his nurse."

"You are both?"

"Most of us have more than one job here in Lily Rock. At least, those of us who have lived here for ages. We call ourselves the Old Rockers." The woman chuckled.

Olivia watched Skye unlock a cabinet. After swinging the door open, she inspected each bottle on the shelves. Then she closed the cupboard, locking it with a key that hung from a lanyard around her neck.

Exploring her forehead with the tip of her finger, Olivia winced as the pain from her injury shot down the left side of her face.

Skye's sharp voice corrected Olivia. "No touching until the doctor has stitched that up. Let me have a look." The woman took a step toward her, extending cold hands to inspect the head wound. "No glass shards. Looks clean. I suppose Michael must have tidied you up with a first aid kit." Olivia heard a harshness come over the nurse's voice.

"I don't remember the exact details," admitted Olivia. "It may have been Michael."

Skye frowned. "You don't remember? There are many women in this town who find Michael irresistible. They would love to be rescued by the likes of him."

Not wanting to be caught lusting after the local ladies' man, Olivia looked down at her lap. The woman lingered in the room, adjusting a photo on the wall behind the door.

Was Skye waiting for the doctor to return or did she wanted to advise her further? Skye turned to face her.

"You're Marla's friend?"

How does she already know I'm Marla's friend?

Skye Jones's lips pursed. She held her hand over her mouth, then with a quick adjustment, a smile replaced her grimace. "I only asked since Marla is new here. She's had a few run-ins with the Old Rockers; she's not one of us. If you know what I mean ...

Unable to focus on the nuance of the woman's remark, Olivia closed her eyes, hoping Skye would stop asking her questions. *Make her go away.*

Another knock on the door caused Olivia's head to throb. Her eyes opened again, this time wide with anxiety.

Skye stepped backward, making way for the doctor. He carried a black kit in one hand. "I'm ready to stitch if you are. But let's start with a little numbing first."

Knowing she'd feel less pain if she thought about something other than a long, sharp needle coming toward her forehead, Olivia pointed to the wall. "What's up with the dog?"

The doctor arranged his instruments without speaking. He pulled a syringe from a drawer in the cabinet by the sink. "Not my dog. At least, he isn't at the present time. He resides with Meadow McCloud. She handles all of his appearances and mayoral duties."

"Don't tell me that dog is really your mayor. What kind of a town is this?"

The doctor applied the anesthetic, which smelled sharply of rubbing alcohol. Working as he spoke, the doctor continued to explain. "He is our mayor. I think we're a pretty good town, and we'd appreciate it if you'd just go along with our ways since you're a visitor."

Olivia winced as the needle pricked her forehead.

"Don't move now, girly. I've got a couple of stitches to finish, and with a little time you'll be as good as new." He patted her shoulder with his free hand.

Then he added, "Not to change the subject, but what happened to your car? Do you need help towing it back into town?"

"I forgot about my car." Olivia watched closely as the doctor slid the empty syringe onto the counter. Taking in his compact frame and white hair, she assumed he must be in his late sixties.

Threading a surgical needle with a steady hand, considering his age, the doctor turned back toward her. "No worries. When I'm done here I can contact my nephew at the garage. He'll arrange to pick up your vehicle. You do have car insurance, right?"

"Oh, I do have car insurance. My Ford is old but reliable. At least, she has been in the past."

The doctor put aside his instruments and cleaned the surface of the small cart. "Well, little lady, won't be long until you are as good as new." His head lolled to one side as he inspected his handiwork.

The doctor continued, "My nephew, Brad, will handle the details of the repairs, and if you give me a contact number, I'll have him call you in an hour or so."

"That would be amazing." Olivia slipped gingerly from the examination table to the floor. Her knees wobbled, but she stayed on her feet. "How much do I owe you, Dr. May?"

A gnarled finger reached toward her as he gently lifted her chin. He smiled as he looked directly into her eyes. As quickly as he grasped her chin, he dropped his hand. "You remind me of someone," he commented softly. "Someone I knew back in the day."

"Everyone says that," she replied. "I always remind someone of their long-lost sister or auntie. It must be my average face."

"Nothing average about that face, dear girl. You are beautiful. You just don't know it."

Olivia felt heat rise up her cheeks. Apparently feeling embarrassed did not go away with a minor head injury. She liked the doc.

He opened the door and, with a sweep of his arm, gestured for her to leave. "Check in tomorrow about the bill and the test results. I think you can go ahead and get some sleep. If you have trouble with anxiety from the accident we can talk about it then. I am the local doctor and apothecary; I can prescribe some herbs or oils for relaxation."

Resisting an urge to kiss his cheek on the way out of the door, Olivia exited the office, colliding with Skye Jones in the hallway. She stood right outside the door, holding a vape. Strawberry scent wafted in the hallway. "So sorry," the nurse mumbled.

The doctor called after Olivia. "Do you need help finding Marla's place? Without a car, you may need a lift. She's way up the hill, on the left-hand side, back from the dirt road."

"Don't worry, Dr. May. I'll call Marla on my cell and explain. I think she can pick me up, or one of her people can."

In the reception room of the doctor's office, Olivia dug into her purse for her cell phone. She held it in her palm, her mind flashing on the image of a man with a cheeky smile. He wore a plaid flannel shirt. Her memory clicked into place.

"I do remember now," she yelled in the direction of the doctor. "I remember the guy named Michael. He rescued me from my car and then drove me into town."

She heard the doctor chuckle from down the hall. "Most women in town don't forget Mike that easily. I'm happy you remembered him on your own. Michael dropped you with us, but it was Skye who brought you into my office."

Olivia poked her head back around the corner and grinned at the doctor. He had another question. "If you don't mind me asking, how do you know Marla? You don't exactly seem to be her type."

"We were friends in high school. She connected with me

on Facebook a year ago and then decided to invite me up here. That's how it all happened."

He blinked. "Well, Little Bit, take it easy with Marla. She has some issues, you know. She has her share of enemies on the hill. I'm just saying."

"It may not surprise you to know that Marla had a lot of enemies in high school. She rubbed people the wrong way," Olivia said.

Dr. May looked up at the popcorn ceiling. "The last time she was in here, she had her share of complaints. But I'm not supposed to talk about that—you know, doctor-patient confidentiality and all."

Olivia turned her shoulder toward the exit. "Thanks again. I'll be back tomorrow with money."

A bell over the door rang as Olivia walked outside. Despite the jab of pain in her head, she welcomed the sunshine. Stepping back into a shadow of the building, she paused to blink and adjust her eyes.

After a brief search in her purse, she lifted a worn pair of sunglasses. The second dive into her handbag revealed her cell phone. She scrolled through her recent calls for Marla's name and tapped on it to phone her.

"This is Marla. Leave a message."

Apparently Marla was not at home. *What do I do now? Maybe Marla forgot I was coming this weekend.*

A sign swung in the wind, colliding against the wood building. The sign was labeled *Apothecary* and pointed to the doctor's office. Another sign, labeled *Library*, was chained underneath. Both were printed in bold italic letters.

I'll see if the library has any information on lodging. Olivia willed her wobbly legs to move forward. Each step brought a dizzy twinge to her head, but she pushed on anyway. She slowly made her way to the library entrance, where the doors swung open in front of her.

"Welcome to the Lily Rock Library," greeted a woman who stood behind the desk. She wore a denim jumper over a neatly ironed long-sleeved white cotton shirt. The sleeves stretched over her slightly chubby arms; the cuffs barely covered her plump wrists.

Gray-streaked hair, pulled back into a messy bun, was held by a scrunchy. The librarian's smile felt genuine.

"Hello," Olivia said, walking toward the desk. "I've just come from the doctor."

"What did you think of old Cal? Did he fix you up?" The librarian's eyes drifted up to the stitches on Olivia's forehead.

Olivia steadied herself on the library counter with both hands. Before she could answer, a small boy interrupted. "Can I check this out?"

The librarian leaned over the counter. "Right over there, honey. I keep telling you to go right to the computer. You can check the book out all by yourself."

Olivia noted the well-worn volume held in his small hand. "He's reading *Lassie*? Does anyone read dog stories these days?"

"Kids read about dogs if they live in Lily Rock. Oh, they also read *Harry Potter*, but the old books have a certain following too."

Olivia smiled. "The doctor took an X-ray, and he stitched up my head. I'm feeling a bit better. Since my car is broken, I think I need a ride to my friend's house."

"Who might that be?" she asked, collecting a returned book from a woman with a small child.

"I've got it, Suzanne. No charge," she told the mother.

Olivia glanced around. The smell of old books reminded

her of her childhood in Playa. She'd spent days reading in an overstuffed chair located behind the mystery section.

"I like the Lily Rock Library. Where I come from, they shut down our local branch. Now a van rolls into our neighborhood once a week. I tried visiting the downtown Los Angeles library, but I don't feel as comfortable there. At least the homeless found a place to rest for the day."

"We like everything old-school here in Lily Rock, including our library. More books than computers is my motto. So far no one has objected, especially since I now handle Mayor Maguire." *Ah, so this woman must be Meadow.*

Olivia laughed aloud. "I saw his photo on the doc's wall. He's a Labrador?"

"He's not just a Labrador," she explained in a voice librarians used when they had information to share. "Mayor Maguire is a labradoodle. His poodle part shows up in the curly hair. His curious part is the Labrador. And then there's another side that we can't quite explain. He's psychic."

"No way." Olivia's incredulous tone brought a smile to Meadow's face.

"Yes way! Speaking of way, I'll be done here in ten minutes, and I can swing by your friend's house to drop you off."

"The doc said she lived up the hill, off a dirt road. Are you certain you're up for that?"

Meadow's eyes narrowed. She directed a black stare at Olivia. "Is Marla Osbourne your friend? She's the only one I know who lives up there."

Dizziness overtook Olivia again. After a deep breath, she nodded toward Meadow. The mood had shifted in an instant, from trust to fear at the mention of Marla's name.

"The doc didn't seem that fond of Marla either. She just got back in touch with me recently. We were—"

Meadow turned her back to walk into the inner librarian's office. She returned with a worn handbag clutched under her arm. "No worries. Let's go. I told my associate to lock up."

Olivia followed Meadow out the back door, toward the library parking lot. Taking small steps for balance, she arrived by the time Meadow had turned on the ignition of her old Toyota pickup.

Meadow's withdrawal at the mention of Marla's name felt like a beesting to her already hurting body. At first Olivia had warmed to Meadow's gentle presence, but now she realized Meadow had only offered to drop her off so that she could get away quickly.

Neither woman spoke as the truck made its way up the hill. This time Olivia fought the urge to close her eyes. She forced herself to focus on the curves in the road to stay alert.

When they reached the dirt road, Meadow shifted gears.

"I can walk the rest of the way, if it would be easier for you," suggested Olivia.

"Oh, I don't mind taking you all the way, especially since you have stitches in your head. Did Marla tell you about her place?"

"She told me that she'd bought a large piece of land, and then months later that she'd built a cabin on the property, with a view of Lily Rock from her master bedroom."

The front tires hit a pothole.

"Sorry about that," Meadow mumbled. "Not much longer until we get to Marla's place. I wouldn't exactly call it a cabin. More like a mansion for these parts. Just wait until you see."

The road rolled hypnotically in front of the car. As Meadow turned the next sharp corner, Olivia gasped.

A tall three-story structure made from redwood and glass stood on the hillside, surrounded by trees. A glare of sunshine streamed off the front of the house. Meadow reached for her visor.

"See what I mean? The place is mostly glass—very modern for these parts. Not my idea of a cabin."

Olivia agreed with Meadow. The architecture of the home did contrast sharply with the folksy Lily Rock setting. The quaint cabins they had passed on the main road looked nothing like Marla's place. Shading her eyes, Olivia glanced up to see smoke rising over the top of the house, wafting into the surrounding forest.

"I guess she's home. I see smoke coming from the chimney. Maybe she didn't hear her phone when it rang."

Meadow pulled the car into the circular driveway. Cedar and redwood trees shaded the front of the house. "Well, dear, here you are." She stopped the car in front of the steps, which led to the massive wooden doors.

"Do you want to come inside?" Olivia half hoped that Meadow would accompany her when she greeted Marla for the first time. Nervous tension tightened her stomach.

"Not today. I have to get home to feed the mayor. Come by the library any time. I'll see you then." The barrier between them was gone with Meadow's kind smile. Her warm voice had returned.

Stepping quickly from the truck, Olivia waved at Meadow. She heard the Toyota's bumper thump against the potholes.

Something flickered in her peripheral vision. Olivia turned around, expecting to see Marla emerge from the front door. No one appeared.

Taking care to keep her balance, Olivia stepped toward the front of the house.

Before knocking, she glanced up at the corner over the

entry. A small camera light flashed. *I wonder if Marla is watching me?*

When no one answered her knock, Olivia pushed the doorbell, which rang two solid tones. She waited. Still no sign of her old friend.

CHAPTER THREE

Overheard in Lily Rock

"You know, here in Lily Rock the billionaires are kicking out the millionaires."

Olivia knocked on the solid-wood door once again. She rang the doorbell. Still no response. For an instant she second-guessed herself. *Did Marla invite me for today, or did I get the date wrong?*

Stepping back from the front entrance, Olivia looked up. Smoke still puffed from the chimney. Her eyes traveled down the wood siding, where pine-tree boughs bounced against the upper-story windows of the glass exterior. *It must cost a fortune to heat and cool this place.*

Placing both of her palms against her temples, she pushed into her skull, hoping to calm her nerves and the dizziness she'd experienced since her near scrape with death.

When Marla still didn't appear, she considered her options. *I might as well look around. Maybe she's out back doing some work.* A smile crossed her face. *Someone may be doing work, but it won't be Marla—not now that she has the cash to hire people since her divorce.*

Olivia carefully walked away from the entry to the house. She checked in with her body. The dizziness and accompanying nausea felt less intense. *When did I last eat? Must have been before the drive up the mountain. Maybe Marla will have lunch for me.*

A single bead of perspiration dripped down Olivia's spine as she directed her gaze to the expanse of glass that wrapped around the corner. Holding her hands next to her face to shut out the glare, Olivia peered into the interior like one would do at the reptile enclosure at a zoo.

What if she doesn't recognize me and thinks I am an intruder? I hope she doesn't call the cops.

Olivia took in the corner room's interior. An enormous bed made from roughhewn timber filled one entire wall. Artwork covered the space across from the bed. Two massive barn-style interior doors remained open, exposing a spa-like dressing room that Olivia assumed led to the bath and toilet area.

After careful scrutiny, she concluded that the rumpled bed was empty. Unable to see Marla, Olivia removed her hands from the sides of her face. She continued her search, walking around the side of the house. Trees lined the pathway, which led to an expanse of forest beyond the home. *Marla may be doing errands in town. She may have forgotten to take her cell phone. Surely she'll be back soon. Or she may be behind the house. I'll wander around to see if I can find her.*

Feeling more confident, Olivia inhaled deeply, welcoming the scent of damp earth and pine. She noticed a cordoned-off area surrounded by a picket fence. Over the gate a sign read *Herb Garden.*

When did Marla become a gardener? Olivia could not

think of a less likely occupation for her friend, who was not known for her appreciation of freshly grown herbs.

She ambled down the main path, opening the gate to the garden. Raised beds displayed kitchen herbs, neatly labeled. Rosemary grew low to the ground next to a leafy plant that Olivia could not identify. *Maybe marijuana,* she thought. *You never know.*

Olivia remembered smoking weed with Marla in high school. They'd hidden behind Marla's house to do it. They bonded as girls with single mothers and absent fathers.

A gate stood on the side of the prolific herb garden, directly opposite the entrance. Olivia opened the latch to step through. She held her breath, taking in the wildness of the forest.

To her surprise, a hot tingle ran up her spine. She gasped, standing still on the path before turning her head to look right then left.

A towering giant sequoia stood some two hundred feet ahead. *That must be an old one,* she thought. She looked up at the wide expanse of the trunk and the blue sky beyond. *At least eighty feet high.*

Feeling drawn to the big tree, Olivia walked forward. Another ripple of hot anxiety rolled down her spine. *Maybe I'm not alone?*

She inhaled deeply. Turning abruptly, she called out pretending to be confident, "Is anyone there?" Only the rustle of tree branches answered, along with the caw of a crow that flew overhead. She watched as the bird drifted from another tall tree over to the top of the giant sequoia's uppermost branch.

Olivia continued to walk forward, feeling a connection to the tree, as if she had been beckoned by an unknown primal presence. Then she stopped again. *Is that a whimper?*

Listening more carefully, she heard a soft moan. "Marla," she called out.

Breaking into a jog, it only took seconds for Olivia to stand directly underneath the giant sequoia. She glanced around again but saw no one. Then she listened. A rustle from behind the tree startled her. Holding her breath, she stood rigidly straight, quiet and waiting.

"Who's there?" she asked again in her strongest voice.

A dog with deep-black eyes peeked around the trunk of the sequoia and stared at Olivia with a piercing gaze. Her heart pounded. Olivia stepped back, her hands trembling.

The furry-headed dog moved forward, coming out from behind the tree trunk. It stood still and then looked in her direction. Olivia smiled tentatively.

Holding her silence, she waited. When the dog made no movement forward, she unclenched her hands and cleared her throat again. *Wait a minute, I know that dog ...*

"Well hello, Mayor Maguire," she called to the labradoodle. "You are much more handsome in person than in your photo at the doc's."

The dog's tail wagged, then he cautiously took a few steps closer to Olivia. When he reached her knees, he obediently sat at her feet, looking up into her face.

She smiled down at him, lifting her right hand to hold under his chin for sniffing. Mayor Maguire bobbed his cold nose on her palm. Inching her hand upward, Olivia scratched his soft, curly neck, her fingers moving to the side and digging slightly behind his right ear.

"What brings you to this part of the woods?" asked Olivia, adding, "To scare the bejeezus out of me?"

Satisfied, the dog disconnected from her fingers. He took one more look at Olivia before walking closer to the giant sequoia. Then he stopped to glance back in her direction.

"You want me to follow?" asked Olivia.

When she didn't move toward him right away, Mayor Maguire circled around her back before sitting. The dog looked up at Olivia as he waited.

"Okay. Let's go, doggy. Show me what you've got."

Together they strode forward. Mayor Maguire remained close to her left knee. To test him, Olivia stopped. The mayor also halted then sat.

"You're well-trained," she told him with a pat on his curly head. Again she took a step forward toward the base of the sequoia. He followed, his nose right behind her knee.

Olivia stopped again. This time Mayor Maguire broke rank to approach the tree, disappearing around the trunk until she could no longer see him. In minutes he returned from the distant side to sit down in the loamy soil in front of Olivia. He stared at her, willing her to understand.

She felt his beckoning, along with rolling, hot anxiety that moved down her spine. Stepping toward the dog, Olivia lost her balance. Dropping to the earth, she felt her head rumble, then heard a click.

Consciousness came back slowly. Unsure how long she'd been lying facedown in the dirt, she opened her eyes. After a moment of disconnect, Olivia felt Mayor Maguire's cold nose sniff her ear. She reached up to reassure him. "I'm okay, big dog. I'm just a little clumsy since my accident. You've probably heard all about it since you're psychic, right?"

Olivia's eyes closed as the now-familiar blackness swirled around her head. She waited to lose consciousness. Instead her head twinged. *I guess I am done passing out for now.*

Stretching out her legs she felt a sharp pain in her lower back. With eyes fully open, she looked around, wondering how she'd lost her balance. Then she knew. Beside her body her leg brushed against a thick branch. *That's what tripped me.*

Olivia heaved herself to her feet, turning to face the tree.

Bending over to examine the dirt where she'd fallen, her throat closed to stifle a scream.

Not a branch but a human arm had tripped her. The fingers of the hand were partially exposed, each nail covered in bright pink polish. Her eyes took in the arm and finally a body, turned over on its side, covering the identity of the corpse.

Olivia already knew who lay under the giant sequoia. She picked up Marla's hand and then dropped it, her heart pounding against her chest.

Brushing aside the dirt and pine needles, Olivia ignored her own pain to kneel over the body and peer at the face. Her friend Marla hadn't changed that much over the years.

Olivia screamed, the loud wail echoing through the forest. Tears streaming, she reached over to touch her friend's cheek.

Marla Osbourne lay dead in the forest, stone cold gone.

* * *

Nausea rolled up to the back of Olivia's throat. Struggling to stand, she stepped away from the body. *I have to call the police.* She found her purse in the dirt, where she'd first fallen.

Olivia grasped her cell phone. She punched in 911, hastily walking away from Marla's body toward the house.

"I've found a dead body," Olivia reported to the voice who answered. "Come quick. I'm in the town of Lily Rock, near the top of the mountain. There's only one giant sequoia. Here's the address."

"Your name?" asked a disinterested voice on the other end of the line.

"My name is Olivia Greer, and this is the address: 945 Mesquite Mesa. It's the closest to Lily Rock Mountain. You can't miss it. I'm in the back—in the forest," she repeated.

"Your name?" inquired the voice.

"Olivia," she shouted for the second time. As she clicked off, another voice startled her.

"Olivia Greer, we meet again. Only this time in the forest!" Michael joked.

"It's you!"

Before she could say more, he strode toward her, placing his hands on her shoulders. "You're all dirty. Have you fallen again?"

"Take a look!" Olivia pointed to the giant sequoia. Michael followed her gesture, walking around the tree. She inhaled a deep breath as he disappeared into the forest. When she didn't hear his voice, Olivia followed Michael and discovered him leaning over the corpse of Marla Osbourne, wiping tears from his eyes.

"It's Marla. She's dead!" Olivia's voice quivered. "I can't believe I found her like this."

Michael looked over his shoulder, wiping his sleeve across his eyes.

"I am so sorry, Olivia. This is just awful. I don't know what to say. I have no words. Did you get a chance to call 911? Are you okay?"

He seemed quite emotional. I wonder what Marla meant to him?

Michael rested his hand against the trunk of the tree. "This isn't my first rodeo with a dead body."

"So are you a cop?"

Michael's face fell. He folded his arms over his chest. "Not exactly. I help out when I can. You are a difficult one, aren't you? It's been two times in one day that I've found you in trouble."

Olivia ducked her head. All the fear and pain and the rawness of her day erupted at once. No longer able to hold back her feelings, she burst into tears. Her sobs echoed throughout the forest.

Michael stepped toward her, his arms reaching around her body. He pulled her into an embrace. "I'm so sorry. You've had a very bad day."

She cried even more, hiding her head in the soft flannel of his shirt. Olivia's body shook with sobs while Michael just held her, saying nothing. After a few minutes, she sniffed, rubbing her hand across her wet face. As her tears subsided, she pulled back from his arms.

He smiled at her. "Do you think you can stand on your own? How is the head, by the way?"

Olivia nodded touching her finger to the recent stitches.

Michael held up his finger, listening. A siren wailed in the distance. "I'd say they're five minutes out and will be here shortly. I suggest you brush yourself off and dry your eyes. The day just got a whole lot more complicated for the both of us."

Olivia looked in the direction of the dead body. "And Mayor Maguire. Where did he go?"

Michael's brown eyes widened. "Mayor Maguire? How do you know about him? I don't see a dog anywhere!"

"I saw his photo on Doc's wall. He told me about the Lily Rock mayor. I recognized him right away."

A group of three uniformed officers appeared around the corner of the house. Michael smiled at her first, then he moved toward the officers, reaching out his hand. "Good to see you, Walt. You too Sam."

"Hey, Mike. You on the scene already?"

A female officer stood quietly by the two men. She didn't offer a hand as the first officer had done. She held open her arms and walked right into Mike's bear-hug embrace.

"Good to see you, Janis," Michael mumbled loud enough for Olivia to hear, before he ducked his head into her shoulder.

Olivia's stomach lurched again, this time not from hunger.

After a longer-than-necessary hug, the female officer dropped her arms to her sides to speak. "Well, Mikey, I see you've found another emergency situation. Who's this, then?" She gestured toward Olivia.

"This is Olivia Greer. She's had a bit of trouble today, beginning with that incident on the way up the hill on the 64."

Janis looked Olivia up and down, her eyebrows raised. "She's the one who fell over the cliff and landed in the ditch? She's pretty lucky, if you ask me. Any other curve on that mountain would have flung her to the bottom of the canyon. Yet she picked the only one without a steep drop on the entire way up."

Olivia's face registered alarm. *Why do I feel like she's blaming me for the accident? It's not like I planned to kill myself on their precious highway to hell. This place may sound simple—Lily Rock—but the longer I stay the more I want to get away.*

The female officer reached into her back pocket to pull out an electronic tablet. She walked toward Olivia. Her partner Walt circled the body of the late Marla Osbourne. The other officer disappeared into the forest.

"You can interview the lady now," stated Walt. "I'll call the doc."

"Sure, I will interview Ms. Olivia Greer. That's your name, right?"

Olivia took a gulp of air into her lungs. She'd been breathing shallowly since finding the body, but she did not want to feel faint during the interview.

"Hey, Janis? Why don't you take Olivia into the house?" said Michael.

"I would if I had a key," replied the policewoman.

"I have one. Right here." From his pocket Michael pulled out a key, which he handed to Janis.

She looked him over closely before saying, "Sure you do. Why am I not surprised?"

She gestured to Olivia. "Follow me, Ms. Greer. Let's talk while we walk to the house. Did I hear you say Mayor Maguire found you by the body?"

Olivia shrugged. "When I was looking around for Marla in the forest, he led me to her body. Took me right here. I stumbled and fell into her corpse. Then he left."

Janis turned her face sharply toward Olivia. "So the mayor and Michael were here with you when you found the body, right?"

Olivia shook her head. "Oh, no. Michael didn't show up until later."

The cop took Michael's key to unlock the massive door. Stepping aside, Janis watched Olivia's expression as she walked into the room.

Olivia gasped, "This is incredible."

"So you've never been here before?" asked Janis.

"No. Never. Marla described the home she was building, but she never sent photos, nor did I have any idea that it was so majestic."

"Then you didn't know Michael before either?"

Now Olivia glared at the policewoman. "Why would you assume I knew Michael before? I just met him today. He stopped to help me out on the highway."

"Now don't get your tail in a knot. Michael built this place. He's the architect and the general contractor. That's why he has all those keys. Between us, he says he's gonna give them over, but I don't think that's ever gonna happen. He's too in love with his own creation." The officer shrugged.

Olivia felt a settling in her gut. So she'd been right all along. Michael wasn't a guy who happened past her car accident. He was a solid Lily Rock citizen with deep pockets.

Janis walked further into the great room. Olivia followed, glancing from the floor to the ceiling, where the windows looked out on a one-hundred-eighty-degree view of a white mountain beyond.

"That's Lily Rock," explained Janis. "They named the town after the rock. You can see the whiteness. Reminds us of a lily."

"The flower everyone sends to funerals," Olivia remarked. Tears flowed down her face. *Will I be the one to organize Marla's funeral? Who else is left? Just me ...*

Janis nodded. "I suppose. But for now let's sit down. I have a few questions to ask you." She pulled out a chair from the massive dining table.

Olivia sat down, wincing as her back twinged. Janis seated herself across the table, holding her tablet with one hand. The compact policewoman leaned forward, her blue eyes unabashedly staring.

"Are you memorizing my face before you book me?" quipped Olivia, clenching her hands under the table.

"Instead of second-guessing my motives, why don't you begin by telling me how you know Marla Osbourne."

CHAPTER FOUR

Overheard in Lily Rock
"I'm gonna pray that everything that doesn't have our best intentions at heart be removed from our lives."
"Don't do that, I'll lose my boyfriend."

Olivia looked down at her folded hands, which rested on the table. Before she could ask for a drink of water, Janis supplied one, placing the glass on the table between them.

Sitting herself back down, Janis opened a black notebook that contained yellow legal paper and sharpened pencils. She selected a business card from a side pocket of her portfolio. "Here you go," she said, sliding it across the table toward Olivia.

A gulp of water helped clear Olivia's throat and her thoughts. "So your name is Janis Jets," she commented after glancing at the card. "Before I tell you about Marla, do I need a lawyer? Am I in trouble?"

Janis stared across the table into her face. "I don't know. Do you think you are in trouble?"

As she swallowed back her fear, Olivia's words stuck in

her throat. Her heart pounded. *I've been in a car accident, visited the doctor, met any number of odd people, and I've discovered a dead body who just so happens to be my friend.*

I didn't need to ask her. Even I know I must be in trouble.

Olivia wasn't certain how to proceed with the officer, who continued to stare at her as if she were the perfect piece of ripe fruit for the picking.

Officer Jets dropped her eyes to glance at her tablet. She typed a few words before she looked up. "You are not charged with any crime, so you really don't need a lawyer. From my perspective, you were in the wrong place at the right time. You can't take my perspective to court, but it's a small town. We play a little fast and loose, even in the constabulary. If we know people, we let the rules slide. People understand that life doesn't necessarily go as planned."

Jets continued, "On the one hand, a lawyer can be help-ful, but on the other hand, I think you are safe without coun-cil. Plus getting someone up here today would be difficult, and it would make you look more guilty." Janis Jets stared at Olivia, making her neck tingle with fear.

She swallowed. "Okay, I'll tell you about Marla. We were friends in high school. We took the bus together every morn-ing. Over time we became friends."

Pushing back her previous nausea, Olivia could almost forget the sight of her friend's face and the realization that she was dead. "Where is Marla, by the way? What did they do with her body?"

Her guilt burst through. *What if ... what if I had arrived earlier, like I was supposed to? If only I had not had that acci-dent coming up the hill, I might have prevented the death. If only—*

"Don't say a word, Olivia!" Pushing past the cop on duty,

a thin man sporting a trim beard barged into the house. He stopped to stare down the two women sitting at the table.

"No more questions until Olivia can get a lawyer," his crisp voice ordered, looking to Olivia for confirmation.

Now she recognized him. *He's the guy who drove by the accident and stopped to ask if I needed a ride into town. He owns the local pub. He told me his name.*

"You're Arlo, right?"

"That's me. I wondered if you would remember. Mike contacted me when the cops showed up." He shifted from foot to foot. "Sorry to hear about Marla. I have a law degree, so let me help you out here. You should postpone this conversation until you've at least gotten some rest. After all, this must be a pretty bad day for you, what with your accident and now Marla."

The Lily Rock grapevine strikes again. Do they text each other to spread rumors?

"I am feeling kind of woozy. I haven't eaten since early this morning, and my head—"

"Right, your head. I almost forgot." Arlo's eyes drifted to the recent stitches on her forehead. "The doc says hello, by the way. He wanted you to come back to his office early tomorrow so that he can check your head. On that note, Meadow says she has a bed for you all set up for tonight. You can stay as long as you want."

Olivia rubbed her tired eyes. *A village overrun with helpful citizens. I have a doctor, an attorney, and a librarian with a guest room. A cop wants to hear everything I have to say, and to top it all off? Some guy named Mike is stalking me, along with a psychic dog who just happens to be the mayor.*

Reaching for the water provided, she watched her hand shake. As she bent her head to get a sip, some water spilled on the table.

Arlo and Janis exchanged glances. Then Arlo spoke again.

"Even if Olivia said something incriminating already, you couldn't hold her to it, now could you, Janis? She's in no shape to make a statement with her head injury. Can it wait until tomorrow?"

Janis Jets pressed both hands on the tabletop. Her knuckles turned white. "On the one hand, I'd like to shove you right out the door, Arlo. Olivia and I were getting along just fine without your help. On the other hand," she paused to close her notebook and to shut down her tablet, "you are right. This conversation can wait until tomorrow."

She faced Olivia again with her direct glare. "Promise me you won't leave Lily Rock. That would look really suspicious. Why don't you stay here at Marla's? You were going to anyway. That way I can keep my eye on you."

Looking over Olivia's shoulder, Jets nodded to an officer standing by the door. "I got the go-ahead. The scene is clear, at least inside the house. Outside is a whole other story. Stay away from where you found the body, do you hear me?"

Before she could agree, Arlo tugged on the back of Olivia's chair, urging her to stand. Taking her by the elbow, he walked with her to the front door. He shouted over Olivia's head to Officer Jets, "Call me tomorrow if you want to talk to Olivia. When she's ready, we will both meet you at the constabulary or Frontier Town. Your choice."

"Frontier Town?" asked Olivia, following him out of the door.

"The next largest community off the hill. The county police station is located there."

"I see." But Olivia did not see. After walking out the door, she tripped on her way to Arlo's truck. She could barely hoist herself into the vintage pickup. After two tries she landed safely on the worn leather seat, then reached for a seat belt. None to be found.

Arlo jogged around the front of the truck, still talking as he sat himself behind the wheel. "The truck is really old. I have a lap belt. You can find the clasp down by the floor on the right-hand side."

Past crumpled papers and crumbs, Olivia located the belt. She pulled it out and then wrapped it around her middle. Arlo reached over her body to help her with the clasp. He clicked it into place before shoving his truck into gear, popping the clutch.

Yesterday I would not have made such a big deal about the seat belt, Olivia thought. *But that was before I nearly killed myself going over a cliff.* Her eyes closed, pushing back more nausea. Arlo drove over the curves on the mountain road, passing slower vehicles with the honk of his horn.

Without opening her eyes, she asked, "So are you some kind of town messenger guy who shows up unexpectedly?" She'd not hidden the sarcasm from her voice.

Rather than take offense, Arlo chose to ignore her tone. "I'm taking you to Meadow's cabin. You'll be warm and comfortable there. Do you have a suitcase?"

"I did," she admitted. "Probably still on the side of the road or in my wrecked car on Highway 64."

"I meant to tell you. Your car has been towed to Brad's Garage. He'll call Meadow tomorrow to get your phone number. He can fix anything. He'll give you a loaner for a couple of weeks."

Olivia's eyes flipped open. "I only plan to stay a weekend. A one-weekend getaway—that's what I planned for."

"It will take longer than that for you to recover from the head injury, plus you have some talking to do to the cops. Just so you know nearly everyone who is a current resident of

Lily Rock drove up for a weekend and ended up staying longer—some people for a lifetime. It's how things work here."

"Not for me," Olivia responded with as much confidence as she could muster. "I have a life in Playa. Or at least I did." The second sentence got lost in the front of her shirt as her chin slipped downward, her eyelids heavy.

The last conversation she'd had with Marla came to her mind. "Come to Lily Rock," Marla had begged. "You will find yourself here."

At the time Marla had sounded so positive. By the end of their conversation, persuaded by Marla's enthusiasm, Olivia had postponed a new job.

Marla had known that moving past the eight-year relationship with Don had not proved easy for Olivia. Her friend had been trying to help.

"Oh no you don't." Arlo reached over to lift her chin with his hand. "No falling asleep on me now. You really have to stay awake, at least until we get you to Meadow's."

Olivia kept her eyes closed, ignoring Arlo's hand. She exerted all of her energy to push back the dark cloud of unconsciousness that circled her head.

The ten minutes down Lily Rock Hill to Meadow's cabin felt like a lifetime. Arlo pulled into a driveway, his tires crunching along the gravel. "Here we are. And there's Meadow." Olivia opened her eyes to see the librarian walking toward the truck.

Arlo leaned over to release Olivia's seat belt. As it snapped back, Meadow cautiously opened the passenger door. "Oh, you poor dear. I am so sorry about Marla. Let me help you out of that seat. We can walk together."

Still wearing her denim jumper and white shirt, Meadow offered an arm to Olivia as they walked to the house. "I am so sorry to inconvenience you this way," Olivia told the older woman.

"Not an inconvenience. I am happy to be helpful and could use a bit of company. Now watch out for the cats. They get under your feet."

As Olivia entered the warm cabin, the smell of lavender enveloped her. When she inhaled deeply, her shoulders voluntarily relaxed. Looking around the cozy room, her eyes rested upon a familiar figure. Olivia smiled at Mayor Maguire. He looked past her, facing an empty metal food bowl.

"Hey doggy," she called to him softly. He turned his back to her, facing the other side of the bowl. Before Olivia could call him again, she heard a door slam from down the hall.

"Mom. I've got the suitcase from Brad for the crazy lady driver. It's here." A young woman entered the room and immediately stopped. Her cheeks grew red. "I am so sorry. I didn't know you were here already."

Olivia nodded. This must be Meadow's daughter. Though she didn't have the same body build, her voice rose and fell in a similar cadence. *She's around my age,* Olivia assumed.

Slim in distressed jeans, the young woman wore a sweater that fit snugly. Scuffed boots covered her trim calves. Her golden blond hair lay on her back, neatly braided. *She looks like she belongs,* thought Olivia. *A Lily Rock girl, born and bred.*

"To be honest, you aren't the first person to call me crazy. Just ask my ex." Olivia felt a surge of surprise—mostly at her own honesty. She'd made it a point not to talk about him since their breakup two months ago. Maybe these Lily Rock people had worn down her defenses already. Now she volunteered her business to them, like a sacrifice to the village gods to appease them.

The younger woman's smile turned her startling blue eyes up at the sides. "My name is Sage, by the way. Nice to finally meet you." She reached across her mother to shake Olivia's limp hand.

Sage grabbed the suitcase from the floor, lifting it easily to take down the hall. She opened a door and slid the suitcase inside a room, then she closed the door again.

"I've been hearing about you all day from one person or another. You made quite the impression on Mike. And then Arlo told me about the cop interview. It seems like you've been here forever."

"Enough of that, Sage," Meadow interrupted. "She's only staying for a short while. I want to show Olivia her room and get her acquainted with Mayor Maguire. But first I think Olivia could use a little sustenance. Am I right?"

Olivia nodded her head. Words escaped her, buried under the rubble of exhaustion.

Touching Olivia's elbow, Meadow ushered her through a doorway into the kitchen.

Olivia noticed the table first. Scratched and oiled, with a bench seat on one side and chairs on the other.

"Come sit down. I'll get you a calming tea. Or would you prefer something stronger?"

Alarm bells rang. "Tea is fine. I don't drink, you know, alcohol."

Meadow's eyebrows lifted as she turned to fill a kettle at the sink.

"You are not the only recovering alcoholic in these woods. Many of us have been down that path and found our way to sobriety."

Olivia's heart sank heavily. She'd confessed about her ex, and now she'd already told them about her problem with booze. The news would most certainly spread through the entire town of Lily Rock before she added honey to her first sip of tea.

Oh well, I won't be here for more than a couple of weeks, she reminded herself. *By then I'll be gone and no one will remember me. Back to Playa to pick up the pieces I've left, none the worse for wear. Time for my new life to begin. Sober and single.*

Olivia's hunger gnawed in her gut as Meadow placed the tea on the table. Reaching her hands around the mug, she appreciated the warmth traveling up her arms before taking her first sip. Chamomile and lavender wafted through her nostrils, along with another scent that smelled familiar. Once she started drinking the comforting tea, she couldn't stop, and she soon finished the mug.

Meadow placed an old chipped plate with a piece of lightly buttered toast in front of her. "That should help with the hunger," she commented. Lifting the empty mug from Olivia's hands, she refilled it to the brim.

Olivia munched her toast. When she tasted the last bite, she unconsciously swept the crumbs from the table, holding her hand under the edge to catch them. She shook out her palm over the chipped plate.

"My, my, you are a tidy one," Meadow commented, taking the plate from the table.

Olivia watched the woman, reminded of her own mother, who rarely sat down in the kitchen, so busy with small tasks. Olivia wanted to stand, but her legs felt rubbery. She hunched over her mug of tea as her head nodded, her eyes half shut.

"How about a warm bath?" murmured Meadow. "Or do you want more tea?"

Olivia did not answer. Aware of movement, she felt Meadow walking around the kitchen table. Inching her chair out, the older woman helped Olivia to her feet. With an arm under her shoulder, she guided Olivia away from the kitchen, toward the hallway.

"There are clean towels on the rack, and there's plenty of hot water. You can take a bath or a shower—whatever you'd prefer."

Olivia shut the bathroom door behind her. She reached for the toilet seat, sitting down slowly. Forcing herself to open her eyes, she noted a neatly appointed bathroom. The walls held a fresh coat of white paint, and the curtain, which wafted in the breeze, looked like it had been recently starched.

The smell of bleach filled her nostrils. "I like tidy," Olivia admitted to herself as she stood to strip off her clothing.

Pushing back the shower curtain, she turned on the tap. She eased the dial around, searching for more heat. As she stood under the stream, her shoulders relaxed and her knees wobbled.

Olivia discovered a homemade herbal shampoo on the windowsill. She squeezed a liberal amount into her palm, running the soap through her short-cropped hair.

Finally she stepped out of the shower to stand naked and dripping on the mat. *What do I wear?* she wondered. *I wish I'd thought of that before I got all wet.*

As if on cue, Meadow's hand appeared through a space in the slightly opened doorway. "I pulled out some yoga pants and a shirt from your belongings—along with clean underwear. I hope it's okay. I figured you'd want clean clothes." She tossed the clothes on the counter before withdrawing her arm and closing the door. *Not sure I like a strange woman rummaging through my belongings.*

Tears welled in Olivia's eyes. It felt so good to see the familiar items she'd packed only yesterday. *Maybe I've overreacted. Maybe it's okay to be taken care of by Meadow. My mom might have done the same in a similar circumstance—when she was alive.* She quickly dried off and started to dress.

"Time to get you to bed," she heard Meadow say from the other side of the closed door. "You can get some sleep, and then we'll talk when you awaken." Olivia opened the bathroom door, exposing the hallway. Meadow put her hand under Olivia's arm to escort her a few steps, into a room that smelled like lavender and sage.

Meadow pulled back the sheets and directed Olivia's body to the edge of the bed. Olivia plopped backward but struggled to get her legs onto the bed. Meadow lifted one of Olivia's legs, then the other, stretching them out on the smooth surface. As Olivia relaxed into the scent of a freshly laundered pillowcase, she felt a bolster pillow being nudged under her lower calves.

"This will support your lower back," Meadow told her, sounding more like a nurse than a librarian.

As the comforter fell gently over Olivia's body, she sensed Meadow's hand sweeping over the top of the covers, moving in opposite directions. "North, south, east, west," Meadow muttered under her breath. Olivia heard her deeply inhale, then exhale.

Now Meadow smoothed her hands over the comforter. When she reached Olivia's feet, she lifted her hands together in a ritualistic motion, taking another deep inhale and exhale.

The bedroom door closed quietly. Nestled in a sweet repose, Olivia felt sleep approach. Only a minute later, her eyes abruptly opened. She heard Meadow's voice from the hallway.

"I put the drops in her tea as you suggested. Added more herbs and three capsules of the other. She's asleep right now. Do what you need to do—she's out for the night."

CHAPTER FIVE

Overheard in Lily Rock

"What's your astrological sign? I need to know what kind of tea to brew."

The warmth of Saturday's sunshine poured into the room. Olivia opened her eyes, following a shaft of light above her head. Remembering her accident, she inched her hand out of the covers to gently explore the wound. "Ouch," she admitted to the empty room.

Raising herself on one elbow, she waited for the dizziness to return. After a deep sigh, she realized, *My head isn't spinning.* Now pushing against both elbows, she swung her legs over the side of the bed.

At the new elevation her head protested. *Thump, thump* in her right temple. Instead of immediately standing, Olivia looked over the bedroom. Her eyes settled on an open suitcase perched on a straight-backed chair in the corner of the room.

Standing up slowly, she paused for another head check. *At least no overall headache,* she admitted. Just a persistent throb at her temple. Her eyes moistened as the events of the past day tiptoed from memory into consciousness.

What about Marla? Poor, poor Marla.

With a deep sigh, Olivia tentatively stepped toward the mirror placed over an old oak dresser. Tousled brown hair poked up on her head, forming spikes. *I look like a porcupine.* She ran her fingers through the mess, remembering that she'd showered the night before. *I must have passed out right afterward.*

Her marine-blue eyes stared back from the mirror. *Eyes just like Mom's.* Since they were only seventeen years apart, people had often commented on their similarities, mistaking them for sisters. The stitches on her forehead stood out against her pale skin.

Olivia turned to push back the curtains. More sunlight filled the space. As she looked outside, the pine forest reminded her of people cued up, waiting for their coffee at a local shop.

Back at the mirror she inspected her face for more damage. Admiring her stitches, Olivia bumped into the bed. "Close quarters," she mumbled.

A rummage in her suitcase revealed a toothbrush and paste. She opened her bedroom door to look out into the hallway beyond.

"Hey," said a voice. Sage stood in the hallway, brushing her hair in long strokes. Olivia stared at her smooth movements. Sage tucked the brush into the back pocket of her jeans as she deftly braided the mass into a neat design, whipping a rubber band around the end.

"You're pretty good at that—the braiding," commented Olivia, gazing with fascination at the hair that lay in a tidy stream across her shoulder.

"I've gotten pretty good at it over the years. My mom taught me when I was small."

"Oh, that makes sense," commented Olivia. She pointed to the closed door in the hall. "That's the bathroom, right?" Olivia held up her toothbrush kit as if she needed to explain.

Sage smiled. "It sure is. When you're finished, meet me in the kitchen. I've got a pot of coffee and some time before I head off to work."

Olivia disappeared behind the bathroom door. After brushing her teeth and washing her face, she returned to her room to pull on rumpled jeans and a soft pullover. The blue color of the yarn matched her eyes. At least, that was what people told her when she wore the sweater.

Closing her bedroom door behind her, she followed the scent of coffee until she discovered Sage sitting at the kitchen table, reading a newspaper.

"Help yourself." Sage pointed to the coffeepot.

"Is that a real newspaper?" asked Olivia, sitting down at the table with her mug.

"I know. Kinda campy, even for Lily Rock. We do have an online presence, but the Old Rockers still publish this antique twice a week." Sage held up the newspaper, with *Lily Rock Reports* printed in dark ink across the top of the page.

Olivia sipped coffee. "Tell me about the Old Rockers. I think the woman at Doc's mentioned them yesterday."

Sage folded the paper. "People who have lived in Lily Rock for ages call themselves the Old Rockers. My mom, for instance."

"Not to contradict, but aren't you also an Old Rocker? You've lived here your entire life, right?"

"Technically I am. But in here?" She pointed to her chest. "I'm the new breed of crazy, according to my mom's crowd. I want the town to attract more people by inviting better restaurants and lodging. I want my school to take on a bigger presence too."

A common complaint between generations, Olivia mused. *The epic struggle expressed in the phrase, "We've always done it this way."*

"What school? Are you a teacher?"

Sage's chin dropped and she frowned.

Olivia realized that she'd inadvertently touched upon a difficult topic.

"Before we get into that, would you like an egg or a piece of toast with your coffee?"

"I'd like both," admitted Olivia, her stomach growling at the thought of food.

Sage stood and moved to the stove, then rummaged under the counter. After pulling out an old iron skillet, she placed it on the burner to heat. Then she turned to the refrigerator for the other ingredients.

"I'll get the toast," Olivia offered. She remembered where Meadow stored the bread from the day before. Olivia yanked on a drawer, revealing a home-baked loaf. "Can I use this?"

"Sure. Mom bakes bread every Sunday for the entire week. Let's dive into that fresh loaf."

As Olivia sliced through the whole wheat crust, Sage picked up their conversation. "I am the headmistress and principal of the Lily Rock Music Academy. We've been up here on the hill for the past thirty years. Since I went to school there and graduated, they hired me just last year to take over for the old principal."

Having a music academy in such a remote location surprised Olivia. Yet this did not explain Sage's earlier frown when she'd first asked about the school.

"Is it a boarding school too?" Olivia asked. "Wouldn't driving up the hill every day be difficult for students?" Olivia knew that for a fact, considering her first experience yesterday.

Cracking an egg over the hot skillet, Sage nodded. "It is a boarding and day school. I audition students every month with a rolling admission policy."

Sage paused, another egg in her hand, ready for cracking. Olivia smiled at her from across the kitchen.

Sage shrugged. "No one asks me about the academy. I guess it kind of startled me when you did. Do you want to hear more?"

"Of course I do."

Sage continued, "The board of trustees hired me to unearth financing for a new performance center for the student recitals. We'd like to build an outdoor amphitheater. The more students we enroll, the more tuition we charge and the quicker we get the plan for the theater rolling."

Olivia gingerly lifted a slice of bread from the toaster. "I bet some of your students are really good."

"All of them are prodigies," commented Sage. "Special students are the core of our problem and the core of our solution. We have to soothe the egos of the parents and the attitudes of the students daily."

Both women sat down across the table from each other. Olivia felt a warmth in her chest, reminding her of how isolated she'd been the past several months, since her breakup with Don. A moment of companionable silence circled them as each bit into hot buttered toast.

My mom would have liked Sage, thought Olivia. *She'd have appreciated her passion for her work and the way she knows her way around the kitchen—her warm presence.*

Licking her butter-coated fingers, Sage said, "My turn. Do you like music or play an instrument?"

"Kind of," Olivia admitted.

"What does 'kind of' mean?"

Meadow entered the kitchen. Dressed in black yoga pants and a flowered tunic, she smiled at the two young women.

"Looks like we're feeling better today. How did you sleep?" Meadow asked as she walked directly to the cupboard. She removed a teapot from a nearby shelf.

"I slept so well, I don't remember a thing. Plus my head feels a lot better."

Meadow smiled. She glanced over at her daughter. "I see you're ready for work this morning. Isn't it time for you to head off to school?"

A tight line formed on Sage's lips. Her chair scraped across the linoleum floor. After rinsing her plate in the sink, she leaned over to put it in the nearby dishwasher. On the way past the table, Sage rested a hand on Olivia's shoulder. "Let's pick up about you and music later. Maybe at the Brew Pub? In a day or two when I have a little more time to chat?"

"I'm not sure where the famous Brew Pub is located," Olivia laughed.

"Didn't Arlo tell you? Usually his first sentence is about his pub."

"I think we were too involved in my series of mishaps yesterday for him to mention the location."

"In another day you'll know everyone and everywhere in Lily Rock. Everything is very close and pretty obvious."

Meadow frowned. "Not that obvious," she muttered. "And Olivia won't be here that long. She's going home very soon."

Sage faced her mother. "Maybe you and the Old Rockers think this place is complicated, but to visitors and young people, Lily Rock is more than obvious. It's downright predictable. And I'd like Olivia to stay just as long as she wants to."

Olivia felt a thump in her head. The pain inched its way across her forehead, settling over her left temple. Rather than rub her head in front of Meadow and Sage, she kept the smile on her face. She'd already become a point of contention between the mother and daughter.

The sound of the land-phone ringing interrupted any more arguing. Sage took the opportunity to escape the kitchen as Meadow answered the phone, which hung on the wall near the back door. The caller identification could be read from the kitchen table.

"What's up, Skye?" she said, a smile in her voice. Glancing at Olivia, she added, "Your patient is looking very well this morning. If I'm not mistaken, she ate eggs and toast for breakfast, plus at least one mug of strong coffee. Would you like to speak to her?"

Meadow stretched the phone cord over to Olivia.

"Hello," she said into the phone. "I did get a good night's sleep. Thanks for the inquiry."

Meadow stared at Olivia, making no pretense of giving her privacy.

"May I speak to Dr. May?"

"May I ask who is inquiring?" came the formal reply.

"This is Olivia Greer. You remember me?"

"I will put you on hold." In a few seconds, Skye returned. "The Doctor is busy. He told me to convey that your friend Marla died of heart failure. Do you have any other questions?"

Olivia gulped. "I'll come over in an hour to look over my bill and check in. Thanks again." Olivia walked the phone receiver to its place on the wall as Meadow lifted a singing teakettle.

"Well? What about Marla?

Olivia blinked to force back tears. She filled Meadow in on what she'd heard over the phone.

Marla was a young woman. How could it be heart failure? Olivia dropped her eyes, her thoughts scrambling. "Marla's body will be taken to a larger medical facility down the hill to determine the exact cause. According to Dr. May they won't know the answer for at least another week."

Meadow shook her head. "I suppose it could happen to any of us, what with the polluted air and the chemicals in our food."

Olivia stopped listening to Meadow's summation of the ills of the world, resisting the idea that everyone was going to hell in a toxic basket of waste. She needed some time alone to think about the doctor's report. Unlike the easy companionship she felt with Sage, Olivia struggled with discomfort around Meadow—or at the very least distrust.

"If you don't mind, I think I'll lie down for a few minutes and then call the garage about my car. Thanks for the breakfast. It hit the spot."

"Oh, you can thank Sage. She's a good cook. She even cooks for the vegan cafe on occasion."

"She ate an egg this morning," said Olivia.

"She doesn't have to be a vegan to cook for one," Meadow replied defensively.

"I suppose that's very true," admitted Olivia, wondering how the topic had shifted so dramatically. "Anyway, thanks again for your hospitality. I'll let you know as soon as I hear about my car."

Olivia made her way down the hall. "No hurry," she called after her. "You're welcome to stay as long as you want. I love the company."

That's not what she told her daughter just a few minutes ago. She wanted me to get going as fast as possible.

Olivia stood in the center of the guest bedroom, behind the door, which stood ajar. She stared at the slightly open door, feeling something familiar about it—then she remembered. Before falling asleep the previous night, she'd overheard a conversation outside the same door.

It must have been last night. Something about— Then her memory slipped, like gears that failed to fit.

Instead of remembering the conversation, she imagined Marla's face when she'd discovered her dead body under the giant sequoia. Marla was *dead.* Olivia held her hands over her chest, taking in the enormity of her loss.

When she slowly returned from her mournful thoughts, she noticed her cell phone perched on the edge of the old dresser. Three missed calls: one from the apothecary, one from the constabulary, one from Brad's garage. Olivia connected with the garage first.

"Hello, this is Brad."

"Hi, Brad. This is Olivia Greer. You have my old Ford in your shop. I was in a crash coming up the hill yesterday?"

"Hello, Olivia. I left a message on your cell. Did you listen?"

"Actually, I never listen to my messages. I just call back. Can you explain again?"

"The car is all fixed. We can bill your insurance and drop it off this morning. I did the basics. You may want to have some of the body work done later, when you go down the hill. We don't do that kind of stuff up here."

Olivia felt relief. Apparently she wouldn't be held in Lily Rock as a prisoner much longer. "Could you drop the car at Meadow's place? That's where I'm staying."

She hoped Brad knew the way.

"Sure will, Olivia. Could you get me that information about your insurance and call back? That way I can complete my paperwork." Brad dropped the call without waiting for her response.

She pushed redial.

"This is Brad."

"Brad? This is Olivia Greer. The insurance paperwork is in the glove compartment of my car. You can get going on your end, and I will make a call to my insurance company after I hang up with you. Thanks."

This time she ended the conversation. *I'm tired of being told what to do,* Olivia thought. *Lily Rock residents have a bit of an attitude about the rest of us mortals.* Plus Brad sounded stoned. Too early in the morning to be smoking weed. Having lived for eight years with Don, Olivia recognized the softened edges of Brad's voice.

Looking over the room one last time, she took a moment to straighten the sheets on her bed. She fluffed her pillows and comforter.

Olivia heard a scratching at the partially closed bedroom door. A wet black nose poked its way into the room. The last time she had seen this nose, she'd fallen headlong into the dead body of Marla Osbourne.

With another shove of his black snout, Mayor Maguire slid past the door to jump up on the freshly made bed. He stared at Olivia before circling three times to lie down in a ball. She reached over to scratch behind his ears. His eyes closed as he buried his head into his back haunch.

"This must be your room, M&M. That's what I'm going to call you. M&M. Mayor Maguire is too serious for a dog with your sense of humor. I hear you're psychic?"

One ear twitched but no sign of a tail wag. A deep snore erupted from the dog's quivering lips as he continued to snooze on the bed.

CHAPTER SIX

Overheard in Lily Rock

Man watching dog sniff people in line for coffee: Marijuana is legal, right?

Girlfriend: Yes.

Man: How do the dogs know if it's legal, though?

"Goodbye and thank you," Olivia said as she completed her call to the insurance company. They'd assured her that she could get the body work on her car done when she returned home.

A conversation with Marla rushed back to her mind.

"It's not the man," Marla had explained. "You miss your dog. Come up here to visit me in Lily Rock. We'll find you a new pet at the animal shelter."

She did miss Don's old dog. Over the years Rusty had become a better companion than Don himself. Sliding her cell phone into her back pocket, Olivia turned the knob of the bedroom door, and Mayor Maguire rose to his feet. He growled.

Before she could close the door, Meadow appeared from

down the hall. She held a set of car keys in her hand. "Brad dropped these off. He's got your car up and running— There you are, Maguire!"

Meadow pushed past Olivia to curl her fingers around the dog's collar. She ushered him out of the bedroom. "We have an appointment with the town council." To him, she said, "I need to get you brushed and ready."

Olivia kept her face immobile. *They take the dog so seriously in Lily Rock. People really think he's the mayor.*

Turning around, she smoothed out the bed where the dog had lain. Olivia glanced over the room, feeling like she'd forgotten something.

Snatching the keys, she glanced in the mirror one last time. Her hair stood up on end in the regular pattern she'd become accustomed to since having it cut two weeks ago. She noticed that her cheeks looked flushed from the heat.

"Thanks, room," she commented, rolling the suitcase out the door.

Olivia stood in the hallway, listening for Meadow. "Just wanted to say thank you," she called out.

Meadow appeared. "Oh, you're leaving so soon? I thought you'd stay for the whole weekend at least."

Talk about mixed messages. She leaned over to kiss Meadow's cheek. "I think I'd better get my car down the hill as soon as possible. It needs more work, and I'm a little worried about the drive—you know, since my ride up was a bit rocky."

Tugging on one of the pink curlers, Meadow nodded. "It is risky travel, what with the sharp curves and steep cliffs. I'm just happy you avoided a catastrophe."

Stitches on my head plus flying off the road, plus a car they can't even fix here—feels like a catastrophe to me!

"Thanks again, Meadow."

"Oh, Olivia? Before you go, will you stop by Marla's house? I mean, did you leave anything there?"

Something about the question bothered Olivia. It felt excessive, even a bit intrusive. "I won't go by the house."

Meadow pulled out another curler. Her hair bounced to her shoulder. "Oh. No worries. I just wondered if you'd gotten all your stuff. Lily Rock is off the beaten path. You most likely won't come this way ever again."

Olivia wondered why Meadow felt so concerned about her belongings. Did she want her to leave quickly or to stay awhile longer? Olivia shrugged.

She released her discomfort, forcing her shoulders to relax. *If only I could skip all of this and return to the time before I fell into that ditch a day ago.* Olivia sighed deeply. Other than Jets, she had no plan to talk to any of the Lily Rock people again. *I can check into emergency care if my head feels worse. I really don't need to see the Lily Rock doctor after all.*

Walking out Meadow's front door, Olivia sighted her old Ford parked under a shady pine tree in the driveway. Dents along the front end gave the car a new identity, as if it didn't care about appearances.

She turned the key in the lock, yanking the driver's side door handle. Bent from the accident, the door did not budge. Nothing happened with a second pull either. With a third pull, the door opened wide enough for her to slide through and sit in the front seat.

For a moment Olivia panicked. Another obstacle for her to contend with. Even her car refused to cooperate with her planned exit from Lily Rock. *I hope it starts,* she thought. Her hands shaking with nerves, she twisted the key a couple of times before the engine finally turned over.

Olivia backed the car out of the driveway, shifting gears to head down the road. Before she could travel one hundred feet, her cell phone buzzed on the driver's seat. Afraid to talk and drive unfamiliar roads at the same time, she pulled over to the side of the road.

"Is this Olivia Greer?" a familiar male voice inquired.

"Yep. I am Olivia Greer."

"This is Michael. You remember me?"

His voice brought a smile to her lips. She would have withheld the smile had he been able to see her. She didn't want him to think she was another one of his female admirers.

"I do remember you."

"Have you gotten into any more trouble that I don't know about?" He chuckled.

"Actually, I'm driving down the hill, back to Playa, this very minute. How did you get my number?"

A puff of air met her ear. "I got your cell number from the information in your glove compartment. Brad found it. Gave it to me."

She remembered telling Brad he could go through her paperwork in the car. She knew she had not told him to share her contact information with anyone else.

"Just to let you know, Officer Jets wants to have a word as soon as you can manage."

Janis Jets wants to talk to me in person.

Michael repeated, "Officer Jets would like to see you at your earliest convenience."

"Are you her secretary or something?"

"Not exactly—"

Olivia's throat constricted. Maybe Michael and Janis were a couple. She'd seen how Janis had hugged him at the crime scene. "Oh, I get it. You're just making calls for the police since you are best friends."

"Well, we do help each other out in Lily Rock. I did make this call, but more for myself than Officer Jets."

"Would you just call her Janis? It's obvious you two know each other." She cleared her throat, adopting a quieter voice. "Sorry I'm being so ill-tempered. Let's try again, shall we? Hi, Michael. How can I help you?"

He exhaled into the phone again. "I can come pick you up and take you to see Janis—I mean, Officer Jets. I also have another thing I want to talk about. I've found a letter addressed to you in the guest room at Marla's house. I didn't open it, but I wanted you to have some company while you read what's inside."

Olivia blinked, confused. "Did the police let you back in the house by yourself?"

"Yeah, Janis and I go way back. She lets me hang around in an unofficial capacity."

How very entitled of you, thought Olivia, adding aloud, "I'm surprised Marla wrote me a letter. She could have called to talk to me. By the way, you don't have to drive over. I can come by her place. I have my car. Brad got it out of the shop faster than he originally thought."

"He did?" Michael's voice deepened. "When did he deliver your car?"

"You mean you didn't already know? I thought the Lily Rock grapevine would have told you that I'm leaving town, and of course what I'm wearing by now—jeans and a sweater, by the way."

"Nope. No news about you leaving. Are you?"

"I'm supposed to meet with Janis Jets first."

"Okay then, at least you aren't leaving town just yet."

Olivia felt her stomach knot. "Crime?"

"I figured you heard already. The police are not convinced that Marla died of natural causes."

"The doc told me she had heart failure and that they were taking her body down the hill—and that they wouldn't know anything more for weeks."

"I'm not sure why the doc said that." His voice sounded grim. "I just know what the cops told me."

Olivia turned the key in the ignition. It was one thing to have her business become everyone's business but quite another to have conflicting reports about Marla's cause of death. "Where do I meet you?"

"Back at Marla's. I live in a cottage on the property. I'll wait for you in her driveway. Take it easy on the roads, okay?"

Apprehension filled Olivia, driving a shiver of anxiety down her spine. The skin on her arms tingled as she made her way onto the main road. She drove slowly to negotiate the steep curves of the winding mountain terrain.

Glancing at her rearview mirror, Olivia flashed back to her drive up the hill. She'd felt chased by the car who tailgated her—the feeling of being pushed out of her safety zone. The unfamiliar roads, along with that fog. Touching her forehead, she winced.

No more running away, she scolded herself. Dropping her speed, she continued her self-imposed critique. *I'm driving like an old person. So sue me. This time I won't give in to panic—for once.*

By the time Olivia had bumped her way across the dirt road to Marla's home, her shoulders slumped from exhaustion. Michael stood in the driveway, waving his hands over his head. He walked to her car to open the door. "Took you long enough."

She grabbed her purse from the front seat.

He hovered over her, standing close to her shoulder, looking down. She met his eyes directly without flinching.

Realizing she was not going to talk, he leaned past her body to shove the car door closed. "Let's lock it, shall we?"

Taking the keys from her grasp, Michael locked the car. "I think a certain amount of caution may be necessary." He looked over his shoulder and then turned back to Olivia. "I will explain more later. Let's go into the house."

As Olivia followed him toward the entryway, she caught a moving reflection on the glass in the corner of her eye. This time she was ready for him.

"Mayor Maguire! I thought you had a town meeting to attend to."

Michael faced the dog. "You're as bad as the rest of them." Olivia ducked her head. He'd compared her to another Lily Rock resident. A flush of warmth grew pink on her cheeks. "He's not really the mayor, you know." He patted his thigh, but Mayor Maguire ignored his invitation.

"He's not exactly obedient," commented Olivia. "He was sleeping in my bed when I left Meadow's. He didn't sleep there during the night, so far as I remember. But he spent the entire morning lounging on my pillows before Meadow grabbed him for a meeting."

"The Mayor gets around. You'll see pretty soon for yourself. You think he's following you, but he disappears with hardly a goodbye. Meadow thinks she has a hold on him, but she has no idea how often he hangs out with other people."

She turned to greet the dog again.

"Hey M&M! Shouldn't you be at that council meeting?"

Michael laughed. "What's up with the nickname?"

"I suppose the name isn't dignified enough." She smiled and pointed at the house. "Are we going in? I wonder if we could make a pot of coffee."

Michael used his key. He paused before swinging the door completely open. Olivia felt herself inhale in anticipation of the spectacular view she'd seen the day before. It was even more stunning than she'd hoped, and her face showed it.

"According to the rumor mill, you designed this place." She faced Michael.

The corner of his mouth curved up. "I have to admit I loved watching you come in that door. You get this place, the majesty of the outdoors moving inside to greet and welcome. Yes. I am the architect and builder."

Olivia detected pride in his voice. "I am so small. The instant view of the trees and the rock put me in my place."

"I knew you'd understand! That is the exact impression I was going for when I drew up the plans. I must also admit—I wanted Marla to get that too. I wanted the connection with nature to assure her that her problems weren't as insurmountable as she thought. I don't think she realized why I did what I did with the design, but she appreciated the end result. I guess that's all an architect can ask."

Olivia looked down at her feet. She did not want to meet his eyes when she felt so vulnerable. He'd shown her a side to his personality that she deeply admired—a sensitivity to nature.

"The letter?" she asked to change the subject.

"Right this way. You didn't get to see the rest of the house yesterday." Michael walked toward the staircase as Olivia followed. When she reached the landing at the bottom of the stairs, she stopped to take in the entire space, upstairs and down.

Unlike the upstairs great room, this space welcomed the visitor into its center with a cozy vibe. Lower ceilings and the fireplace in the corner drew her eye to the four-poster bed that dominated the room.

My entire apartment could fit inside this suite, Olivia thought, admiring the overstuffed chairs placed on each side of the fireplace. The scent of smoke and pine filled the room.

"Is this all pine?" she asked.

"Sure is. What do you think?"

"Smells amazing. A complete mood contrast to the upstairs. Is this where Marla intended for me to stay?"

"It is the guest suite. There's a bathroom behind this door and a walk-in closet over there. But that's not what led me to believe Marla set up the room for you. It's the letter she left."

Michael pointed to a massive pine dresser with a mirror balanced on the back. The mirror, framed in darker wood, stood out against the roughhewn wall. Only after she'd admired the texture did she notice a cream-colored legal-sized envelope with her name printed on the back. It lay propped up against the mirror.

Olivia stared at her own name as if it belonged to someone else. *Why would Marla leave a letter when she expected to see me face to face?* Olivia turned toward Michael, the question reflected in her puzzled expression.

"I guess Marla wanted you to have something in writing. Maybe she left it there so she wouldn't forget to give it to you?" Michael looked down at his feet.

What is he hiding? He knows more about this letter than he's saying.

Olivia reached out for the envelope. Her hand shook as she grasped the letter. For a moment she felt doubt. *Has someone else read this letter before me?*

Sliding her short fingernail under the flap, Olivia lifted the document from within. Four pages, each numbered, displayed typed words. Olivia flipped to the last page. Marla's notarized signature jumped out immediately.

"It's notarized," she commented to Michael.

A voice from upstairs called out. "Yoo-hoo. Anyone home?"

Olivia hid the letter behind her back. Then she blushed. "I guess I don't have to hide this, right?"

Instead of disagreeing with her, Michael stopped to listen. "I hear Officer Jets at the door. Why don't we walk upstairs and see what's on her mind?"

Folding the document in half and then half again, Olivia shoved it into the back pocket of her jeans and patted it down to look flat.

Michael shouted, "We're down here. We'll be right up."

He took her hand, pulling her toward the stairway. When they reached the top, he slid his hand away. Olivia looked up to see Officer Jets staring at them both.

"There you are." A weapon hung on her black leather belt.

"Relax, Janis. I was just showing Olivia the guest suite that she never got to stay in. Here she is, delivered as promised. Is it a problem if I start a pot of coffee while you talk?"

Olivia ignored Michael's question. "I'd like to get this interview over with as soon as possible. Getting my car to a shop down the hill is my highest priority. I have to get back to my job."

"What is your job, by the way?" asked Officer Jets.

"I do a little of this and that. Next week I'm scheduled to temp for a paralegal. It may not seem like much to others, but for me the work pays the bills."

At the word *paralegal*, Michael's eyes widened. "So you have some legal background?"

"Some," Olivia said. "Enough to take the job."

"Interesting," remarked Michael. Then before she could

ask more questions he added, "Why don't you two begin the interview? I'll start the coffee. Be right back."

Olivia's stomach dropped. The letter from Marla burned in her back pocket. *I wish I'd read the entire document before speaking to Officer Jets.*

She sat down directly across from Janis Jets, who opened her electronic tablet.

"Okay, let's get this over with," Olivia prompted the police woman. "I'd like to get back home sometime today."

CHAPTER SEVEN

Overheard in Lily Rock
"Isn't it crazy that I was a baby at one point?"

Officer Janis Jets sat upright in her chair, a badge hanging from her neck. Olivia tried to read her dangling credentials as Jets stared her down.

"Is that my photo?" Olivia asked, pointing to an upside-down image of herself on Jets's electronic device.

"Got it off the internet." Jets turned her tablet around for Olivia to get a better view.

Her photo showed a young woman with a tentative smile. She had long brown hair that hung over her slim shoulders. Her eyes drooped. She looked distant and sad.

That was taken when I was deciding to leave Don. After eight years of emotional upheaval, I'd had enough.

"According to your Facebook page, you are in a relationship?"

Olivia wondered why her personal life was of any interest to the cop, unless of course she was a suspect, which would confirm her worst fear.

"I didn't update my status. I've broken up with my boyfriend."

"Your famous boyfriend, the bass player. What happened?"

"I know my love life is of infinite interest in Lily Rock, but would you just tell me more about my friend Marla? According to Michael, she didn't die of natural causes; she was murdered."

Officer Jets tapped the table next to her tablet. She turned the tablet back toward herself, shading the words with her right arm. "Okay then. I was just trying to be friendly. Sorry about your breakup, by the way."

Olivia waited, twisting her ankles under the table.

"According to the coroner down the hill, Marla Osbourne died of a drop in heart rate, brought on by anaphylactic shock. They found an unusual amount of CBD oil in her blood. Did she have allergies to any plants that you knew of?"

"CBD oil?"

Officer Jets closed the screen on her tablet. She leaned into both folded arms, stretching herself closer to Olivia. "That's right. CBD stands for cannabidiol. It's like marijuana without the THC. Helps people with all kinds of problems. On the one hand, CBD is very easy to get. But on the other hand? No one has tested the long-term effects. Now, how do you suppose your friend overdosed on CBD?"

Olivia stared at Jets. "Marla and I did some weed back in the day. You know, high-school-girl kind of experiments. I'm pretty certain Marla would just smoke the weed if she wanted to, instead of taking that—what is it? CBD oil?"

"Maybe an allergic reaction slowed her heart? That's the mystery and where our investigation will lead us. We need to answer how she came to have the oil and also why—" Jets pressed her hand to her forehead as her voice became more accusatory.

Olivia stopped listening, pushing away the implication that Marla's death was her fault. Instead she remembered how she had met Marla on the bus going to high school. One day Marla had invited her to spend the night, and that was when their friendship became close.

Olivia returned to the uncomfortable conversation with Jets. "Like I said, we did smoke weed a couple of times. She didn't have any other medical problems except for ... I think she had an allergy to beestings." Olivia closed her eyes to bring up an image of Marla when she was eighteen. A beautiful young blond woman, tall and thin. Two years older and much more sophisticated than Olivia.

Her eyes popped open. "She wore one of those bracelets. You know the kind? It says what you are allergic to, in case someone finds you and you need help. She showed me her bracelet once. She was allergic to beestings. I do remember that."

Officer Jets kept typing intently on her tablet with her index fingers.

"Okay. That's helpful," admitted the officer. "Doc has her medical records. We can check with him. We can also look through her personal belongings for the bracelet. She didn't have it on when she died."

Olivia gripped the table edge with both hands. She wanted to bolt from the conversation. The confusing details and Jets' intense glare frightened her. "I keep getting a cramp in my foot since the accident." She stood to stretch, eying the door across the room with longing.

As Olivia considered the option of running away, Michael popped his head out from the kitchen. He held three mugs by their handles in one hand and a coffeepot in the other. "Time for a drink, ladies?" he asked.

"Bring the coffee, but I need to talk to Olivia alone for a bit longer. We'll let you know when to come back." Officer Jets did not look up from her notes.

Mike's jaw tightened. He placed the coffeepot between them, along with three empty mugs. "Okay then. I know when I'm not wanted." He poured coffee before saying, "I'll check on the mayor. By the way, sorry to interrupt again, but Olivia? I'd like to take another look at your car, just to make sure it's safe to drive. Would you mind?"

Olivia hesitated. Michael might want to take her car back to the garage, and then she'd be stuck in Lily Rock. His interest in her car seemed unnecessary since Brad had given it a clean bill of health. But then, everything Michael did felt overly protective. Just when she thought she'd ditched him, he showed up unexpectedly, like when she had found the dead body. Then the letter discovery—that had come from Michael.

Olivia looked him over. His flannel shirttail hung out of snug-fitting jeans, while his sheepish grin hid something he was not talking about. *I've fallen for that guy before—the one who has so much potential, who needs me to take care of him. Like Don, only less famous.*

She starred at him a minute longer. *Maybe I'm over thinking. Not everyone is like Don.*

Reaching into her purse, she pulled out the car keys. "Have at it," she told him with an easy underhanded toss. He grabbed the keys midair, smiling back at her.

"Okay then. Thanks for trusting me." With the last remark, Michael left the two women to continue their conversation.

Still standing in the middle of the great room, Olivia got to the point with Jets. "Is this a fact-finding mission, or are you interrogating me?"

Instead of smiling as Olivia hoped she would, Jets' elbows popped up on the table as she cradled her chin in her palms. "I am the one asking questions here, and I am trying to figure out how you got into the middle of this murder."

"I have no idea how I got here. I was on a getaway vacation, just coming to visit an old friend," Olivia said, unable to hide her growing irritation. "Marla thought Lily Rock would help me get over my recent breakup. I planned to drop in for a couple of days and then leave Sunday afternoon."

"Take it easy. I'm not saying I don't believe every word. I have one more question, okay? Do you have any idea what that envelope in your back pocket is about?" The officer's cell phone lit up. She clicked the red icon to silence the ringtone.

"How did you know about the envelope?" Olivia's hands grew moist as she fumbled with the mug of coffee in front of her. She took a sip to steady herself.

Running the flat of her hand across the table, Officer Jets took her time before standing. "I can't force you to read me the contents of that envelope, but I do find it suspicious. Why would Marla write you a letter if she was planning on seeing you face to face? It just seems odd to me."

Olivia nodded. "I know. It seems odd to me too. I do have the envelope. But first, how did you know about it?"

Jets ignored the question. "I think I understand why you may not want to talk about what your friend wrote to you before her death. Even if you've already read the contents, you may not have had time to digest the information. I want to warn you—you may want to consult an attorney."

Olivia felt her gut twist. "I still don't understand why you would think I had anything to do with Marla's death. I was on the other side of the hill, sitting in a ditch with my head bleeding when it happened."

"Were you? Maybe you had a friend who was in on this with you. We know you pitched that car over the only bluff without a serious drop. The only bluff with a ledge that would break the fall. You could have done some research. Maybe you and an accomplice drove the hill before finding just the right place to stage the supposed accident. Maybe you planned the whole thing to cover up killing Marla."

Olivia wanted to scream. She had traveled from victim to murderer in less than twenty-four hours. *I've gotta get out of Lily Rock. This is a crazy place.*

Jets's cell phone lit up again. This time she answered. "Jets speaking."

Her ear pressed into the plastic case. "Are you okay?"

While Jets continued to speak in soft tones, Olivia walked to the front window. No car.

Mayor Maguire stood outside the window, looking in. His sad eyes traveled around her face, searching for a clue.

Olivia opened the door and the dog happily trotted in.

"Have you seen my car?" she asked him.

He pawed gently at her leg. She bent at the waist to scratch his ear. Breathing into his neck, she inhaled the scent of dog.

"It's Mike," explained Jets from across the room. "He's found some problem with your car. The brakes. He wants to talk to you as soon as possible."

Olivia felt her head rush. "Did he get into an accident?"

"He is just fine. He's returning your car to Brad. He said he'd meet you here in twenty minutes. Can you wait for him? I have to go now." Jets closed her tablet.

Olivia glanced around the room. The custom sectional in front of the fireplace looked inviting. "I'll hang out with the mayor while I wait. I'll take him to get some fresh air first."

"Don't dig into the crime scene," warned Officer Jets, and she headed toward the door. "We've got that taped off. Just stay away for your own good!"

After the officer disappeared down the driveway, Olivia called to the dog. "Come on, M&M. You heard the cop. Don't play with the crime scene, you old dog." After mocking the warning from Officer Janis Jets, Olivia slammed the front door behind her.

The dog circled Olivia, stopping to sit on her left-hand side behind her knee. He'd done the same when he'd led her to the dead body the day before.

"Let's go." Walking past the front of the house, dog and human turned the corner together. Breathing deeply, they moved toward the woods. When Olivia reached the entrance of the herb garden, she unlatched the gate, gesturing for the dog to go first.

Mayor Maguire rushed past. He bounded to the farthest corner of the garden, stopping to lift his leg. Olivia smiled. "Good doggy."

The last time she'd walked through the garden, she'd been in a hurry. This time, with Mayor Maguire so occupied, she stopped to inspect the plants. Herbs with carefully written labels filled the raised beds.

Olivia bent over the first to take a branch in her fingers. She crushed the familiar leaf, raising her fingers to her nostrils. *This must be lavender*. Olivia moved along to each plant, sniffing her way through the herbal bouquet.

To clear her senses from the herbal smells she stopped to admire the carefully placed rocks. Each one separated more vigorous growers from their less inclined counterparts. Olivia looked up, her eyes drifting to the top of the closest pine. A crow bounced on a branch overhead. Raising her glance even higher, she sighed. The giant sequoia, where she had found Marla's body, stood unfazed by the previous events.

Opening the back gate, Olivia called, "Let's go, M&M." The crow cawed overhead.

Mayor Maguire trotted to Olivia's side, sitting at her knee again. She moved away for him to pass. He waited for her to move first.

Olivia noticed the yellow police tape that surrounded the area where Marla's body was found. Tears formed in Olivia's eyes. The area held emotion for her, the memory of her friend. No matter how challenging Marla had been, she didn't deserve to be killed and left on the ground, under a tree, where no one could see her. She didn't deserve to be hidden away, taken from her own life.

Wiping the wetness from her cheeks, she walked around the tape to look at the scrambled earth, disrupted by the people who'd taken charge of the body.

Not hampered by the official rules, Mayor Maguire slid under the tape, his tail waving for Olivia to follow. He stopped to sniff the dirt more closely. "Don't do that!" Olivia warned. "No one is allowed, even if you are the mayor."

The dog tilted his chin up toward the sun, which peeked between the trees. Shadows played against his curly brown fur. He sniffed the ground and then continued his journey away from the police tape, moving deeper into the woods.

Remembering the last time she'd followed Mayor Maguire, Olivia stood her ground. "I am not going after you," she warned the dog. His tail disappeared behind a section of ferns.

"M&M. I mean it. Don't go any farther. Come back."

No sight of his curly brown head.

Olivia glanced backward at the place where she'd found

the body the day before. She didn't want to follow the dog, yet she worried. Still no sight of Mayor Maguire.

Instead of walking away, Olivia inched slowly forward to the place where she'd seen the dog disappear. "Mayor Maguire," she called in her most winsome voice. "Where are you?"

Ignoring her initial apprehension, Olivia decided to play along with M&M. *Is that you barking?* After walking briskly toward the sound, she found him. He bent over a spot under a nearby mesquite bush in the brown earth.

"Nice doggy." She looked more closely at the ground where he stared. As she bent over she inched her fingers around his collar, grasping him firmly to her side.

"It's just a pen, you silly mutt. I suppose you want it to sign important documents back at the office?" Holding the pen in her open hand, she squinted in the sun. The dog leaned over to sniff for himself.

Examining it more closely, Olivia read a list of written directions on the side of the plastic case. *Place the orange tip against the middle of the outer thigh. Swing and push the auto-injector firmly into the thigh until it clicks. Hold firmly in place for 3 seconds—count slowly.*

Her eyes widened. *This isn't a pen for writing. This is a pen for injecting.*

Mayor Maguire stopped sniffing her open palm. He looked up into her eyes, his tail wagging. She patted the top of his head.

Unsure whether to take the pen with her or leave it where she found it, Olivia stared at the dog as if asking for advice. His tail stopped wagging.

"You lead me to trouble, but no help after that?"

Closing her fingers around the pen, she slid it into her back pocket, next to the envelope from Marla. *I'd better put this in a plastic bag for evidence,* she thought. *Of course, my fingerprints will be the most obvious.*

At that instant Olivia knew what she had to do next. "I'm going to find out who killed Marla, M&M, if it's the last thing I do!"

The dog's tail quivered, then wagged again as his tongue slipped past his smiling jowls. He leaned toward Olivia, once again moving behind her to sit at her knee.

"Let's go." Dog and woman walked toward the house, a new determination in their step.

CHAPTER EIGHT

Overheard in Lily Rock

"Her forty-two-year-old best friend is living in her guest house right now."
"Why is he living in her guest house?"
"He's trying to pay off his Tesla."

Olivia stopped to catch her breath before going inside. Transfixed by the light dancing off the windows of Marla's new home, she stood in place. *Breathe deeply,* she reminded herself.

Mayor Maguire sat by her side, his ears slightly forward.

Reaching into her back pocket to secure the envelope and the EpiPen, she explained to the dog, "If I am playing detective, I'd better start thinking ahead. But where do I begin?" Olivia gazed down at the dog. "It's your fault I got into this situation in the first place. I might have gone home thinking I'd gotten the date wrong. You were the one who took me to Marla's body."

Just for a moment, Olivia felt tempted to change her mind about staying.

"Oh, don't worry. I'm still on the job. You can relax," she assured the dog.

Olivia pulled the EpiPen out of her back pocket. Clearly the device had not been activated. The plastic catch remained intact. *Now my fingerprints are all over this thing.*

She shoved it back into her pocket, underneath the letter. *If Jets finds the pen she'll have it tested in a lab, and this may be just what she needs to arrest me on suspicion of murder.*

Looking down for Mayor Maguire, she saw that he'd disappeared yet again.

* * *

The hum of a vacuum roared from somewhere in the house as she walked in the front door. Looking to the left in the entry-way, Olivia saw her purse hanging on a wall hook. Someone had moved it from the table. *Maybe Marla's housekeeper?*

A cursory inspection in her bag revealed the one hundred dollars in twenties she carried around for emergencies. Tucking the EpiPen into the side pocket of her purse, Olivia zipped it shut.

Since Michael had not given her a tour of the entire first floor, she walked around slowly, taking in Marla's home one glance after another. The great room opened to a floor-to-ceiling stone wood burning fireplace. The scent of smoke filled her nostrils.

There was smoke coming from the chimney, she recalled. *Who lit that fire? Was it Marla or maybe a guest? Did the killer linger in the house waiting for someone to discover the body, only to run away when the police arrived? Or did the killer come upon me and pretend to help out, infusing himself into the crime scene as an observer?* Olivia shuddered.

The vacuum sputtered.

Setting aside her thoughts, she moved around chairs and small tables tucked behind several massive support posts. Alongside the windows facing the forest, Olivia stopped to admire the expansive deck reaching into the trees.

Looking on the nearest wall, she touched first one knot-hole, then another. On the third try her finger sank into the paneling as the entire bank of windows slid up like a garage door. Now the scent of fresh pine filled the interior.

Leaving the windows open, Olivia turned to face the great room, admiring the oversized boulders placed in groupings throughout the indoors. Plants surrounded the boulders, covering and exposing the random surfaces. *Nice touch, bringing the outdoors inside.*

She saw solar blinds, operated with carefully disguised wall remotes barely visible from where she stood.

Olivia remembered looking in from the outside the day before. She turned toward the hallway. *That must be the master suite,* she concluded. The rumble of the vacuum started up again.

Olivia pushed in the door of the master suite. She stared at a tall woman with broad shoulders who effortlessly pushed the vacuum across the thick area rug. Her dark-black hair, swept back into a ponytail, exposed her ears, which held white earbuds.

Olivia remained still. She waited for the vacuum to switch off.

"Hello?"

Despite her precautions, the startled worker swung to face her, ripping the earbuds out with both hands. "Who are you?" The woman's deep voice surprised Olivia.

"I'm Olivia Greer. Marla's house guest."

The woman looked older than Olivia had first thought. Maybe mid-forties but in good shape. Her shirt exposed strong forearms, the muscles of which rippled as they pulled the vacuum closer to turn off the switch.

"I'm Cayenne. Cayenne Carson. I am Miss Osbourne's housekeeper."

"Marla invited me to spend the weekend."

"So you're the one who found her dead body?"

Olivia nodded.

Cayenne let the headphones hang over her shoulders as she stepped around the vacuum to extend her hand. "I'm sorry for your loss."

At the mention of loss, Olivia's eyes filled with tears. Kindness often unsettled her—especially from strangers. Rather than cry more, she changed the subject.

"I don't mean to interrupt your work. I think I'll look for a bite to eat. Do you want anything?"

"I had breakfast. Thanks." Cayenne rolled the vacuum down the hall, toward the next room.

In the kitchen Olivia opened the refrigerator door. A line of takeout boxes, carefully labeled with dates, filled the top shelf. Picking up one container, she peered inside. The aroma of lemon and pepper wafted to her nose as if asking to be appreciated. The next box revealed a beautiful piece of salmon with a crumbly coating.

Closing the lid, Olivia shut the doors. Since hunger had been an excuse, she wasn't sure what to do next.

"There you are!" Michael stood in the kitchen, smiling at Olivia. "You left the window open in the great room."

Olivia watched as Michael pushed the button of a remote he held in his hand. The enormous glass panels swept downward. "These were Marla's idea. She saw them on some television show and wanted them for her great room. What do you think?"

Michael continued. "We planned to build a downstairs

patio on the bottom level, along with an outdoor firepit. We planned it but didn't quite get around to the execution. Marla didn't feel well toward the end."

Michael's voice dropped as he spoke Marla's name.

"You miss her ... I mean, you're grieving her loss?" Olivia wondered what Michael really felt.

"I do miss her. We worked together for nearly two years. I built my cabin first and moved in shortly afterward. She stayed in town until her place was habitable."

"Then you weren't ... lovers?"

"We weren't like that! I made it clear we were strictly business from the start. Lily Rock thought we were a couple. I didn't argue with anyone who assumed. Thinking I was with Marla kept other people away, and I was happy with that arrangement."

The story sounded plausible. Or maybe Marla had just rejected him and that was what he told himself.

"Do I hear a vacuum?" Michael asked. "Must be Cayenne. I didn't realize she'd be here on a Sunday. I'll go and have a word with her. I'm not sure who will pay her from here on out." Michael reached into his pocket to bring out a flat wallet. He extracted a hundred-dollar bill. "I'll take care of this and be right back."

Left to her own devices, Olivia looked for a coffeepot. Sparkling-white quartz countertops ran down both sides of the kitchen. She opened a cupboard close to the sink. Rows of carefully marked bottles filled the shelves.

Some containers were still in their original packages, others in decorative jars with chalkboard labels. Rosemary, turmeric, garlic—there were several varieties of each.

"All set." Michael appeared at her elbow.

"Look at all this stuff." Olivia pointed to the bottles and containers. Lined up next to the spices were supplements including abhwagandha, echinacea, and grape seed capsules. "Was Marla worried about her heath?"

"She adapted to the culture. Lily Rock is known for the liberal use of lotions and potions. Marla dabbled a bit. You saw her garden, right?"

"She didn't actually dig in the garden, did she?"

"Oh no!" Michael laughed. "You got that right. She hired people to harvest and bring the vegetables and herbs into the house for cooking."

"She didn't actually cook."

"Marla had a chef for each night of the week, who delivered her dinner, bringing in a variety of cuisines from the local restaurants, including vegan and Mexican. You name it, she ate it. Very open-minded in that regard."

Olivia looked over the kitchen again. "So this kitchen played host to any number of cuisines, depending on the day?"

"You seem really interested in Marla's habits. Any reason?"

Olivia felt a sneeze coming up. "Must be the herbs," she explained, shutting the cupboard door. Rather than alarm Michael with more questions, she answered in a careful voice, "I guess I'm fascinated by Marla's life here in Lily Rock."

Michael looked her face over closely. "You had a pretty bad day yesterday. How about we head to the Lily Rock Brew Pub? They have an excellent lunch for everyone's palette. You remember Arlo? He stopped at the accident—"

"Oh, I remember Arlo. He also rushed to my rescue when I was being interviewed by Officer Jets. I guess he's an attorney?"

"I think he practiced law briefly, but then I don't really know. Lily Rock doesn't expect people to divulge all of their secrets. Kind of like a town in the old west, or so I've read."

"Lily Rock does feel like a town that appears and then disappears. A throwback to another time—with the modern convenience of a local brew pub, just to keep people off-balance."

Michael laughed. "The past is very murky here, and people make up the most unlikely stories to tell everyone else. The difficult part is that they don't stick to the same story; they keep changing them. The last I remember, Arlo did not have a law degree. But if you ask him, he could change the story and not feel one bit ashamed."

"Since he offered to help me, I'd like to know for certain."

A slow smile spread across Michael's face. "How about this instead? I know very little for certain, except that you need some rest and a good meal, and I'm the man to make it happen."

He took her hand to guide her out of the front door. His large pickup truck waited in the driveway. "I have to tell you about your little car. It's back in the shop. Let's drive my truck to the pub, and I'll fill you in."

She climbed into the passenger side with no need for help, fastening her own seat belt.

"You are feeling better," Michael remarked as he slung himself behind the steering wheel.

Her cheeks flushed.

He pulled out of the circular driveway and onto the main road. He did not speed, taking the curves cautiously, watching Olivia out of the corner of his eye.

With one hand on the wheel, Michael turned to her. "Your car had some pretty iffy brakes. I left it at the garage to get them worked on."

"I can't afford any more repairs. I need to get back to my job."

"Don't worry. We can use credit, or maybe we can get you

a part-time job up here for a while—you know, until you're fully recovered and the car is ready."

"I'd prefer to leave sooner than later."

"I know. But you have to admit, things have gotten a lot more complicated than you anticipated. And by the way, have you opened that envelope yet?"

Her chin dropped. "I feel like a big baby. I don't want to know what's inside."

His free hand reached over to pat her knee. "Don't worry. No matter what's in that envelope, we'll figure it out. That's why I want you to stay a couple of weeks. Plus I have to admit, things have gotten so much more interesting since you arrived. I hate to see you go."

He brought his hand back to the steering wheel, smoothly pulling into a parking area.

"I have the envelope right here," Olivia remarked as they climbed out of the truck toward the pub. "Maybe after lunch we can open it."

High-top tables with chairs surrounded the bar in the outdoor seating area. Roughhewn lumber outlined the deck and siding of the pub. Even the most astute observer would have difficulty telling where the outside stopped and the interior began.

"This looks a lot like Marla's place," Olivia remarked.

"Good eye." He grinned. "I also designed the pub. Marla and I planned to bring Lily Rock into the twenty-first century. We were going for a more upscale theme to attract a different clientele. Less biker crowd, more hipsters, if you know what I mean."

Olivia glanced around, looking for a hostess. Sure enough, Arlo stepped right up. "You made it! Welcome to the Lily Rock Brew Pub." Arlo turned to Michael. "Good to see you,

Mike. There's a table right over here." He led them to an outdoor table.

Sitting near the metal rail, Olivia looked out into the woods that surrounded the pub. She held up her menu and glanced over its offerings. The waitress stopped by and waited patiently at the side of their table.

"They have a great burger," suggested Michael. "Lots of good beer choices as well, plus a full bar with every cocktail imaginable."

Olivia knew this conversation. It happened every time she went out with someone she hadn't met before.

"Water is fine for me," she commented.

He closed his beer menu.

"I'll have water, too, with lemon."

No more questions. Just acceptance and support. Olivia felt relieved.

I don't know this man. He may be sincere, but I've been tricked before. Eight years of my life gone since I thought I'd found Prince Charming. I didn't come here to get involved in another relationship.

CHAPTER NINE

Overheard in Lily Rock

"I thought I was playing footsie with you—but it was just my own shoe."

Arlo cleared the table as Olivia patted her full stomach. "A really good burger."

Across the table Michael shoved the last bite into his mouth. He chewed slowly, staring over her head as Arlo walked back inside with their empty plates. Olivia shifted her glance to the bar.

"Isn't that Marla's housekeeper?" She pointed to the tall woman behind the counter.

"That's Cayenne. We call her Cay. She's also Arlo's wife. She works at the bar and manages a cleaning service here on the hill." Michael wiped his mouth to continue. "Cay supports some hefty clients, including the local parks, along with cabins owned by wealthy individuals. During the evenings she tends bar."

"Do I owe you for her cleaning fee at Marla's?"

"I have a contingency fund as Marla's property manager. I can pay for Cayenne for as long as you want her."

Olivia made a note in her head. *Contingency fund.*

"Want dessert?" he asked, looking over the menu again.

"I'm pretty full. You were right, I was famished. I am thinking a lot more clearly now."

Arlo reappeared holding a slip of paper. He slid the bill to the center of the table between them. Olivia reached out, but Michael's hand slid under hers.

"Oh no you don't. This is my treat. Plus I have a tab here, and they give me a discount, since I'm the architect-builder and all." He smiled, then added, "Certain privileges came with my contract."

I wonder if Marla's contingency fund pays for his meals?

"Well, okay. I'll pay next time."

He frowned at her.

She'd made it a point to take care of her own finances since her breakup with Don. At first it had felt good to be taken care of, when their relationship was new and his rock-star fame brought in so much money.

But for the past two years, as he'd floated in and out of rehab, money had become scarce. She'd gone back to working. "Never again," she'd told Marla in one of their Facebook Messenger conversations. *I'm going to take care of myself from here on out.*

"I do have some money. You don't have to be my savior or anything," she told Michael.

He held his hand in front of his chest. "Far be it from me to think I can rescue you. But remember, it's a small town. We are bound to run into each other again."

For a moment they stared at each other openly. He didn't blink, inviting her to look into his eyes for as long as it took.

Olivia's glance broke first. Her heart beat quickly. *I so wish I could just get in my car and get out of here right now.*

"So what did you see?" he asked her quietly. "Do my past, present, and future pass muster? Can we be friends?"

Her cheeks flushed. She reached under the table to grasp her purse. "I'd better read the letter now." By the time she sat back up, her cheeks were no longer bright red.

She extended her fingers into the purse. No envelope. She shoved her hand deeper into the depths. Reaching back, she patted the pockets of her jeans, coming up empty-handed. Panic drew her eyes wide.

"It's gone. I don't have the envelope. It must have dropped out when I was in the truck!"

Michael shoved his chair back. "I'll go check," he said as he strode out of the pub. In just a minute she could see him in the parking lot from their table.

"Can I bring you anything else?" Cayenne stood at her table. Her eyes looked over to the parking area below. "Is that Michael Bellemare outside?"

"I left something in the car," Olivia explained.

"If anyone can find it, he can. He's like our resident detective. Very observant kind of guy."

Olivia considered the housekeeper's voice. Something's different here.

Noting the woman's hair she said, "I'm so envious of your thick hair." Olivia pointed to her own short crop.

Cayenne leaned against the table. "I'm sorry if I frightened you this morning. I didn't know if I was supposed to keep up my cleaning schedule since Marla died. So I decided to go ahead. I can give you back the house key whenever you like."

"You probably knew Marla pretty well. Did you happen to see the letter she left for me?"

Cayenne looked over her shoulder before answering. "In the guest suite in front of the mirror, right? I did see it the last time I was here. I hid it from the cops. I only put the letter back after they left."

"I had the letter, or at least I did before I came here. Michael is looking for it in the truck. Speak of the devil."

Holding the folded envelope in his hand, Michael said, "Must have dropped out when you were hoisting yourself into the truck. It's quite a distance from ground to seat." He slid the envelope to Olivia, who stared without touching the paper.

Cayenne looked on with interest.

"So what did Marla have to say?" Cayenne pulled an extra chair to the table to sit down.

At the bar Arlo stopped polishing a glass to stare at them. Perspiration formed on his upper lip.

"It's not the Academy Awards, Olivia. Just open it," Michael insisted.

Olivia unfolded the envelope. Arlo joined them, placing his hand on Cay's shoulder.

Smoothing the paper in front of her, Olivia read aloud:

Dearest Olivia,

If you are reading this letter, I am most likely in the hospital or dead. I did not intend to have the document ready for you on your visit; I really wanted our time together to be about you and you alone, but my Marla-self got in the way again, and I made everything about me.

I might have been able to give you a good time without getting in the way, except for the fact that I don't feel well. Over the past several weeks, I've been congested and headachy. At first I thought it was a cold, but the symptoms did not go away. Instead of visiting my internist down the hill I consulted with the doctor here in town. He's so kind and grandfatherly. Why aren't there more like him in our age group?

Anyway, he gave me some kind of drops, which helped for a while, but then I got worse again. I am feeling very weak. Head spins all night, so no sleep for me. I can't even take that damned Mayor Maguire for a walk when he shows up at my house. So my conclusion is that someone in Lily Rock is poisoning me! My other conclusion? I'm not sure I care. I no longer have any confidence in my ability to read people or to trust anyone, except for you, of course. I've lived my life well —up until now. I think it may be time to let go.

Don't be sad, Olivia. I can come back another time as a reincarnated person, a natural blond, or an important celebrity. Thirty-six years of some pretty good living. Maybe I need to say, "Enough." At least, that's what the town psychic (the woman, not the dog) told me.

Please find in this envelope all of the signatures necessary for you to take over my entire estate. It will be some work to put together, but I figure the financial gain will be worth the effort. Plus you can live in that amazing dwelling designed by Michael Bellemare. If you haven't met him already, he's the guy with the flannel-shirt wardrobe and the big Dodge truck. He's from the famous Bellemare architectural firm in Chicago, the one that wins all those awards given out by *Architectural Digest*. He designed and built my house. Only the best for Marla, right?

That's it, my love. I remember fondly our time together in high school, how we longed for our fathers who never showed up, and the way you never could smoke a joint without gagging. And how you stood by me even when I was such a ... Just say it, Marla. B-I-T-C-H. Love you. Sorry I turned out to be such a lousy hostess.

See you in the next life,

Marla

Olivia brushed tears away with her finger. She looked at the second page. The formal language stated:

Since I have no living next of kin, I hereby give all of my estate—including my house, my jewelry, my personal belongings, the contents of my bank accounts, my stocks and bonds, and anything else I fail to mention—to my old friend, Olivia Greer.

At the bottom of the next page were signatures. Two witnesses had signed: *Michael Bellemare* and *Cayenne Perez*. Underneath the notary stamp was the name *Arlo Carson*.

Olivia searched the faces before her. Michael's eyes filled with tears as she stared at him. Cay circled her arm around Olivia's shoulders. Arlo looked relieved.

"So you three knew what was in this envelope all along?" Olivia wiped her eyes again. "Is that why you rushed over that first day, to see if I got the letter?"

"I called Arlo. We both knew that you had to open it and find out for yourself," insisted Michael. "It's better that way."

"Is that why you took my car away? So I wouldn't leave until I read this?"

Michael nodded. "And for other reasons."

"Yep," said Arlo, standing to his full height. "We needed a fourth for bridge, and you're it."

Laughter rippled around the table as they all looked each other over. Olivia carefully folded the papers, fitting them back into the envelope. "I should be feeling good about this newfound income, but instead I feel like I've profited from my friend's demise."

Michael reached to pat her hand.

"I can't take this money—at least, not until I figure out who killed Marla."

Cayenne smiled. "That's what I told these men. You

wouldn't accept the money unless you knew how Miss Marla died. But don't worry, Olivia. We can help you, what with Mr. Nosey over here, and of course my husband the bartender —the guy everyone talks to—and me. My staff covers nearly every house inside and out of this town. With us four, we will find the one who killed Marla."

Lifting her glass of water, Olivia said, "To us: the barkeep, the architect, the business owner, and the old friend of the dead woman."

Cayenne nodded.

On the drive back to Marla's house, Olivia posed a question to Michael. "What I don't understand is why you three didn't encourage Marla to find help when she first started feeling ill."

Michael explained. "We did. I even offered to drive her down the hill to Frontier Town, where they have lots of city facilities, not like here in Lily Rock. She refused."

"Couldn't you have gotten a real doctor up here to look at her?"

"Well, she did call on Doc. He said she was probably allergic to ragweed and that her symptoms would go away soon enough."

"He told me he prescribed over-the-counter medications."

"Most likely he gave her CBD oil. People around here believe in that stuff."

"I heard about it for the first time yesterday. Meadow is a big fan."

Michael smiled. "So you know all about it then. Saves me mansplaining. Aren't you glad?"

Olivia looked out the window. *See you in the next life.* She wondered if Marla really believed in reincarnation or was trying to sound lighthearted.

Michael waited for her to turn away from the window

before picking up the conversation. "It's known around town that the doc uses CBD oil for nearly every ailment. I'm surprised he didn't give you some after your accident for the headache."

"Maybe he was saving that particular remedy for the follow-up visit. I was supposed to return to his office yesterday."

"You probably couldn't catch him today. The doc goes back to the Palms to Paws Animal Shelter to feed the livestock and check on the animal rescues in the afternoon."

"He's not busy enough with people—he also fixes pets?"

"Doc handles all the animal rescues here in Lily Rock."

"Again with the double-purpose employment."

"You're so right. No one can afford to live up here without taking part-time gigs; not even the doc has enough money to live on. He takes jobs down the hill."

Turning in to Marla's driveway, Michael navigated the truck over crunching gravel.

"I have a small problem," mumbled Olivia.

Michael pulled the truck to the side and turned off the ignition. "You have nowhere to stay tonight?"

"I am not staying with you," she added as clarification.

"I completely understand." His voice dropped slightly. "But you do realize that Marla's will"—he pointed to her purse—"means this house and everything in it is now yours. You can sleep wherever and whenever you want. For as long as you want."

The mention of Marla's will quickly overwhelmed Olivia, and she found her eyes welling with tears, even as she tried to remain calm. It was impossible not to cry when she thought about what had happened. She rubbed her face with her sleeve as Michael waited for her emotions to pass.

"Let's walk in together. Maybe we can start a fire and get

you settled in." He pointed to a path in the forest. "I only live over there. Tomorrow I'll show you my place so you know I'm close. You'll feel more secure then."

He strolled around the truck, opened her door, and lent a hand for her to step down. They walked in silence to the front entrance of Marla's darkened home. Instead of opening the door, Michael reached into his pocket to hand her a ring of keys. "Your place. You can open up."

As she leaned forward, something brushed against her legs. Olivia dropped the keys.

Michael's arm slipped over her tense shoulders. "It's okay, Olivia. You're safe. Look here." He pointed to her right knee.

She stooped to pat Mayor Maguire's head. "You show up at the darnedest times."

Mayor Maguire walked through the open door first. He pivoted to stare out into the dark night. Before Olivia could close the door behind her, the dog turned to lick her outstretched fingers, then disappeared back into the darkness.

"Mayor Maguire," called Olivia.

Only the dog's tail was visible, disappearing into the grove of trees.

Olivia pulled the door closed behind her. She waited. No scratching. She'd hoped Mayor Maguire would change his mind and come back inside.

"A solid door means good construction," remarked Michael, oblivious to her concerns for the dog. "I know the builder."

Michael strolled into the great room, turning on lights one at a time. He talked as he moved.

"If you don't mind, I'll check the house before saying goodnight. Just want to make certain everything is secure. Tomorrow I'll call the lock guy. I have no idea how many keys Marla handed out."

Maybe, despite his protestations, Michael does expect me to invite him to say the night.

"I appreciate you looking out for me, but I'm sure everything is fine. No need to make a fuss." She waited for him to edge toward the front door.

Instead Michael disappeared around the corner.

"Everything looks good," he commented from down the hall. "I checked all the doors. There are double security locks on the windows."

"I really appreciate your help and your company tonight." She spoke with firmness, hoping he'd realize she'd offered him another exit line.

He walked back in and stood in front of her. "We can talk more tomorrow when we go to see the doc."

Grateful that he didn't insist upon staying longer, Olivia smiled. "Thanks again. I'll sleep in the guest suite for now. I'm not ready to take over Marla's personal space."

"I understand. Plus her room is at the front of the house, surrounded by glass. It's as safe as we could construct, but the back room has more privacy. It just feels cozier."

Opening the front door, Olivia looked into the night one last time. "I don't see the dog. Will he be safe?"

"He doesn't stay with one person for very long. He moves about at night and shows up somewhere different nearly every day. Some say he's psychic."

"I heard that rumor. You don't believe it, do you—a psychic dog?"

Michael's hands slipped into his pockets and he rocked back on his heels. "I don't believe in love at first sight either. Doesn't mean it never happens."

He turned and made his way into the darkness.

CHAPTER TEN

Overheard in Lily Rock

*Patient: Hi, I forgot my appointment yesterday, and I'm hoping
to slide into today's schedule.*
Receptionist: I love that journey for you. I so get that.

Olivia opened her eyes the next morning. She appreciated the
pattern of the ceiling over her bed. Roughhewn boards lay in
diagonals, creating a symmetrical design. Lifting her body on
both arms, she inhaled, then flopped back to the pillows. *If
only I could close my eyes and not wake up. I guess I'd better
get moving ...*

Moments later Olivia stood on the floorboards next to her
bed. *Heated floors, thank you, Marla.*

After her shower Olivia searched for a pair of clean jeans.
*Last pair. I know I saw a laundry room when I looked over the
place. I'll start a load later.* She slid her feet into clean socks
and wool clogs, pulling a blue cashmere sweater over her
head.

Olivia ran her hands through her hair. *Wash and wear,*
she'd told the stylist. Not only had the woman complied, but

in a twenty-minute shearing she'd turned Olivia from a sweet young thing to a woman who could handle everything.

The complicated coffee maker in Marla's state-of-the-art kitchen required experimentation with dials. Olivia stared at the water level. Then her cell phone buzzed.

"Hey, you—up yet?" Michael's lazy voice filled her ear with warmth.

"I am trying to figure out this coffee maker." Olivia poured in water. The phone clicked off as she measured the ground beans. *Rude.* Then a few minutes later she heard a knock on the back door.

"I brought my own mug," commented Michael, sauntering into the kitchen. She sniffed. *Patchouli soap. Very Lily Rock. Next time I lock the door.*

She took the mug from his hand, turning back to the counter. "Coffee is ready. Cream and sugar?"

"Lots of both. I actually hate the taste of coffee."

Olivia groaned. That was the last straw. A man who did not love coffee could not be a friend.

Ignoring the frown on her face, Michael added, "I'll get the sugar. I know where it's kept. I bet there isn't any cream."

"Actually, there is cream. Someone supplied us with a full refrigerator, and here's the container." Olivia lifted a glass bottle, which she tipped over Michael's mug of coffee. *Did everyone in Lily Rock have access to Marla's house?*

Olivia swallowed back her fear.

Settling into a chair at the kitchen table, she took in the view out of the nearby window. "Lavender blooms in early spring?" she asked Michael.

"I have no idea. It blooms whenever it feels like it in Lily Rock. Just like everything else here, you can't always predict."

"Remind me again—how long have you lived here?"

Though her mind felt less fuzzy, Olivia did not quite feel herself.

"Four years next spring. Marla signed me on early to design her house. We built my cabin first so that I could also be the caretaker." His forefinger circled the rim of the mug. "There was some resentment in Lily Rock, you know, about her moving here."

"I picked that up," admitted Olivia. "I would have thought the town would appreciate added resources, jobs for people, and of course you—a famous architect."

He ducked his head to hide a sheepish grin. "I'm not that famous. It's my father who's the big deal." His now purpose-fully bland expression caught her attention. *That's his hiding-my-feelings resting face.*

"You don't like working with your dad?" she prodded gently.

"Let's just say I prefer going my own way without his advice. He can't help himself. He has to take over everything. I learned that the hard way."

Sometimes people tell you more than they realize. Like father, like son, Olivia mused.

"So how did you meet Marla?"

"She read an article about me on the internet. I guess she liked my photo." The grin returned. "Anyway, the article went on about my innovative ideas, so Marla called me. Hired me on the spot. It was a fast connection, which I came to appreciate more as time went on. Marla meant well."

Olivia nodded. "Of course, I would be the last to criticize, since she just gave me a house."

Michael glanced over Olivia's shoulder to the clock above her head. He added, "How about we get over to the doc as soon as his office opens? We can ask him about Marla's health issues. Plus we can get his opinion about your recovery. I'd feel better if he checks you again for a concussion."

She got up and poured herself another full mug of coffee. "Want some?" she asked Michael.

He held up his mug in response. Olivia filled his cup half-way. *No sense wasting a good brew on a guy who drowns his coffee in sugar and cream.* She sat at the table, facing him.

"In all honesty, I liked the doc, but that woman? The one who works as his receptionist?"

"And nurse," added Michael. "She insists that she is also a nurse."

"Her name is Skye something?"

"Skye Jones."

"She kind of gives me the creeps."

"Is that so?" Michael leaned over the table. "Say more."

"I just felt odd when I first saw her. A gut reaction."

"You get those often?"

"I used to. I stopped paying attention a few years ago. I guess now that I think about it, I felt pretty woozy that day, with the thump on my head. But you've got to admit, even her name, Skye Jones, feels a bit off. Sounds more like a Bond woman than a resident of Lily Rock."

"Why did you give up on your own gut feelings?"

The question surprised Olivia. Michael had a way of picking apart a conversation, like selecting a particular apple from the tree. She decided to give him a taste but not the entire piece of fruit.

"A long story about the person I used to be before my hair-cut." She smiled at him, lifting the short hair on her neck for effect.

"So you're Olivia 2.0—that explains everything." He laughed under his breath. "For what it's worth, I suspect Skye made up the name back in the sixties. Who knows? She may have thought she was a Bond girl then."

He took a sip of coffee with a grimace. "Skye is also the town occult expert, and she does the dispatch for the police and fire department."

Olivia gently pushed against the stitches on her head. "Is Skye the one Marla talks about in her letter? You know, she said she consulted a psychic in town that was not Mayor Maguire."

"Skye is the best-known occult expert in Lily Rock."

"Do you think Marla told Skye about her health concerns? Maybe she mentioned my visit too ..."

Frown lines appeared across Michael's forehead. "I had not thought of that, but you know, lots of people confide in their psychics. Off-the-wall kind of information that you wouldn't necessarily tell anyone else. You may be on to something. Let's give Skye Jones a once-over this morning."

"Does that mean I'll hold her down while you interrogate?" Olivia grinned. "But seriously, how many jobs do you have in Lily Rock? Like, do you wash windows or hunt venison or work for the *Daily Rock* newspaper?"

Placing his empty mug in the sink, Michael spoke over his shoulder. "I am an architect and a property manager for now. Marla and her projects kept me pretty busy."

"For a guy who's so busy, you've certainly been right on the spot for me."

"My pleasure, ma'am," he drawled, assuming the cowboy accent. "Shall we make our way to the doc's, little missy?"

Olivia scowled. She rose from her chair and walked toward the dining room, where her purse lay on the table. Staring into the contents, she noted her important belongings. Sunglasses, wallet, comb, car keys.

She turned abruptly. "I nearly forgot. Is my car ready yet?"

"The brakes gave out when I was driving it. I suspected a problem; that's why I took it back to the garage. We can call Brad for his diagnosis. In the meantime, I'll drive you in my truck."

Then he added, "You have the house keys, right? The ones I gave you last night."

"I think I left them in the pocket of my jeans from yesterday. Give me a minute." Olivia walked lightly down the stairs. When she returned, keys in her hand, Michael stood at the fireplace, poking ashes.

Glancing around the room, she saw her purse. *Did I leave it unzipped?*

Michael spoke first. "I'll clean up the fire remains when we get back. Might as well start with a fresh bunch of wood, you being the new owner and all."

Olivia felt a niggle in the back of her mind. Her thoughts arrived and disappeared quickly since the accident.

"I remember something about that fire. I can't remember just what, but it feels important," she told Michael.

"Maybe you'll think of it on our way to Doc's. Better grab a jacket." Michael opened the front door.

Olivia rubbed the back of her head. "Since the accident, a thought will pop into my mind and then poof—gone. Leaves a bad feeling."

"I'll keep you on track until you feel better."

Olivia swallowed back a sigh as she followed Michael toward his truck. "I feel a bit overwhelmed when I think of myself as a property owner," she admitted to him, climbing into the passenger seat.

Then another random thought popped into her head. *My*

letter from Marla. I don't remember seeing it in my purse this morning. I'll check again later.

By the time they arrived at the doctor's office, Olivia had forgotten about the vague feeling of importance surrounding the fireplace in the house. She reached down to grab her purse before unfastening the seat belt. *Silly me. Every time I forget something I reach for my purse like the thought is somehow stored inside.*

Still in the truck, she asked Michael, "Isn't it Sunday? I've lost track of the days. How come the doc works on a Sunday?"

"Doc has worked at two different locations for years, including one down the hill. He keeps the office open on Sundays here in Lily Rock." Michael got out and came around to Olivia's side, taking a quick glance at her huddled against the seat. "Do you want me to go inside with you? Or I can meet you after you talk to the doc. I'll stop in at the library to wait. Meadow is holding a book for me."

"I've got this," she assured him through the passenger-side window. She got out of the truck on her own and walked toward the familiar building without looking back.

A warm blast of heat covered her face as she stepped into the doctor's waiting room.

A cool voice greeted her. "Hello. How may I help— Oh, it's you!"

Skye Jones leaned over an old wooden desk, her intent gray eyes staring directly at Olivia. A few wrinkles around her mouth indicated her age to be at least sixty, most likely a smoker.

Glancing down at Skye's hands, Olivia confirmed her opinion. The slight swelling of the blunt ring finger revealed a woman edging closer to seventy years.

"I was wondering if I could see Dr. May? He asked me to

stop in for a quick check about, you know, my head." Olivia pointed to the stitches with her forefinger.

Opening her laptop, the receptionist clicked around, then typed rapidly. "He has someone in his office, but he can see you in ten minutes, if you don't mind waiting."

Skye pointed to a small leather sofa and forced a smile.

"I can wait. Thanks." Olivia sat down, pretending to read her cell phone.

"I hear you inherited the Osbourne estate."

Olivia's chin raised. *She* is *a psychic!*

"How did you know? About the inheritance?"

"Oh, honey. Word gets around. I bet you've figured that out by now. My niece works for Sage at the music school. Her mother told her. I think she heard it from Cay, her house-keeper, who witnessed the will."

Document, Olivia corrected Skye in her thoughts. *Now I remember what I was worried about earlier.* Reaching her hand into her purse, she pushed aside her wallet. The folded envelope lay in the bottom, underneath the ring of keys.

Skye Jones continued to stare at Olivia. "Missing something?"

"No. I have everything."

The doctor's door opened, revealing a tall woman. Her jet-black hair reached past her shoulders to the middle of her back. Olivia recognized Cayenne.

"See you later," the doctor's voice boomed from within the office. "Take that medicine as directed. Don't skip any doses, and you should be feeling better in a day or two."

Cayenne brushed past Olivia without a greeting. By the time the front door shut, Skye was leaning her head into the doctor's exam room. "The woman who got the stitches is here to see you."

"What's your name again?" she asked Olivia over her shoulder.

"Olivia Greer."

The doctor's inviting voice called out, "Do send Olivia in. How are you this morning, little bit?"

When she entered the exam room, he extended his hand, a broad smile on his face. She took his grasp, welcoming his concern.

"I'm feeling a lot better," she reported.

"Why don't you hop up here on the table while I examine my handy work? Do you need anything for the pain?"

The doctor stood in front of her. His hand reached toward her face, and he lifted one eyelid, then the other. "No concussion that I can see," he said. Afterward, he touched the wound on her forehead. "Healing quite nicely," he mumbled, turning to wash his hands at the small sink.

Olivia could not remember what the doctor had asked her; she was mesmerized by how much better she felt in his presence.

"I heard you were the one who found Marla Osbourne's body—right after you saw me, if I'm not mistaken. That must have been very difficult for you."

"You could say that," Olivia admitted. She waited for the tears to come, the ones that arrived whenever Marla's name was unexpectedly mentioned. "I'm doing better, though."

"Why don't we check the rest of your health while you're here? Take a deep breath." He stood close to her again, moving the hard metal stethoscope toward her chest. He smelled like sandalwood and vanilla. Probably aftershave.

The physical exam completed, Olivia eased herself off of the examination table. "Since I'm healing to your satisfaction, I do have a few questions—about Marla."

He didn't turn around at first. She saw his shoulders stiffen from behind.

Olivia continued anyway. "Marla left me a letter. She wrote that she'd not been feeling well for the past several weeks. Did she consult you with her concerns?"

For a moment she thought Dr. May had not heard her question. When he turned away from the sink, his hand reached up to stroke his chin.

"Without revealing too many details due to patient-doctor privilege, I can tell you that Marla did experience some common symptoms. She was new to Lily Rock, and many people take several years to adjust to the weed pollen count here, since the blooming season lasts longer than other places."

"What kind of symptoms exactly?"

"I don't suppose it hurts to tell you now that Marla's gone. She came to me for sneezing, watery eyes, congestion. She even felt nauseated at times, complaining that spicy foods did not agree with her anymore. I wasn't too concerned. Prescribed some antihistamines and cough suppressant. Over-the-counter medicines, nothing complicated."

"Her symptoms didn't improve?"

"Now that you mention it, I had her down for an appointment for today. I think she was coming in to talk about the possibility of allergy shots. Maybe the drug store remedies weren't strong enough."

He opened the examination room door and glanced into the hall. "My next patient is coming. I can talk to you more about this later. How about having dinner with me tonight?"

For a brief moment Olivia reconsidered the man in front of her. In his seventies, he cut a pretty dashing figure. Still athletic in build, his gray hair swept back from his tan face into a ponytail. Was he asking her out on a date?

Since she wanted to know more about Marla, Olivia decided quickly. "Okay. Where would you like to meet?"

"How about we meet at the Lily Rock Brew Pub around six?"

"I had a great burger there recently," she mentioned, just to make conversation.

His eyebrows raised. "Arlo hired the new chef from down the hill. Arturo brings excellent flavor to his cooking. A bit spicy for some."

"Oh, I can handle the spice." Olivia laughed. "See you at six."

She hurried to the waiting-room exit. Out of doors, the cool air stabbed the stitches on her forehead.

"All ready?" asked a familiar voice. Michael stood by his truck, a steaming paper cup in his hand. "Hot chocolate," he explained, watching her eyes. "Meadow makes it for all the library patrons. Quite good too. Want a sip?"

Olivia shook her head. Already regretting the dinner date with Dr. May, she wondered if she should tell Michael. *That's just what he wants, for me to check in with him every two minutes. He's a bit of a control freak, just like Don. If I have dinner with someone, it isn't any of Michael's business!*

"I'm ready to go if you are. I've got a few phone calls to make, one to Marla's attorney. Do you mind driving me back?"

Michael emptied the chocolate remains from his cup into a plant along the boardwalk. "Let's go," he said reaching into his pocket. Jingling the keys, he opened the passenger-side door of his truck. She heard his cell phone ring.

He put the phone to his ear. "Hi Brad. Okay then. I'll tell her. Are you certain it's safe? Good. We'll be by in a few minutes." He walked around the truck after shutting her door and got behind the wheel.

"That was Brad," he explained to Olivia. "Your car is ready to pick up. Brand new brake linings and pads. I'll take you to his shop." His lips tightened as he put the keys into the ignition. The truck drove smoothly onto the road.

He doesn't seem very happy about the car, Olivia thought. "Are you okay?"

He nodded.

"Are you sure?"

Michael pulled off the main road. A sign that said *Brad's Garage* pointed down a dirt road. The truck wobbled along, coming upon an old military Quonset hut surrounded by trees. Cars and trucks lined up in front of the makeshift building. Olivia's old Ford stood on the side, first in line.

"I'll walk in with you," Michael grumbled, swinging out of his seat.

Okay then. Just be a grumpy bear. At least I have my car.

CHAPTER ELEVEN

Overheard in Lily Rock

"He asked me lots of questions, over and over. I finally asked him why he was so obsessed with me."
"You were on a date, right? What did you expect?"

A few hours later Olivia backed her car into the last parking spot at the Lily Rock Brew Pub. As she approached the outdoor stairway, voices buzzed from the heated patio nestled in the pines. Trees rustled around the building, depositing a fine dust of pollen over the deck's railing.

"Would you like a table?" asked the red-lipped waitress, who had a small bar apron tied at the back of her thin waist.

"I'm looking for Dr. May."

"What's that? You have to speak up over this din," said the waitress, holding one hand over her ear.

"Doctor—"

"Oh, you're the one. The doc said to look out for you. He's at his usual table by the fire." The waitress pointed to the back of the outdoor seating area, where Olivia caught sight of the older man, his head cocked, watching the television over the fireplace.

Doc looked up as she approached. He stood to pull out a chair, waiting for her to sit down. Like a spicy cologne, his warm presence made her feel welcome.

A male waiter stood next to the doc's shoulder, smiling down at Olivia. "So you're the one he's been waiting for." Turning toward the doctor, he added, "You're right. She's beautiful, just like you said."

Olivia felt a blush coming up her neck. *How do you handle an old man's praise without feeling slightly pleased, yet a little annoyed at the same time?* Being objectified by the one who had just stuck a stethoscope down her shirt felt a tad awkward.

Turning back to the doctor, the waiter asked, "Your usual, Doc? Do you want the sticky wings, too, or just a plate of calamari?"

Without asking Olivia, the doctor ordered. "We'll take the wings and the calamari." Looking over at her he said, "I assume you drink beer. Take a look at the choices." He handed her a menu.

"Actually, I'd prefer a seltzer with a squeeze of lemon."

The doctor's face fell.

I guess he wanted a drinking companion, thought Olivia.

The waiter smiled and left their table as Olivia folded her hands in her lap, waiting for him to lead the conversation.

Dr. May sat quietly, gazing into the nearby fire, as Olivia took a moment to observe the rest of the outdoor restaurant. Propane heaters placed between the tables provided enough heat for the restaurant to be filled to capacity on this chilly spring evening.

The stone fireplace and oversized television screen made their spot the most desirable. Olivia wondered why the doctor deserved his own table and how long they held it for him. *He's important here in Lily Rock. Maybe that's how they roll.*

As if reading her mind, he opened the conversation. "This is my table. They make sure it's available when I get here. Of course, I'm a steady customer, and I was the deciding vote on the town council when they required a permit to build. How do you like the structure?"

"Oh, I think it's charming," replied Olivia without hesitation. "The roughhewn construction among the pines looks so cozy. It feels a lot like Marla's place."

Doc took his time looking around the outdoor seating area, staring through the glass toward the indoor bar. He didn't speak. The waiter placed a sparkling water in front of Olivia and a full beer glass at the doctor's place. The doc smiled before taking a long sip.

Holding the glass in his hand. He turned to catch the eye of the hovering waiter. "Another one when you get a moment."

Olivia sipped from her glass of sparkling water. She waited for him to respond to her earlier observation.

"You know Michael Bellemare designed this place and Marla's home as well?"

Olivia nodded her head.

"So were you just testing me? Don't worry. I have no beef with architect Michael. He did a good job. Of course, he was paid outrageously for his work."

"He didn't mention his fee."

"He wouldn't be so tawdry as to speak of money. He's trying real hard to impress you. You might even be a little alarmed at the millions going his way just to make a name for himself in Chicago."

Instead of disagreeing with the doctor, she smiled. If he wanted to get between her and Michael, he'd have to work harder; she had no dog in that fight. She just wanted to encourage him to keep talking. The more information she could get on the mysterious Michael Bellemare, the more she would learn about Marla's last weeks prior to her death.

"All of us wondered how he would continue to rake in the money from Marla after her place was completed. He made himself real cozy on her property, holding all the keys, making big decisions for her."

Warming to his topic with a second beer, the doctor continued. "Bellemare managed to get the bid for the pub. We thought he'd be leaving Lily Rock when he finished with Marla's place, but oh no! He got another job so he could stay longer. Of course, he and Marla—"

Her gut clenched. *Here we go again about Michael and Marla.* Talk of their couple-hood annoyed her. Not like she cared one way or another.

"Oh, they most certainly were a couple. All over town he'd follow her like a puppy. They could be seen everywhere together, him looking inscrutable and her like she swallowed sunshine in a jar."

By the time the wings and calamari arrived, Olivia knew more than expected about Marla and Michael and the town's opinion of them both. Yet she'd heard very little about Marla's health.

"He went to all the council meetings with her," said Doc, with his fingers wrapped around a sticky chicken wing. "Have some." He gestured toward the plate.

Olivia shook her head. "I'm not that hungry."

"Try the calamari. It's the best in town."

Giving in to his eagerness, Olivia reached her fingers toward the basket. She selected a small sample to place on her own plate. The fried coating made her stomach turn.

The doc kept talking. "So all of this is to say—stay away

from Michael. I don't mean to order you about, but you're new to town and recovering from a head injury. I just don't trust him."

Rather than respond to the doc's warning, she drew in a deep breath, pushing her chair away from the table. "If you'll excuse me, I'll be right back. Have to use the ladies."

People filled the indoor area, where she glanced toward the bar. Arlo smiled at her from behind the burnished counter. He polished a glass, giving her a big wink. "Olivia. I didn't see you come in!"

Ignoring the sign to the restroom, she walked toward him. Arlo reached over the counter to give her a small hug. "Good to see you. Here with Michael?"

"I'm here with Dr. May," she answered, speaking into his ear over the din of voices.

Arlo reached for another wet glass from the sink. "I see. He comes here every day. You sitting at his table?"

"I am."

"I'll stop by in a few minutes. Doc likes an update on the kitchen. He especially likes to sample all the food. We put it on his bill, of course." Arlo smiled. "How are you getting along at Marla's place, now that it's all yours?"

"I don't feel like the place is mine. One piece of paper and an overnight stay do not make a home for me. It will take time."

"Will you go back to Playa del Rey or stay here in Lily Rock?"

"I've thought about it. I have a temp job waiting for me in a Los Angeles law office. I let them know I'll be staying here for a while, at least until the legalities of the estate are in motion. I'm not sure what to do with the property. Maybe put it on the market?"

"I am real sorry to hear that, Olivia. Cay and I like you

and hoped you'd stick around. We even figured out a paying job for you. If you're looking for work, you are more than welcome to hang out with us here at the pub. Ever done any waitressing?"

"I've done a little bit of nearly everything." Olivia nervously fingered the hair over her ear. *I wonder if the doc misses me yet?* She glanced around the room, her eyes drifting past a small performance stage, then back to Arlo.

Once upon a time, I would have been the one on that stage. Nostalgia swept over her, but she packed it back down quickly.

"I'd better find the restroom and get back to the doc. Thanks for the suggestion about a job. You're a good person, Arlo. You and Cay."

Placing another dry glass on the counter, Arlo reached over to give Olivia another quick hug. "I'll be out to your table really soon," he mumbled in her ear.

When she returned, Olivia found the doctor staring at the television screen. He pushed his chair back to stand as she approached. "Not necessary." She smiled at him, pulling out her own chair.

Just as Arlo had promised, he showed up with a small plate that he placed in the middle of their table. "Pulled pork sliders," he commented, "with a secret ingredient."

"Did you order this, Olivia?" The doctor's jaw tightened, displaying a deep vein that slid up the left side of his face.

"I saw Arlo in the bar. He mentioned a new item on the menu."

The doctor looked over the plate of sliders.

"So what's the special ingredient?" Olivia reached for a slider to put next to her calamari.

The doc grabbed one and quickly took a bite, washing it down with a sip of beer. "Lily Rock has attracted some new attention from foodies in Los Angeles. I suggested to Arlo that he hire a new chef to bring distinction to the cuisine at the Brew Pub."

Olivia's face showed surprise. "Are you a part owner with Arlo and Cayenne?"

The doc finished his slider by licking his fingers. "I do have ownership in several Lily Rock businesses. No harm in that."

Olivia poked at a slider with her finger. "Looks like the pork was cooked with some kind of coating." She pressed her index finger into the meat.

"I think the chef coats the pork in a special blend of his own, made from local plants here on the hill."

As the doctor spoke, Olivia's attention wandered to Arlo behind the bar. Tall and thin, he did not look like a man who cared for food or drink, while the doc obviously enjoyed both in abundance. Are they friends or some kind of business partners?

She glanced at her cell phone. An hour had passed, and still no talk about Marla's health and what may have caused her heart failure. Clearing her throat, she waited. "So Doc, what about Marla? Were you aware she had heart problems?"

He dabbed the barbecue-stained cloth napkin around his mouth. Turning to look over his left shoulder, he signaled to the waiter. "Time for one more beer."

Rather than be ignored again, Olivia redirected: "But about Marla—"

The doctor scowled. "Let me just say this one more time, and then we can drop the topic for some pleasant discourse. Marla had allergies. She never complained about heart problems.

"There was no record of cardiac arrest in her medical files. I don't know why her heart stopped. But I do know it happens, especially up here where the altitude is higher than most people are used to. She may have stopped exercising, what with the construction, and she may have turned to more cocktails to cope with the stress of building. One thing led to another, and her heart just stopped. That's the best I can offer —from my professional opinion."

Olivia leaned back in her chair. Though he'd invited her to dinner on the pretense of saying more about Marla's heath, in fact he'd said nothing new. This puzzled her.

After another delivery of the doctor's beer, she pushed her chair back to prepare to leave. "Thank you so much for dinner."

This time the doctor did not stand up. He forced a smile. "This has been quite pleasant. Perhaps we can meet another time, for a local concert maybe?"

In her gut Olivia knew that brushing him off would not be well received. She smiled at him without agreeing to another —was it a date?

Now Doc stood up from the table. "Before you go, did you check out your car? My nephew said Michael brought it back."

Relieved that she had not given in to his request, Olivia's words tumbled out quickly. "I got the car. Drove it here, as a matter of fact. The brakes were wonky. He fixed them. Nice guy, your nephew. Thanks for recommending him to me."

Dr. May pulled a wallet out of his back pocket. "Let me offer you some money for the repairs and for the next few days while you're here. I feel like Lily Rock owes you that for the unfortunate road and the inconvenience we've caused you."

Olivia felt shock overtake her face. "Oh no, that won't be necessary." She playfully pushed his hand away, adding, "I can take care of the expense."

Shoving the wallet back into his pocket, the doc said,

"Well then, why don't I walk you to your car?" As if a window shade had been pulled down over the previous scowl, a smile appeared on the doc's lips.

He thinks I'm funny. I wonder why?

Olivia waited for Doc to pull on a leather jacket. Weaving her way through the crowded patio, they headed toward the exit. On the way down the metal stairs, the doctor grabbed her arm. "Do you mind? I'm a little wobbly on these stairs."

Too much to drink, or showing his age? She took his hand to wrap into the crook of her elbow. They walked slowly, taking one step at a time. As soon as they reached the pavement at the end of the stairs, Olivia disengaged his hand.

Doc stood in front of her, shifting from foot to foot as if to find his balance. Olivia felt her hand at the ready, should she need to steady him.

Finally he spoke. "Olivia, I don't want to alarm you, but my nephew called me this afternoon. He felt uncomfortable telling you. The brakes on your car? Despite Michael's insistence, there was nothing wrong with them. Brad won't be charging you for any repairs."

"But Michael said—"

"That confused Brad too. He wasn't sure why Michael brought the car back to him, but he wanted you to know he didn't charge you for the labor of inspecting the brakes either. He's like that. Brad's a good kid."

The doctor cleared his throat. He reached over to rest his hand on her shoulder. "Stay as far away as you can from Michael Bellemare," he warned again. "He's not a good person."

"Thanks, Doc. I appreciated our conversation and the food. See you around."

Sliding behind the wheel, she looked through her

rearview window. The doc stumbled toward his vehicle, stopping several times to regain his balance.

She shifted her car into reverse as her cell phone rang.

"Hello."

"It's me, Michael."

That's interesting timing. He's sticking close to me, like the doc said he did with Marla.

"What's up?"

"Would you like to have dinner at my place?"

At the pub, Olivia had felt no hunger. But now her stomach grumbled. She was ravenous. Ignoring the doctor's warning, Olivia asked, "Why don't you come to Marla's place for dinner? I can find something in my full refrigerator. Do you like salmon?"

"Salmon sounds great, but how about this—I can throw something on the grill and bring it up to your place. I can cook; I am a man of many talents."

Her stomach growled. "Sounds good. Let's grill."

Michael laughed. "See you in fifteen minutes."

The phone clicked.

CHAPTER TWELVE

Overheard in Lily Rock

"My boyfriend isn't a vegan—he's a free-gan. He will only eat free food."

Once through the front door, Olivia walked downstairs to the guest room suite. She yawned, taking a moment to fold back the comforter. *Maybe I can stretch out and take a small nap before Michael gets here. I can think about what I learned at the pub.*

Doc says Marla had no previous history of heart problems. She did have lots of allergies. Is there a connection between her allergies, the EpiPen, and her death?

Olivia's eyes fluttered, then opened abruptly. *And what about the smoke the day I discovered the body?* Her eyes closed again.

"Olivia," Michael's voice called from upstairs. "Are you here?"

She sat upright on her bed, rubbing her hand over her eyes. *How long have I been asleep?* "I'll be right there," she called up to Michael.

Standing in front of the bathroom sink, she splashed cold water on her face. Her cheeks turned rosy as she patted her skin dry. A touch of lip gloss made her look presentable.

Michael has to know more than he's saying.

Twenty minutes later, Michael sat at the dining room table, watching Olivia eat. She vigorously chewed on the last bite of sirloin, thinking, *The man can grill, I've got to admit.*

"Coffee?" he inquired, glancing at her empty plate. "Unless you want me to grill another steak for your dining pleasure?"

"Coffee would be great. I think I've made good work of this piece of meat."

Olivia noticed a shy smile at the corner of his mouth. *Why does my appetite amuse him so much?* she wondered.

When he returned with two full mugs of coffee he suggested, "Let's move to the great room. We can sit more comfortably."

She glanced past his shoulder. *Be careful. He might want to start something on that really comfy-looking sofa.*

I'll fix him. Olivia moved toward the great room. *But I am a sucker for the smell of leather,* she thought as she sat primly on the edge of the seat cushion.

"You don't want to sit over here where we can hear each other better?" Michael patted the cushion next to him. He sat at the opposite end, stretching his arm across the back of the sofa.

So comfortable in his own skin. I wish I had his confidence. She took a sip of coffee. Then she blurted, "I had a drink with Doc May earlier."

Michael's eyes widened.

"After he checked my head and the stitches, he asked me to meet him. I had more questions about Marla's cause of death. I thought he'd be more comfortable talking to me away from his office, so I said yes when he asked."

Why am I talking so fast? Olivia felt puzzled at her own behavior.

"That old scoundrel," muttered Michael under his breath.

She placed her empty coffee mug on a side table, leaning back into the cushions.

Michael watched her closely.

At least he's man-spreading on his end of the sofa, she mused to herself, enjoying his obvious discomfort. "The doc was evasive about Marla. He said she visited him a month ago, and he diagnosed allergies. I suppose he didn't want to break his doctor-patient privilege. Maybe he thinks someone will sue him if he tells me any more details."

Michael raised his eyebrows. "You'd be surprised. The lawsuits in this town outnumber the inhabitants, going back decades. People hold grudges, and they don't give in readily. At least four attorneys make a good living here, passing clients back and forth, showing up in the city for court, and not settling a damned thing."

"Sounds like you speak with the voice of experience."

"I have three cases pending at the moment. All from Lily Rock."

"You haven't lived here that long. What's the deal?"

"Meadow, on behalf of the Lily Rock town council, sued me for not getting all the permits approved. She says the building is okay, but we need another permit approved for the parking. You would think, since this is a project for her own daughter, that she'd give us a break."

"Sage mentioned the plan for the performing arena to me when I stayed with them. Her mother doesn't like the idea?"

"Neither does Meadow's posse of followers, who think I've had too much influence in the town. They don't appreciate the hipster vibe either. The pub, as you may have noticed, attracts younger people. Big no-no for the group that calls themselves the Old Rockers."

"I would think the influx of tourist cash would be welcome."

"You would think, but it's not true. The Old Rockers want money, but on their terms. They complain about all the new Airbnbs that court young people who party for a weekend, leaving the mess on Sunday afternoon for the residents to clean up. I understand their concerns, but I think there are ways to accommodate the younger crowd without keeping the place back in the last century."

"So how can Meadow sue you for something that's in a planning stage?"

"Oh, she claims that I've taken her council authority for granted and that I've overstayed my welcome. She's also accused me of misusing the funding from the school, and she's determined to prove it one way or another. I'm kind of tired of fighting her off. She may get her way after all, though I do like Sage and think she has the best interests of her students in mind."

Olivia nodded. "I like Sage too. But now I wonder how she gets along with her mother, living in the same house with such disparate views."

"Apparently you don't live with your mother," Michael commented quietly.

Olivia laughed. "Oh no. I moved out when I turned eighteen. I do miss her, though. She passed away four years ago."

"That must still be fresh. What about your father? Is he still in the picture?"

"He died before I was born. I don't know much about him really. My mother rarely spoke of him."

"So you are without parents. I must admit I have had

123

moments when I wished my dad would pass to the great beyond and get off of my back."

"Your dad? The famous architect in Chicago?"

"The very one. He's not over the idea that I don't want to continue on with his business and his legacy in Chicago. I love my work. I just don't want the complications of fame and more fortune. Learned that the hard way."

Olivia's mind wandered. *How come he's so interesting? I like that he wants to split from his father's fame. I wonder if that's real or just what he says to people to make them think he's his own person—*

Alarmed that she'd let down her guard, Olivia reminded herself, *Nice guy or not, he might have murdered Marla. Don't forget how quickly he showed up on the scene after I found her dead body.*

She picked up the conversation. "That's why you moved here to Lily Rock? To get away from the city and your dad?"

Michael nodded.

I can't help but think he'd look more tense if he'd murdered someone only a few days ago. Look at him, spread out on his end of the sofa while he sips that sugary brew he calls coffee. Looks like he doesn't have a care in the world.

"So, Olivia, I want to spend the night. Do you think that's possible?"

Aha! He does have an ulterior motive. Here it comes. Am I the next victim?

She stared at Michael, her eyes glaring across the length of the long sofa.

He cleared his throat. "Oh, not like that! I didn't mean sleep-with-you-in-your-bed kind of spend the night."

"What did you mean then?"

Michael's face flushed red. He reached his hand toward

her. She crossed her arms in front of her stomach, feeling her jaw tighten.

"Look, Olivia. I admit I am attracted to you, but we've only known each other for a few days, and you're still recovering from shock and a bad car accident. Please don't be mad at me."

"What did you mean then, about spending the night?" she repeated.

"I'm concerned about your safety in this house. I would feel a lot better if you'd take over Marla's old room and let me sleep in the guest suite until we get more information about her death."

"So you are suggesting a friendly sleepover night?"

Michael grinned. "Sort of, if that's what you want to call it."

Olivia stared at her lap, thinking, *There is no chance in hell you are spending the night with me, buster.*

"I can see having me stay here might be a problem for you. I get it. I'm a stranger, and you must be feeling protective of your own space. How about a compromise?"

Olivia sighed deeply.

Michael stood. He picked up her coffee mug along with his own.

Good, he's being useful.

When he returned she had tucked her legs back under her body as she stared into the darkness across the room.

He sat at the other end of the sofa, speaking in a quiet voice. "Okay, let's explore another idea. Tomorrow I'll have my guys come over to inspect the house for any possible ways someone could break in. Along with that inspection, I will have them change every lock in the place. One new set of keys will go to you."

Keep talking, cowboy—

"I've nearly finished the house electronic security system, so I can complete that in less than ten days."

"Will I be safe, with everyone running in and out of the house?"

"No, you won't be safe. That's why I want you to stay in my cabin. I'll find somewhere else to bunk while you are there. No hanky-panky on my watch."

He uses the cowboy drawl when he's nervous.

"I like your idea—at least most of it. If you don't think it would be too much trouble, I'd like to stay close to the house and observe the workers during the day. That way I can also get in touch with an attorney and sort through some of Marla's stuff. But Michael, I don't want to sleep in your cabin. Nothing personal."

Except that it is personal—very personal. I do not want to be murdered in my bed.

"Not a problem."

You may say it's not a problem, but your face speaks otherwise.

"I'll make sure you're secure for tonight. You can call me with any emergency. Then let me get things rolling with a few phone calls early tomorrow."

I'll take him at his word, she grudgingly admitted. *At least for now.*

He pulled a cell phone from his back pocket.

"It's nine o'clock. Isn't it too late to be calling people?" she asked.

"Just the right time. My crew likes to hear my voice before they go to sleep every night. I tell them my own kind of bedtime story."

She raised her eyebrows.

"Knowing you have work the next day always brings a

better night's sleep, no matter when the call comes in," Michael explained with a laugh.

He stared at his screen. "It looks like Janis has been trying to get a hold of me. Maybe she has information about Marla. Do you mind if I call her back now?"

Just when I was starting to trust him, Officer Jets steps in. Olivia walked toward the kitchen.

When she turned off the water faucet, she overheard Michael say, "Okay then. I'll see you bright and early tomorrow morning at the station. Goodbye."

Olivia dried her hands on a nearby towel as Michael entered the kitchen.

"Looks like our plans for tomorrow may be a little more complicated than I thought. It seems Janis wants to interview me this time—at the station."

Hair rose on Olivia's neck. "Why do they want to talk to you?"

"Janis figures I was the last one to see Marla alive. They think I spent the night with her and that I was in the house the morning she died in the grove."

So Janis is finally tuning in to my vibe. Took her long enough. Olivia hesitated, then asked, "Well, were you in the house the day she was killed? Did you spend the night?"

"I told you, Marla and I were not like that!" Michael turned on his heel to walk out of the kitchen. The next sound Olivia heard was the slam of the front door.

He really is moody. Kind of like my ex. Except he isn't a meth user or a drunk. At least, I don't think he is. What do I know? It's only been a few days since we met.

Olivia turned to switch off the kitchen lights. She looked into the great room, where shadows drifted across the empty spaces. Fear gripped her gut. Her hands clenched.

Now I have to worry about my own safety. Why didn't he

just answer my question? Either yes, he was in the house that morning, or no, he was not. He must be guilty, or he would not have stormed out.

The bottoms of Olivia's socks slid over the wood flooring as she tested every door and window on the upper level. Finally she opened the front door to check on her car, nearly tripping over Mayor Maguire, who was lying just outside. The dog rose up on all fours. He smiled at her, his tongue slipping out the side of his wide jaw.

"Hey, M&M."

The dog took a step forward, sniffing the hand at her side before walking past her into the house.

Olivia closed the door, testing the lock to make certain that it held while the dog waited expectantly behind her back.

"So you're my body guard tonight?" Mayor Maguire's nails clicked against the wood floors as he followed her across the room. "Do you want to sleep in my bed?"

The dog ran ahead. He waited at the foot of the stairs. For the next twenty minutes they both continued the security check on all the windows and doors on the lower level. Feeling satisfied, Olivia moved toward her bedroom, and she reached out to flick on the light near the door.

Mayor Maguire stood in front of her, preventing her movement into the room. He held his nose in the air to sniff. Then with two strides and one leap he landed in the middle of the bed, turning himself three times before resting his curly head on the pillow.

"Do you need me to read you a bedtime story?"

The dog's ears flicked and his eyes remained closed.

CHAPTER THIRTEEN

Overheard in Lily Rock
"Those tattoos are from the rough streets of Beverly Hills."

Olivia awakened in the dark to Mayor Maguire's gentle snore. She pondered the previous day's events with her eyes closed. Resting a hand on his curly dog fur, she ran her fingers across his body.

He's so comforting.

For a moment she reveled in her feeling of well-being— and then she wondered about Michael's angry departure. Olivia sighed, closing her eyes.

Why did he offer to protect me and then leave so abruptly? He probably slept with Marla and the cop, both at the same time. He just didn't want to admit it to me.

I wish I could trust people again—this is ugly Olivia right here, lying in bed with a dog in the middle of the night. She doesn't trust anyone human; thank you, ex-boyfriend.

"That girl is following you," she'd said to her ex after a concert.

"Oh, that happens all the time," he'd answer. "Nothing to worry about. She's just a groupie."

"All the guys sleep with the groupies," she had commented to Don.

"They do, but not me. I never get attached."

I never get attached. Sure, Don. Only one-night stands for you. I bet Michael plays with the truth just like Don.

Maybe Dr. May would be a welcome change from a younger man. *At least he has a profession and cares about people other than himself. Not his fault Marla didn't make it to the next appointment.*

Mayor Maguire's breathing transitioned into a loud snore. Olivia draped her arm over his body. Sleep approached. As her eyes drooped, her mind drifted back to Michael.

All of his talk about surveillance. He must feel pretty bad about Marla being dead on his watch. I'll let him install more cameras. Cameras—he could already be watching me right now. How would I know?

Olivia opened her eyes. The clock glowed. Two a.m. *Now that I'm fully awake, I'd better check to see if there are cameras in the room.*

She shifted her head to the left, looking at the wall a few feet away. Her heart thumped against her chest. Her feet hit the warm floorboards first. She walked around the guest suite, looking for evidence of cameras.

What am I looking for exactly? Maybe a blinking red light?

Finding no evidence of a camera in the guest suite, Olivia tiptoed along the wood planking down the hallway, running her hand against the wall in the darkness.

Maybe there's a camera in a corner of the spare room. She opened the next door on the left.

Two twin beds, made up with linens and fluffy pillows. No blinking lights or any sign of a camera in here. She opened the next door, which revealed a washer and dryer stacked next to each other, both white.

The door to the dryer was not fully closed. When she opened the door fully, clothing tumbled out on her feet. She pulled the remaining pieces from the back of the appliance, placing a bundle on the folding table. Three armfuls later, the large-capacity dryer was empty.

Olivia stared at the mound of laundry. *Might as well fold it. I'm wide awake.*

Marla's underwear. What do I do with a dead person's panties? Olivia continued to fold as her mind wandered. Four neat piles of Marla's clothing lay before her. She patted each one. "Thank you for serving Marla," she mumbled, a ritual she'd learned in some book on closet organizing.

A gleam of light came from the laundry room window. The full moon shone against the panes of glass. Turning away, Olivia lifted a pair of distressed jeans from the table. *They might fit me. As if getting her house isn't enough, now I'm going to wear Marla's clothes.*

Olivia shook out the wrinkled jeans, holding them away from her body. With the light from the full moon at the window she could read the tag. *We wore the same size in high school.*

Gathering the jeans under her arm, she walked out of the laundry room. *I'm sure Marla wouldn't mind. She hated for good things to go to waste. Even if they don't fit, I can throw in a load of my own dirty clothes tomorrow.*

Oh. I forgot to check for a camera light in the laundry room. Olivia dropped the jeans on her dresser. She walked back down the hall, toward the laundry room. Standing in the center, she looked around. Her gaze traveled to the corners, to the machines, and then back to the moonlit window. A trickle of apprehension tickled up her spine.

She gasped.

Illuminated eyes from the window stared back at her. Human eyes.

Olivia ran to the window, whisking the curtains closed. She darted from the room, her hand held over her thumping chest.

Someone is watching me. Should I call 911? Would Janis Jets respond?

Her thoughts jumbled in her head. *Michael said they rarely get instant help up the hill. I could call him, but what if he was the one outside looking in? I don't know who that was.*

But then Michael has keys, he wouldn't need to stay outside. I am so confused!

In the guest suite, she stopped to catch her breath.

I have to get out of here—by myself.

"You can't do anything yourself," Don's voice sneered in her memory.

"Oh yes I can," she said aloud, overriding her fear.

Marla's jeans fit her perfectly. Just like in high school.

From the bed, Mayor Maguire lifted his head.

"Go check in the laundry room, you big mutt. Do some barking. Protect me from being murdered in my bed."

The dog's head rested on his paws as his eyes closed again.

Maybe he isn't alarmed. Maybe—just maybe—the intruder is familiar to him?

Olivia hurried, pulling a thick sweater from the drawer.

Now fully onboard with dressing in Marla's clothes she stood beside the bed with a backpack full of essentials, watching Mayor Maguire. *He's not mine,* she told herself. *He belongs to Lily Rock.*

"Goodbye, M&M. You are the best."

The dog's eyes followed her to the doorway.

Get back to sleep. I've got this.

Once upstairs she opened the browser own her cell phone to search on the internet.

That's it! I can take the hiking trail to the desert tram. By the time I arrive it will be operating for the day. I'll buy a ticket. No car for me. They may have bugged it or even messed with the engine. All that confusion over the brakes must have meant something.

Fearful that she might be followed through a GPS in her cell phone, she left it in a drawer. *I can call Ted from a pay phone when I get to Playa. He would be happy to pick me up.*

I feel pretty good right now. I can do this. She inhaled deeply, remembering the person outside her window. *I wonder if the intruder is still there?*

Grabbing her purse, Olivia stood in place, bracing herself to open the front door. *Go out the back,* she told herself.

The clock in the kitchen ticked; the hands pointed to minutes before 3 a.m.

She let herself out of the back door, leaving it ajar for the dog. Backpack full of essentials slung over her shoulder, Olivia disappeared into the dark.

Onward and upward. Let's get the hell out of Lily Rock.

Olivia walked along the path, within the shadows of the trees. She quickened her pace to stay ahead of the sunrise. Past the berm in the road, her shoes slid a few feet in the loose dirt along the trail. Arms outstretched, she kept her balance.

Am I going in the right direction? Olivia reached for her cell phone. She patted all her pockets. Then she remembered that she'd deliberately left the phone back at Marla's house. *Now I don't even know what time it is.*

Light seeped over the tree-lined path. She inhaled deeply, making her steps easier, walking further into the forest. *I can do this,* she coached herself. *I can ...*

By the time Olivia reached the entrance to Pines to Palms Park, visitors were lined up at the booth to purchase tickets to the tram. Olivia stepped up to the open window.

"May I help you?"

"One ticket for the tram."

"Certainly. The tram doesn't start for another hour, but the ticket gives you access to hiking trails. Have you hiked here before?"

Olivia handed over her cash. "No. I haven't."

The ranger reached under the counter to bring up a map. He spread it out on the counter between them. Then he explained what she already knew from her previous research on her cell phone. Rather than act disinterested, Olivia opened her eyes to take in any new information.

"Be sure to keep in touch with your cell phone," the man warned, folding the map. "That's how we help people if they get into trouble. There are mountain lions up here, and it's rattlesnake season."

Fear made a knot in her belly. She forced her face to remain calm. *I hate snakes. Me and Indiana Jones.*

"Do you want to sign the guest pass now?" the man asked, shoving the pocket-sized paper over the counter.

She looked into his eyes. Had this been a week ago, she'd have signed in a heartbeat. She may have even agreed to a cup of coffee with this attractive young man.

No you don't, Olivia Greer.

"I'll sign it later. Thanks so much!" Olivia waved at his stricken face.

As she turned to make way for the next customer, a car pulled up a few feet from the booth. Stepping quickly toward the outdoor restrooms, Olivia disappeared behind a group of trees.

She took up her observation from there. Someone familiar sat behind the wheel. Olivia gasped as Cayenne Perez stepped out from the driver's side.

Cayenne pulled out a plunger and a mop from the trunk of her car. Next she held up a red bucket and an industrial-sized bottle of bathroom cleaner. Olivia recognized the brand; she'd seen it before—at Marla's.

Cayenne must have a cleaning contract with the park facilities—or she's following me. After a few minutes Cay returned from the toilets and headed back to the car, carrying the mop and a full bucket.

She's very sporty—more like a—

As Cay bent over the bucket to insert her mop into the sudsy water, Olivia observed more closely. Standing to her full height, Cay's shirt collar slipped, revealing a strong neck and—a very visible Adam's apple at her throat.

Oh. Olivia finally knew what had bothered her since first meeting Cay. *So that's what's so different about her—I mean him—no, I mean her.*

Olivia swallowed. She wanted to call out to Cay. To tell her that she knew and that everything was okay. Not that Cay had asked for her approval. *Why do I care so much about people I hardly know?*

Leaving Cayenne with her work, she found a worn path heading toward the woods. She began her self-talk. *I have to get out of here,* she warned herself in a rhythmic chant. *I—have—to—get—out—of—here,* she repeated. One foot, then another.

I—am—not—safe.

CHAPTER FOURTEEN

Overheard in Lily Rock

"I don't date. I just exist—some of the time with other people."

As the sun sparkled behind the trees, Olivia stepped to the side of the trail to let hikers pass. She didn't recognize anyone from Lily Rock. *They must be weekenders,* she thought.

After her short time in the mountains, Olivia suspected that the divide between the full-time and part-time residents lay just beneath the surface of the idyllic town veneer. The need to make a living hugely influenced the residents. Many toggled together several jobs just to make ends meet. The overlapping roles alone confused her. Plus just in the past few days her gut told her Lily Rock held many secrets.

The further Olivia hiked toward the tram, the less frightened she felt. Distance brought her a wider emotional perspective. When she thought of Michael, his easy grin, and the warmth of his gaze, she did not suspect a hidden agenda. Remembering the doc, she sighed. The old fool had a drinking problem. Olivia had personal experience with that particular demon. How could she judge him without judging herself?

Meadow and Sage, they acted like a typical mother and daughter, bickering over the small stuff, forgetting how much they loved each other. And Skye—well, she was an aging woman with a decades-old crush on a man who did not reciprocate her feelings. *Skye and the doc would have made a good couple back in the day. I wonder why it never happened?*

And then what about Arlo and Cayenne? Ever since they'd revealed to her the letter from Marla with their signatures, she'd looked upon them with suspicion. As she hiked and relaxed, she realized she knew what made them seem out of sorts with each other. A transitioning spouse may disrupt the most stable of relationships.

Even Janis Jets and Michael Bellemare felt off to her. Maybe they were friends—maybe with benefits—or connected on some other less obvious level.

Olivia paid attention, keeping a safe distance behind the family ahead. She didn't want to engage in any conversation. Deeply inhaling the scent of pine and sun-baked earth, her mind wandered.

You are such a sissy. You had nothing to be afraid of. But what about the EpiPen? Okay, that was kind of suspicious.

Had Marla dropped the pen by accident, or had someone pitched it into the forest and out of reach? Not knowing which—if either—of the options was relevant to Marla's death, Olivia admitted confusion.

Police business. That's what Janis would tell me.

So what if Michael and Janis had a thing between them? So what if Michael had a past relationship with anyone, for that matter? *I don't own Michael.* She stopped to catch her breath, leaning against a tree. *Time for a snack.* Lifting a peanut butter sandwich from her backpack, she took several bites.

Now I'm thirsty. What was I thinking? Peanut butter on a hike?

Olivia sat in the dirt. She shoved her back against the trunk of the tree. Unused to hiking she closed her eyes to rest. Her hand clutched the crust of the sandwich she'd made hours before.

A leg cramp woke her up. She rolled to the right to point her foot, then stretch her calf. Standing, she lifted her arms over her head. Leaves and dirt clung to her jeans, which she brushed away with her hands. Looking toward the horizon, a breeze rustled the trees overhead.

Olivia admired a mesquite tree that grew in the midst of some granite boulders. She watched a branch shake over the sun-drenched rock. *Strong wind—maybe a storm is coming. Better get moving.*

As she turned to grasp her backpack, she heard a faint rustle. A gray boulder caught her attention; she saw a coiled rope nestled in the dirt nearby. *Someone must be a serious rock climber. Probably dropped—*

Olivia felt hair rise on her neck. Her eyes, drawn to the rope, watched it carefully. *There—it did move. Not a rope. When is a rope not a rope?*

When it's a snake!

Her jaw clenched as she froze in place. Her heart beat rapidly in her chest. She wracked her brain. What had that ranger said about snakes this time of year? Keeping her arms at her sides, she clenched and unclenched her fists.

Be very still, Olivia. Very still.

The coiled snake shuddered down its length, untangling to move toward Olivia. Longer than she had originally thought, the body slithered toward her, its head pointing the way. The tongue darted rapidly, in and out of the open mouth, as if sensing her to be prey.

The tail shook. Two rattles. With a surge of motion the snake slithered, stopping at her feet. The head jutted forward. She remained frozen in place.

Go hide. I won't hurt you. Just go curl up for another nap under that boulder. I will walk away—no harm, no foul.

The snake slowly coiled around her foot, looking away.

That's it. Look at the sun on that rock. Go back and finish your nap.

An intense pain shot through her leg, so severe that Olivia stopped breathing. Her eyes grew wide as she slumped to her knees in pain.

Having completed its work, the reptile slid away, disappearing into the brush.

On the ground she folded into a ball, clutching her searing leg. *Inhale deeply,* she willed her body. Sitting forward Olivia inched up the leg of her jeans and discovered two puncture holes. Blood oozed, a stream rolling steadily down her leg into her sock.

She eased her head down to the ground, lifting her leg up to place her foot on a nearby rock.

Branches overhead showed no interest in her circumstance. The breeze rustled the needles, the sky remained blue, the clouds hovered gently. *I suppose someone will find me. I can't believe I'll die of a snakebite after surviving a roll over the cliff in my car.*

She admired the blue sky overhead. Just before losing consciousness she heard a muddle of voices. Sounds came from the distance.

* * *

Olivia felt her eyes move behind her eyelids. A dull pain in her leg reminded her—the snake. Then she recognized a voice.

"I'm with Olivia Greer. She's still asleep. I'll call you with a report when she wakes up."

Sage. It must be her. Thank God it's not someone else. My hand is being touched.

"She's right here, Doc. I think she's waking up. Take a look."

Dr. May leaned over Olivia's face. She smelled his warmth—Old Spice aftershave.

"I see you returned to us," he commented. She felt his hand pull at the clothing on her chest, followed by the cold metal of the stethoscope. He listened to her heartbeat as she opened her eyes. An intravenous needle taped to her inner arm pushed liquid through a tube. A plastic bag hung from a pole next to her shoulder. *I must be in a hospital.*

"We were able to find the exact anecdote for the bite. Since you elevated and didn't wash your wound, you made it easy for us. You'll be feeling a lot better soon."

Dr. May removed his stethoscope, turning toward Sage. "Call your mom and see if she can stay with Olivia after the hospital releases her. I don't want her to be alone until she's completely out of the woods." The doctor laughed. "Out of the woods. Pretty good. I'm a funny guy."

Sage laid her cool hand on Olivia's forehead. "Are you okay, honey?" she asked.

Olivia nodded against the pillow. "Thank you so much ... you know, for saving me." Even to her own ears, her voice sounded weak.

Reaching for Olivia's hand, Sage sat on the edge of the bed. "I didn't exactly save you. Some hikers found you and decided to call the Lily Rock paramedics. They put out a bulletin, and I was free to drive up to the tram. Once the hikers brought you in, I took you to the closest hospital. Doc met me here, and he dealt with all of the medical stuff. You were very lucky!"

Olivia squeezed Sage's hand.

"Just want you to know, we couldn't find your cell phone."

Should she tell Sage the reason for her hike without a phone? "It wasn't exactly a hike. It was more of an escape, truth be told."

For the next twenty minutes Olivia described her night, with Michael leaving in a huff and her seeing an intruder from the laundry room window. "I didn't know what to think about the safety of the house. I felt like I was being watched."

"Oh, I don't think your Peeping Tom was Michael. He has the perfect alibi. Janis Jets arrested him last night, and he's in jail."

"Arrested him?"

"Apparently they got news from the toxicologist down the hill. Marla had a huge amount of marijuana in her system. They think she was allergic to the plant and that someone was responsible for poisoning her."

"Do they suspect Michael of being her dealer?"

"No, they think Michael was the last to see her alive. Something about smoke in a chimney before her death."

"I wondered that too—except Michael was busy rescuing me from the car accident. He didn't have time to kill Marla."

"That's what they thought at first. But Doc didn't determine the time of her death accurately. He thought she'd had heart failure, so he didn't take a look at other factors, and it seems the coroner down the hill thinks she died only an hour before you found her body. That would make Michael available as a possible suspect."

Olivia leaned back into the pillows. Maybe her suspicions

about Michael were well-founded. "Were Michael and Marla ... you know, lovers?"

"He's always claimed he didn't have a personal relationship with Marla, other than being the architect and builder for her house. No one believed that, of course."

"Why not?"

"He's too handsome, and she was way too clingy. Put that together, and you get personal. At least, that's what the town believes. Lily Rock also suspects that Michael wanted to inherit Marla's estate. Not completely unthinkable. She could have willed him the property. You know, just in case something happened to her."

Olivia kept quiet. She wasn't certain that Sage had heard about the inheritance from Marla, and even if she had, she must not have known that Michael signed the will as a witness. Olivia rolled onto her side. Her injured leg throbbed. Looking up at the intravenous bag, she asked, "Are they giving me pain medication?"

"I don't know what they're giving you. I can certainly find out. Give me a minute, and I'll ask a nurse."

Sage patted Olivia's hand before she turned to walk from the room.

Olivia felt a tug in her heart, remembering Michael's hurt expression the night before. Surely he hadn't killed Marla. The more she thought about Michael—well, he didn't seem to have what it would take to kill a woman.

A nurse walked into the room. He stood at the end of Olivia's bed, picked up her chart, and scanned the information. "They didn't give you pain medicine. I think they didn't want your heart to over-function, which would risk moving the poison faster. If you need something, I'll text the doctor."

Olivia shook her head. "No, I'm okay. Just a little bit of throbbing. I'd prefer to keep aware of my situation."

The nurse smiled. "You may be the first patient from Lily Rock who refused more drugs."

"I'm not from—" She stopped mid-sentence. For all intents and purposes she was from Lily Rock. She owned property there, and she had a friend who lived there.

Olivia had known when she opened her eyes in the hospital that Sage was her friend. Just hearing her voice had brought her a wave of peace.

* * *

Olivia checked out of the hospital the next morning; Sage waited in her car to drive her back to Lily Rock. Olivia propped up her foot on the dashboard of Sage's old Toyota truck, leaning back into the worn seat.

As Sage shoved the keys into the ignition she turned to Olivia. "I wondered about your head wound after the snakebite." The engine turned over as Sage looked out the windshield, snapping the gear shift out of park.

"My head's fine. Healing nicely. Not even dizzy. Let's stop with my problems." She wanted to shift the conversation away from herself and onto Sage. Though Olivia didn't think Sage would kill Marla, the young woman might know more than she realized about who did.

Bumping along the road, Olivia reached over to pat Sage's arm. "Didn't mean to sound so rude before. What I meant to say is we know so little about each other. How old are you anyway? Do you mind telling me?"

"I'm thirty-six years old. I'll be thirty-seven in two months. And you?"

"Close to you. I'll be thirty-five my next birthday." Olivia dropped her feet to the floor to sit up straight. "So have you always lived with your mother?"

"Except for the time I spent off the hill, going to school. I have a college degree in human resources. But even when I went to school in Los Angeles, I'd come home nearly every weekend."

"That's very dedicated of you."

"My mom needed me. She used to drink excessively, and she did some pills. I never knew if she'd be alive when I showed up on the weekends. The constant not knowing made me stay more and more. Finally, when I graduated, I moved back into my old room. Just easier to watch over her that way."

"You've been taking care of your mother when she's the one who should be taking care of you. What about your dad?"

"Oh, he's no problem whatsoever! I have no idea who my father is, and I've never met him."

"Really? You mean your father is not an Old Rocker gone to rest in a mountain cabin in the forest?"

Both women laughed.

"You could say my father never existed. My mom refused to talk whenever I asked about him, so I just gave up. I even tried to prod her when she was drunk, but her lips were sealed."

"So you have no idea?"

"None. And get this, Olivia. No one in town ever talks about my father either. You'd think they would spill the beans at the pub or the library, but no. Silence is golden around the topic of my sperm donor."

"Now that is odd," agreed Olivia.

So we have the missing father in common. Just like Marla and me. Her head buzzed, a familiar loneliness creeping into her thoughts. "Did you miss having a father when you were growing up?"

"Not really. Doc kind of stepped in as my male role model."

Olivia yawned. Talking sapped her strength. Instead of asking another question, she paid attention to Sage's expert driving as she navigated the steep curves up the hill and back to Lily Rock.

After a few minutes of quiet, she couldn't help herself. "Does the doc also have a drinking problem?"

"What do you mean?"

"We had dinner at the pub a couple of days ago. He got kind of inebriated. I had to help him to the parking lot."

Sage sighed. "He and my mom were drinking buddies before she got sober. I thought he'd cut down a bit now that he's nearly seventy. Sorry to hear he was such a pain."

"No problem. I was just wondering."

"And that is important—"

"I suppose his drinking over the years may have impeded his ability to be a really good doctor."

"You can trust him with his medical knowledge." Sage's mouth tightened. "He's been there for me and Mom. Plus he's a saint with animals. Did you know he runs the animal sanctuary in Lily Rock?"

"I did hear something like that from Skye. She talks a lot about Doc."

"Speaking of Skye, stay on the right side of that woman. She's a handful, and she protects the doc. Skye has had a crush on him going back decades. She is particularly difficult with the women he finds attractive, which can be anyone female when it comes right down to it."

"So Doc has lived on the hill his entire life?"

"Mom tells me he worked down the hill for a few years after medical school at some kind of clinic. She's pretty knowledgeable about the doc if you have any more questions." Sage's voice lowered.

I am asking too many questions. Apparently Sage has a limit when it comes to talking about her male role model.

The road leveled in front of the truck, revealing the sign: *Welcome to Lily Rock.* Olivia's stomach tensed. Before she could figure out why, Sage asked, "Should we drop by Marla's to get some clothes, or do you want to go to our place to rest? We can go back later."

"I want to go to the police station."

"Okay then. I'll drop you there. I have to get back to the school office. Let me know if you need a ride when you're done. Just use the phone there, and I'll come pick you up."

I have to find the truth, even if it means staying here in Lily Rock.

CHAPTER FIFTEEN

Overheard in Lily Rock
"She's not my girlfriend ... we just make content together."

Olivia stood on the boardwalk in the middle of town. She took a moment to run her fingers through her hair. *I nearly escaped this town. Yet I feel hiccupped back to where I began.*

Lily Rock Constabulary, read the sign above her head. *Lily Rock can't have an ordinary police office; they have to name it something fancy.*

She straightened her jacket, pulling it around her body as she reached for the doorknob of the constabulary office. With a sweep of the door, Olivia stepped in, ready for a fight. She clenched her fists at her sides, thrusting her chin forward. "Who is in charge here?"

"That would be me," said a familiar voice. Michael stood from behind the computer desk. He rushed around to embrace her in a bear hug. "Olivia! You're back. Are you all right?"

She struggled to keep her balance, filled with indignation. Leaning away from his chest, she placed both hands on his shoulders. He looked into her eyes, and for a moment she allowed him to see what she felt.

Hands on hips, she stepped back farther. "I thought you were arrested!"

Michael's arms dropped to his sides. "I guess Sage did her job. I told her to make my arrest sound kind of desperate."

"Do you work here? Are you a plainclothes cop along with everything else or just a big fat liar?"

Olivia felt her bottom lip tremble. She turned her back to him, hiding her relief. She'd assumed he'd be in a cell, sitting on a bench, with a toilet in the corner for company. Her imagination had led her to believe he'd be contrite, holding his head in his hands, begging for her forgiveness. As usual, this man surprised her.

"So how many of you cooked up this charade? Never mind. I'm leaving."

With a dignified huff, Olivia reached for the door handle. Michael's hand moved faster, grabbing hers in midair. "Not so fast, Little Missy. Please. We are lying to you for all the right reasons. We—Sage and I—worried when you left in the middle of the night without a cell phone."

Olivia shook her hand from Michael's steel grip. She stared at her shoes, feeling self-conscious. *I've overreacted. Not for the first time. Life was easier when I drank more.*

"Can I sit down? My leg hurts."

Michael's brow wrinkled in concern. He moved tentatively toward her. When she didn't resist, he touched her elbow, directing her toward the desk that had a stool next to it.

"Sit here," he said quietly. "Do you need another chair to prop up the leg?"

Olivia sat. Her shoulders curled around her chest. She stretched the sore leg awkwardly in front of her. The old blood on her jeans from the bite had dried brown, making her feel queasy. Adjusting her leg on the stool gave Olivia time to compose herself.

Michael sat across from her, his back to the computer.

Glancing up from her soiled jeans, Olivia swallowed hard. "Time to explain yourself."

"Do you want coffee? I make a good brew here. Not like other police coffee—not that you'd be familiar with a jail, I didn't mean that."

"I'd like some coffee. Black. None of that cream-and-sugar nonsense. Thanks."

Michael disappeared around the corner. He returned with two Lily Rock Music Festival mugs and handed her one.

"Black. Just as ordered."

Olivia nodded, taking a sip, feeling the warmth slide down her throat. She remained silent, waiting for the promised explanation from Michael.

"First of all, I am not employed by the police department here in Lily Rock. I am an architect and a builder, just as I told you. No lies about that."

The way he specifically said "about that" alerted Olivia. *That doesn't mean he isn't lying about something else.*

Michael looked at her intently, watching for a response.

He wants me to admit that I believe him. I'm still sitting here. That should be enough admitting.

He continued to explain. "If you remember, Janis—"

"You mean Officer Jets," Olivia interrupted, taking another sip of coffee.

Michael grinned. "Right, Officer Jets. She knew you'd inherited Marla's estate since she read the letter."

"I figured as much. When she asked me about the letter that first time, it was as if she knew more than I did."

Olivia watched Michael over her coffee mug. He smiled, eager to explain himself. *He's trying to get back into my good favor.* She took another small sip of coffee, waiting for him to explain further.

"After we discovered Marla's body—"

"You mean after I discovered Marla's body." Olivia shuddered. *Has it only been a few days since I discovered Marla's dead body?*

"Right. You. Anyway, after Janis arrived on the scene, I told her about Marla's will. Last night she demanded that I meet with her to spill the details of Marla's estate. She saw my name on the letter Marla left you, but she wanted more."

Michael cleared his throat. "Since I was the one to help Marla put it together. I arranged for Arlo to notarize and Cayenne to witness. I did ask Marla a lot of questions at the time, but she was very certain she wanted her friend Olivia to have her estate.

"Right before she invited you up for the getaway weekend, Marla was worried about her failing health. Such a young woman but so consumed with her own fate."

Olivia's eyes filled with tears at the mention of Marla's health. She looked at her lap while she composed herself.

Michael continued. "At the time, I didn't know you, so I was skeptical, but I went along with Marla since she was my boss. Now that I know you ..." Michael swallowed.

"Now that you know me?" Olivia wanted to hear the rest of the sentence, his thoughts, his feelings.

"Let's just say, I think Marla made the right decision." Michael reached out to gently pat her foot. "How's the leg?" he asked, changing the subject.

Olivia bent over to rub her stiffening knee. "Getting better," she admitted. "Faster than I thought it would."

"I heard it was a really big snake," he teased.

Olivia stretched out both arms. "This big—times ten. Huge."

Michael laughed. "I think you may be more suited for Lily Rock than you ever imagined. Now you can make up a story of how you wrestled with a snake over one hundred feet long, with three heads. No one will argue with since you have a bite scar for proof. In fact, we'll admire you even more on account of we would expect nothing less from one of us."

One of us. Olivia let the expression wash over her. Had he just included her in their midst? *Am I really one of them? Do I belong here? Then why do I feel so afraid, and how come I ran away without looking back until the snake—*

Olivia pulled both legs underneath her chair. She leaned forward toward Michael.

Was this what belonging felt like? A man smiling at her, explaining himself, encouraging her to tell her own stories? "So everyone knew about me inheriting Marla's house before I did?"

"I knew, and of course Arlo and Cay. My niece heard rumors in town. Seemed to come from Meadow. Janis knew once I told her about the letter, and she found it when they searched the house. I don't think Janis told anyone else. She's the cop around here, and she had trouble admitting she knew even to you."

"She did have trouble. Why was that?"

"So here's the difficult issue, Olivia. I am not sure where to begin with this part of the story, and I'm not sure I want to say more right now. Your safety may be in jeopardy. Can we leave it there? Would you just trust me for another twenty-four hours?"

Olivia blurted out, "I'm not sure I can go back to Marla's house. There was someone outside when I left. Looking in the laundry room window."

Gone was the face of warmth and affection, replaced by a resolute set to Michael's jaw.

"Potential intruder," she corrected herself. "I got out before he got in. I told Sage."

Michael reached for his cell phone. His thumb traveled over the lettered keyboard. He paused to read. "There it is. I didn't read that text, and I see now that Sage told me about the intruder before she drove you up the hill." Instead of pocketing his phone, he reached over to show Olivia the text:

Bringing Olivia home. She left. Someone was trying to break into Marla's house. Stop worrying. I've got this.

Olivia raised her brows. "Stop worrying?"

"Of course I was worried. I didn't leave under the best of circumstances that night. I felt terrible when Mayor Maguire reported that you were missing."

"Come on now, Michael. Mayor Maguire?"

A sheepish grin came over his face. "Okay. So now you know. Mayor Maguire is also Officer Maguire. That's his second job. He reports to Janis every morning. When he didn't show up, she went to find him."

"And where did she find the mayor—I mean, officer?" Olivia inquired with a snicker.

"Not at the pub or the music academy. He did not show up at Meadow's place either. The doc hadn't seen him, so we concluded he might be at Marla's. When you didn't answer your cell phone nor come to the door, we used my spare key. Sure enough, we found Mayor Maguire curled up under Marla's kitchen table."

"That's where I left him." Olivia nodded. "I'm surprised he didn't report to the constabulary as usual. I left the back door ajar so that he could come and go."

"I noticed the open door immediately. What were you thinking? Anyone could have come inside. Apparently the mayor was waiting for you to come back, so when we arrived he led us around to the window in the laundry room. We saw some footprint evidence outside under the sill."

He ran his hand through his hair before continuing. "I was worried. Sick. I'd left you in such a huff. And then I found your cell phone in a kitchen drawer and felt even worse." Michael pointed a finger at Olivia. "Why the hell didn't you take your cell phone with you? Things would have been so much better if we could have called you. You might not have been bitten by a damned rattler!"

Olivia felt perplexed. *Maybe this is what belonging feels like, when people care about you enough to worry? I like being looked after.*

When he didn't admonish her more, Olivia changed the subject. "I think now is the time for me to get cleaned up a bit. Sage said I could stay with her and Meadow tonight. Would you mind dropping me there?"

Michael slapped his hands on his knees in exasperation. "So I'm not getting an explanation about why you left your cell phone? Okay. Just so you know, I'm happy you're okay. Maybe you can tell me more later. Since I'm supposed to be behind bars as the only suspect, I'll call Arlo to drive you to Sage's place. Gotta keep playing my role."

Olivia's curiosity returned. "How does arresting you help find Marla's killer?"

"We want the killer to get overconfident, thinking that I've been arrested and that the police are no longer looking for other suspects. That's why I'm hanging out here. Arlo knows since I told him. You know. Both of you have an alibi, and I should know—I was there with you."

"You mean she was killed when you stopped to help me on the road?"

Michael sighed. "It seems I was not able to help Marla,

but I was there for you. Karma sucks. I don't know how else to explain what happened."

Would Michael have been able to save Marla if he hadn't stopped on the road to help me? As if reading her mind, Michael interrupted.

"I'd been down the hill doing some errands. Marla knew she could get me back quickly on my cell if she needed anything. I did get a call with a quick hang up. I thought she'd hit my number by accident. I didn't call her back but I did cut my errands short. That's why I was driving so fast up the hill."

So that was the real explanation for his tailgating her car. Realizing her leg had gone numb, Olivia caught her hand on the side of the desk. She stood up. Michael jumped from his seat to help. She brushed him off.

Then when she saw his hurt face, she reached out to touch his elbow. "Thank you," she whispered. "I appreciate the help."

Michael's half smile flooded her with relief. Before she could say any more, he lifted his cell phone with one hand to text with his thumb. The phone immediately pinged back. "Arlo will be here in five minutes. Take a deep breath. I'll help you to the door," Michael said.

They made their way toward the constabulary exit. Michael dropped behind the door so as not to be seen. He gestured for Olivia to walk through the entryway and then waited until she sat on the bench outside. The door closed silently behind her.

* * *

Ten minutes later, Arlo's truck stopped in front of Meadow's home. Meadow opened the door. "So happy you can stay with us for a few more days," she said, guiding Olivia by the hand.

Arlo followed them into the living room. "If it's all right, I'll check back later. Maybe I can bring a change of clothing for you?"

Thinking of Arlo rustling through her underwear made Olivia feel uneasy.

Meadow interrupted, "I have a washer right here, and Olivia, you are welcome to use it whenever you like." Taking charge of the domestic quandary, she added, "Bring her suitcase. For now she can wear Sage's clothes. Sage doesn't mind sharing."

Olivia looked around the living room, aware of the heavy scent of plants and earth. Meadow watched her and then pointed to the kitchen. "Why don't you sit down at the table? I'll make us some tea."

Too tired to resist, Olivia followed her suggestion. As she sat down at the kitchen table, she heard Arlo's engine turn over from outside.

Meadow bustled around the stove. "I'll just put the kettle on, dear. We'll have tea in a jiffy."

Olivia took a deep breath. *The earthy odor must be coming from the kitchen.*

"That's right, dear. Breathe deeply. Here's your tea. All ready. Drink up now. You will feel so much better very soon."

After the first few sips Olivia became aware of a buzz in her head. She felt her eyelids droop. Minutes later she put down her mug of tea, resting her head on the tabletop. Aware of Meadow bustling around the kitchen, Olivia closed her eyes.

Then she felt Meadow pull her chair away from the table. Unable to stand due to the heaviness in her head, she felt herself being lifted to her feet from the kitchen chair.

Meadow struggled, pulling Olivia's arm over her shoulder. Lifting her from the chair, she shifted Olivia's weight to half lift and half drag her, heading toward the door. "You're just sleepy, Olivia. Don't worry. I'll put you in bed, and you'll feel much better after a good nap."

Olivia felt a familiar tingling in her arms and legs. Trying to walk herself, she heard the buzz in her head, and then silence.

* * *

The cool feeling of linen under her face brought her to semi-consciousness. *I'm in bed.*

"Sleep well," Meadow's voice whispered. "I'll be back soon."

The door to the hallway closed. Olivia heard Meadow's voice on the phone.

"I've got her right here in the next room. She's out, just as you said she would be. Send someone to the house while she's asleep to collect the evidence. I hear Sage. Have to go."

The front door opened as Meadow called out, "I'll be there in a minute!"

CHAPTER SIXTEEN

Overheard in Lily Rock
Guy: She postponed.
Bartender: Reason?
Guy: Wind.

Both of Olivia's feet tingled. The sensation traveled up her legs. Then her eyes slowly opened. She saw Sage staring at her, her brow wrinkled with concern.

"Am I back in the hospital?" asked Olivia with a yawn.

"You're here in our house; you've been sleeping like the dead for two days. The doc came to check on you, but he said you were just exhausted from the hike and the snakebite. So we decided to let you keep sleeping."

"So it must be Wednesday then." Olivia slipped her hand over her mouth to stifle another yawn. Before Sage could respond she asked, "The doc looked at me?" Olivia's legs went from tingling to quivering instantly. "I feel really weird," she added, resting her hand on a bouncing knee under the sheet.

"Can you stand? I can help you to the restroom." Sage held out her hand for Olivia to grasp.

She tried twice before managing to remain on her feet. Sage placed one hand on Olivia's lower back and the other on her elbow to guide her down the hall to the bathroom. "I'm gonna wait outside, just in case you call out."

"Thanks."

After the door closed Olivia looked at herself in the mirror. She observed the same puffy, pale face she'd encountered the first time she spent the night at Meadow and Sage's house. *Is it the mirror or me?*

Minutes later, she still faced the sink, holding on to both sides with her hands for balance. Splashing water on her face helped steady the trembling in her legs. When she finally opened the bathroom door, she discovered Sage leaning against the wall on her cell. Olivia looked up over Sage's head. "Family photos," she mused aloud, staring at one in particular.

Sage looked up from a text to smile at Olivia. "Almost done with this," she told her, head bending as thumbs continued to tap.

Olivia took time to observe the photos that ran along the wall for the entire hallway. She remembered something her mother had told her long ago. "You only take pictures of the ones you really love." Surely Meadow loved Sage; all the photos had Sage in them.

Before her mother's death, Olivia had gone through all of her photographs, which her mom had collected over the years and stored in shoeboxes. Most of the photos were of Olivia. *I guess single moms with one child take lots of pictures out of love.*

From one end of the hallway to the other, Sage matured in photographs. There was one with her on a pony that reminded Olivia of a picture her mother had of her at a similar age. As Sage pocketed her phone, Olivia pointed to a tousle-haired blond child. "You and I looked kind of the same at that age," she commented with a smile.

Coming closer to peer at the photograph for herself, Sage squinted. "I think I was around five years old. We went to a fair down the hill and stayed in San Diego for the weekend. I loved animals even then. After that, my mom took me to Doc's animal shelter every Saturday. I learned from him how to care for horses and dogs."

Sage sighed. "Sometimes I wish I still worked at the animal shelter instead of the academy. Animals are less annoying. Talented musicians and their rich parents have high expectations." Sage turned to Olivia. "If you're feeling better, why don't you come up to the school for lunch? I can show you around, and we can eat in the pub. The food is pretty good."

Olivia glanced at her dirty jeans. "I'm not sure I have anything to wear. I've been in this outfit for way too long."

"I've got you covered. Cay brought your suitcase a day ago. I guess Mom called her since she has keys to Marla's place. Anyway, you may want to look. If you don't have clean clothes we can pop these in the washer, and I can lend you some."

Olivia nodded, pushing away her annoyance. *Why are my clean clothes everyone else's business?*

When she returned to her room, she saw her suitcase in the corner. The top was propped open. Apparently Cay had done the laundry at Marla's. Or maybe Meadow had washed her clothes while she slept. Rummaging through her belongings, she searched for a fresh pair of jeans.

Two pairs of folded jeans nestled into the bottom of the suitcase. Holding them to her face, Olivia inhaled. A quick image of Marla's laundry room came to mind. Her brain fluttered, then zapped—she could see a set of eyes staring at her from the window. Olivia dropped the jeans, her hands trembling. She gritted her teeth. *I feel like I'm losing my mind.* Time to take a shower.

Dressed in freshly laundered clothing, Olivia looked in the mirror to apply sunscreen. Her face had lost most of the puffiness. Pinching each pale cheek, she stared harder at herself.

Closing her eyes, she remembered the voices outside her room before she had completely lost consciousness. The low voice of Meadow speaking in hushed tones. *What happened before I passed out? I remember sitting in the kitchen and—the tea. That's it. Meadow put something in my tea.*

Opening her eyes, she stared at her reflection in the mirror. She brushed her hair back from her forehead with a sigh. After quietly closing her bedroom door, Olivia walked to the kitchen. Listening for Meadow's voice, she opened each cabinet to look inside.

Rows of vials marked with exotic herb names were lined up like soldiers ready for battle. Each bottle was carefully labeled: anise, bergamot, asafoetida, angelica. Some of the bottles held capsules. Some contained crumbled leaves. Olivia picked one vial from the shelf. She unscrewed the top to sniff. *Smells like marijuana.*

"What are you doing in that cabinet?" Olivia's stomach clenched. Instead of hurrying, she carefully screwed the top back on and placed it where she found it on the shelf. *Take your time, Olivia. Consider your response.*

Stepping away from the cabinet, Olivia turned to face Meadow. "I was looking for some cereal for breakfast. I didn't want to bother you."

Meadow swallowed the outrage from her voice. "I am the town librarian, but I also operate the Lady of the Rock boutique and tell fortunes two days per week. I read tea leaves for some of my clients."

Olivia willed her face to register no surprise. Meadow had more jobs than most: that was the Lily Rock solution for economic stability. However, Olivia was surprised that Meadow included psychic reader in her portfolio of employment. "Did you happen to read my tea leaves the other day? Before you put me into bed?"

The older woman's jaw dropped. "So you remember me getting you to your room. I thought you might, since you weren't entirely asleep—and no. I only use my psychic abilities when invited. It's part of my professional code."

"Is drugging people to sleep also a part of your professional code?"

"Don't be ridiculous." Meadow glared at Olivia. "I added chamomile and lavender to your tea. Nothing remotely unsavory. You had a snakebite. It doesn't take a psychic to realize the venom may still be in your system. No wonder you were so sleepy." The older woman closed her mouth, offering no further explanation.

Back in charge, Meadow assumed her fluid librarian tone. She had seamlessly shifted personas. "Would you like a piece of homemade toast with strawberry preserves? I can make that for you."

"Oh no," Olivia replied. "My appetite has gone. I'll get something in town. Sage invited me to come up to the music school for a tour and lunch. I think I'll do that."

"What a splendid idea, dear. I advise that you stay away from Marla's for the time being. I think the vibrations are not healthy for you." Meadow smiled at Olivia. "By the way, do you know what will happen with Marla's house now, since her passing?"

"The future of the house is up in the air, as far as I know.

Did Marla ever talk to you about her family? You know, from before she moved to Lily Rock?"

"Oh no," said Meadow hastily. "I knew very little about Marla. No one here got that close to her except Michael. She did annoy some of the Old Rockers with her spending."

"You've lived here a long time?"

"Since before Sage was born. We've been very happy here, the two of us. She's my life, you know."

Single mothers and their daughters, mused Olivia. *A very close relationship.*

Olivia wanted to ask about Sage's father, but the time did not feel right.

"Will you stay another night?" Meadow began wiping the counters.

"Thank you for the invitation, but no. I need to get back to Marla's house."

"Why is that?"

"I want to contact her attorney. She has a sizable estate."

"So you will be staying in Lily Rock a while longer?"

"I can do most of my work on the phone. It doesn't really matter where I am."

Meadow ran water down the drain, her back to Olivia.

"I'll get my stuff together and be out of your hair in a few minutes. By the way, are you the one I can thank for doing my laundry?"

"I am. I did the wash while you were asleep."

"I could see that everything was rearranged in the suit-case. I hope it wasn't too much trouble to go through my things."

Meadow frowned, drying her hands on a kitchen towel. "Happy to help."

Sarcasm must not be one of her strengths.

Moments later Olivia snapped her suitcase shut. After closing the bedroom door behind her, she made her way to the front of the house. "Thanks again," Olivia yelled into the empty space.

No one answered.

With suitcase in hand, she walked down the driveway and onto the road toward Marla's house. The wind swept against her cheeks. Feeling more steady on her legs, she swung into a comfortable stride.

A truck rumbled around the corner. Olivia recognized Cayenne, who smiled and pulled over to the side of the road. The passenger window rolled down. "Like a lift?" asked the woman.

Olivia nodded. "I would. I'm not feeling that energetic. Plus I have a few questions to ask you." Olivia wondered how often people asked Cay about being trans and if the question felt old to her new friend.

Cay stepped out of the car to help Olivia with her suitcase. "Ask away," the woman said, climbing back behind the driver's seat. As she pulled away from the curb, she turned to Olivia. "You probably want to know if I am trans?"

Olivia laughed. "Of course I want to know, but I would not have asked you. Such a personal question, and none of my business. Plus I didn't want to say anything. I didn't want to cause you any discomfort. I just assumed you were a transgender woman. Is that right?"

"That's right. We can be girlfriends, you know share lipstick and swap stories about old boyfriends. I identify as she/her."

"Me too, and I certainly need a Lily Rock girlfriend."

"Aren't you getting close to Sage? At least, that's what I heard this morning."

"Who told you?"

"Honey, I work at the pub. We hear everything. You sneeze anywhere on the hill, and we provide the tissues."

Olivia laughed and changed the subject. "The first time we met, you didn't tell me that you and Arlo are a couple."

"Before I go talking about my husband, I like to size people up first—you know, to see if they are for me or against me. Lots of people don't like transgender people. I have to be very careful."

Olivia knew how cruel people could be. She also knew about people talking. She and her mother had endured lots of discrimination over the years, with no father in sight. Rarely ruffled, her mother would say, "You are my one and only," as if that would compensate for anyone else's critical opinion.

"Any other questions?" Cay asked. "People are always curious."

Olivia swallowed. "I was wondering if you were the one who brought my suitcase to Meadow's house the other day?"

Cay pulled into Marla's driveway. "I did not bring your suitcase to her house. In fact, no one asked me to. Did someone tell you I did?"

"Meadow said—" A thump against the passenger window interrupted her words.

Two dog paws splayed out on the glass. Mayor Maguire's big head filled the window while his tongue hung out the side of his mouth. Olivia lowered the glass while the dog leaned in. He licked her face as his tail wagged in greeting. She reached out to scratch between his ears.

He jumped back, excitedly barking.

Cayenne shook her head. "That's his *let's play* bark. I think he's taken a liking to you. Be careful, though. Meadow hates it when the dog likes anyone but her. She's been known to cause a lot of trouble for people just to keep the mayor in her yard."

Olivia opened the passenger door. "You don't mean Meadow is that competitive?"

"She kept the mayor away from all town meetings for an entire month the one time when he took a shine to the guy who owned the vegan restaurant. Then she told everyone to boycott the place, which they did—no one wanted to be on Meadow's bad side. He finally shut down the restaurant and moved."

Olivia shook her head. "Small towns have surprising dynamics. I understood that part of M&M's mythology is that he belongs to everyone."

"You would think that, but Meadow disagrees. She's an Old Rocker and holds some clout here. Plus everyone just loves Sage. They don't annoy Meadow on account of they don't want her to take it out on Sage."

"Not to change the subject, but would you like to come in? I make a mean peanut butter sandwich and could use some company."

Cayenne's eyes glistened with tears.

"If you don't have time—"

"Oh I have time, Olivia. I'm just a bit surprised—in a good way. I've only cleaned that house. I've never been invited to sit down as a guest, let alone eat a peanut butter sandwich."

Olivia and Cay got out of the car and walked toward the house. Olivia unlocked the front door, and Mayor Maguire raced ahead, spinning on the floor to rise up on his back legs. He placed his front paws on Olivia's knees. She looked down into his black eyes. "Hey, big fella. You're not supposed to jump up on people."

As soon as she finished her sentence, his big tongue

pushed out of his mouth to give her one lick on the lips. Then the dog jumped down.

Looking around the space, Olivia inhaled deeply. The house welcomed her. She blinked away tears.

Don't get too comfortable, she warned herself.

CHAPTER SEVENTEEN

Overheard in Lily Rock

"I'm just gonna stay in and drink with the ghost in my house."

Cayenne stared out the kitchen window as Olivia spread peanut butter over whole wheat bread. A look of longing came over Cay's face.

"Are you okay?" Olivia asked, placing the knife in the sink.

Cayenne forced a smile. "I think I'm okay. I just remembered, when Marla first came to Lily Rock, she knew right away that I was transgender. She approached me at the pub. I appreciated her candor, like I appreciate yours. Not many people here like me. I suppose they're afraid."

Olivia offered the simple sandwich on a plate, handing it to Cay. "I know what you mean about Marla. One thing I liked best about her was that she accepted people. That's probably how we got along so well in high school. I was raised by a single mom, and so was Marla. Other kids' families seemed so simple compared to ours."

"No dad in the picture?"

They sat across the table from each other. "I never met my father. My mom barely mentioned his existence. After she died, the secret went with her." Olivia bit into her sandwich, then continued, "I did one of those DNA tests online. Have you ever done that? Sent in a sample to see about your roots?"

Olivia watched Cayenne's Adam's apple slide up her throat as she swallowed down a sticky glob of peanut butter. Finally she spoke. "My parents have always found me confusing. In fact, they joke about me being adopted. My gender issues blocked every conversation I might have had, you know, about the smaller stuff. Despite the constant conflict, I look just like them. So I never did the DNA thing. I can't imagine that my parents are not mine. So what did you find out from your DNA test?"

"A bunch of stuff about my health, which scared me. Potential heart attacks, and some relatives' thyroid issues long ago. But then I discovered a few DNA matches. I think my father may have been a sperm donor." Olivia laughed. "Marla told me that I could check a box if I wanted to connect with other people with the same DNA markers. I didn't pursue any of those leads. By the time I read the information, I felt like I was betraying my mother. So I just left it. That was right before Marla invited me to Lily Rock for the weekend."

"I get it." Cay smiled at Olivia. "When I did the counseling for transitioning, we often said, 'Life is already complicated enough.'" Swallowing the last bite of her sandwich, she looked over Olivia's shoulder to the garden below. "Marla probably never told you, but I helped her start the kitchen garden. She didn't know a thing about herbs when she moved here."

Olivia followed Cay's glance out the picture window.

"I've never lived anywhere where I could cultivate a kitchen garden. It surprises me that Marla wanted one. When we were in high school I never imagined her damaging a manicure to dig in the dirt."

"Oh, everyone here in Lily Rock spends some time in the garden. So, speaking of our quaint little village, are you staying?"

Sometimes a question was just a question. This one from Cay felt layered, as if there was something underneath that she wanted to ask. Olivia scanned the great room.

For a moment she lost focus on her conversation with Cay to stare at the fireplace. *I guess my brain is healing from the car accident. I know that fire is important. There's something else about the great room—hidden cameras. I didn't look in there.*

"I'm not sure Lily Rock is for me. I came up because I was invited by Marla. I intended to stay for a weekend."

"I'm sure the Old Rockers will be relieved to hear that. They're worried you'll take up where Marla left off and start infusing outsider money into our small town."

"Why is the source of money such a problem up here? Why not celebrate the new jobs and opportunities instead of pushing them away?"

"Old Rockers don't like giving up control of their town. Marla's new money threatened their way of life."

Drifting from their conversation again, Olivia wondered, *What about the cameras? I'd better call an attorney. Got things to do. Time to let Cay go.* She picked up the empty plates. "Not very gourmet, but excellent company," she assured Cay. "I'm thinking of looking through some of Marla's stuff to get to know what I'm up against when I decide to put the place up for sale."

Cayenne stretched her arms over her head. "I've got a few inches on you. Do you want me to stay and help with the higher shelves that you can't reach?"

"Let's check out her bedroom. I've been afraid to go in there since her death."

Together the women approached Marla's sanctuary, opening the door quietly as if entering a sacred space. "So peaceful yet vibrant in here," Olivia observed. "You would never know that she's dead."

"Come look at this. Most people don't know what's behind here." Cay ran her hand over the shiplap planking across the room. She pushed against one board and another. Finally, a panel popped back.

An entire doorway opened.

Olivia stepped forward, expecting a walk-in closet. She stopped in the doorway to gasp. "Another entire room!"

Two chairs faced each other in the center of the room, inviting people to sit down for a conversation. Olivia stepped in farther. When she turned she saw a wooden table and an upholstered lounging sofa. The walls held storage: some open shelves, some with doors to cover the contents. Poles stretched across one area, and clothing filled the top and bottom racks.

Cay pointed to a line of sweaters hung at eye level. With a sweep of her arm, she exposed a small window hidden behind the clothing that looked out to the front of the house. Standing next to each other, the women observed Mayor Maguire, who lay asleep on the mat at the front door.

"Good security idea, the window hidden in the closet," remarked Olivia. "This would have felt like a safe space if Marla needed to hide."

Cayenne nodded. "Most likely designed by Michael. He's very good at security."

"Lily Rock feels so harmless. I wonder why Marla felt afraid in her own home?"

"The first time she showed me this hidden room, she wanted me to clean in here. I thought she was a tad eccentric. But now that someone's killed her, I guess she knew best. They say that even paranoids have enemies."

I still don't know just who Marla was most afraid of or why.

Cayenne pointed to a wall of storage. Decorative baskets lined the entire top shelf. "Let's start up there. I can hand you boxes, and you can set them on the carpet to look at later. Would that help?"

For the next half an hour Cayenne lifted baskets and unmarked boxes and handed them down to Olivia, who would then turn to stack each one on the floor. When they had cleared the shelves, Olivia lifted the top of one box, revealing file folders neatly stacked.

"Ugh," she groaned. "I hate paperwork. It looks like she never got rid of anything. She just kept storing things in a new box and shoving them up on those shelves."

Cayenne laughed. "I was hoping you'd find an old fur coat. I would have done anything to try one on. Or maybe a pair of red high-heeled boots. I think Marla dressed in those one time for a town council meeting. I sure envied those beauties."

Olivia giggled. "If I find them, they're yours. The very least I can do after your help." She closed the box and sneezed. "Lots of dust around these parts. No wonder Marla complained of allergies."

Walking back to the bedroom, through the hidden door, Cay rubbed her finger under her nose. "I have a stuffy nose from that closet. You know, the allergies are so bad up here, some people have to take injections just to ward off the symptoms."

Olivia sneezed again. "I'm going to find a tissue. See you in the kitchen!"

Cay walked into the kitchen, "Doing any better?"

"I think so." Olivia sniffled. "How about some tea before you go?"

"I'd love some."

"Open that cupboard, and take a look in there. I've never seen more dried leaves and tea labels. I bet you'll find any tea you'd like. I'm sticking to my own mint blend that I brought from home. You can have some of that, if you'd prefer." Olivia put the kettle on.

Cayenne moved to the cupboard to look inside. With a quizzical face she turned toward Olivia. "There's nothing in this cabinet. It's completely empty."

She dropped a spoon to look inside for herself. Olivia's mouth hung open. No bottles. No bags of leaves. No labels. No marking chalk for the labels. Just empty space.

She ran her finger inside the cupboard. "I don't believe this; not even a speck of dust! Just a couple of days ago the entire cabinet was filled with tea and herbs. Somebody must have cleaned me out."

"Someone was here when you weren't around."

"But why would they empty a cabinet with leaves in it? Makes no sense."

Both women looked up as the teakettle whistled. "Guess I'll have mint tea with you," Cay added, walking to unplug the electric kettle.

Olivia dispensed the tea while both women sat down at the table in silence.

Cayenne spoke first. "Did you hear about Michael getting arrested?"

Olivia nodded over her mug. *I don't want to tell Cay about Officer Jets's ruse. I'll just go along and ask more questions.*

Cay continued, "He's at the jail, waiting for his attorney to arrive from down the hill. I can't imagine Michael murdering Marla. I mean, why would he? She was his paycheck, and it looked like Marla had any number of projects to keep him in business."

"Tell me more about Michael and Marla. I mean, were they more than friends?"

"Most people think so," admitted Cay. "But I know for sure they were not. Since I cleaned the place twice a week, I could tell they weren't shacking up together."

"You could tell?"

"Sure. No sign that he occupied her bedroom or the bathroom. No extra sheets or toothbrushes."

Olivia felt her cheeks flush. Investigating Marla's death required her to be nosier than she was comfortable with, especially when it came to Michael.

"Why would they arrest Michael, then? What evidence do they have to keep him?" Olivia wanted Cay's perspective.

"I don't know. For some reason people don't care whether there is evidence or not. Once the cops arrested someone, they breathed a sigh of relief and got on with their lives. At least, that's the way it seems to me."

"So, I was wondering, what does Arlo think about Marla's death and Michael's culpability?"

"Oh, you know Arlo. He doesn't care about anything other than his next brew. I'm not sure he even cared when I told him I'm transgender."

"You have got to be kidding!"

"I told Arlo about the surgery, and he barely blinked an eye. He's not said a word since. For months I took pills, and bit by bit I changed my wardrobe. No word from Arlo. Then the day of the first surgery, he dropped me off, and he picked me up three days later as if I had gotten my tonsils out. Arlo made the transition better than I did."

Olivia and Cay smiled at each other.

"Men," they said in unison, chuckling aloud this time.

"I know. You can do pretty near anything, just don't get in the way of their conveniences. I am proof of that."

A scratch at the door drew Olivia's attention. "I think Mayor Maguire may be ready for an afternoon treat. I'm going to let him in." When the front door opened, the mayor trotted into the house, followed by Arlo.

"Speak of the devil," Olivia muttered before adding, "Look who's here."

"Is my wife around?" Arlo took a cursory glance around the great room. "Oh, there you are! We need you at the pub."

Cayenne stood obediently. "Right. I'm ready. Just give me a minute to grab my purse."

Arlo waved at Olivia as he headed back toward the open door. "Sorry to interrupt, but two of our waiters called out sick. See you later. Be sure you drop in for a drink." Olivia watched Arlo jog to his truck.

Cayenne hopped into the passenger seat next to him. She rolled down her window to add, "We'll pick up my truck after work if it's okay."

"There's plenty of room to park." Olivia gestured, her arm sweeping over the expanse of driveway. She waved at Arlo and Cayenne.

Noticing her own car in the shade, she sighed. Dry pine needles collected on the windshield wipers. She whisked them away with her hand.

After walking back into the house, Olivia grabbed her car keys from her purse. Mayor Maguire followed. He trotted toward her car, waiting on the passenger side as she unlocked his door first.

Olivia held the door open to watch Mayor Maguire settle into the passenger seat. With three turns, he plopped his rear end down to face the windshield. She slammed Mayor Maguire's door shut.

Feeling oddly pleased with the dog's company, Olivia glanced over at her furry companion. *He's worth the extra effort—like having a kid, only better.* "Good boy, M&M," Olivia told him as she turned the ignition with the key. On the third attempt, the engine started.

She pulled out from the expansive driveway and onto the main road. At the time she'd invited Cayenne to lunch, she'd forgotten about her previous engagement with Sage. "Let's go visit Sage. She must be closing up the school office, and I want to explain why I'm late."

The dog did not turn his face at the sound of her voice. Instead he remained vigilant, his eyes staring out the windshield. He blinked, then his mouth closed.

Olivia's car bumped along a dirt road for nearly a mile when an old wooden structure caught her attention: the Lily Rock Music Academy. She turned off the engine before leaning over to open the car door for Mayor Maguire. He jumped right out. The top branches from trees overhead waved in the wind as children's voices from behind the building filled the air.

Turning the knob on the front door of the music academy's office, Olivia stepped into a darkened room. She could hear voices from the grove where the classrooms held students and teachers, yet no one sat behind the computer. The screen saver blinked photos of intent young people smiling at the camera. An open door behind the desk caught her attention. She stuck her head into the office, looking for Sage.

The smell of rosin and dust itched her nose. Olivia coughed into her elbow. Several guitars, both acoustic and electric, decorated the wall behind an old wooden desk. Next to the guitars, two violins and a viola hung, fully strung—waiting to be played. Next to the violin, an odd rectangular instrument with one corner cut off caught her attention. Her heart beat quickly. "Look what I found," she said aloud to the room.

Making her way to the display wall she reached up to touch the instrument. Her neck tingled. "Are you tuned?" she asked, strumming her fingers over the dusty strings. Years of corrosion made them feel sticky to her touch.

Mayor Maguire sat on Olivia's right side, looking up with an interested expression.

"It's an autoharp," she explained to the dog. "I'm not going to play, no matter how much you beg. Plus this one needs repair—and tuning. No one even likes autoharp anymore. Trust me."

Olivia reached up to remove the wooden instrument from the wall. She ran her thumb across the strings again, a grimace coming to her face. She held the instrument tenderly in one arm as she scrubbed the wood to reveal a stamp: *Oscar Schmidt* appeared from under the dirt.

Turning the instrument over, she wiped the dust off the back with her hand. "You could use some work," she spoke aloud. With careful precision, Olivia placed the autoharp back on the wall where she'd found it.

Now Mayor Maguire padded around the office, sniffing under the chair and desk, into each corner. When he finished his investigation he stood in front of Olivia, his ears poking out from his head. "Hear something, buddy?" A creeping sense of fear moved up her spine. The dog stepped closer to Olivia, nosing her knee.

"Yoo-hoo," came an unexpected voice. "Anyone home?"

Caught snooping, Olivia felt guilty. She did not want to be found alone in Sage's office. Eying the back-door exit, she gestured to Mayor Maguire. "Let's go," she hissed in his ear. "I think I recognize that voice."

CHAPTER EIGHTEEN

Overheard in Lily Rock

Girl: "I was having a beer at the pub, and I was attacked by a crow. But that's my spirit animal, so I'm not sure if it was an actual attack or if it was trying to remind me who I am."
Boy: "If you aren't Native, then it was just a crow and not about you."

Olivia grabbed Mayor Maguire's collar, guiding him out of the door as the familiar voice called again, sending a chill up her spine.

"Sage, are you in the office?" Skye sounded innocent, but Olivia wasn't so sure. She grasped the door handle, pulling backward when Mayor Maguire twisted out of her hand, running out the doorway ahead of Olivia.

"Olivia! You're here." Sage stood just beyond the open door, arms filled with files. She looked the part of the perfect administrator.

Holding her finger to her lips, Olivia pointed to the other room. "Skye is looking for you. I was in there alone and had a desperate urge to run away."

Sage smiled. "No worries. I've got this." Standing outside she started to close the door when Skye appeared from the outer office. Her spectacles were perched on the end of her nose, her gray hair brushed away from her face. For a moment she appeared unworldly.

Looking back and forth between Sage and Olivia, she addressed them both. "So you've been here all along. Trying to get away before I noticed?"

Olivia ducked her head as Sage answered in a smooth voice. "We just walked in from the back door. Didn't hear you call. Can I help with something?"

Not satisfied with the logical explanation, Skye crossed her arms over her ample bosom. "Have I caught you two in flagrante? Is there something you want to tell me?"

Irritation tickled at the back of Olivia's throat. "We're friends, Skye."

Sage added, "And we're going out for a late lunch. Care to join us?"

Olivia shuddered. She did not want Skye to join them at the pub. She wanted to talk to Sage alone. Glancing at Olivia, Sage raised her eyebrows. Olivia closed her eyes, hoping Sage would read her mind.

Skye's less than genuine voice broke the silence. "Oh, that is so kind. Actually, I have other plans, but I wanted to ask you about the young man, Dennis Oqwatan, who applied for a scholarship." Skye sat down in a chair. She continued to speak.

"The town council would like to add more money to the scholarship fund if you think he'd be good for the school. A Native American student makes us look more diverse. It would be good for the academy's demographics, don't you think?"

Sage walked behind her desk, assuming the role of

academy director. "We haven't heard his audition tape yet, but when we do the committee will come to a decision. How did you know he was applying?"

"Oh, he's a friend of Dr. May," Skye explained. "As you know, the doctor is quite popular with the Native community down the hill."

Sage, still standing behind her desk, glared at Skye.

"He's so well respected. Dr. May worked for years at the clinic. Very popular—everyone loved him."

Before Skye elucidated more of the doctor's finer qualities, Sage interrupted. "Now that you mention it, I heard a different story. Not everyone loved our doc. Wasn't there some upset with his fertility clinic in the office?"

Hands on her hips, Skye jutted out her chin. "None of our business, is it. Not really."

Walking around the desk to stand in front of Skye, Sage looked down at the older woman. "Please thank Dr. May and tell him that the academy no longer accepts specific donations from the council. If they want to donate, the money will go toward the general scholarship fund. Dennis may or may not be our scholarship candidate this year. It wholly depends on his talent."

Rising to her feet, Skye stood chin to chin with Sage. "Just so you remember, the town council supports your school. Without us, where would you get the money?"

Skye exited the office, her door slam indicating the last word.

Sage turned to Olivia. "So now you know what I deal with day in and day out. The town council wants to run the school. When they appointed me, they thought the connection with my mother would make me a pushover for their ideas." Sage shuffled papers on her desk. "Just so you know, Marla was the main contributor to our scholarship fund. She doubled the town council contribution for the past three years."

"I bet the Old Rockers weren't too happy with that," said Olivia.

"No, they were not. Even my mother, who supports the academy, didn't like losing her influence over our decision-making. Without their money after Marla's death, I'm not sure how we can go forward with the groundbreaking for the new performing arts center. We may have to scrap the plan."

Olivia nodded. "Speaking of Marla's money, I need to contact an attorney about her estate. Do you know one down the hill? I don't want to ask anyone else in Lily Rock. You never know the hidden agendas of small towns."

Sage walked back to her desk. She reached into her bottom drawer, pulling out an old cigar box. "I do have a name. A guy who helped me with the academy finances, and so far as I know he's never spent one weekend in Lily Rock." She handed Olivia a business card.

"He's from the desert?" She stared at the card in her hand before putting it into her back pocket.

"He is," answered Sage.

"Speaking of desert," remarked Olivia, smiling. "Should I assume the doc had a clinic down the hill?"

Sage smiled back at Olivia. She began to tidy her desk, shifting papers into one pile before placing them in a drawer. "My mother told me back in the day the doc would spend most of the week in Desert Hot Springs and the rest up here in Lily Rock."

"What about our friend Skye? Was she ever a couple with Doc May?"

"Now that's a story that deserves a beer," said Sage, reaching for her purse. She looked up at the wall of instruments behind her desk. "Someone must have taken down that old autoharp."

Olivia grinned. "I guess I didn't put it back just right when I was snooping."

"The placement doesn't give you away; I see a shadow of dust across the front."

"I did take it down. I haven't seen one in years."

"No one plays those things anymore."

Olivia smiled. "Autoharps retain a sentimental place in my heart. My mom taught me to play the autoharp when I was very small. I'd accompany her as she played old-time fiddle tunes by ear."

A look of surprise came over Sage's face. "I didn't take you for a musician."

"I used to play a lot. In fact, there's an old YouTube video of me sitting in with a band. That's how I met my ex. But then when I got together with Don, I gave up playing. He hated the autoharp. Only rock and roll counted with him. I gave the instrument to an elementary school around the corner in Playa."

For the second time that day, the old instrument was removed from the wall. "Here," Sage said, shoving it toward Olivia. "I want you to have this one. I picked it up at a donation store in town just to hang on the wall for decoration."

Olivia felt tears sting her eyes. She took the instrument from Sage's grasp, pulling it close to her body, inhaling the smell of dusty wood. "Thank you." For a moment Olivia felt the strange sensation of having a part of herself returned. Sure, it was old and dusty and no one else wanted it, but that autoharp was her childhood. It connected her with the music she and her mother had made together. Olivia wiped away tears with the back of her sleeve.

"I'm such a baby since the car accident. I feel like every-thing makes me cry."

"It's just an old autoharp, honey. It might as well mean something to someone. So let's go to the pub. You can tell me more about playing. You aren't a kindergarten teacher, are you? I thought they were the only people who played autoharp."

Olivia glanced around. Mayor Maguire was missing again. "I gave the dog a ride up here, and now I don't see him."

"Oh, don't worry." Sage smiled. "The mayor has his own agenda. He'll catch up with you when he's good and ready. Did you know that he's—"

"Psychic?" Olivia laughed. "I've heard from many people that he's quite extraordinary. Psychic seems a bit exaggerated, but he does show up when I need him. He lends me a paw, so to speak."

"He's like that. A Lily Rock treasure."

Olivia still clutched the old autoharp to her chest. Sage touched her shoulder. "Why don't you leave that here, and I'll drop it by tomorrow? I may have a spare set of strings around here someplace. Let me check. Plus then you can give me a tour of Marla's place, if you have the time."

Olivia cradled the instrument in her arms one last time before she offered it back to Sage. "Sure. That would be great. I'm surprised. You haven't been in Marla's place?"

"She planned on having an open house for the town but never got around to the actual event before she died."

As Sage placed the autoharp back on the wall, Olivia felt instant regret. She wondered if she'd ever hold it again.

* * *

The pub hummed with voices as the two women walked up the stairs to the outdoor patio. After a cursory glance around the space, Olivia's eyes rested on Doc. He sat at his usual table by the fireplace, laughing with a waiter who handed him a menu.

"The doc is here. Do we have to go over to say hello?" asked Olivia.

"No, we don't. If you want to keep sane here in Lily Rock you learn not to greet everyone you know in the pub. If you do you won't have any peace."

Sage pointed to a corner table across the way from the doctor. "Let's sit there. If people want to talk to us, they'll come to our table."

Olivia sighed as she made her way to the table. Sage took a seat and placed her menu on the table.

"I'll have a seltzer water and lime," said Olivia to the waitress.

"Embracing sobriety, I see. Says a lot about you. I'll take the same since I'm going back to work."

After ordering their drinks and chicken wings for a snack, the women sat back to look at each other across the table. An outside observer might think they were sisters, with the same hair coloring and deep-blue eyes. Though Olivia's lips were fuller, Sage's eyes were wider, giving her a childlike appearance.

The waitress brought their drinks and appetizer, then left.

"How long have you been sober?" Sage asked, sipping from her glass.

"Just over two years." Olivia grabbed a sticky wing from the plate. "When I stopped drinking, my ex went wild. We lasted for a bit longer, but then it became too much. He hated my sobriety and I hated his drinking."

"So you're single now?"

"I am, and I'm not ready for another entanglement. My sobriety depends on a clear head, and I don't want to fling myself at someone else just to avoid my own problems."

Sage ran her finger over the tabletop. "I don't know personally, but my mother does. She's had her issues with drinking." Sage reached for a chicken wing. "Have to use lots of napkins with these things. Here." She shoved a paper napkin toward Olivia, who gratefully wiped her mouth.

"Thanks again for the autoharp. It kind of called to me when I first saw it on your wall."

"Will you play for me sometime? I know a lot of those old Appalachian songs. I play some fiddle. It might be fun."

"I would love to play with you. Give me a chance to get the thing up and running. I'll have to find a place where they do repairs."

"I have lots of music catalogues in my office. You can come by and look through them and then order online. It won't be hard, especially if you hang out a while longer in Lily Rock."

The pull to leave and the pull to stay in Lily Rock tugged at Olivia. *I'm here to discover Marla's killer,* she reminded herself. Yet her gut told her otherwise. Nibbling on another wing, Olivia wondered why she felt so attracted to the people in this small town. *It's like I have a piece of my destiny here, only I arrived at the wrong time. Either I'm too early or too late.*

"What's going on, ladies?" Arlo stood next to their table, a smile on his face. He looked over the empty chicken wing plate. "You want to order main dishes too?" he asked.

Sage opened a menu. "I'm not quite ready. Come back in a few minutes?" She turned to Olivia. "The pulled pork sandwich or the fish and chips—that's what I usually order. The burgers are to die for. Oh, the mac and cheese is also one of my favorites."

In five minutes Arlo returned and jotted down their order. Lingering at the table, he asked, "So did you get some rest at Sage's house? I heard you were there for a few days."

Glancing up at Arlo, Olivia wondered if now was the time to tell him about being dosed. She felt certain Meadow had put drops in her tea. She stared at the tall man as he shifted from foot to foot.

Instead of mentioning Meadow, she pursued another topic. "Did Cayenne tell you we had lunch?" Arlo raised his eyebrows.

Before he could answer, Sage spoke. "I was surprised Olivia slept so long at our house. We called the doc in just to make sure she was okay. I guess the snakebite and the drugs at the hospital finally hit you." Sage looked to Olivia for confirmation, her eyes asking forgiveness.

Sage knows. She knows about the tea being drugged. Why didn't she warn me ahead of time?

"Cayenne and I don't talk that much," Arlo responded to Olivia. He tapped his fingers on the wood tabletop, then added, "We're both so busy."

Olivia felt uncomfortable, so she changed the subject abruptly. "I lost sight of our beloved mayor. Have you seen him lately?"

Arlo laughed. "Look, he's over by the bar." Sure enough, the labradoodle lay curled up under the bottom row of taps. His eyes closed as if he'd had one too many licks from the overpours.

"So that's where he ended up. I lost him up at the music academy. Happy to know he's back on track."

Arlo glanced over his shoulder, taking in the room filled with customers.

From outside the bar area a bang shot out—a single strike from the forest behind the parking lot. All heads in the dining area turned toward the sound, which echoed in the silence.

Olivia's eyes grew wide. "What was that?" she asked Arlo.

He hurried toward the bar, calling back to Olivia. "Sounded like a gunshot to me, or a car backfiring."

Fear tightened Olivia's gut. She asked Sage, "Is it hunting season in Lily Rock?"

"Not this time of year," Sage assured her. She pointed to two men walking purposefully toward the woods. "Maybe they'll figure it out and tell us later." Sage patted Olivia's hand that rested on the table. "Don't worry. Gunshots happen up here. Everyone thinks they're a cowboy at heart."

The voices in the pub resumed as Sage took her final sip of drink. "How about we pay our bill now?"

Olivia placed her napkin on the table next to her plate. "Good idea. I've got a phone call to make before things shut down for the weekend."

As if on cue, Arlo returned with their check. He dropped the bill on the table, as his eyes remained on the woods.

"Any news?" Sage asked, pulling out her wallet.

He shook his head. "Must have been a backfire in the parking lot." He shifted from foot to foot, anxiously waiting for the check. Olivia wasn't sure she could trust Arlo. He had been around since her accident, but in an odd kind of creepy way. She wanted to take him at face value, but—

Arlo tapped his knuckle on the table. "How are things going with Marla's will?" he asked Olivia, whose face turned white.

"What will?" asked Sage, handing Arlo cash for the check.

"She didn't tell you?" Arlo's face registered surprise. "Marla left Olivia her house and all her money. Cay and I witnessed her last will."

Sage's head swiveled back as her eyes searched Olivia's face for confirmation. "So that's why you need the attorney's name. Why didn't you tell me?"

"I didn't want to say anything until I'd settled the details. The will isn't official—a flimsy handwritten paper. It may not stand up in court, should anyone want to protest."

"Did Marla tell you she was leaving her estate to you before you came up the hill?"

"Marla never said one word to me. I was as shocked as you are."

A smile crossed Sage's lips, her eyes lighting up. "Okay then. Actually, this is good news. More reasons for you to stay in Lily Rock than go."

Olivia pushed back her chair. "I'd better get back to the house. Marla left a lot of paperwork. Maybe I'll find something there that will reveal her reasons for making me the beneficiary."

Sage and Olivia made their way toward the exit. Olivia glanced toward Dr. May's table. He smiled at her from across the room.

Olivia raised her hand with a gentle wave of greeting. The doc held up his glass as a greeting—or was it an invitation?

As the two women descended the stairway, the metal steps shook under their feet. Olivia grabbed at the rail. *My head still feels a bit fuzzy.* In the space between the steps she saw a couple hiding in the shadows underneath the stairs. A familiar voice spoke.

"We never talk anymore." *That's Arlo,* Olivia realized. She kept moving down the stairway, avoiding looking again.

"Whose fault is that? You don't even look up when I enter the room. We never go out anymore, you're always behind the bar," came an accusatory reply. *That's Cay.*

Arlo continued to speak, his voice rising with emotion.

"You are so different now. I fell in love with a man and you became a woman overnight."

"It was hardly overnight. I was in therapy and took hormones for over two years. I underwent surgeries, and it was like you never noticed."

"I was busy! I had the pub to run."

"You were busy all right. It was like you didn't care about me at all."

Olivia wanted to plug her fingers in her ears to stop hearing the conversation. *None of my business,* she thought, hurrying toward Sage's car.

Sage seemed oblivious to Arlo and Cay's conversation under the stairs as she opened the passenger-side door for Olivia. "Great meal. Let's do it again sometime soon."

The two women drove in silence back to the Lily Rock Music Academy.

CHAPTER NINETEEN

Overheard in Lily Rock

"This is the time to use all of your clothes that you never wear in Los Angeles. Like socks. It's that cold."

The moon hovered over Marla's house, casting just enough light for Olivia to see her keys at the bottom of her purse. She glanced nervously over her shoulder. *I wish M&M were here.*

Once inside, Olivia walked from room to room, checking windows and door exits. *Remember the cameras,* she reminded herself. A quick glance around the great room did not reveal any blinking lights from the corners. A thump at the window caught her by surprise. Hair rose on her arms and neck as shadows played across the glass. *Must be a branch,* she assured herself.

Instead of giving in to panic, she decided to sit down across from the expanse of windows. *So beautiful here.* The sense of mystery inside and outside the house felt intriguing—when she wasn't scared out of her wits and discovering dead bodies.

Lily Rock is growing on me, and Sage helped. A kindred

spirit. She feels like the sister I never had. She didn't know her father either. Olivia had always wondered what it would be like to have a father in her life. She envied her schoolmates who had dads to coach soccer or to help make sets for the yearly play.

She'd sit and watch fathers hug children, promising pizza for dinner, wondering if she'd ever have that kind of relationship with anyone. Olivia had envied other children until she met Marla in high school. Two years older, Marla became her sister, advising her through those awkward years of adolescence. Within months of their friendship, Olivia forgot to envy other children with two parents.

Olivia made her way to the kitchen. She started the electric pot for tea, pulling the last bag of mint leaves out of her travel tin. Staring out the window, she noticed a light flickering among the trees. *Most likely another cabin in the woods,* she concluded.

Pouring her mug of tea, Olivia wandered to the great room again to resume her seat. She stared into the massive fireplace. Bracing her sore leg on the rustic coffee table, she leaned back into her overstuffed chair to close her eyes.

Each sip from the hot beverage soothed her active thoughts. Her eyes naturally traveled over the structure of the room. The vast ceilings brought her a sense of proportion. She felt small but cared for in the space. Olivia took another sip, feeling her shoulder muscles relax.

Walking her empty mug back to the kitchen, Olivia glanced down at the dishwasher. *I better learn how to turn this thing on if I'm staying. Am I? Staying in the house that Marla built?*

Her eyes lingered on the row of coffee mugs in the dishwasher. Michael had left his from the other morning, the one that said *Carpe Diem.* Seize the day. She smiled. A cowboy who drowned his coffee in cream and sugar. *What's wrong with that picture?*

She'd not seen Michael since their conversation at the constable's office. Looking through the window over the sink, she felt a longing to connect with him. Maybe she should give him a call? Better not, she warned herself. Stick to the plan.

Making her way downstairs, to the guest suite, Olivia yawned. Then she turned to walk back up the stairs. *Why not sleep in Marla's room? Time to be brave. I'd love to take a steam in her fancy shower.* Olivia entered the master suite and flicked on a switch near the door. Illuminated by the soft lighting, the room reflected serenity.

Olivia's eyes rose from the well-appointed bed to the secret room entrance on the opposite wall. She moved closer. Imitating what she'd seen Cay do earlier, she ran her hand over the boards. One was raised slightly from the other. She pushed against the board to hear a click.

Her tiredness forgotten, Olivia walked into the room. The boxes she'd stacked earlier waited for attention. She bent over, taking the lid off the first one. *Finnegan, Fogerty, and Fine Attorneys at Law,* a file read.

She remembered a pencil and paper stored in the top drawer of an antique dresser. Jotting down the name of the legal firm, Olivia closed the box, sliding it under the table. Intrigued by the contents, she opened another and then another. Marla had saved files dating back at least a decade.

By the tenth lid, Olivia's focus intensified. *Why did Marla keep these files hidden instead of storing them in her office?* After thumbing through each folder, she placed them back in a neat pile on the table.

The final boxes revealed extensive copies of ancestry research. Remembering Marla's search for her birth father in high school, Olivia felt no surprise.

At first Marla had kept hitting dead ends since she didn't have access to the DNA companies that would reveal any information. Then a decade later, things had changed. A sample of hair in the right hands would reveal information dating back to the cave people.

Her chest tightened. Only weeks ago Marla had advised Olivia to search for her birth father on the web. She had made the effort but then retreated from reading the results. She'd told Marla in an email, "I don't want to disrespect my mom. She sheltered me for a reason. What if my father was a serial killer? Do I want to know that?" At the time Olivia had meant to tell Marla about her concerns over the DNA findings. Instead the conversation had diverted to another topic.

Only days later Olivia and Marla spoke on the phone about her visit to Lily Rock. Olivia, darling," Marla's voice had drawled. "I want you to take a getaway weekend with me here in Lily Rock as soon as possible. Set aside the time to drive up. You will love it here. If I can be frank, my house is to die for!"

Olivia laughed. "I figured your house would be fabulous, the way you described the planning on Facebook. How come you didn't post any photos?"

"Oh, I wanted to surprise you. Really, the place has something extra that can't be captured in a mere picture. Do come up this weekend."

"I won't be great company. You may regret your invite."

"A change of scenery will do you so much good. You can read and contemplate nature or go on a hike. I'll have my crew deliver delicious meals from the town." Marla's voice had dropped. "Plus I have something I'd like to show you about my ancestry research. I think you'll be quite interested."

"Do you really? Something about your biological father?"

"Not on the phone, darling, let's talk face to face. Let's

just say that I've received information about my family, and you will be surprised."

Olivia swallowed. She envied Marla's certainty, her unrelenting search for the truth about her father. Before she could explain to Marla about giving up her own quest, her friend interrupted her thoughts.

"Bring your results when you come so that we can compare our experience and chat like old times."

Remembering Marla's hopeful voice gripped her with sadness. She closed the box. *A house to die for.* Really. Hadn't that been exactly the case? Poor Marla, she'd never be able to tell Olivia about her father face to face. She glanced down at the boxes one more time. *The answers may be in here somewhere. Marla went to great lengths to keep all of this information for a reason.*

Olivia yawned. The initial surge of adrenaline plummeted to deep fatigue. She made her way out of the hidden room, closing the entrance behind her. *I would love to try that steam shower about now.*

After some inspection of the knobs on the wall beside the wet room, Olivia turned on the steam. She walked away from the moisture to locate a towel robe in the bottom drawer of the bathroom vanity. Setting the robe aside she stripped away her jeans and sweater and underthings.

After sitting on the stone bench she took deep breaths. Then in another fifteen minutes, Olivia turned on the shower for a tepid rinse. Marla's file boxes forgotten, she dried off and felt ready for sleep.

The crisp white bedding smoothly draped over Olivia's skin. She wore a clean tee to bed, with her hair wrapped in a towel. Olivia drifted back into a nest of pillows, looking up at the ceiling overhead.

If not for Marla, I could not afford to stay in such a beau-

tiful home in this serene location. Feeling grateful and loyal at the same time Olivia reminded herself, *Don't get distracted! I need to find Marla's killer.*

Her eyes closed, then opened. *I forgot to leave a message for the attorneys.* Unplugging her cell phone by the bed, Olivia spoke after the beep. "This is Olivia Greer. My friend Marla Osbourne died unexpectedly, leaving a handwritten will. I would like to talk to you about the next step. Oh, by the way, she listed me as the beneficiary of her estate."

The second time she lay back into the mound of pillows, her eyes closed immediately.

* * *

Thud. Thud. Thud. Someone hammered against the front door of the great room. Olivia glanced at the clock. *It's already eight o'clock in the morning.* She snatched the towel robe from the night before and hurried up the stairway. She cinched the tie at her waist before looking through the front door peephole. Michael Bellemare stood shifting from one foot to the other, hair slicked back, a grim expression on his face.

"I'm out of jail," he hollered at the closed door. "Looks like the killer did not take our bait. We've got another dead body in the trees."

Olivia whipped open the door and ushered him inside with her hand at his elbow. She secured the lock before asking, "Who is it?"

Michael looked down at her, his jaw taut. "Open the door again. I think the mayor followed me to your house." An insistent scratch at the door confirmed his words.

"Welcome back, buddy." She patted his haunch as he sauntered past her knees. Michael leaned over to pat the mayor's head.

195

"I was wondering what happened to him. He was at the pub yesterday in the early evening, sitting behind the bar, waiting for bites of hamburger to be thrown his way."

Michael's eyes lowered, taking in Olivia's bathrobe and spa slippers. He shifted his glance to stare at Olivia's face.

"You were saying—someone was found dead?" she prompted him.

"I could sure use a cup of coffee. Let's head to the kitchen and I'll explain."

Michael filled the coffee filter with scoops of heaping dark roast. He shoved the filter under the pot. Olivia no longer resented his take-charge attitude in the kitchen. In fact, she now found his kitchen behavior endearing ... sort of.

As he poured water into the back of the pot, Olivia leaned against the counter. She waited for him to tell her, not knowing if she wanted to hear the name of the deceased.

"It's not Sage, is it?" Her voice cracked.

"No, it's not. Hikers found Skye Jones. A gunshot to the head."

She backed away from him, holding on to the counter for support.

"Janis figures it's suicide." Michael shook his head. "I have my doubts. Skye was never my favorite, but I hate to think we missed something and could have helped her in some way before she got desperate enough to kill herself." He poured her a mug of coffee and handed it to her.

Olivia nodded. "I wonder if Sage and I were the last ones to see her yesterday?" Her bottom lip trembled against the mug.

Stretching out his hand, he asked, "Are you okay?"

Her cheeks flamed as she turned away. "I've cried more often in Lily Rock than I did after Don left." She wiped her tears quickly, adding, "I have some cream, assuming it's not expired. You like cream in your coffee, right? And sugar?"

"I do like both of those things, and I am delighted that you remember."

Taking her cue to ignore the tears, Michael pointed to Mayor Maguire standing next to the great room table. His head dipped as if he, too, were sad. "That fella found the dead body. He showed up at the constable's office when the sun came up. I opened the door, and he stood in front of me in that way he has, like he wanted me to follow him.

"I tried to explain how I was keeping out of sight, but he just kept nudging my knee. What could I do? I pulled on my jacket and followed him. I didn't want to drive the truck, to avoid attracting too much attention, so we took a back-road hike on foot behind the town."

"That's exactly how the mayor brought me to Marla's dead body," Olivia said.

"I remembered you told me that. So by the time we walked into the woods, I knew something was up. Sure enough, he led me to Skye Jones—sitting under a tree, holding a small gun—dead. Blood everywhere. Just an awful sight."

As he told the story, his voice got softer and softer. Much to Olivia's surprise, he held his hand in front of his face. Michael's matter-of-fact retelling must have ignited his emotions at finding the body. Olivia put down her mug of coffee. She walked in front of him to wrap her arms around his waist. She whispered in his ear, "It's okay. You're all right. We've got this." He relaxed into her embrace. They held each other as Mayor Maguire watched.

After several minutes, they mutually stepped back. Michael wiped his eyes with his sleeve. "Who says men can't cry? But look what I got—a hug from Olivia Greer."

At the sound of Olivia's name, Mayor Maguire nudged Olivia's knee.

"Looks like the mayor wants us to follow him again."

The dog smiled up at her, his tongue poking out of the side of his mouth.

Olivia patted the dog's head. "Two dead bodies are certainly enough for now, even for a psychic doggo. I'm going to make us all breakfast. Scrambled eggs and bacon."

CHAPTER TWENTY

Overheard in Lily Rock
"You got robbed at yoga?"
"Yeah. But they only stole my beauty products and my CBD."
"Best Lily Rock drama ever."

Later that morning Michael and Olivia drove to town, parking on a side street. She pointed to a large group of citizens who had gathered in the center of the village.

"An old biker restaurant used to be the meeting place," Michael commented. "It was leveled. Since a huge renovation, people gather in the park. Looks like the Old Rockers lifted their ban on the park. I see several sitting on the benches, mostly the loudest complainers at the last town council meeting."

"I don't understand." Olivia looked out of the window.

"The park is a symbol of what's to come. Down with the disgusting bar and restaurant that used to be there; up with a carefully cultivated space of redwood shade for visitors." Michael held his hand up to his ear. "Listen. Do you hear the grumbling?"

Olivia laughed. "I think the dogs love the new park."

Scrambling over each other in a circle formed by benches, dogs on leads sniffed and smiled while owners chatted with their neighbors. Olivia saw one pit bull lift his leg toward a tree, only to be promptly yanked back by a cautious owner.

"No dogs under the trees either?"

"That's right." He smiled. "Lily Rock actually restricted dog behavior. See the tasteful wood fence? That marks the path for foot traffic—period. Since the local arborist made her pronouncement a few months ago, the redwoods have flourished; just look at the new growth. Even the diehard Old Rockers stopped complaining."

The limbs from the giant redwoods reached toward the sun, showing fresh new growth. "You can't argue with good conservation," she commented to Michael. Once out of the truck, Olivia walked beside him toward the gathering in the park.

People sat shoulder to shoulder on the benches, chatting with each other. Mothers cradled babies in their arms. Dog owners chided their pets. Older people hovered together, whispering. Tourists looked from group to group, wondering what was going on.

Michael took Olivia's hand, guiding her around a group of people who blocked the path. As they passed she heard someone say, "I didn't like Nurse Jones, but she was kind to my children when I made appointments with Doc."

Another man mumbled to his companion, "I heard she left a suicide note. She confessed to killing that new woman—Marla something or other. Do you believe that?"

"Just shows how you don't really know people like you think you do."

Olivia grabbed Michael's elbow. "Did you hear that? There was a suicide note."

"I guess I was so enthralled by your fluffy bathrobe this morning—you rocked it, by the way—I didn't tell you that part. She left a note claiming she'd been poisoning Marla for months."

"How can that be?" Before Michael could answer, Olivia's eye caught one head that bounced higher above the rest of the crowd. Arlo. He smiled at her, moving closer for conversation.

"So what's all the ruckus?" Arlo shook Michael's hand before turning toward Olivia.

"You didn't hear the news?" she responded.

"I guess not. I had a long night. Cayenne and I were up talking until two in the morning."

As Michael filled Arlo in on Skye's death by apparent suicide, Olivia took a moment to look at the crowd for a familiar face. Next to two Dobermans and an English bulldog she found Sage. Meadow stood close by. Sage waved at Olivia, who walked away from Arlo and Michael.

After dodging a dog chasing his tail, Olivia found Sage, reaching over to give her a hug. Sage felt small in her arms. "Since you came to town, we've had nothing but excitement." Sage smiled at Olivia.

Ten days ago Olivia would have personalized the remark. But now she knew that was how Lily Rock people talked to each other. In the difficult circumstances she'd become one of them: an unfamiliar feeling but not entirely unwelcome.

"There's nothing funny about a woman dying," hissed Meadow. She stood behind Sage, her face a mask of grief.

Sage took her mother by the hand, leaning against the wooden rail that separated the trees from the walkway. "Remember what you used to say to me when others passed away? Skye is in a better place now. She's at peace."

Running over the tried and true words in her mind, Olivia

disagreed. People had said the same to her when her mother passed away, but Olivia had never thought her mother was in a better place. She suspected that the dead took their problems with them.

Meadow's mouth curved downward, her chin dipping into her neck. Olivia took advantage of Meadow's vulnerability by asking a question. "You and Skye were close?"

Would Meadow be one of those people who grieved without speaking, or would she be one of those people who liked to talk about the one who was gone? A moment later, Olivia had her answer.

"Skye and I were friends for as long as I can remember. She helped me a lot when Sage was a baby. Skye's nursing experience got me through the initial months of caring for a premature infant."

Sage added, "Mom was pretty scared for me the first year. That's why she never had another baby." The words poured from Meadow and Sage in an easy cadence. They tag-teamed the story as if they'd told it often.

After listening to the mother and daughter, Olivia added, "That must have been challenging for you, Meadow. But look how well Sage has turned out! You'd never know she was so small in the beginning. You had Skye Jones to thank for her success."

Sobs overtook Meadow, her shoulders shaking as tears streamed down her face. Sage glared at Olivia, taking her mother in her arms. *Too soon. Skye just died. Not the right time for gratitude yet, not until Meadow gets over the shock. Mistake on my part. What's the matter with you, Olivia?*

Olivia tried to catch Sage's eye as the young woman dabbed at her mother's swollen face with a tissue. "I'm so sorry, Meadow," Olivia said quietly. "That was insensitive on my part. I do apologize." Feeling that the women wanted to be alone, Olivia stepped away, finding a spot on a bench to sit down.

"We'd rather stand," commented Sage. "Better for hugging."

Olivia's stomach rumbled. She touched her belly while glancing around the crowd. *There's Michael.* She watching him leaning forward, listening intently to—Janis Jets.

Nearby Arlo had distanced himself from Michael and Jets, but only a few feet away. He could easily listen in on their conversation. Olivia made her way toward Arlo. "So what do you think about Skye's suicide?"

He shuffled his feet and said, "Sorry, Olivia. I didn't hear you. Repeat the question?"

"Do you think Skye killed herself?" This time Olivia raised her voice to be heard over the crowd.

For a moment Arlo's eyes glanced upward, then back down to Olivia's steady gaze. "I never took Skye as the suicidal type. She liked controlling people and would manipulate unmercifully, but she liked herself too much, and suicide doesn't ring true for me. I always figured she was too full of spite to kill herself."

Olivia held the surprise from her face. He must realize that people cover up their inner selves to some degree, especially from people they see every day. Of course, Arlo may not know about how suicidal people pretend. She suspected Cayenne kept her feelings out of reach to protect herself.

Olivia knew. Don had taught her what to expect. Once you'd been around a person seriously considering suicide, you recognized the signs. You walked on eggshells waiting for the next attempt. You overthought every word. You worried. What if you said something that pushed the suicidal person over the edge—how would you forgive yourself?

"Will you miss Skye?" Olivia asked Arlo.

He shrugged. "I never thought about missing her. She was such a pest. Actually, I won't miss her. Skye was always in Cay's face about her medications, before her surgery and after. She was so judgmental and annoying. It hurt us both."

Olivia's heart beat faster. She felt this way when someone confided in her. She reached over to touch Arlo's hand. "I like Cayenne a lot. We had a chance to get to know each other better just the other day."

He glanced down at his feet. "I've been so afraid to say anything to her about the transition. It's put distance between us. I'd forgotten why we got together in the first place. She reminded me last night."

So that was what was going on under the stairway at the pub. They had started to talk and then took it home. No wonder he had been up all night. Olivia touched his elbow, then dropped her hand. "So happy to hear you two are connecting again."

Both Arlo and Olivia smiled. "There's the doc." Arlo nodded. "Wonder how he's doing with all of this?"

Olivia concluded her conversation with Arlo. "Catch you later," she told him, making her way to the boardwalk.

Dr. May sat by himself in the middle of the bench outside of his office. His hands rested on both knees. He looked toward the mountains at Lily Rock, the town's namesake.

"Hi, Doc," greeted Olivia.

He patted the seat beside him, inviting her to sit. Keeping a distance between them, she sat down, following his gaze, looking to the mountains behind the wooded area. "Still some snow," she commented.

"For another month," he said. "In late spring things will heat up, and we'll be heading to tourist season before you know it. How are you today, darlin'?"

Olivia leaned against the wooden bench. Recoiling from

the term of endearment, she pulled her arms closer to her sides. "I'm feeling fine. My leg is healing, and my head doesn't hurt. Must be time to get back down the hill. I have a new job waiting for me."

"So you're leaving, then?" The doctor shifted his body around to face her.

Not wanting to seem rude, she drew her eyes from the mountains to meet his. The doctor crossed his leg over one knee. His eyes looked bloodshot and his hair uncombed. He reached out, taking her hand from her lap. He turned it over in his grasp to trace her palm with his forefinger.

"My nurse is gone now. I feel so alone. Would you consider taking her place in the office, just as my receptionist? I could sure use your help." The invitation was made in a soft, pleading voice. A persuasive tone. Olivia felt her heart bump against her chest. She wanted to help the old man, but something held her back.

"Don't you want to wait a bit before you interview for a new receptionist? At least until after the funeral arrangements for Skye?"

Realizing he'd made a mistake, the doctor dropped her hand. Hunched shoulders covered his chest. "Now don't take it the wrong way, Little Bit. I was just thinking you may want an excuse to stay here in Lily Rock." The doctor's voice lowered. "Looks to me like you and that Michael fella are becoming kind of chummy."

A current of anger slid up her spine, surprising Olivia. With a quick inhale, she spoke. "First of all, stop with the little endearments. We hardly know each other, and I find them condescending. Second of all, your nurse of decades just killed herself. Don't you think you might be feeling a little bit responsible? Didn't you notice her despair or at least a bit of depression? And finally, my relationships are none of your business. If I want to stay in Lily Rock I will because I want to, not because you've provided me employment."

Olivia knew what to do next, and it wasn't waiting for the doctor to recover from her tirade. She stood up and walked briskly away. *What's the matter with me? First I make Meadow cry, and now I've blasted the most influential Lily Rock resident?* Turning the first corner of the building, she exhaled her remaining anger as someone's hand grabbed her shoulder. "Let go of me!" She turned toward her assailant.

"It's me." Michael held her at arm's length. "What's going on with Olivia Greer?"

Her face turned red as her shoulders sagged in defeat. How different it felt to be called by your full name: Olivia Greer.

"I've been giving the doctor a piece of my mind, if you must know."

"Have you now?" Michael dropped his hands. "I want to hear all about that. What if we head over for a late lunch. You can tell me every juicy detail." Michael reached to touch her shoulder and then dropped his hand instead. He gestured with a nod of his head toward Casey's Kitchen. People had already lined up outside.

The smell of bacon wafted past Olivia. Her stomach growled. She walked toward the cafe as he followed.

"One booth left," the waitress assured Michael when it was their turn. "Good to see you, Mike."

"Mike," sniffed Olivia.

"You don't like my name?" he asked, sliding into the booth opposite her.

"I like your name just fine. Only Mike just sounds silly."

"Good to know," he mumbled, looking over his menu. "The waffles and omelets are excellent here. In case you want a suggestion." He stared into her eyes. "Still mad at the doc?"

Olivia sighed. "No, I'm not mad. I'm just getting used to being not mad. It takes me a moment to calm down." The waitress brought the coffee, then she took their order. Olivia told Michael about the heated conversation.

"I feel like Doc May slips in and out of personas, using his role as a doctor to assume unwarranted intimacy. Then when he gets in there, he keeps pushing. Do you know what I mean?"

Michael's face drew a blank. "I've never been to him for a medical problem. I do know he has a good reputation down the hill. I think he worked for the Cahuilla Indian tribe, mostly the young women in the reproductive clinic."

Maybe he's right. I've overreacted again. Michael knows the doc better than I do. If the rest of Lily Rock trusts Doc May, then maybe I need to give him the benefit of the doubt. He might have been in shock when he asked me to take over for Skye.

"It's probably me," she admitted to Michael. "I'm a bit edgy with Lily Rock and all the happenings. Had I met Doc in Playa I may not have had the same reaction."

"I'm not dismissing your feelings, Olivia. Please hear that."

Nicely done. Never dismiss a woman's feelings. Number one in the playbook. Point in Michael's favor. "It's okay. I don't feel dismissed. You don't have to agree with me, you know. I can handle opposite viewpoints."

"I did notice that the first time we met." He sipped his coffee.

When their meals were delivered, the waitress refilled their coffee mugs.

"So did Jets know any more about Skye's death? Had Skye been showing any signs of depression?" asked Olivia, pushing her empty plate to the side.

Michael leaned over the table to whisper, "I'd like to tell you what I just heard. I could use your perspective."

Olivia smiled at him. Another point in his favor. He trusted her to listen. She hastily looked around the room to see if anyone in the crowded restaurant was aware of their conversation. She nodded at Michael. "Did Officer Jets say what kind of poison?"

"No details. That's why the police from down the hill have been called to investigate Skye's cabin. They've roped off the place to keep nosey neighbors away until the team arrives." Michael glanced at his watch. "Shouldn't be much longer. We may hear sirens very soon."

Olivia looked into her empty mug of coffee before speaking. "I noticed something the last time I went into the doc's office several days ago. Anyway, Skye had a locked cabinet over the sink in the examining room. I felt kind of uncomfortable when she opened the cabinet. It was stuffed with small vials with labels."

Michael nodded. "So far that doesn't sound too odd, considering it was a medical examination room."

"Oh, you are so right. I didn't feel that odd until I realized I'd seen something very similar in another place. At Marla's. She had a large cabinet with the identical bottles and chalk labels an exotic array of herbs in her kitchen—oh, and so did Meadow, in her kitchen."

Michael's eyes widened. "You're certain they looked similar?"

"I am certain. But there is something else. Remember when I stayed at Meadow's the second time, after the snakebite, when you were hiding at the constabulary?"

"I was not hiding. Just for the record. I was keeping a low profile to ferret out the real killer. It's done all the time in crime novels."

"Okay, so when you were hiding but not really hiding? When I got back to Marla's, Cay and I were having a sandwich for lunch. She opened the cupboard to look for tea, and Marla's entire cabinet of herbs and containers had been cleaned out. Not a trace of what had been there before. Even the shelves were wiped clean of all residue."

His eyes widened. "Like someone went into your house when you were staying at Meadow's and cleaned out the stash?" Olivia nodded.

Michael paused for a moment. "Maybe someone took the key out of your purse. Would that be possible?"

She thought back on that night at Meadow's house. She remembered drinking tea and waking up two days later. She did not remember where she'd left her purse when she arrived at the house. "I do remember Meadow dragging me down the hallway to my bedroom," she told Michael slowly. "By the time she lifted my legs onto the bed, I was out. Anyone could have taken my purse and my keys."

Michael leaned back into the booth. His hand grazed his chin. "Do me a favor? Close your eyes to help you remember details. Think back to the tea-drinking scene." Michael's voice lowered. "What kind of brew did that old witch make up for you?"

"Old witch?"

"Meadow is the local crystal-toting New Age herbalist fortune-teller of Lily Rock. Did she not mention this to you when you first met?"

"She did mention her other day job of reading fortunes. Don't you guys ever get tired of acting out this small-town drama by playing all the parts?"

Olivia clamped her lips closed. *There I go again. What's up with my brutal honesty and probing questions all of a sudden?* She didn't mean to insult Lily Rock, or at least not the entire town. *First Meadow, then Doc, and now Michael. He'll probably get in a snit and walk out again.*

"Lavender and chamomile," she blurted aloud, hoping he would not be angry. "The tea smelled like lavender and chamomile," she repeated.

"Nothing else?"

He didn't look upset. Olivia inhaled deeply with relief. She dutifully closed her eyes again. "I smelled another earthy scent that the lavender and chamomile covered up. I kind of remember seeing a capsule on the counter. I wonder ..."

He nodded. "Who knows what she put in your tea. The woman is a bit wacko. But now for the other remark?" He sat back into the red cushion of the booth. "I am going to say something that may annoy you. You're a fine one to point out how other people play various roles. One minute you're the femme fatale lost on the road up the hill, and the next you're the Nancy Drew of Lily Rock, ferreting out who murdered Marla Osbourne. Sound familiar?"

Shocked at his insightful remark, Olivia did not know what to say at first. She noticed a small smirk on his face.

"I guess we're done here." She grabbed her purse from the bench seat, looking toward the exit.

CHAPTER TWENTY-ONE

Overheard in Lily Rock

Girl: Do you have lemon fruit juice?
Bartender: You mean lemonade, right?
Girl: No! Lemon juice!
Bartender: Okay, concentrate.
Girl: I am!

Michael reached for Olivia's hand. She stopped in her tracks. "Don't get your panties in a bunch. Just an observation on my part, Nancy Drew." Michael grinned at her. "How about I show you another quaint Lily Rock place, formerly known as the plain old animal shelter, now called Palms and Paws Animal Shelter?"

Her stomach unclenched. "Sure. I'd like to go there."

"Good." Michael left cash on the table. "I have a funny suspicion. Skye spoke to me recently, kind of unexpected, really—not like we were close—about some odd business going on over there."

"Sage mentioned that Skye loved animals. I think I heard Mayor Maguire liked her more than Meadow." Olivia glanced at the wall to her left. A sign read, *If a man speaks in the forest and no one's there to hear him, is he still wrong?* She smirked.

"Skye took care of every stray cat, dog, and mouse here in Lily Rock. Her tenderness toward animals helped the town excuse her irritability with humans."

Olivia shrugged on her jacket. "I know you made an exception for Skye, but where I come from, she would have been written off and unemployed."

Michael ran a hand through his hair. "Now, now, Olivia, you must not discredit the fine people of Lily Rock until you move here. Then you can pile on with the rest of us."

"I've been here nearly two weeks, and I can't wait to get back to my own life, humble as it may be. I can't imagine myself staying in Lily Rock much longer."

Michael ignored Olivia's lament. He glanced over the crowd in the diner before taking Olivia's hand. Pointing to the restroom sign, he pulled her along.

"But I don't have to—"

Michael leaned over to mumble in her ear. "Just trust me for once. Okay? We're leaving through the back door."

Sliding past the recycling cans and boxes of restaurant supplies, Michael glanced around again. He reminded Olivia of a furtive detective in a B movie. After shoving the door with his foot, he yanked her over the threshold.

Olivia pulled her arm back from his grasp to adjust her coat.

"If you walk around the building and head down the main street we can meet up at the constable's office. Time to get some answers from Janis."

Olivia nodded. Wrapping the coat against her body, she strode down the back alley at a quick pace. Her cheeks flushed as she remembered, *I've spent the entire morning asking questions of vulnerable people in Lily Rock Park. But let's face it, I don't think Skye killed herself—and neither does Arlo. Janis Jets needs to give me an update. Even if Skye did kill Marla, there are still a lot of unanswered questions. I want to know why two dead bodies have been discovered in this idyllic town in less than two weeks.*

Twenty minutes later Olivia and Michael met again, this time in front of Janis Jets's desk. Without looking up, Janis stared at her desktop computer. Michael leaned over to wave his hand in front of the officer's face. "So, Janis? I'd like some information about Marla. Have you heard from the coroner?"

Olivia expected Jets to push Michael back with one of her withering glares. Instead she twirled her wheeled desk chair to face them both, a smile appearing on her lips. "I suppose you do want information. On the one hand, I might give it to you. But on the other hand"—she extended her left arm—" why should I give it to her?" Jets pointed at Olivia.

"Of course, on the other hand"—she gestured with her right hand—"you'll probably tell her everything I say anyway, so I might as well tell you both at the same time." She paused to reconsider her conclusion. "Yet on the other hand—"

"Enough with the hands, Janis!" barked Michael. "What did Marla die from?"

She turned from the desktop to flip open her laptop. Officer Jets scrolled. "Here it is, the medical report on Marla Osbourne. How about if I just summarize? Marla Osbourne, a healthy woman, died of heart failure."

"You have got to be kidding. That's all you've got?" Michael's face turned red.

"Don't be so impatient, Mike. I'm not done reading. Here we go. She—Marla—died of heart failure brought on by anaphylactic shock due to—"

Both Olivia and Michael leaned forward at the same time, waiting for what came next.

"—an allergic reaction from exposure to cannabis."

"Weed?" Michael's voice rose with incredulity. "Marla died from smoking weed?"

"According to the notes, she may have ingested rather than smoked. The medical examiner found a lot of THC in her blood, along with significant traces of hemp CBD oil. The combination must have activated her other allergies, which over time led to anaphylactic shock. Apparently she did not carry one of those EpiPen thingies with her. A shot of that may have stopped the reaction. Since she didn't have one, her heart rate plummeted, and she died."

Olivia felt faint. "Would you mind if I sat down?" she asked Jets. "I need to absorb this information." Michael pulled out an old wooden chair, and she sat down heavily. He reached over to pat her leg.

Olivia's hands began to perspire. As soon as Janis Jets had mentioned the importance of the missing EpiPen, she knew she held a valuable clue that she'd failed to disclose. Olivia closed her eyes, imagining the worst.

On the day she died, Marla had most likely clutched at her chest and reached for the EpiPen she carried with her everywhere. The killer saw a moment of opportunity, grabbing the pen from Marla's shaking hand to throw it away into the undergrowth, letting Marla tremble and then die without the needed injection.

The killer may know I found the EpiPen. Her hands began to shake. Olivia closed her fingers into fists so that no one would notice. *Maybe that's why I feel so uneasy and spied upon in Marla's house. Someone knows that I found the pen.*

Olivia opened her eyes. *I can't tell Janis or Michael. They may think I'm the one who took the pen from Marla just so that I would inherit her estate. Maybe they think Marla told me about her will earlier. Am I one of those obstruction-of-justice people like the ones they arrest on* Law and Order?

Janis looked intently at Olivia. Her eyes traveled to the closed fists she held on her lap. "On the one hand, I think you know more about Marla's death than you're saying. I suspected you right away. Our entire town has come unglued since you decided to fall off that cliff on the way up to Lily Rock."

"Now just a minute—" Michael interrupted.

Jets ignored Michael, continuing to speak. "On the other hand, I took you off my list of suspects as soon as you got that snakebite. If you really wanted to escape you would have driven a fast car down the hill, not put on your old sneakers to hike a back road. Not even an idiot would get themselves bitten by a poisonous reptile to avoid suspicion. Oh, I also respect Mayor Maguire's opinion, and he likes you a lot. That cannot be discounted."

Olivia shook her head in disbelief. The oddest logic she'd ever heard, yet Jets had come to the correct conclusion—that she did not kill Marla.

Michael locked his arms across his chest. "Enough about Olivia. We came to find out about Skye. I know you think she killed herself and that she'd somehow poisoned Marla. But I don't feel it, you know what I mean? Skye the drug dealer?"

"I don't either," admitted Jets. "I've looked at her letter over and over. Whoever wrote it disguised themselves pretty well. Only Skye's prints are on the paper. The writing belongs to her. It looks to me as if the letter was written to someone, and they took out the part that sounded confessional so that we'd believe Skye killed herself.

"The suicide is straightforward, as far as self-inflicted wounds go. None of that movie crap either. She pulled the trigger with her dominant hand. One shot from a gun she purchased down the hill only a month ago killed her. Done and done."

All three of them paused, silently contemplating the information they'd shared.

For a moment Olivia wanted to tell Jets and Michael her secret. She imagined the look of surprise on their faces when she admitted, *I found an unused EpiPen one hundred feet away from where Marla's dead body was discovered.* She knew in her gut the pen had not dropped from Marla's pocket. Someone else had thrown the pen aside to hasten Marla's death. That person was the killer.

Before Olivia could process whether to tell Jets and Michael about her discovery, Michael revived the conversation.

"Olivia, tell Janis about how you were drugged."

Jets looked up with interest. "Drugged?"

Giving Michael dart eyes, she clamped her lips shut. Jets and Michael looked at her expectantly. She swallowed and then spoke.

After hearing the entire story, Jets drummed her fingers on the desk. "So you think Meadow drugged your tea. Why would she do that?"

"At first I thought she was just trying to help me sleep. I was offended that she didn't ask me first, but with everything else going on, I kind of forgot the whole thing.

"It wasn't until the second time, when I slept for so long, that I began to wonder what Meadow was up to. I mean, she's an educated woman, a librarian. She's an animal lover. She's Sage's mother. Why would she want to drug me?"

"Why would she?" echoed Janis.

Not wanting to hear Janis ruminate aloud one more time, Olivia continued. "The other thing that kind of bothered me is how my suitcase kept coming and going, showing up with clean clothes, as if by magic. At first I figured my head injury made me forgetful. Now I'm not so sure. Whenever I was asleep, stuff happened. Even my car was fixed, then it wasn't. I started to feel uneasy, not knowing who to trust. By the time I saw someone spying in the laundry room window, I tried to get away on foot; I wasn't sure if the car could have been tampered with."

Michael looked down at his hands, a sheepish grin on his face. "Okay, I can explain some of that. I had nothing to do with the suitcase," he said. "But I did kind of tell a small fib about your car—the brakes."

"What do you mean, a small fib?"

"I kind of lied about the brake problem for my own reasons." He looked down at his lap. "You fell right into my life. I felt confused at first, and I wanted to keep you close until I figured out my own ... you know ... feelings."

Both women stared at Michael. His confession shocked Olivia. She felt her cheeks grow warm. Then she clamped her lips closed. *I don't want to hear about his teeny-tiny feelings right now. I'm trying to solve my friend's murder.*

Jets turned to Olivia. "Be that as it may, drugging you is not normal Lily Rock behavior. I think I need to have a word with Meadow McCloud."

Olivia agreed. "Meadow seemed really upset in the park. I didn't realize that she and Skye were so close."

Jets reached into her top drawer, pulling out a pad of paper. "Let's think this through. On the one hand, if I go and talk to Meadow, her suspicions will be aroused and she will most likely clam up. On the other hand, if I send Michael to talk to her, she will certainly go silent. Michael is good for the odd police job, but the Old Rockers didn't like his relationship with Marla from the beginning."

Jets turned to Olivia. "I think you could help me out here.

Why don't you go and talk to Meadow again? Chat her up a bit. See what you can find out in casual conversation. But whatever you do, no more tea! She's a menace with those herbs!"

Olivia liked being included in the informal investigative team. Apparently Jets trusted her—on account of Mayor Maguire. Michael smiled appreciatively at them both, looking from one to the other, his personal confession forgotten in the moment.

Then a shadow crossed Michael's face, a stern voice to follow. "I'm worried about Olivia and the Old Rockers. If she's not the culprit, then she may be the target. Everyone knows she's inherited Marla's estate. None of the Old Rockers want new money to keep pouring in for the hipster restorations."

Janis Jets raised her hand. "You have a point," she admitted. "So that's why I'm sending you to go with Olivia. You can hang around to make sure she comes away from the conversation awake, in one piece, on her own two feet. Not drugged or bitten by a snake this time!"

Olivia smiled. The friendly banter felt so comfortable. *How did I wander up a hill, a temp from Playa del Rey, and end up in this mess of intrigue and death? I feel like an entirely different person in Lily Rock. A much more interesting one.*

Bidding Jets goodbye, Olivia followed Michael down the boardwalk to his truck.

"Thanks for taking care of my car. I just wanted to say that out loud. I wasn't sure about your motives for sending it back to Brad's. But I'm beginning to trust you more than I did."

Michael smiled at her, making her chest feel warm. *Better stop this right now,* she warned herself.

"Do we have to talk about your feelings anymore?" she asked, keeping her voice light.

"We don't have to talk. We never have to talk about my feelings. I just want to hang out with you, that's all."

Olivia sighed with relief. *I believe him.*

On the short drive to Meadow's, she leaned her head out the open window, filling her lungs with the pine-scented air, feeling the wind against her cheeks. *Just like M&M*, she realized. *What am I going to do without that silly mutt?* Pulling her face back from the open window, she spoke aloud, "I wonder what Marla was thinking those last minutes, as she lay in the dirt underneath the sequoia? I think I know what I'd be thinking, should I have a few minutes left. I'd be thinking, what a relief. Now I know how it's gonna end."

Michael's face looked grim. "Knowing how you're going to die after a lifetime of speculation may be some comfort."

"Do you think Mayor Maguire was there at the end?"

"I don't know. Wouldn't he have dragged her body to the house, making a heroic effort to save her?"

Olivia imagined Mayor Maguire next to Marla, injecting the EpiPen into her thigh with his mouth.

Michael turned the truck onto a side road. "Where are we going?" Olivia asked.

"There's a good chance that we'll catch Meadow at her afternoon job. Pines and Paws Animal Shelter, right over there." His finger pointed to a sign. "Meadow and Skye used to work together at the shelter. If Meadow is there, she may feel like talking."

"You said that the shelter has a bit of history?" Olivia looked at him expectantly.

"Just so you know, the doc owned the place for years. He employed people to run things for him, including his nephew Brad. The mechanic guy who fixed your car? Doc hired lots of part-time help, which worked out well for Lily Rock. Just a year ago, the doc built another shelter—state-of-the-art—quite beautiful."

"Why did he build a new shelter—any particular reason?"

"That's the part I want to tell you about. Let's pull over here." Michael drove into the dirt road, stopping to pull on the emergency brake. Slinging his right shoulder over the seat, he looked at Olivia. "So, in the past, the doc got into trouble at the animal shelter.

"It turned out to be Marla's doing," continued Michael. "Three years ago Marla stopped by the shelter to talk to Meadow and Skye about the town council's decision to block her building permit for her house. As an aside, it took us months to get approval. Too much glass, not enough drainage, soil unstable, you name it. We finally succeeded, though."

Olivia nodded.

"When Marla visited the shelter, she didn't like what she saw. Behind the closed doors were cages with dogs lined up, no outdoor access. After getting nowhere with the two employees and her request, she marched herself down to the constabulary to report the squalid conditions."

"So the shelter was investigated?"

"Officials from down the hill, from the ASPCA arrived in two days."

"And—"

"If you go on their website you will see photos and a write-up on the shelter before they shut it down. Unknown even to Marla, Doc had his employees injecting CBD oil into the dogs' food for experimental purposes."

"Unbelievable!"

"As you probably know, CBD doesn't have a hallucinogenic effect like cannabis, but it has been known to help dogs with seizures. At least, that's what the doc told the officials.

They gave him a warning and shut down the shelter. It took him months to reopen with a new building and under a different business name."

"They actually gave him a new license?"

"Of course they did. He's an Old Rocker. The town council practically paid him to start up again. Animal shelters are big in Lily Rock. People bring their pets from down the hill and all over just to have them adopted here."

"But no more CBD injections, right?"

"The doc stopped that, and I have to admit, he redesigned the shelter so that the kennels are much bigger and the animals have access to the outdoors. He did fix things."

Having finished his story, Michael turned the key in the ignition. He steered the truck back onto the open road. "So now that you have some backstory, let's see if Meadow is working this late Friday afternoon."

CHAPTER TWENTY-TWO

Overheard in Lily Rock

"Lily Rock is where a dog runs the town while people bark and sniff at each other."

As the sun began to set, Olivia got out of the truck and took off her sunglasses. Then her eyes grew wide. When she heard about the Pines and Paws Animal Shelter, she had expected a hut-like building surrounded by a chain-link fence. Instead, a state-of-the-art two-story structure rose within the forest, redwood siding freshly stained. Lily Rock, the actual namesake of the town, glimmered white from the mountain range in the distance.

The sign, *Pines and Paws Animal Shelter,* looked familiar. Olivia had seen other similar designs in the village, mostly advertising the businesses supported by new residents. As they approached the building, dogs barked a warning.

"Were you the architect for this building as well?" Olivia asked Michael, carefully noting the structure.

"I was not. However, I think they drafted off my ideas. You can see the similarities if you look closely."

"I do see! From outside, the use of wood and glass makes this building your distinctive style." She pointed to the roofline above. "I'm pretty certain there's an atrium indoors, which reflects your philosophy of bringing the outside to the inside."

Kicking his toe in the dirt, Michael smiled. "You know my work. I'm flattered."

The double glass doors automatically opened. Olivia braced herself for the usual odor of cleaning fluids and dog feces that accompany a visit to the veterinarian. Instead she inhaled once—then again. Cool air brushed past her cheeks, bringing with it the scent of rich soil. The center of the reception room was a lushly filled atrium, where plants grew from floor to ceiling.

People sat in chairs with their animals. Concealed by the indigenous potted plants and large boulders, there was very little mingling. The woods outside, easily viewed through the floor-to-ceiling glass windows, brought a serene feeling to the waiting area.

Behind the atrium, a long counter made from rough-sawn pine supported three new computers. She stepped to the front, noticing a series of pamphlets with photos of cats and dogs. Olivia picked up the first one that caught her eye: *How to Welcome Your Pet to Their New Forever Home.*

"If I get bored I'm going to consider suing the company for stealing my designs," Michael muttered in her ear.

"I thought you were all about Lily Rock moving into the twenty-first century. Isn't imitation the sincerest form of flattery?"

"Not for me, it isn't. There's something wrong, as if the builder intentionally wanted this place to look like my design —like getting away with my ideas without acknowledging me."

"What would be the purpose of that? I think you're good at what you do, and you've captured the essence of Lily Rock in Marla's home and the pub. Didn't *Architectural Digest* pick up some photos of both?"

"They did." He nodded. "But this just feels wonky to me, and oh, by the way, it's creative infringement. I could sue them!"

Olivia wanted to argue more with Michael. Instead she looked at his hardened expression and the stubborn chin that jutted out in disgruntlement. She had to admit that his genuine indignation felt much more authentic than the laid-back cowboy persona he usually wore.

"How can we help?" A young man interrupted her thoughts. He stood behind the desk, his hands poised on a computer. "Here to adopt?"

Before Michael could respond, a door behind the counter opened to reveal another young man sporting a full three-inch beard and a baseball cap turned backward. He pushed aside the greeter to pull open a drawer from the front desk. Rummaging about, he pushed the contents aside, only to shove the door closed.

"Grant. Where are the keys to my pickup?" the bearded man asked the greeter. "I was told to get them in the usual place at the desk."

Shoving his hand through his short-cropped hair, he replied, "I have no idea what you're talking about. I'm trying to set these people up with an adoption, okay?"

Much to Olivia's surprise, Michael greeted the impatient man. "So Brad, you're not working at the garage today?"

Ah hah. This bearded guy must be the famous mechanic who worked on my car.

Brad blinked at Michael. "I help out my uncle here at the

shelter." Instead of pausing for friendly banter, he resumed his search through the drawers.

Olivia's superpower kicked in. She could pinpoint a person with alcohol issues from across the room. She could also spot a person coming off of weed or meth since she'd observed Don and his bandmates for years. Brad's nervous gestures and sense of panic reminded Olivia of people she'd known from the past.

Michael raised one eyebrow. "Come here a minute, Brad. I'd like you to meet a friend of mine."

The young man turned around reluctantly. "Hi," he mumbled, averting his gaze.

"I'm Olivia. You fixed my car a few days ago? We talked on the phone."

A shy smile came over the young man's face. "I figured that's who you were. Just sayin'." Brad turned his back on them again, eager to continue his search.

Michael shifted from foot to foot. Now Olivia sensed his impatience. Before she could speak, Michael blurted out, "We're here to adopt a dog."

She pretended to brush hair out of her eyes to disguise the surprise on her face.

Ignoring Brad's search under the counter, Grant launched into action. He grabbed a clipboard. "You have to fill out this form, and then I can take you back to visit the dogs." He handed them a packet of papers and a pencil.

Michael thumbed through the papers. "We're not applying for a bank loan. Just want to adopt a dog."

"I know the questionnaire seems lengthy," explained Grant. "Just fill out the front and back. After you select your new family member, we will schedule an inspection of your home to make certain you're ready to take on the responsibility of caring for a new pet. Do you have other animals?"

"Not at the moment," Olivia said, playing along with Michael's ruse. *We came to talk to Meadow, and now I'm adopting a pet? I've been Lily Rocked for sure.*

"That will make the process easier. Otherwise we'd have to introduce your new family member to each of the other pets. Gives us a chance to observe their interaction before we can deem your home a safe environment."

"Actually, we have an occasional dog visitor. Mayor Maguire spends a lot of time at our place."

Grant looked up from his clipboard, interest showing in his eyes. "So you're residents of Lily Rock? The mayor visits you? Well, that will probably expedite your waiting period. We rely upon the mayor's opinion in our adoption process."

Olivia worked to keep her face in a neutral pose. *Maybe playing undercover for Janis Jets isn't my deal,* she thought. *How can I take an interview seriously when my relationship with a dog is my most important reference?*

"Before we fill out this paperwork, could we take a tour of the facilities? I want to make sure you people are up to our standards, right, Olivia?" Michael looked to her for confirmation.

Surprise showed on Grant's face. It must not have been often that customers turned the tables on the shelter. He grabbed a set of keys behind the counter.

"Follow me," he said, striding across the center of the atrium toward an exit door. A long hallway appeared on the other side. The door slammed behind them.

Hand-drawn pictures of dogs and cats and hamsters and rabbits lined the walls. "We give lots of tours to schoolchildren," Grant confided as they walked together.

"Where do all of these go?" Michael asked, pointing to the lineup of closed doors.

"Some are offices, and the rest are exam rooms." He took a

left turn at the end of the hall, exposing another set of double doors.

The sound of dogs barking intensified as they passed through the doorway. A sign at the end of the hall read, *Kennel*. Grant opened yet another door, where two dogs waited, both smiling a welcome.

"This is Sidney and his partner, Jeff," he told them. "They are permanent residents of the shelter. The rest of our adoptees live toward the back." He pointed while Jeff took a moment to sniff Michael's jeans.

All shapes and sizes of dogs greeted Olivia and Michael. Some smiled, running to the front of their wire kennels. Others huddled in the back, where the outdoor exits gave opportunity for escape, should it be necessary. Olivia counted over fifteen dogs in residence. Only three cowered in their kennels, while the rest wagged tails at the visitors.

"Do you have records on your rescues?" Olivia questioned. She suspected that the shy dogs may have been abused.

"We do have extensive files on the adoption, including the circumstances of their rescue, along with specific characteristics of each animal. In case you're interested, we also have an entire cat wing, separate from the canines."

For a moment Olivia imagined having her own dog—like Mayor Maguire, only a bit smaller. One who could ride in the car with her and sleep in her bed. A pet to feed and care for now that she was single.

As if on cue, Michael said, "I called a day ago to ask about your adoption process. I spoke to my friend Meadow."

"Meadow answers the phone most afternoons."

"Will she be here today?"

"She should be. Do you want to talk to her again? She

may have told you about a specific dog, so I can get her on the phone."

Michael shook his head. "It's okay. We can talk to you."

At the conclusion of the tour, Grant walked them back to the main desk. Olivia felt herded, as if Grant only wanted her to look in the direction that he pointed. She didn't ask further questions about the other closed doors, since Grant did not encourage her curiosity. When they got back to the atrium, their guide handed the stack of papers to Michael once again.

Glancing at the pile, Michael said, "I think we'll bring these home to fill out and then bring them back later. In the meantime, we'll walk around the grounds, if you don't mind. I like the way you've built the kennels with indoor and outdoor space. Maybe I can do that for her new fur baby," he pointed to Olivia.

"Feel free to look around. I'll tell Meadow to expect you this afternoon. Thanks for stopping by."

As they exited the atrium, Olivia questioned Michael. "Fur baby?"

"I'm so sorry," he laughed. "That kid took himself so seriously, and I didn't know what else to say. Obviously it would be beneath you to call a dog your fur baby. What was I thinking?"

Walking next to Michael behind the facility, Olivia considered. "I might call a pet a fur baby. If he was like M&M, let's say. It's not entirely beyond possibility."

"Maybe under that city-girl exterior you're just a Lily Rocker at heart." Michael patted her shoulder, a look of affection coming over his face.

"Maybe I am," she admitted, enjoying his attention.

Michael lowered his voice. "So there's an advantage to somebody stealing my designs. I know the building, the possible ways to disguise hidden rooms. I kept a close eye during our walk behind the scenes. I had the feeling that the most obvious building space was used for the kennels and exam room. If I calculate correctly, there could be hundreds of unaccounted-for square feet."

"Maybe they store equipment and stuff there?"

"That could be possible. I know I'm acting suspicious. This place puts me on edge." He looked past his cowboy boots, staring at the dirt path.

Olivia took a moment to consider. "You do seem more tense. Tell me, how do you intend to find out about the hidden space?"

Michael swerved abruptly to the right, standing at the corner of the building. He pulled Olivia with him into the shade and pointed upward. Olivia saw a camera pointing straight in their direction. Michael stepped away from the building, gesturing for her to follow. Two horses looked up from the paddock, chewing their afternoon meal.

"There was a camera right in the corner," Olivia noted as she reached over to pat the nose of a gray mare.

"Cameras are all over, not that carefully hidden either. But I think I can find a space where there's a blind spot." He gestured with a nod. "Do you want to come with me or stay here? I won't be long."

"Oh, I'm coming with," she insisted, leaning over to kiss the soft nose of the horse.

Grasping her hand again, Michael briskly walked ahead, making a wide circle around the corral. Heading back toward the building, he took careful steps within the shadow cast by the afternoon sun.

Olivia followed Michael into an area sheltered by bushes. They stood huddled closely together while Michael assessed the situation. "No camera," he confirmed to Olivia. He ran his hand over the exterior wood planking. After feeling the surface of each board, he pushed the top edge of one, and the plank flipped up, revealing a hidden door.

After he pulled on the handle, the rest of the door gave way, revealing an opening into the building. She followed him into the dark space as the door closed behind them.

Blinking, Olivia expected to see a hidden room like the one at Marla's. Instead she faced an empty corridor. As she inhaled deeply, the scent of cedar filled her nose.

"This feels like a person-sized gerbil cage," Olivia mumbled, staying close to Michael's side.

"Or an obvious way to disguise another smell," Michael added, jingling two keys on a ring in front of her face.

Olivia asked, "How did you get those?"

"When Grant ducked down to retrieve his clipboard, I snagged an extra set of keys out of that drawer behind the counter. You were reading the pamphlets and probably didn't see me. So we'd better get going before he misses his keys," added Michael.

After two tries, the larger key released the lock. Taking her elbow, Michael ushered Olivia into the next room, closing yet another door behind them.

Though hidden, this space still held no resemblance to a clothes closet. No boxes full of documents here. No dry cedar smell either. Perspiration broke out on Olivia's palms. The atmosphere felt damp, like a steam room.

"Feels like a greenhouse," Michael said, echoing her thoughts.

Olivia inched forward. She noted rows of boxes that lined the sides of the warehouse. No more fancy wood planks or sweet-smelling cedar in this part of the building. Just the scent of damp cardboard.

Michael turned to examine the rest of the room. "Over there." He pointed to a corridor neatly disguised behind a stack of cardboard boxes and walked toward it. She strode in the direction he pointed, passing rows labeled *Restaurant Supplies*.

Michael waited for Olivia to catch up. He made his way behind the stacks.

"Which restaurant in Lily Rock requires all of these supplies?" she asked.

"I'm not sure. Kind of odd. Let's go this way."

Olivia followed Michael down another narrow hall. As they walked along, the light grew more dim. By the time they turned the corner, she stood next to him in complete darkness. This time Olivia reached out for Michael's hand. He grasped hers immediately, giving it a squeeze.

Reaching toward the closest wall, he ran his hand along it until he found a switch. A bright light surrounded them. Olivia blinked.

Buzzing and popping noises came from overhead. Olivia's skin prickled. Lining the room were rows of wooden tables, with a narrow space between them for a person to pass by. She sniffed. The smell of rich earth filled her nostrils, followed by a distinctive musk. *Kind of like Meadow's tea.*

Michael pointed to the electrical cords strung overhead. Each cord connected to a light that dangled from a beam over the wooden boxes. In each planter box, a mister on a tube sprayed. *That's why the earth smells so moist.*

Several of the wooden boxes contained green sprouts in various stages of growth. Each seedling had been carefully spaced three inches apart. The more mature plants had produced a few buds.

"I believe we've discovered the best-kept secret of Lily Rock," remarked Michael, a smile appearing on his lips.

"A marijuana greenhouse." Olivia added. "Wait till we tell Janis about this!"

CHAPTER TWENTY-THREE

Overheard in Lily Rock

"I'm not really trying to jump into a friendship right now."

After returning to the horse corral, Michael spoke first. "Dropping the keys unobserved may be problematic for me. Why don't you wait outside in the parking lot while I figure out how to make this happen?"

Olivia nodded in agreement. Standing to the side of the building, she leaned into the trunk of an old maple tree, her breath shallow in her chest. Two children emerged from the parking lot.

"Hurry up, Dad," yelled the little boy. "The shelter may be closing soon!"

"Wait up," the father yelled. The small boy carried a red leash, the younger sister a huge smile. Olivia felt happy thinking of the joy a small dog or cat would bring to this family. Pushing the family aside in her thoughts, she texted Michael in a hurry. *Family of three heading your way. They may be the distraction you need to return the keys.*

Within seconds, a thumbs-up emoji came her way.

Michael emerged through the automatic doors and sprinted toward Olivia. "Let's get out of here," he whispered to her.

"Did anyone see you?" she asked as he unlocked the truck.

"No one saw me, but I did talk to Meadow."

Olivia's stomach fluttered. She'd put Meadow out of her mind. "I kind of forgot that's why we came here in the first place."

After they got into the truck, Michael leaned his arms on the steering wheel, collecting his thoughts. A sudden knock came from the side window. Olivia's head jerked toward the noise as she pushed backward into the seat.

"Hey, guys," shouted Arlo. He looked down through the closed window, at Olivia's hand holding a brochure from the Pines and Paws Animal Shelter.

"Are you adopting a pet?"

Olivia rolled down the window of the truck to explain. "Michael brought me here to look around. Plus we wanted to check in on Meadow. She seemed really upset when we saw her in town earlier."

"I came to check on her too. Such a sad situation, and she was really close to Skye."

Olivia touched her forehead, remembering her accident up the hill. Something tugged at her understanding of the relationship between Meadow and Skye. At times both women blended into one person in her mind. *I guess I didn't know Skye that long.*

"Was Meadow in Lily Rock before or after Skye?"

Arlo shrugged his broad shoulders. "I don't know for certain. I just got here a few years ago. But I think it was Marla who told me that Meadow moved up the hill with baby Sage. Skye must have been here already, working for Doc. Why does the timing matter so much?"

Unsure how to answer Arlo, she looked at her hands folded in her lap without speaking.

When he realized an answer was not forthcoming, Arlo looked over Olivia's head to address Michael. "What do you think, Mike?"

"About what, exactly?"

"You know, Skye's suicide."

Michael's smile faded. "I don't know what to think. Skye did not impress me as the suicide type, if you must know."

Olivia opened the passenger door, gently shoving Arlo back from the window. "Why don't we just go talk to Meadow and ask her about Skye?"

"I'll go back with you." The truck door shut as Arlo walked toward the shelter entrance. Olivia followed. She heard the driver's door shut with another thud. Michael joined them.

As the door swished open, Olivia turned to Arlo. "You came here expressly to visit Meadow?"

He smiled. "Let's just say I have business here."

The center of the atrium hummed with activity. A chew toy let out a loud squeak. The family with the two children played at one side with a small black cocker spaniel. The dog pulled at the toy, which the boy grasped firmly in his small hand.

"I'll go find Meadow," Arlo said. "Looks like you're in good hands. He's on patrol." Arlo laughed, gesturing at Michael, who was carefully observing every corner of the large room.

As Michael turned around to face Olivia, she smiled. His eyes traveled over her head, to where the ceiling met the opposite wall. Before she could turn to see what he stared at, Arlo appeared from around the reception counter.

"Did you find her?" Olivia called out.

Arlo said, "She was in the back, sorting through invoices. Some key is missing. She's been looking all morning, and then she found it at the back of a drawer. She'll be out in a minute."

Michael glanced at his watch. "She's taking her time. I'm getting kind of hungry." He turned toward Olivia. "Are you up for a Brew Pub burger?"

Is he really hungry, or is he looking for an excuse to leave the shelter?

"Well, you two have a good lunch. I'll catch up with you at the pub later. Still have a little business to attend to out back." Without more explanation, Arlo ambled toward the atrium exit. Olivia followed Michael as he made his way to the main desk.

"We could check the back office if no one's around," Olivia offered, pointing to the door behind the counter.

Michael knocked first. When no one called out, he tried the door handle, which turned easily in his hand. Posters of dogs and cats and happy families decorated the carefully appointed walls. No papers on the desk surface; no computer either.

"Obviously Meadow isn't here," grumbled Michael. He glanced around the small room as Olivia watched.

"Do you think there's another hidden room?" she teased in a quiet voice. "I bet there's another hidden closet at the very least."

"You and your secret passages." He smiled. "But you may be right. Look over there." Sure enough, one raised panel stood out from the rest of the wall planking.

"I'm no Nancy Drew, but do you think there may be another hidden office behind that panel? Oh, I hope so!"

Michael grinned. "You try first, Miss Drew. See if you can get it to open." She began tapping the wall where he pointed.

One board sounded hollow, so she tried again. The panel slid under her touch, revealing a hidden door.

"No way!" Michael exclaimed. "You were right. Another door behind a door."

"Or maybe a staircase," she added, stepping into the space. "Nancy Drew always found hidden staircases."

Now standing within a ten-by-ten room, Michael pointed to the row of file cabinets.

"This could be a safe space for the business paperwork," suggested Olivia.

"Or it could be a place to hide another secret doorway to who knows where." Michael pointed to the outline of a door in the opposite corner.

"No hardware," agreed Olivia. "You may be right."

Michael pushed against the wood. Panels slid back revealing another darkened hallway.

Olivia stared. "This place is a maze of hidden doors and closets. I feel trapped in a 1940s mystery novel. I wonder, who did design this place?"

"I know. Do you want me to explore by myself? You can meet me back at the truck." He held out the keys as an offering.

"I'm coming with you," Olivia said, leaving no doubt in her tone of voice.

Michael slid through the narrow door. Without a switch on the wall, the only illumination came from above, where a skylight had been built directly overhead. He held his finger to his lips, gesturing for her to follow. Olivia heard a low mumble, which turned into distinct voices as they drew closer.

Two people quarreled in another room.

"Who's back there?" Olivia whispered to Michael.

"Not sure," he said. "Keep listening." They walked closer to the people arguing.

"I'm going to see Jets right now," a woman's high-pitched voice threatened. "You can't stop me!"

"You're overreacting as usual," the other voice responded.

Michael turned toward Olivia, "I think that's Meadow."

"If they keep snooping around, they will certainly discover the greenhouse," the woman's voice accused, growing louder with each word.

Michael's eyes narrowed. "It's Meadow. We've finally found her. Is she talking to Arlo?" Before Olivia could answer, the woman's voice continued.

"It will only be a short time before we're outed to the police. We might as well confess and get ourselves some goodwill."

Michael inched his way along the hall, edging closer to the open door. Arlo's voice became more distinct. "I just saw Olivia and Michael in the atrium. I have the feeling she's not here to adopt a dog. They were looking for you. I told them to wait until you got back—"

Meadow spoke quickly, "They'll be wondering where I am. I can deal with them later. Just so you know, Arlo, my decision is final. Consider yourself warned. I am going to tell the police everything." Sniffles could be heard, followed by a torrent of sobs.

Michael reached around, shoving Olivia behind his back. "Stay here," he hissed before walking into the room to make himself known.

"I knew I'd find you here," he called out to Meadow.

Her hands drew away from her face, exposing eyes that were red and swollen from crying.

Arlo stepped in front of Meadow, as if to stop her from saying more.

"I'm so ashamed," mumbled Meadow, wiping her face with the back of her hand.

"There's nothing to be ashamed about!" Arlo erupted. "I don't understand why women back out when things get just a bit challenging. You know, Mike. You know how women are."

Michael stepped farther away from the door and into the center of the room. He faced Meadow. "I thought we were going to have a talk. At least, that's what you said, so I went to your office. Were you trying to get rid of me?"

Tired of hiding in the shadow behind the door, Olivia took a step into the room. "We've been looking for her for ages," she said pointing past Arlo to Meadow.

Meadow's head swung upward as she glared at Olivia. "What are you doing here?"

"We came to see if you're okay," Olivia said.

"Never mind that!" Arlo shouted. "How did you know where to find us?"

Michael wrapped his arm around Olivia in a protective gesture. "We waited for a long time and didn't know where to find you at first. So we looked around. After some—okay, call it what it is—snooping, we discovered any number of hidden doors and hallways leading to secret closets and storage spaces. We found restaurant supplies and the weed being grown under the skylights. You don't have to hide any of that from us. We already know."

Arlo's shoulders slumped. "I guess there's no use pretending any longer. So we grow and distribute a little weed. I don't understand what the big deal is. I use the space for the restaurant supplies, and I grow some weed to distribute here and down the hill. It's not exactly illegal in California."

"Are you his partner?" Olivia looked directly at Meadow.

"Not exactly," she muttered. "More like his distributor. I don't get any of the profits for the growing, only for what we sell."

"So this is the real business at the Pines and Paws Animal Shelter. The production and distribution of weed. I get it now. Since weed isn't illegal, I suspect you don't have a business license to sell in Lily Rock. No wonder you kept it hidden." Michael's face looked stern as his eyes darted from Arlo back to Meadow.

Arlo rocked nervously on his heels. "Look, you guys, instead of making a big crime of all this, why don't I just cut you in on the profits? We're up and running now, and I think we could all make a tidy sum to support our lives here in Lily Rock. Talk about a backyard enterprise—"

Michael's arm dropped away from Olivia's shoulders. "I don't think so," he said quietly. "Olivia doesn't need any more money, she just inherited Marla's estate. I don't need any more money either. I have projects lined up for the future. It looks like you two are in this alone."

Olivia spoke up. "I have a question, if you don't mind. Did you drug my tea with some herb to make me sleep? I saw your cupboard full of herbs and teas with carefully labeled vials. Now I'm wondering just what I drank that I don't know about."

Meadow's eyes opened wide. "Well, I helped you sleep with a little of my special brew. I put a few drops of cannabis oil in your tea. It's not marijuana, but it does assist with healing and relaxation."

"Was that the only reason? To help with healing and relaxation?"

"Of course that was my only reason. Why would you think otherwise?"

Remembering how she'd fallen dead asleep on both nights at Meadow's house, she doubted the woman's simple explanation.

"I heard you talking on your cell phone that first night,"

Olivia admitted, hoping Meadow would fill in the details.

Michael interrupted, "What I want to know is, what did you intend to tell the police? We both heard you talking about going to Officer Jets."

"Oh, that." Meadow's chin touched her chest. When she lifted her eyes, she added, "I was going to tell the police that Skye didn't kill Marla."

There it is. That's what we came for. Neither one of us believed the suicide story, and neither did Meadow.

Meadow's monotone voice continued, "Skye is—was my best friend. She didn't like Marla, and neither did I. Marla had no regard for the Old Rockers. Plus her unlimited resources bought her everything she wanted. So irritating."

Michael said, "Your dislike of Marla was pretty obvious, especially at the town council meetings. After the first couple of times, things turned pretty tough. People threatened Marla, demanding that she move off the hill. She got concerned about her safety, so she hired me to watch after her."

"You mean like a bodyguard?" Meadow asked.

"Yep, just like a bodyguard. I was salaried to keep Marla safe, along with my other work at the house. It wasn't that hard since everyone thought we were a couple."

Now Michael looked apologetically at Olivia. "I wanted to tell Olivia right off that I was Marla's bodyguard." When Olivia frowned at him, he kept explaining. "Since you knew people had at least two jobs up here, I figured I didn't have to say much. Now that I'm confessing, Marla wanted me to look after you once you made it up the hill."

Olivia felt her gut turn over. "You mean it was all professional, you rescuing me from the accident?"

"Please don't misunderstand. It wasn't all professional. It was at first, but after Marla died—" Michael's eyes pleaded with her. Unable to comprehend his explanation, rational thought became impossible for Olivia. A door slammed in her buzzing head.

"You can't take care of yourself," Don screamed. *"You have no way of earning a living. You're weak. I put you on that pedestal and no one else will ever do the same."*

"I have no idea who to trust around here," Olivia announced in a clear, decisive voice. "No more excuses. I'm done. All of you with your small businesses and sneaky behavior and lies. I don't want to see or speak to you again." She pointed to Michael, turning on her heel to run from the room.

"Don't go like that, Olivia. I'm your bodyguard." Michael's voice followed her.

Emerging from the office door, she nearly ran into the boy who held his new black cocker spaniel puppy in his arms.

"Sorry," she said quickly, pulling her cell phone from her back pocket. Feeling her heart beat in her throat, she placed a call.

"Hello," said a familiar voice.

She swallowed before speaking into the phone.

"Hi, Sage. Do you have a minute to swing by Pines and Paws? I need a ride home."

"I sure do. See you in five." The phone clicked off.

Olivia walked through the parking lot and up the dirt driveway toward the main road. All the while her mind tumbled in anger. *The more I get to know these people, the less I trust them. Meadow blatantly admitted she drugged my tea. Arlo has a real nasty side, plus he sells weed without a business license. And then Michael—my bodyguard? He said he wanted to be my friend. He held my hand and teased me about being Nancy Drew.*

"Lily Rock is dead to me!" Olivia hollered aloud into the tree-lined road.

CHAPTER TWENTY-FOUR

Overheard in Lily Rock
"Why did you decide to take a retreat day?"
"Well, isn't there a saying that your body is a wonderland?"
"Temple. Your body is your temple."

Saturday morning brought sunshine and gentle breezes. Still dressed in her pajamas, Olivia stood outside on the deck to look into the forest. She knew the time had come. Running away from Michael felt cringeworthy. Not her finest moment by any means. A lifetime of avoiding conflict had made what she called the Great Escape her first instinct.

He reminds me of Don, Olivia admitted to herself. *The controlling way he hangs on to the keys gives me the creeps. It may not be my house officially yet, but it isn't his either. Plus he keeps saying he'll change the locks but he doesn't. Promises, promises. If I had a dime for every time Don promised me he would change.*

Olivia deeply inhaled the smell of moist earth coming from the garden below the deck. *I must change. That's why I came up here in the first place, to get back to myself. First I'll address my overly active mind.*

Michael's words interrupted her thoughts. "I'm your bodyguard," he'd said. *Why does that bother me so much?*

In the moment Olivia had felt shame, like an ill-fitting jacket. Rather than probing for more details, she'd given in to anger. She'd heard a lie rather than the beginning of a deeper truth when Michael admitted he'd been her bodyguard, assigned by Marla. If she'd not gotten angry, she might have inquired more fully, maybe finally understanding his real relationship with her old friend. Yet one of the things bothering her was that Don said something similar all the time. When he left her in their house, deliberately taking her car keys with him, he'd say, "It's for you own good. I am protecting you."

Assessing the past several days, she knew where she'd gone wrong. When she discovered Marla's body, she'd forgotten her goal, her quest. She'd left herself due to unforeseen circumstances—granted, they were extreme.

Driving to Lily Rock that first day, she knew what she was about. She planned to connect with her inner self and see an old friend on a getaway weekend. During that time she wanted to strengthen her resolve as a single person. Since leaving Don, she needed to rediscover herself.

Instead, one turn of her clammy hand on the steering wheel of her car had tossed her into a ditch, where fate took her off course. From that moment she'd been unable to rescue herself. She'd needed a "bodyguard." At the word, a tingle tiptoed up her spine. That was it. When Michael had appointed himself as her bodyguard, anger had erupted. She wanted to take care of herself. He'd gotten in the way of her plan, much the way Don had years ago when he'd offered to take care of her and she'd given in.

With a swallow, she placed her coffee mug on the deck

railing. *I need to reset my priorities, remember why I came here originally. I must find my own way.*

Her nerves tingled as her body began to tremble. Inhaling deeply, Olivia remained in the same spot. By the third breath, the hurricane in her head had been reduced to a storm. Only then did Olivia hear her mother's voice.

"Get away to a safe space where you can reflect," Mona, her mother, would advise. "Do it as soon as you realize your inner confusion. Don't wait. Cancel everything to be reunited with your inner wisdom. Pray the Psalms. Just turn to the middle of your Bible and begin."

For years Olivia wrote off her mother's advice calling it hippie-gone-dippy, good-for-some-but-not-good-for-her suggestions. She'd dismissed her mother's Christian upbringing along with her prayers since the time Don said, "I thought you were smarter than to buy into all that Christian mumbo jumbo."

Only after her death did Olivia realize her mother's advice may have been the most important wisdom Mona had left her, along with the music, of course—the music they shared together.

Olivia knew how to retreat. Mona taught her a combination of Native American and Christian spiritual practices to clear her mind and access her inner wisdom. *I'll begin now. I'll look for the Psalms—maybe online.*

Later she stood at the sink. After unplugging the coffeepot, she wiped down all of the counters. She put away all the dishes, including the soap and brush. Under the counter they went, accessible but not visible. With a soft cloth she polished shiny surfaces until they gleamed. Then she stepped back to inhale, then exhale. No extra appliances on the counter nor dishes in the sink. Clear surfaces, clear focus.

Keeping clean surfaces helped her racing mind slow

down. "Outside matters. Your inner life aligns with what you see, feel, and hear," Olivia's mother would say. Energy tingled in Olivia's gut, telling her she'd made the right decision.

Her next task drew her to Marla's suite. Walking past the bed into the bathroom, she stood in the center of the space to once again deeply inhale. Behind the tub there was a glass wall revealing a secluded courtyard surrounded by a redwood plank fence, the boards placed equidistant from each other in a horizontal pattern. Olivia opened a window over the tub, allowing a fresh breeze into the space.

She took another clean cloth from under the sink to wipe down the windowsill. She used vinegar and baking soda for the tub and the counter, placing all of the extra cosmetic bottles underneath the sink. "I promise to look at you very soon," she told the beauty lotions.

Rinsing her cleaning cloth, Olivia tackled the steam shower. Gray tiles gleamed when she finished. After whisking the old towels from the heated rack, Olivia walked slowly to the laundry room, where she dropped the cloth and the towels, along with everything she'd worn the past few days, into the deep drum of the washer.

Having cleaned the bathroom, Olivia pulled the sheets off of her bed. She gathered the mattress pad and the comforter. She bundled them immediately into her arms to take down the hall to the laundry room.

Now that her environment felt refreshed, Olivia worked on herself. "Outside in," her mother had told her. She accomplished her personal ritual with ease, holding her face under the tepid water from the shower and rinsing her hair twice, before stepping out on the woven mat placed on the tile floor.

Drying off with the recently laundered towel, Olivia pulled on fresh jeans and a soft sweatshirt. She inhaled deeply, lifting her arms over her head. Her confidence grew, slowing down her mental chaos.

Finished with the bedroom, Olivia paused at the landing before walking down the stairway. *What about those boxes?* Still in slippered feet, she padded against the plank flooring, back to the hidden closet where the files were stored. *Don't forget to offer your gratitude.*

"I've forgotten to thank you," she spoke aloud. "You welcomed me and provided me the space to retreat. I am grateful." Holding out her arms from her body, she felt the tingle. Energy coursed, as the area over her heart turned warm.

Following her sense of gratitude, Olivia dropped to her knees in the hallway, bending forward with her hands clasped in front of her as if in prayer. *Thank you, God, for receiving me. I am grateful to be sheltered by you.* Now silence enveloped her.

Relief flooded her, beginning at the top of her head, moving past her shoulders, her gut, her lower belly, and finally her thighs, calves, feet, and toes. The previous shame she had felt ran off her shoulders as the shower water had done moments ago. "Outside to inside. Make the connection to the Creating Spirit," her mother's words came to her again.

Something in those boxes must be important. Something about Marla and her search for her ancestry. Now Olivia had only one desire. To open the boxes in the hidden closet.

She lifted the box on top of the pile. She glanced around, feeling uneasy. *Not here. The boxes aren't that heavy. I want to look at these papers, but not in this hidden space.* Glancing at the stack, she knew her decision was not the most logical. Yet her inner wisdom led her now, not just her logic. *Something in those boxes requires exposure.* She shook her head and smiled. *How do I know that? Well, I just do.*

Opening the boxes with intention would require taking each one individually up the stairs. The certainty of this thought gave her the energy necessary to move forward.

One box at a time, Olivia moved up the stairs. She placed a box on the large dining table and then sat down to read the contents of each folder.

When she completed her inspection, she closed the box and placed it at the end of the dining table. After making the trip down the stairs, she retrieved one more container. By lunch she'd read the contents of three boxes but found no information that would explain Marla's death.

Taking a break she stepped outside on the deck to look over the back garden. A question wafted into her mind: *What do Marla's files have in common?*

Olivia placed her empty tea mug on the railing. When she inhaled, her body yearned to be stretched. First she grounded herself on the woven rug underneath her feet. Then she assumed the warrior pose, her back arched, her arms stretched over her head.

Her back tightened, then released. Before she could continue to the next yoga pose she heard a familiar scratch at the side gate. Releasing the stretch, she looked over to see a curly brown-haired labradoodle who stood with his paws placed on the fence.

"Look at you, M&M," Olivia greeted the dog.

She unlatched the gate as he dropped his paws to the ground. She bent to give him a hug around his neck, and she pushed her face near his ear. She sniffed in and out. He waited for her to stop before he licked her chin.

"Did you drop by for lunch?" she asked the dog.

In the kitchen the dog stood over the food bowl Marla had provided. Olivia searched her refrigerator. After smelling each takeout container, she made a decision. *Marla planned on us eating this food, and she went to a lot of trouble having it delivered. But I can't pretend Marla is coming back any longer.*

Running water in the sink, she pitched the contents of the refrigerator as the garbage disposal rumbled. When she opened the last container, her nose wrinkled. It smelled the worst. As she tossed it into the kitchen sink for the disposal.

As the disposal ran, she added a cup of baking soda to freshen the drain. Turning the water off, Olivia inspected the spacious freezer, where packages of frozen meat were stacked and labeled. Each one displayed a date. Taking ground turkey off the top, she closed the door.

The turkey slowly browned over the stove. She added rice and water. In twenty minutes she had made a lunch suitable for dog and human.

After the silent, companionable lunch, Olivia wandered into the dining room with her cup of tea. The dog followed, waiting until she sat down. Then he curled himself over her slippered feet.

Her cell phone blinked. *I bet it's Michael. He's trying to make up.* Olivia noticed one other message on her phone that was not from Michael. *Probably the attorney. I'll get back to him tomorrow.*

"I wish I had access to a computer," she told Mayor Maguire. His eyes remained closed. "If I'm going to continue the ancestry search, my smartphone screen is too small. Maybe I could use a computer at the library."

Before heading to the library, she needed to complete the task in front of her. Though she dreaded opening yet another box, she made one last journey down the stairs for the remaining box.

Upon opening the container, she looked underneath the lid. To her surprise scrawled in cursive was @lilyROck!.

Underneath the odd-looking letters, there was an abbreviation of Marla's email address: 4MOsbourne. *Marla must have written her login and password!*

Olivia's hands trembled. Since most of the files contained information about Marla's search for her father, the password may be connected to her ancestry account online. *That's the next task. The time is right: to the library!*

"Do you want to go with me?" She patted Mayor Maguire's head.

He stretched both paws in front of his chest, only to close his eyes. Olivia stood up from the table. She grabbed her purse. "Suit yourself," she told him, heading toward the door. Discarding her slippers under a convenient chest, she reached for her hiking boots. Before she could open the door, she heard the click of nails across the wood floor.

"Good doggy." She smiled at him. "Let's go."

* * *

Mayor Maguire walked close at Olivia's side as she entered the library. Not bothering to stop at the desk, she and the dog slid around the corner to where the computer cubicles lined the back wall.

Eager to continue her search, Olivia selected the first available monitor. She used the password she'd found, and Marla's account popped right up on the first try. Staring at Marla's name in the corner reminded her of a conversation they'd had months ago.

"Why don't you search for your biological father online?" Marla had asked.

At the time Olivia felt little interest. "The secret went with my mom. I'm okay with that," she had told Marla yet again.

"But don't you want to know?" Marla asked her in a Facebook message. "We've talked about finding our fathers since high school. If you're scared, we can look at your results together when you come up for your getaway."

Olivia clicked the DNA matches on Marla's account. Her hands tingled over the computer keyboard. Information not revealed in the boxed files drew her apt attention. Marla had a dozen siblings who lived all over the country, two overseas. How could that be possible? Before Olivia clicked again, she felt someone stand behind her shoulder.

"So I see you've found your way to our computer system. Need any help?" Dressed in her denim jumper, Meadow blatantly craned her neck to look at the computer screen.

Clicking Escape, Olivia laid her hands in her lap. "I got what I need, except for privacy. I didn't get that."

"Don't get all huffy with me, Olivia. You're in a public library. Privacy is not available here for anyone."

Olivia stood. She faced Meadow. The older woman looked tired, dark circles smudging her eyes. Without makeup, her skin appeared sallow. Putting aside her impatience, Olivia asked, "Are you okay?"

Clutching her hands in front of her jumper, Meadow said, "I've had trouble sleeping since Skye's death, and frankly, I'm not happy that you and Michael barged into my conversation with Arlo."

Meadow's anger spread over Olivia like a toxic spray. *Stay standing,* her inner voice reminded her. So instead of sitting like a victim, she planted both feet deeper into the thin carpet. *Not going to run this time.* Then the words came with a quiet intensity.

"I'm not surprised you aren't getting any sleep, considering you've been aiding and abetting an illegal business at the animal shelter. Do you and Arlo have a license for growing and selling?"

Meadow's hands rested on her hips, and her mouth froze. Apparently she had not expected the normally soft-spoken Olivia to come back at her that way.

For a moment Olivia hoped Meadow would not respond to her accusation. But instead the older woman's voice rose in volume, carrying over the library. Aware that people were staring at them, listening to the conversation, Olivia cringed inside as Meadow kept shouting.

"You have no right to accuse me of anything. You don't belong here. Just like your friend Marla, you are not welcome." Meadow took a breath to continue her rant. "Get out. Leave the library. I can't stand a liar. You are not a friend of Lily Rock."

Again Olivia considered running away. But she stood her ground. The words came from her lips, though she was not certain they were even hers. The voice sounded confident, more confident than she felt for sure. "I want to be clear about who is lying, Meadow. You lie to Sage about her birth, you lie to me about your herbs and potions, and you lie to the entire town with that hidden cave in the animal shelter. Who is the liar here?"

"You don't know what you're talking about," Meadow screamed this time, her face contorting. She turned her head away from Olivia. Now the library patrons openly gaped at the two women.

Meadow lowered her voice. "Stop making such a scene. Just go."

With deliberation, Olivia gathered her purse. She turned off the computer to glance at Mayor Maguire, who still lay curled under the table. "Let's go, M&M," she said quietly to get his attention.

"Not you, Mayor Maguire," hissed Meadow. "You stay with me. We have town business to attend to."

For a moment Olivia felt protective of the big dog. He'd been her guardian under difficult circumstances since the first day in Lily Rock. Anticipating when she might feel lost and alone, he'd accompanied her. Using a more confident voice, Olivia said, "Let's go, M&M."

The dog stood, looking from one woman to the other. Olivia thought he would choose the more familiar Meadow. Everyone in the room, eyes on the drama unfolding, held a collective breath.

With a wave of his tail, Mayor Maguire made his decision. He walked around Olivia's body two times before he sat next to her left knee.

"Good boy," she told him, patting his head.

Library patrons nodded before ducking back to their own business.

As Olivia left the library she heard one man say, "The mayor has good sense."

CHAPTER TWENTY-FIVE

Overheard in Lily Rock

"Can you tag me on Instagram as the red pepper flake to your avocado toast?"

Olivia dropped her folder and purse on the table. When she pushed the button to release the glass wall, the outside deck revealed a thick carpet of pine needles that crunched under her feet. After choosing her favorite oversized chair, she sat cross-legged, resting her open palms in her lap, preparing for Centering Prayer.

The tension along her spine released as she closed her eyes. Meadow's angry face rose up in her imagination as three soft gongs from an app on her phone began her time of silence with God. She entered into the silence, drawing her eyes toward her skull. She noticed nothing outside herself, since she'd crossed to the silent side.

Breath becoming regular, she inhaled softly, then exhaled.

Twenty minutes later, the sound of the gong from her phone app brought Olivia back. She repeated a prayer to accompany her breath's inhale, pause, and exhale. Reaching for the Bible she'd found in Marla's nightstand, she turned to the middle. "The Lord is my shepherd," she said slowly, "I shall not want." After reading Psalm 23 and then 139 Olivia closed the book, holding it in her lap.

She noticed a tingling in her left foot, so she stood to stretch her arms over her head and shake out her foot. Thoroughly refreshed, she made her way to the kitchen for a cup of herbal tea. Before praying, she'd marked each task as a conscious goal. Now she felt keenly aware of each movement, from filling the pot to pouring the contents, effortlessly moving from one task to the next.

Olivia found a pencil in a drawer. Her hand hovered over the small pad of paper waiting for input. Finally she listed *vegetables* and *dog food*.

Mayor Maguire's warm body stood beside her, his breath on her knee. "I suppose you want to eat dinner," she said to him. "I wonder what Meadow feeds you?"

The mayor did not reply.

Olivia smiled. "One day you'll surprise me and start speaking words." She reached to scratch behind his ears. "We can both eat turkey and rice one more time. Then I'll go to the market."

Mayor Maguire hovered over his bowl, staring at his own reflection. Olivia dished up the rest of the turkey and rice. Instead of focusing on eating, her mind drew her to another task: Marla's legal boxes in the great room.

I'd better see if there's space to store these boxes in the office. She'd deliberately avoided Marla's office before. As soon as she opened the door she knew why. Entering her friend's business space would be an acknowledgement of both the untimely death and of the inheritance, the responsibility for which lay at Olivia's feet alone.

Since recently resolving her mother's estate, Olivia

dreaded another phone discussion about paperwork with banks and attorneys. Her mother's death and then her breakup with Don had derailed her from the path she had wanted to take. Now that Olivia was back on her feet and moving forward, Marla's inheritance threatened to derail her yet again.

I need to have legal death certificates sent to all the places Marla held her accounts. A sigh filled Olivia's chest before she released her frustration into an exhaled breath.

Olivia's heart ached. Using her own inner voice for encouragement, she said, *I did this with my mother; I can do it again. I can.*

Olivia pushed open the door to Marla's office. *This space reminds me of the design at the animal shelter.* Her eyes glanced at the wall behind the desk. She began her inspection, first for cameras in corners and then for hidden exits.

Sure enough, one panel behind the desk stood out from the rest. As she pushed against the panel, a door slid open, revealing another entrance. She walked into a room identical in dimensions to the one at Pines and Paws. Shelves lined the walls from floor to ceiling.

Fresh paint, Olivia thought, sniffing. *Maybe that's why Marla didn't keep her research boxes in here. She was waiting for the paint to dry.*

Olivia left the door to the hidden closet open as she made several trips from the great room to the office, stacking each box on the empty shelves. The task completed, she closed the hidden door behind her.

Ten minutes later, her car puttered its way down the road. Mayor Maguire poked his head out the open passenger-side window, his jowls spreading across his smiling mouth.

Olivia grabbed her reusable shopping bags from the back seat.

"I won't be long," she told the dog.

Inside the market, Olivia inspected the romaine lettuce. Then she selected vegetables for a fresh salad. Feeling a bump on her elbow, she turned. Cayenne smiled at her.

"How's it going?" Cayenne moved her cart next to Olivia's. "Shopping for dinner?"

After discovering Arlo and Meadow in the warehouse, Olivia felt uncomfortable talking to Cayenne. How much did she know about her husband's extra business in Lily Rock?

Unsure how to proceed, Olivia swallowed her anxiety. *Mention the obvious. Let Cayenne bring up Arlo if she wants to.*

"I like to pick up fresh food every day if I can."

Cayenne pointed to the contents in Olivia's shopping cart. "A lot of what you have in your cart already grows in Marla's garden. I should know, I helped her plant the seedlings."

"I forgot all about the garden."

Cay's face grew thoughtful. "Or maybe it's too close to where you discovered the body. That would be painful. I understand why you don't want to go back there."

Olivia nodded. Sometimes people understood her feelings better than she understood herself.

"Not to change the subject, but I heard you had it out with Meadow at the library earlier."

No longer surprised at the speed with which gossip traveled in Lily Rock, Olivia nodded.

"Just so you know, I think Meadow is drinking again. It happens. Being sober in this small town takes an act of God. Everyone falls off that wagon at least once or twice. Just ask me."

Olivia picked up a tomato. It felt ripe. She placed it in her cart. "Or you could just ask me about sobriety. I've had my rounds with alcohol. Do you ever go to meetings?"

Surprise registered on Cay's face. "I do go to meetings, and I'm happy you asked. Maybe we could go together some morning and then have breakfast afterward. I'd love your company."

Of course Lily Rock would have meetings. Now that I'm not finding dead bodies and running away, there are things to appreciate, especially my connections with Cay and Sage. My relationship with Don isolated me from other people. I won't make the same mistake again now that I know what healthy relationships look like.

"I'd better get back to shopping. See you later."

Cay moved her cart in the opposite direction with the wave of a hand.

Olivia placed the green onions and peppers and tomato back where they had come from. Looking at her own garden would bring a necessary connection to the outdoors. She'd take M&M with her to the garden to begin the process of cleaning out her memories of finding Marla's dead body.

She reached for a carton of eggs, then she held them in her hand. *Make a quiche* came immediately to her mind. She put the eggs in her cart. Next she tried a tub of margarine. She returned the tub. Then she held the package of yellow butter in her hand. She placed it into her cart.

Each decision, no matter how small, felt important.

Anyone watching her move through the market might assume she had an obsession with groceries. As she traveled up and down the aisles, Olivia stopped at another cold case displaying several types of gourmet dog food.

She picked it up and closed her eyes, releasing the inflated cost to hold the package of buffalo meat. It felt right. Disregarding the price, she placed it into her cart.

After checking out of the market, Olivia greeted the dog in the front seat. "So, M&M, do you like buffalo?"

The dog lifted his head, a smile crossing his face.

As she drove home, the sun drifted behind the trees, sinking into the range of mountains. Olivia quickly entered the house with the dog. She chose a lamp to illuminate the room before she headed to the kitchen to unpack her groceries.

"There's just a little light left, let's go outside and pick some vegetables."

Mayor Maguire walked close to her left knee as they approached the garden gate. Olivia inhaled the rich smell of earth, admiring the leeks and green onions poking through the stakes of the picket fence. A basket hung on a nail—perfect for gathering produce.

After closing the gate, she bent over to lift the top of a cold frame where tomatoes rested in red clusters. She chose a ripe red tomato along with a green pepper for her basket. Next Olivia inspected other rows for vegetables ready for harvest. Since spring came early in Lily Rock, she found an excellent head of red leaf lettuce.

As she straightened her knees to place the lettuce in her basket, she hesitated. Something felt out of place. Olivia glanced over the rows in the garden. Her eyes stopped when they reached the far corner. Where the two picket fences met, she saw a freshly dug hole. After walking closer, Olivia bent over to sift her fingers through the dirt. Using her foot, she kicked the rest of the loamy soil back into the hole.

Her mind struggled to make sense of what she saw. Had an animal, maybe a possum, dug up a plant?

That explanation satisfied her until she turned to look over her shoulder at the opposite corner. Another empty hole. Olivia's eyes quickly traveled to the two remaining corners of the square garden space. Sure enough, all of the corner plants had been uprooted in a similar way.

She walked from corner to corner to inspect more closely. A person, not an animal, had most likely pulled up all four plants. *I may not have noticed if they'd filled the holes back in. Must have been in a really big hurry.*

Mayor Maguire sniffed the space she'd been inspecting. He lifted his face to the sky, nose quivering, and then ducked his head with a big sneeze.

"Are we allergic, M&M?" Olivia laughed.

She and the dog strolled back toward the house as the sun disappeared behind the mountains. Olivia clutched the basket of vegetables close to her stomach. Thanks to her heightened awareness since her day of retreat, she felt her fingers tingle.

Is someone watching me? Glancing around, she saw no one. She looked at Mayor Maguire, who sat by her feet.

The dog wagged his tail.

"You don't seem worried."

She closed the kitchen door carefully, taking the time to double-check the locks.

Olivia washed the fresh vegetables, laying them on a rack to dry. She dried her hands before circling the great room once again. Instead of looking for cameras, she considered each chair and the overall seating arrangement. She selected one chair with a cushion in the corner. Folding her legs under her body, she closed her eyes for the second meditation of the day. With her app set to twenty minutes, Olivia disappeared to the other side.

At one point during the silence her mind led her to the recent scene at the library. *Remember for later,* she told herself. The silence returned.

Later, when the sun had set, she remembered. She stood in the kitchen, pulling apart leaves of romaine and spinach. She wrestled with her thoughts. *Do I keep this information to myself, or do I share it with others?*

No warmth came from within. Just a tingle of uncertainty.

Later Olivia lay in her bed, watching the moon through the skylight overhead. Stars shimmered in the night sky. She felt sleep creep over her as she closed her eyes. The round shape of the moon appeared on the backs of her eyelids.

Why did Skye confess to killing Marla? She clung to the question, knowing it held something important for her to consider. *I'll talk to Dr. May tomorrow.*

Her eyes drooped again, only to fly open when she heard a buzz from her phone. By the time she slid out from under the bed covers, the phone lay silent.

A new message popped up on her screen. *Still mad? Please let me explain. Talk tomorrow over coffee—I hope.*

Am I ready to speak to Michael? she asked her inner wisdom. Her stomach felt calm. She texted him back, *See you in the morning. I'll bake fresh banana bread.*

Olivia returned to her bed. M&M's curly head rested on her pillow. His body stretched out, blocking her from lying down.

"Move over, silly mutt."

In seconds they both fell asleep.

CHAPTER TWENTY-SIX

Overheard in Lily Rock
"Have you talked to her?"
"Not exactly. I did send her a few memes, but she's only double-tapped *them."*
"Wow. It's over."

By early Sunday morning, Olivia had showered, dressed, and baked banana bread. Leaving Mayor Maguire behind, she walked the short distance to Michael's cabin. The smell of coffee met her at the front doorstep. She knocked.

Clean-shaven with a bright smile on his face, Michael stood in the open doorway. She felt an eagerness to reconcile radiate from his body. The unabashed delight of finding her on his doorstep shone from his eyes, making it hard for her to resist reaching out for a hug.

"Ms. Greer, fancy finding you this fine morning," he spoke with a drawl.

She ignored his greeting, telling herself, *I can't afford to get too cozy.* He moved his body to the side, giving her room. She slid past.

The cabin felt familiar, like an old sweater you found in the back of your closet. The rock fireplace on one side dominated the room. Light from the glass wall on the opposite end created a kaleidoscope of color over the inner beams of the A-frame structure.

After shrugging out of her jacket, she placed it on an available hook in the entryway. "Do I remove my boots?" she asked Michael, who stood back to observe her reaction to his house.

"Not necessary." He smiled. "Are you ready for coffee?"

She nodded, handing him the promised banana bread.

"How about breakfast too? I make a mean omelet."

"Maybe later," she said. "Not quite ready for food."

"Do you want a tour?" He handed her a mug of coffee. "I want you to know that I don't take my cabin for granted. It was never meant to be my permanent home, even when Marla was alive. I built it as a guesthouse for her to take over as soon as my work was finished."

Olivia sipped from the coffee mug. "Maybe I could take the tour later. I wouldn't mind sitting out on the deck." She pointed to the expansive glass door, which led to a seating arrangement suspended in the trees.

"Let me turn on the outdoor heater. It's still a bit chilly. Grab your jacket, and I'll meet you outside."

As the glass-sided wall slid open, Olivia walked onto the deck. Pine trees stood tall and quiet. She pulled her jacket closer around her middle.

As she stood looking outwardly, she felt the presence of Lily Rock. Upright in the distance, the town's namesake transmitted an aura of confidence, shadows playing off of the white exterior. Postcards of this very angle were displayed in every shop in downtown Lily Rock.

Michael stood beside Olivia, looking out over the forest. Expectation oozed from his body. She knew he wanted to explain himself. Instead of waiting for him to begin, she took the lead.

"I didn't intend to stonewall you yesterday. I took a day of personal retreat to clear my head."

Michael's expression drew blank. Instead of speaking, he moved two chairs together, placing a small table in between them. He gestured for her to sit down.

She continued, "I do a retreat now and then. It takes an entire twenty-four hour period. By the time I received your latest text last night, I knew I'd overreacted in the warehouse the day before."

His mouth lifted at the corners. "You continue to amaze me. I don't think I've ever met anyone so responsible with her own feelings. I thought we were done—you know, our friendship—when you ran away."

"I run so that I don't say something I might regret later."

"But you sure thought a few things, right?" Michael chuckled as if he could hear the names she'd silently called him.

Olivia took her time before speaking again. She observed the deck. A crafted rustic bench caught her attention. "You also do finished carpentry?" she asked.

"I have an extensive workshop in my basement. When I'm upset I make things. I guess you'd call it my personal retreat."

"To each his own."

"Maybe I can also do some explaining now?" When she failed to stop him, the words rushed from his lips. "I didn't mean to deceive you about Marla assigning me to be your bodyguard. It never came up in our conversation. You must admit, we had a few other things to worry about, including your head wound and the snakebite."

To keep her emotions in check, Olivia fastened her eyes on Lily Rock. Where the mountain had once shown glimmering white, a cloud covered the exterior, casting a gray shadow.

"Plus Marla did not hire me originally to protect her," continued Michael. "That happened after her house drew attention from some architects down the hill. There was an article in the *Los Angeles Times*. People began driving up to Lily Rock to watch the construction progress.

"Then she got a threatening letter, then two more. When she showed them to me I asked if she needed a bodyguard. We both figured no one would pay too much attention, since I'd been hanging out for the past two years anyway. So I took on the added employment."

"That's when the rumor about you being a couple sprang up?"

"That's right. You're getting to know Lily Rock pretty well. There aren't a lot of rules when it comes to relationships, but that doesn't mean people don't talk. Marla and I figured we'd let the rumors alone. It explained my constant presence."

And are you a couple with Janis too? Olivia wondered.

"Do you want to say more about that?" Michael asked, his eyebrow raised.

Staring into her empty coffee cup, Olivia decided to ignore the relationship issues and instead challenge Michael with a question that had bothered her since before she discovered Marla's body. "I saw smoke coming from the chimney the day she died." Olivia's voice quivered, remembering the lifeless form of her friend under that tree.

Michael sipped from his mug. "I lit the fire for Marla every morning to keep up the pretense that I'd spent the night. I'm up with the sun anyway, so I'd let myself in through the back door in my pajamas and robe to get the house warm."

"Then you'd carry on as if you were a couple?"

"Pretty much. When Marla started having more and more

sick days, I started helping her more with the house in the morning. I'd get the fire started and make breakfast. Then I'd go back to supervising my projects from her office."

Michael's voice deepened. "I felt so helpless. Marla kept getting more and more sick."

"Why didn't you take her down the hill for some tests?"

"I did. Nothing turned up but allergies. She spent most mornings gasping for breath, using an inhaler. The docs down the hill made certain she had EpiPens just in case she needed them. One beesting could have taken her out. That's why I thought she'd died of natural causes."

"That's also why you were Johnny-on-the-spot the day I found her."

"One of the reasons. I did keep a good eye on her ... and you. She told me to watch out for you that morning."

"The other reason?"

Michael's chin dipped low. "Not ready to talk about that yet. But don't worry. It's hardly a secret."

Olivia did not inquire further. She had a feeling it had something to do with her, and she did not want to be distracted. To change the subject, she asked, "After my retreat, another question came up for me."

Michael's mouth curved into a smile. "Go ahead, ask away."

"Do you think it was Skye who actually killed Marla?"

"I've been wondering the same thing. I don't think Skye killed Marla. Since Doc May knew Skye the longest and the best, maybe we could ask him."

Olivia laughed. "Were they a couple? You know, back in the day?"

"Skye had a huge crush on the doc. She took care of him as if she was his wife, mother, and girlfriend. I think she held a torch for years, decades even."

"Were they a couple?"

"I don't think so. The doc, let's just say, preferred younger women. He's hit on nearly every woman under the age of twenty in town."

Olivia shrugged. "Apparently he hits on women who are in their thirties as well."

"You too?" Michael's eyebrows raised. "So did he talk about Marla at the pub?"

"He didn't mention Marla. He acted like we were on a date, the silly old man. And just recently he offered me a job."

"What?"

"The day Skye killed herself, he wanted me to take her job."

Michael's face registered disbelief. "What did you say?"

"Hell no, in so many words."

Now his eyes sparkled. "I only wish I could have seen you turn him down. It must have been epic."

A small smile curved at the corner of her mouth. "So we've concluded that the doctor is a lecherous old man. What else do we know about him?"

"I know very little about the Doc. Let's change the subject. Want more coffee?" Michael stood, holding his empty cup.

"I wouldn't mind that omelet now, if you still want to cook."

"Come on inside to the kitchen."

She followed him into the cabin. He pulled out a pan from underneath the counter, along with a dozen eggs from the refrigerator. Olivia cleared her throat. "I have some other news for you—about Marla's ancestry research."

Michael held the carton of eggs midair. "I didn't know she was into ancestry work. She never mentioned—"

"She did extensive research about her biological father. I found all the paperwork in boxes and online."

Michael cracked two eggs in one hand, dropping them into a sizzling frying pan. Olivia admired his deft work. Previously chopped vegetables came next. In minutes he gave the pan a toss, landing a perfect omelet on her plate. "Here you go."

By the time Olivia had eaten half of her breakfast, Michael sat down across the pine table. She waited for him to catch up. He refilled their coffee mugs and then took empty plates to the sink.

"I'll wash up," she told him.

She ran water over the utensils, then she loaded them into the washer.

"You're very tidy," he remarked, watching her progress.

"Oh, you don't know the half." She grinned. "I am the poster girl for neat and tidy."

"Are you also afraid of germs?"

"I have a reasonable concern for germs," she admitted. "Mostly I like to tidy as I practice letting go of stuff. It's a spiritual thing for me."

Michael nodded. "You always know where to find what you're looking for if you put it away every time."

"That's one way to look at it." She sat back down at the kitchen table. "Before I tell you about Marla's research, did you ever find out who was threatening her with those letters?"

"Actually, I have a pretty good idea."

"And?"

"You know about the Old Rockers?"

"I do. Meadow and Sage both told me about them. I think Cayenne even mentioned them, something about the city council."

"I think the Old Rockers hated Marla's new house and all

of the attention it received. Then when she infused money into other projects, like the pub, with more plans to build an amphitheater at the music school, she really worried the old-time residents."

"I suppose Lily Rock was changing in front of their very eyes?"

"The council meetings became even more contentious than usual. People got really upset, threatening each other. I think that's how the letters got started. No one wanted Marla to build anymore, and they probably thought they could drive her out of town if they frightened her with written threats."

"They didn't know Marla very well. Even in high school she did not tolerate bullies."

"Why did she get bullied in high school?"

"She didn't have a father; she was raised by her mother only. My understanding is that Marla's mother conceived her through in vitro fertilization. I think that's why Marla was obsessed with finding the man who donated the sperm."

"And did she find out?"

"She did. At least, I think I've found her biological father, according to her ancestry account."

"She never mentioned her research or her findings to me," Michael said.

Holding Marla's personal information felt like a sacred trust to Olivia. She wanted to tell Michael what she knew, yet she hesitated. *Just admitting Marla did the research may be enough for now.*

Michael continued speaking. "So in answer to your other question, in my estimation, one of the Old Rockers wrote those notes."

"Any idea who?"

"My first guess is Skye."

"So we are back to Skye again. Maybe she felt afraid of

Marla and all the changes to Lily Rock, and she—what? Poisoned her soup? I just can't see her doing that."

Michael smiled. "One thing we know for certain: Marla did not die from overexposure to threatening notes with letters cut out from magazines. She died from heart failure, brought on by—"

"Anaphylactic shock," Olivia finished his sentence.

They locked eyes across the table. Michael was the first to break the gaze. "I think we need to solve the *why* of Skye's death. If she didn't kill Marla, why did she focus the blame on herself? Any thoughts on that?"

Olivia sighed. She'd taken blame for a lot in her past relationship with Don. Rather than push back when he'd accused her, she'd hung her head to avoid the argument. Maybe Skye was like Olivia. Not interested in conflict, and ready to pay any price to keep the peace. "So where do we go from here?" she asked. "Do we need to talk to Meadow about Skye?"

"And then we should talk to the doc," added Michael. "By the way, the town council meets tonight. You can get a front-row seat."

"Mayor Maguire will come with me, and I'll be his plus-one."

"I heard that you and Meadow had a tiff over the mayor in the library. He picked you over Meadow. Now that's Lily Rock news."

"He chose me for now. I'm not sure how long it will last."

Michael's eyebrows raised. "Why is that?"

She felt her cheeks flush. *Just the way it started with Don,* Olivia thought.

"I don't know how long I'm staying. I do have a life in Playa. I really have to get back to work and to my place." Olivia's eyes rested on her folded hands to avoid Michael's look of disappointment.

She heard a scratch at the back door. Olivia opened the door to find Mayor Maguire standing outside. "How long have you been here, M&M?"

Michael looked first at Olivia and then at the dog. He shrugged and stood. "You gotta do what you gotta do. Rather than chase Meadow and the doc around village, why don't we catch up with them both at the town meeting this evening?"

Olivia drew a breath of relief. He'd not argued with her plan to leave Lily Rock. Apparently he'd changed his mind.

"Sounds like a great idea." Shrugging on her jacket, she walked toward the living room. Michael opened the front door, his lips drawn in a straight line.

Olivia smiled. "Thanks for breakfast."

"You're welcome. See you tonight."

The door closed as she and Mayor Maguire walked the path to Marla's house nearby.

CHAPTER TWENTY-SEVEN

Overheard in Lily Rock

"Can you pour a La Croix into mineral water, add three shots of vodka, and bring it to me at Pilates? Thanks, Mom."

Olivia and Michael walked into the community center where people already gathered for the town meeting. Chairs filled with expectant observers made it difficult for the two late-comers to find seats together. The American flag, placed in the right-hand corner, waited for two Boy Scouts to salute to begin the Pledge of Allegiance.

Mayor Maguire stood at the entrance door, his red, white, and blue necktie drawing attention from the town's people. They individually greeted him with a pat on his head.

Sitting next to Michael in the back row, Olivia brought her elbows to her sides so as not to touch him. She wanted to keep clear boundaries between them. "So do they have an agenda—a written one?" she asked him.

"The agenda is determined by Sebastian Green. That guy over there."

Olivia glanced to where Michael pointed. She saw a tall,

skinny guy in his mid-forties, with a scrunchy at the back of his neck holding three inches of thin gray hair. Sebastian's narrow eyes scanned the crowd from the front of the room, stopping at Michael and Olivia.

She spoke out of the corner of her mouth. "He's staring at us."

Sebastian Green dropped his gaze as he reached for the microphone. "Good evening, everyone, I see we have quite a full house. Please stand for the Pledge of Allegiance."

Facing the flag, Olivia placed her hand over her heart along with everyone else in the room.

Viewing the residents from the backs of their heads, she tried to sort out those she'd already met. The one thing she felt certain about was that the town of Lily Rock attracted people who were leaving something behind. Some ran from their past, like a stray dog, while others showed indifference to their past, like a cat who silently licked its paw.

After the pledge, chairs scuffed as people sat back down. A man and a woman in front of Olivia passed a paper cup between them as the town council secretary stood to read the minutes from the last meeting.

"All those in favor of accepting the minutes?"

The voices responded in unison, "Aye."

The moderator took the microphone. "We'll begin with Mayor Maguire's report. Afterward we'll deal with new business. Then Arlo Carson has an announcement. Unless you approach me during the coffee break, I have nothing else to add to tonight's agenda. Any questions?"

"Sebastian?"

All heads turned toward the voice of a woman standing against the wall in the back. Meadow, dressed in her denim jumper, spoke up. "I think the council would like to defer their report until after Arlo speaks."

Sebastian scowled. Apparently he disapproved of meetings being hijacked by other people's ideas. "Is there a reason?"

"Arlo briefed me earlier. His announcement will explain everything."

Clearing his throat, the town council president spoke into the microphone again. "I will defer my report. We will begin with the usual Mayor Maguire slideshow and then Arlo can step up to speak."

Meadow dodged elbows in the crowd as she moved to the front to take the microphone. Olivia shifted in her seat. She felt impatient. Enough with the M&M slideshow. *I wonder what Arlo has to say to this crowd?*

Olivia inhaled deeply. She turned her head, catching sight of Arlo. He stood to the left near the front, staring blankly ahead.

Fifteen minutes later, Meadow had finished her report. She folded her paper. But instead of stepping off the stage she pointed to the back of the room. The lights went off.

"I thought she was done," Olivia whispered to Michael.

"Now we get more of the slideshow," Michael growled back.

Before Olivia could protest, photos of Mayor Maguire dressed in a cowboy hat and scarf brought sighs from the crowd. Photo after photo with Mayor Maguire standing next to one Lily Rock visitor after another continued. Olivia tapped her foot impatiently.

Instead of watching the show, she scanned the darkened room for Arlo. Now Cayenne stood next to him, leaning against the wall. Arlo, two inches shorter, held her hand.

Olivia felt a shiver roll down her spine. She remembered how Arlo had become so intimidating at the warehouse when Meadow confronted him. *You think you know people, but you don't, really, until you see them under pressure.* He'd been under a lot of pressure that day at the animal shelter.

Olivia clenched her hands on the handle of her purse. She planned to bolt outdoors to catch Meadow when the meeting adjourned for a break. She felt certain that knowing the truth about Marla's death depended upon knowing Skye's exact involvement.

By the time everyone had admired the recent photos of Mayor Maguire with his hat and necktie, the lights blinked back on. Silence grew in the room as Arlo moved toward the microphone. His chin touched his chest as he stared at his feet, unable or unwilling to look directly at the audience. Finally he grasped the microphone with both hands, resembling a nightclub singer. Looking directly to the side wall, at Cayenne, he tilted the stand toward his body.

"I have something to say," Arlo said, his voice trembling. He waited for the room to grow quiet before continuing his speech.

"A couple of days ago I found myself in an awkward position. I threatened people I care about." Now his eyes shifted to take in Michael and Olivia. "I nearly ruined my marriage with my secrets." He gazed again at Cayenne, who smiled back at him. "After some reflection, I realized that I must come clean with everyone here in Lily Rock.

"I've intentionally sidestepped the town council on any number of important issues, and I'm here to ask for your forgiveness. I'm hoping that I can correct my course and that maybe I can begin again, only this time I'll fill out all the paperwork and go through proper channels."

Arlo's words rushed from his tight-lipped mouth. "For the past two years I've watched the council turn down people who wanted to start small businesses in Lily Rock. I've seen people move away on account of they can't make a living here.

At times I thought the new business ideas were excellent, and I didn't understand why the council proved so obstinate."

Arlo swallowed again, slightly out of breath. "So I had an idea for a business. Someone in town, a well-respected long-time citizen, suggested that I check out one of his buildings. He told me that nothing gets done here unless you just move forward without asking. So I took his advice. I started a business in the private warehouse hidden inside the Pines and Paws Animal Shelter. At first it was small; I planted a few seeds. Then I installed some raised beds for larger plants."

A low mumble filled the previous silence. The heads of the two people sitting in front of Olivia leaned together. They whispered back and forth. Glancing around the room, Olivia saw people leaning forward to hear Arlo, curiosity aroused.

"I got a few of the young people here in Lily Rock to help me sell my product. Within the first six months my business quadrupled in size. I'd filled at least half of the indoor space with raised beds, added lighting, hired people to do my gardening, and started producing gummy bears and various other bits to attract more business."

So far Arlo had not said the word *marijuana*. Yet Olivia had no doubt that everyone in the room knew exactly what he was talking about.

"It wasn't until recently, when my wife, Cayenne, confronted me, that I realized, in the process of keeping my secret, I'd become a different person. I'd become a man who walked with his head held down, who disconnected from people he cares about. Looking over my shoulder became a habit and I nosed my way into everybody's business whether they wanted me or not. And then just the other day, during a conversation in the warehouse with my business partner, two unexpected visitors dropped in. Well, I became downright surly."

Now everyone in the room looked around to see whom Arlo was talking about. Eyes scrutinized Olivia and Michael. She froze her face to look less guilty. Michael just smiled, like he was listening to a familiar bedtime story that had little to nothing to do with him.

Arlo nervously shifted the microphone back and forth between his hands. Olivia saw perspiration forming on his upper lip. "So you see," he continued, "I'd gotten myself into a mess just because I didn't want to ask the town of Lily Rock for permission to start up a perfectly legal small business. I figured you'd turn me down, and so I moved forward anyway. But now I see it changed me in ways I didn't want to change. I don't want to be a jerk to people I care about."

Arlo reached out his hand in Cayenne's direction. She stepped toward him. Her long legs carried her to the stage, where she stood by her man, facing the crowd. Tears filled her eyes as she took Arlo's offered hand.

As the crowd mumbled, some leaning forward to express their opinions, Michael rose to his feet. "So let's take a vote and get out the paperwork for your new business. If you need help, I can get you past the legal language. We can have it done and in front of the council in a few days."

Arlo blinked, his eyes now shining with tears. "You'd do that? After the way I treated you?"

"Hey, man, you aren't the first guy to take a shortcut when it comes to business. I'll require a few free beers to get the job done successfully. Can you manage that?"

Someone in the crowd began to clap. Olivia looked around. As people stood one by one to give their approval with more clapping, Olivia sighted Doc May and Meadow, sitting next to each other in the front row. They stared straight forward. They did not join the applause. The doctor's jaw tightened, while Meadow nervously twisted her hands in her lap.

Arlo's sincere request for another chance did not meet with their approval.

* * *

During the coffee break, Olivia followed Michael to the back of the room. "That was very generous of you, offering to help Arlo."

"I am a generous man," he admitted.

"What about the shelter stealing your design for the building?"

"I've been thinking about that. If I am not mistaken, I think it belongs to a partnership, and I think I know who did the actual borrowing of my creative work."

"Do you?"

"Tell you later. I'm going to grab a cup of coffee. Meet you back here after the break."

Olivia stood alone, glancing around the room for Meadow. She found her near the back exit, and Olivia picked up her pace to follow Meadow out the door.

The cool evening air lifted the hair on Olivia's neck. She gulped and untied her sweater from around her waist. After pulling it on, she zipped the front to keep warm. *Now, where did Meadow go?*

A puff of smoke wafted from around the corner. Olivia saw the shadow of a person standing in outdoor light at the corner of the building.

"Looking for someone?" the voice asked.

Olivia walked closer. "I didn't know you smoked."

Flicking the cigarette butt to the ground, Meadow

squished it under her beaded leather moccasin. "I don't smoke much. Just when I'm nervous."

"I noticed you didn't seem particularly convinced of Arlo's sincerity."

"Oh, I think he was sincere. After I threatened to go to the cops, I'm not surprised that he took the lead to confess. I just don't want him to get the council approval. We don't need a weed shop here in Lily Rock. When the word is out, weekenders will come up just to get high, and the town will turn into a hellhole before we know it."

"I thought pot imbibers were a pretty tame lot. Mostly they eat and talk. That may be good for business, the eating part."

"You don't know anything about Lily Rock, do you? A few people run things around here, and we are not about to let the decision-making be turned over to a minority of people who are clueless."

Olivia felt confused. "So why did you agree to be Arlo's partner in the first place?"

"I had no choice. If I'd turned him down, he would have found someone else without my civic-mindedness. I had to say yes. Keep your enemies close, if you know what I mean."

Something did not add up. Olivia leaned against the wall next to Meadow, taking her time with the next comment. "It may interest you to know I don't intend to live here in Lily Rock. I'll most likely sell Marla's place. I've got an attorney working on the paperwork. When the police close this case I'll move on. You'll have one less newcomer to worry about."

Pushing herself from the wall, Meadow faced Olivia. "I'm very happy to hear that. Of course, everything changes if you aren't staying."

"Everything changes?"

"We were certain you'd team up with Michael and start

building that amphitheater for Sage's school. One too many of his architectural designs already in this town."

"What do you mean?"

"Your place, the pub, and now the animal shelter. Anyone can see he has his hand in every project. That's why the council will refuse Michael permits from here on out. Time for him to move on to another small community and leave us alone."

"You know the animal shelter isn't his design?" Olivia looked intently at Meadow's face, hidden in the evening's shadow. "It's just made to look like his work."

"The town council doesn't have to know all the details. 'If it walks like a duck'—well, you know the rest." Meadow twisted another cigarette out of the pack. Her hands trembled. "I do what I have to do to keep my family safe."

"You mean Sage? Your perfectly capable adult daughter?"

"Oh, everyone knows I'm the strong one. Sage had always been weak since her premature birth. Her job, for example—she was supposed to be a music teacher. Now she thinks she runs the entire academy." Meadow's voice grew quieter. "At least I think I am the stronger one..."

"Plus Sage is too concerned about what the academy parents think. The school doesn't need an amphitheater. They can use the community stage like everyone else in Lily Rock."

Meadow's resentment of her own daughter surprised Olivia. She disagreed about Sage, but instead of speaking her mind, prolonging the conversation, she changed the subject to ask what she'd been wondering about all along. "How are you doing since Skye's passing? You were her best friend."

A deep sigh escaped Meadow's lips.

Olivia persisted. "I've been wondering what you think

about Skye committing suicide. Do you think she killed Marla?"

The corner light blinked off, casting darkness between the two women. Unable to see Meadow's face, Olivia didn't know how her question affected the other woman.

"Skye did not have it in her to kill Marla, and for that matter, I don't think she killed herself on account of Marla. There's only one person Skye would kill for."

Before Olivia could ask who that was, Meadow continued. "Skye spent her life growing things. She gave life to rescued animals. Why, she'd pick up potted plants from the trash, take them home, and rejuvenate them on her windowsill.

"That's why she worked with Dr. May. She cared about his patients. He introduced us when I needed help with the baby. The doc sent Skye, and we became friends. I had no idea how to take care of an infant."

"So why would she confess to a crime she didn't commit and then kill herself?"

Meadow refused to answer, so Olivia pressed on. "Would you tell the police if they asked you?"

"No one is going to ask me. I'm not a suspect."

"You may not have broken a law, but I think you know a lot more than you're saying. I think you've held back the truth, which has led to any number of complications. Why don't you just come clean so that we can put Marla and Skye to rest? That's all I'm asking."

"You can ask all you want! I'm finished with this conversation."

Meadow inhaled the last drag on her cigarette, dropping it to the dirt in front of her feet. "See you later," she snarled at Olivia, walking toward the parking lot.

Olivia shouted after her, "Meadow, do you really think

you need to protect Sage? Is that why you won't tell the whole truth?"

Meadow turned to face Olivia. "What do you care about my daughter? You've barely known her for, what, five minutes?"

Olivia swallowed. How could she explain the instant sense of kinship she had felt with Sage from the moment they met?

Pulling from deep within, she used her most rational voice. "You're right, of course. I don't know Sage that well." Then she added silently to herself, *You aren't the only one who can keep a secret.* Thinking the conversation over, Olivia turned toward the open door of the community center.

Olivia watched Meadow stride away toward her truck in the parking lot.

"Meeting is being called to order," someone yelled from inside the hall. She turned back to the door.

Michael stood at the back of the room. He raised his coffee cup in greeting. "Meet me outside," he mumbled in her ear.

Once outside, Michael spoke urgently. "I saw you talking to Meadow. Did she have anything interesting to tell you about Skye?"

"I'm worried about Meadow. She admitted she knows more than she's willing to talk about. There's no love lost for you either."

Michael did not look surprised. His lips drew a grim line. "Instead of waiting until the meeting adjourns, why don't we follow her home and ask her about Skye again?" He was already reaching for the keys in his back pocket.

In the truck Michael backed up, then shifted forward, the tires crunching against gravel. The moon illuminated the road, drawing Olivia's attention to the woods. She blinked, unsure of what she was seeing, and then pointed. Michael glanced out the passenger window.

Smoke billowed into the dark air. Catching sight of a flame licking the side of a redwood tree in the distance, Olivia gasped. Then, looking upward, she saw tongues of fire lighting up the night sky. The top of a lone pine tree drew more flames and then burst open, only to topple over, a ball of fire descending toward the ground. It took seconds for the brush beneath the trees to ignite.

She clutched Michael's elbow as he spun the truck around, heading straight toward the fire.

CHAPTER TWENTY-EIGHT

Overheard in Lily Rock
Owner of a dog barking hysterically:
"I apologize, he's still dealing with ancestral traumas."

Slowing the truck, Michael pulled over alongside the main road. "Roll down your window," he insisted. The acrid smell of smoke seeped into the cab, where Michael and Olivia stared out the windshield in horror.

"The fire may be coming from the animal shelter," Michael assessed. He shifted the truck into drive. "Call 911 and report the flames. We have to get on this as soon as possible. A small fire could take out this entire town."

Curving to the right, the truck bumped against the road. Olivia's cell phone flew from her hand. With an instinctive reflex, she caught the phone midair. Holding it up, she dialed the number with her index finger.

"Emergency line, how can I help you?"

"There's a fire in Lily Rock by the Pines and Paws Animal Shelter." Olivia kept her voice calm.

"Can you give me your exact location?"

"Where are we exactly?" Olivia asked him. Before he could speak she held the phone up to his mouth.

The fire reported, Olivia slipped the cell into her back pocket. Her breath shuddered in her chest. "What about the animals at the shelter?"

"My first concern," Michael admitted. "We've got to evacuate the building."

Olivia reached over to clutch his arm. She squeezed her fingers into his flesh. "I'm terrified of fire," she admitted to him. "I may not be much help."

He took her hand in his. "Don't worry. You'll be fine. Just stay calm, and go with your instincts. I just saw you instinctively grab a cell phone midair. Go with your instincts. You don't have to rush into a burning building, you can help on the other side. You can do this."

Rounding the next corner, Michael pulled off the road, driving over the rough field toward the smoke. As he stopped in front of the blaze, a tall pine tree fell to the earth in flames, accompanied by a cacophony of dog howls, which filled the night air. Pushing aside her own terror for the plight of the trapped animals, Olivia slid out of the passenger side of the truck while Michael hurried around to the back. He reached into the storage box behind the cab, then he pulled out a jug of water and another box. Several flashlights rolled around the bottom.

"Here, take this." He shoved unopened batteries into her hands. "Peel back the packaging and put them in the flashlights." Olivia followed his directions, her hands shaking. She dropped one battery in the dirt but retrieved it quickly.

As she worked with the flashlights, Michael soaked a cloth in water from a plastic container that he kept in the back of the truck. He covered his nose and mouth with the bandana, tying the ends around the back of his head.

"Good work on the flashlights. Leave them on the tailgate. People know where to find them if they need one." Without more explanation, he ran directly to the burning building. She watched his back disappear through the front doors of the animal shelter. Her stomach turned over. *What if he doesn't come back?*

She shook her head to clear her emotions. Walking away from the fire, she considered a location for dogs and cats pulled from the burning building. A plan formulated in her mind. *I can form a corral around that group of trees. Maybe Michael keeps a rope in the back of the truck.*

She dug through Michael's survival gear, seizing a rope hidden under several tarps. Along with the rope, she snatched a radio with a crank handle, marveling at how he kept the emergency gear so organized. *I wonder if he was a Boy Scout?*

Olivia glanced back toward the blazing fire. This time she did not feel as afraid. She'd gotten past her reluctance by moving instinctively, just as Michael had suggested. A wail of sirens interrupted. First responders pulled into the parking lot, piling out of a fire truck to the siren of an ambulance only minutes behind. A group of pickup trucks came next. Within minutes, lights flashed all around Olivia as men and women tumbled from their vehicles.

"Olivia!" Cayenne called out. Arlo stood beside her. She reached Olivia in two strides, wrapping her into an embrace. "Are you all right?" She pointed to Michael's truck. "Where is he?"

Olivia gestured toward the burning animal shelter. "He went in to rescue the animals."

"How long ago?" Arlo asked, taking a water bottle from the back of the truck. Grabbing a flashlight from the two left on the tailgate, Arlo tied a wet cloth over his face.

Olivia pushed her hair back with one hand. "I don't really

know. I've lost track of time since he went into that building. I'm worried."

Without another word Arlo ran head long toward the flames.

"Don't worry, hon, this isn't our first rodeo with fire," Cayenne told her, wrapping an arm around Olivia's shaking shoulders.

Instead of wetting a cloth to cover her face, Cayenne unexpectedly dropped her arm from Olivia. Hands rising past her shoulders, she began to rip at her own hair. She yanked over and over until the mass of straight black hair gave way, revealing a bald head beneath. Olivia's mouth hung open.

"Not my best look, but this is an emergency. Appearances don't matter when it comes to life or death."

A bit shaken by what she'd just witnessed, Olivia reached for humor. "You have a great bald head—worth showing off. I'm going over there to wrap those trees with this rope just in case we need to corral the dogs."

Cayenne grinned at her, tossing the wig into the back of Michael's truck. "That is an excellent idea. Some cats and dogs will escape on their own after they've been removed from their cages, but a few might be so frightened they just freeze."

Cay looked around. "The dogs could be contained in a corral. We can put the cats in the cars and truck cabs for now. It will be nasty, but we can deal with that problem later. I'm going in to see if they need more help."

Olivia picked up her rope. Feeling more confident, she made her way to the circle of trees. Voices behind her called to each other in the smoke, as more people moved toward the flames with wet bandanas covering their mouths and noses.

Olivia circled the trees, holding the rope against the trunks to make a temporary enclosure for the rescued dogs.

Beginning her loop, she walked around several times before stepping back to look for gaps. Then she wrapped more rope until, looking up, her eye caught sight of a person in the grove. A man sat on a bench with his head in his hands.

After securing the rope with a knot, she walked toward the lonely figure. "Are you okay?"

Doc May raised his head, staring blankly toward her. "Who's there?" he demanded, blinking but not seeing.

"It's just me, Olivia." She walked closer, reaching out her hand to touch his shoulder.

Shaking his head, he covered his face with his hands. "I can't believe it. That beautiful shelter in ruins. All of my children lost in the flames."

Olivia wasn't certain that he recognized her. Now the doc reached over to grasp her fingers. "Such a loss of property and effort. It breaks my heart."

Before she could identify herself, she heard Doc mumble, "Poor Skye. It's a good thing she isn't here. She'd be heartbroken."

A searing branch cracked overhead. Olivia ducked by instinct, pulling on the doctor's arm. She yanked him to his feet, only to have him sit down again. Olivia longed for Michael's familiar voice to find her in the forest. What would he do in this circumstance? Her heart pumped wildly in her chest.

When she could not budge Dr. May with another tug, Olivia sat next to him, still holding his hand. *How awful this must be for a man who loves this town so much.*

She held her other hand over her chest, to hold back her grief. Closing her eyes, she imagined what courage would look like. Within a minute she felt a nudge to her knee.

Mayor Maguire sat in front of her, looking into her face. His soulful eyes glanced over to Doc but settled back on

Olivia's face. His mouth drooped as he collapsed to the dirt beneath the bench.

Olivia dropped the doctor's hand. She knelt beside the dog, reaching both arms around the labradoodle's furry neck as she buried her face in his fur. He smelled like smoke. Had he been inside the shelter?

"Mayor Maguire, where have you been?"

The dog's wet nose nuzzled her ear. Then he lifted his curly head to glance at the doctor again. He insistently nudged her knee one more time. As the dog got up, so did she, recognizing Mayor Maguire's command to follow. The doc, who sat against the bench, still held his head in his hands. She followed Mayor Maguire, leaving the doc to his grief.

Minutes later a familiar voice caught her attention.

"Hey, I've got a cat and two pit bulls for you. Where do I put them?" Michael stood at the edge of the forest, his blackened bandana wrapped around his neck. He bent over to greet M&M. "Take this, would you?" A yowl from a paper bag startled Olivia. She took the bag from his hands.

"I'll put the cat in the cab of the truck, and I've got a place for the two dogs over there." She smiled at Michael. "Good to see you." *Probably the biggest understatement I've ever made,* she thought.

Michael's face was covered in black soot, and his teeth glistened as he smiled. "Back at you. I found Arlo inside. He said you were setting up a temporary enclosure for the dogs. You found where you could help. I never doubted you would."

"I guess I did," she admitted. Her genuine need to secure the animals had pushed back her fear of the fire.

The two pits huddled next to Mayor Maguire. Before they could bolt, Olivia inched her fingers under both collars, walking one dog on each side toward her makeshift kennel. "Follow me," she called to Michael over her shoulder.

"I'd better go back for more animals. It won't be as long this time. I found my way." With a small wave, Michael turned toward the blaze. His body disappeared into the smoke.

Olivia coaxed the soot-covered dogs toward the trees, lifting a rope to admit them into the makeshift enclosure. Since she'd left, plastic buckets had been placed along the perimeter. Both dogs gratefully entered the ring. They walked together across the space, one separating himself to drink from a bucket of water while the other waited.

Olivia looked around the enclosure. She recognized Meadow, who refilled the bucket after the dogs drank their share. Glancing toward Olivia, Meadow briefly nodded, then returned to her task.

Olivia stepped outside the enclosure. Instead of following her, Mayor Maguire walked toward Meadow. He sniffed her shoes. *Maybe he'll go back to her now,* Olivia thought, observing the dog from a distance. Paws in the dirt, instead of following either woman, Mayor Maguire took up his observation post right outside the pen. With a heave he lay on the dirt, his eyes directed toward the corral.

"Looks like my dog adopted you," said Meadow. "I was hoping he'd come back after the library incident, but I guess not."

"I'm sorry, Meadow. I can bring him back to your house when this is all over."

"The mayor has always been free to choose where he goes in Lily Rock. I'm just his handler for official events." Meadow stared at Olivia.

"For what it's worth, I think Mayor Maguire finds the rescue dogs more interesting than either of us." Olivia gestured to the dog, who watched the pen, his eyes alert to intruders.

The hum of an engine overhead caused Meadow and Olivia to look up into the sky. The twin engines of a small aircraft buzzed as the plane swooped behind the flames, toward the animal shelter. Fire-retardant spray spewed from the back of the airplane, settling over the flames.

"Mayor Maguire! We have to go now." Olivia spoke firmly to the dog. He rose to his feet, making a circle around Olivia, stopping to sit by her left knee. He nosed her thigh.

Walking with the mayor, Olivia glanced over the now-full parking lot. In the center she recognized the marked vehicle of the town constabulary. Sure enough, Janis Jets leaned against the hood, holding a walkie-talkie to her mouth.

Olivia knew the time had come. She walked toward the officer. "Officer Jets, do you have a moment?"

Jets turned. "I've been waiting for you."

"Not exactly a convenient time to talk," Olivia admitted.

"You are so right. Thanks for your phone call, by the way. Looks like we can stop this fire before it takes over the town. Good timing."

Olivia felt a surge of gratitude toward the officer.

Jets kept talking. "On the one hand, you were very helpful with reporting the fire so quickly. But on the other hand? You've been a pain in my ass when it comes to this investigation.

Ignoring Olivia's embarrassment, Jets gave directions. "This is how the arrest will go. I won't be needed here much longer. Afterward, I'm going to round up the usual suspects, and I'd like you to meet with them at the constabulary tomorrow."

"The suspects—in Marla's murder?" Hair prickled on Olivia's neck. Then she added, "Am I still a suspect?"

"Of course not. I eliminated you and Michael right from the start. I told you that Mayor Maguire's trust in you was all I needed."

"But he's a dog. I thought you were kidding, you know, to set me at ease so that I'd confess." Olivia felt her face flush. "I actually have evidence that I've been withholding. It's at home. I'll bring it to your office as soon as the fire is contained."

Jets looked deeply into Olivia's wide eyes. She scratched the back of her neck before adding, "So tell me now. What evidence do you have?"

"I have Marla's EpiPen."

Janis's eyes narrowed. "And where is that evidence, pray tell?"

"I found it in the woods after Marla's body had been removed. Your people must have missed it." Olivia looked at Janis, realizing she'd just criticized the police force of Lily Rock. "Oh I didn't find it, Mayor Maguire did, actually. He led me to the evidence."

Jets's brow smoothed. "Oh, the mayor led you, did he? Not the first time my guys missed something that the mayor led us to later. Anyway, that doesn't explain why you kept it from the police."

"Yes it does," insisted Olivia. "If I brought it forward, you'd think I took it from Marla and killed her."

"And you figure I'm that stupid, right? I *am* a trained investigator. I joke around about the mayor, but that's to put people at their ease. I actually do a good job around here you know." A huff of indignation pushed past Janis's lips. She stared Olivia down, daring her to disagree.

"I'm sorry." Olivia hung her head. *Not only that, I underestimated Janis Jets from the very beginning.* "You're right. I did assume a lot of things when I first got here. But hey, I kept the Epi in a plastic baggie. Does that help?"

Jets grimaced at Olivia and then smiled. "Not much. We can try to get some prints. Just so you know, you're not the first to think my job is a joke. What the hell? The entire town claims they have a psychic dog as the damned mayor. A pack of lunatics lives here. What else would you think? No wonder you underestimated me."

The defensive energy between the two women, born of their unlikely first encounter, dissolved instantly. Now they both grinned at each other. Not only a truce but a connection formed in that moment.

Jet's continued to explain." I want the fingerprints for my case, and I'll get them if you bring the EpiPen to me as soon as you can. Then we'll set up our denouncement. It will be fun."

"Denouncement?"

"That's right. You figured it out. If Lily Rock is the town of mythological ambiguity, then we need an amateur detective, and she requires a professional investigator. Jets and Greer. This is us."

Olivia's shocked expression brought a smirk to Janis Jets's face. "Sometimes you are the last to know your role in a drama. We're gonna end this crazy situation and get it under control once and for all."

Maybe, thought Olivia. *Or maybe this is just the beginning of the next act.*

A crack echoed in the air. Shouts echoed in the distance. "Look out!" For a moment time stood still, as Olivia and Janis glanced at the Pines and Paws Animal Shelter.

The once state-of-the art building lay in the rubble, a mass of burning embers, flames licking along the concrete slab. Beautiful windows, now shattered with the heat, exposed a load-bearing main beam that had once supported the atrium. Charred remains threw sparks into the cool air.

Shaking her head, Olivia heard a dog barking from the direction of the temporary corral. She nodded to Jets. "See you in the morning." As she ran toward the barking, Mayor Maguire trotted at her side.

Along with the two pit bulls, a dozen wild-eyed dogs of various breeds cowered, watching the fiery spectacle beyond. Alongside the dogs, volunteers shaded their eyes from sparks, looking toward the destroyed shelter.

Olivia noted each volunteer wore a bright neon-green T-shirt that said *Lily Rock Fire Volunteer* on the front. Oversized dog and cat paws decorated the back.

In the corral, one elderly woman bent over a Chihuahua mix to comfort him. She lifted the small dog into her arms, whispering into his ear. Olivia felt Jets stand next to her. She asked, "Will the pets all be adopted now?"

Jets nodded. "As you know, the town likes dogs and cats more than people. No one would refuse to shelter a pet in crisis in Lily Rock. On the other hand," Jets continued, "just because someone is good with animals doesn't mean they won't kill a human, especially if that human got in the way."

CHAPTER TWENTY-NINE

Overheard in Lily Rock
In the constabulary office:
Accused: Not guilty, officer.
Officer: Okay. Your court date is April 16th.
Accused: Ummm, can't make it. Isn't that, like, Mayor
Maguire's birthday?

When the first responders declared a 30 percent containment of the fire, the Lily Rock volunteers were sent home. Olivia waited by Michael's truck until she saw his familiar grin.

"Let's go. I'll drop you off and then head to my place." He ripped away the filthy bandana from his neck.

They drove back to Marla's house in silence, with Mayor Maguire sitting between them in the front seat. "Move over, Mayor," Michael grumbled as he reached for the gear shift to put the truck in park.

Olivia opened the door, climbing out of the cab. The dog scooted across the seat to follow her. "I guess he's staying with me tonight."

"A dog with his own mind," admitted Michael. "Get some rest. I'll see you in the morning."

"I'll give you a call when I'm awake."

Olivia and the mayor made their way in the dark to unlock the front door. Michael waited in the truck until she entered. She waved at him before closing the door, hearing his truck shift into first gear.

Mayor Maguire's tongue hung out of the side of his mouth. She walked directly to the kitchen to fill his water bowl. Then her cell phone rang and lit up with the name *Sage* on her screen.

Setting the bowl on the tile floor, Olivia answered. "What's up?"

"Olivia?" Sage's voice sobbed into the phone. "Can I come over? I know it's late—"

"Of course you can. The door will be open. I'm going to step into a shower. Just come in and make yourself at home. In fact, since it's so late, why don't you stay in the guest suite? Plan on it."

"Oh, Olivia. Thank you. I'm so grateful. See you in a few minutes."

Though exhausted, she felt a surge of new energy. Even though Sage was a few months older, Olivia felt like the older one. Sage needed her. *I need to be needed.*

She stripped off the smoke-scented clothing, discarding the heap on the laundry room floor.

Running her hands through her short hair, she felt the stickiness of the fire retardant on her scalp. After a hot shower and fresh clothing, Olivia looked in the mirror. Dark circles appeared under both eyes. Her skin felt crackly like old paper. She bent over to open a drawer, looking through Marla's skin products. *Skin Renew with CBD Oil*, she read. She smoothed the contents over her tired face. *I do feel better. At least I don't look like an old newspaper left for days outside.*

When she wandered back to the kitchen, she found Sage hugging Mayor Maguire around the neck.

"Tell me everything." Olivia filled a kettle for hot tea.

With another hug for the dog, Sage brushed her tears aside with the sleeve of her sweatshirt. "Let me get the mugs," she offered, moving toward the cupboard.

For the next few minutes they made tea in silence, each moving around the other in an intuitively choreographed dance. Finally the two women sat down facing each other, with the teapot and mugs between.

"Start at the beginning," Olivia suggested, taking her first sip as the peppermint aroma cleared her air passages.

* * *

Olivia felt a prickling up her neck. "Aren't you a bit relieved now that you know?"

Sage's turned-down lips indicated otherwise.

Olivia remembered how she and Marla had spent their teen years speculating about their fathers and how frustrated they both had been. They had each other, but not knowing left them both feeling abandoned. She admitted to herself that over the years, many of her worst decisions had been based upon the threat of another abandonment. She'd stuck with Don years longer than necessary to avoid being alone.

Sage stood to pull a paper towel from the roll by the sink. She patted at her face. When she returned to the table she no longer looked teary. Her hands lay beside the mug of tea. Her long, tapered fingers did not tremble as they had when she first arrived.

"The problem is, I don't think Mom told me the entire

truth about my biological father. I'm not certain she even knows who my father is. She told me I'm not her biological child, but she said nothing about my birth parents."

"So then how did she get you—I mean, adopt you?"

"She said she had connected with a young mother at the clinic down the hill. Arrangements were made, and I was handed over to her as soon as they stabilized my breathing—I was just three pounds."

Olivia reached over to pat Sage's hand. "I know you were small, but look at you now! Full-sized and ready to rock and roll."

Both women smiled. "I am a bit of a handful. Being small in the beginning must have made me strong."

"So I see why you felt so unhappy. You thought you'd finally learn about your father, only to discover your mother isn't even your biological parent."

Tears formed again in Sage's eyes. "The thing I don't understand is why Mom kept the secret for all these years. It's not like adopting an infant is a crime or something, unless—"

"That's it! Maybe she didn't adopt you. Maybe she took you from your real parents. Have you thought of that?"

Sage's eyes widened. Olivia saw that she had not considered that possibility. "You mean I may have another mother and father out there, alive and well and wondering where I am?"

Olivia felt her gut clench. *Why did I say that?* "I'm not sure about that. But I don't think I'd trust Meadow's stories anymore, especially since she's been telling this whopper for your entire life."

Sage stared down at her hands, resting on the table. "Is it a coincidence that I've become brave enough to question Mom since you arrived in town?"

Olivia did not know what to say. She reached over to pat

Sage's folded hands. "I know. I feel the same. I think we're kindred spirits. Not to change the subject, but Officer Jets wanted me to come by the constabulary tomorrow. I have something to hand over to her. Do you think you could get some sleep now? The room is all set with fresh sheets."

Sage stood on wobbly legs. She took the two mugs to the sink. "I am exhausted. I hauled at least a dozen cats in crates out of the fire tonight, and I could use a hot shower and a good night's sleep."

"Off you go. I'll show you the room."

After settling Sage into the guest suite, Olivia eased herself into bed, resting her head on the pillow. She cast her eyes to the ceiling. *Do I tell Sage what I know now, or do I invite her to Jets's meeting?* Her eyes fluttered as sleep arrived.

A few minutes later Mayor Maguire woke Olivia up. He circled three times and curled himself up next to her. His eyes closed. Both were asleep within minutes.

The following day Olivia decided not to awaken Sage. Instead she called Michael. "Meet me at the constabulary. We can have coffee there."

The phone clicked.

Fifteen minutes later they both stood in front of Jets's office. Michael hadn't shaved but looked none the worse for the short night's sleep. "Do you think she's inside?" asked Olivia, pointing to the *Closed* sign hanging in the window.

"Oh, she's there. She starts her day before dawn." His hand slipped into his pocket to pull out a key ring. After unlocking the door, he ushered Olivia forward to the beeping sound of an alarm.

Michael reached behind a panel to punch in a code. The alarm stopped. "Where is she?" asked Olivia, looking around the room.

"I'm back here," came Jets's voice. "I'm making us coffee."

Down the hallway, closed doors lined up on both sides. Three jail cells had been constructed on the opposite side, with bars across the front and a toilet in each corner. No one was under arrest, as far as Olivia could see.

The pungent smell of French roast drew them toward the end of the hall. Olivia took the mug offered by Michael, slumping into a wooden chair next to a large round table.

"Now that you have your coffee, do you have something for me?" Janis Jets asked, her mouth drawing a grim line.

Olivia rummaged through her purse. She handed Jets the EpiPen. "Here you go. You'll most likely find my prints on there."

Jets took the bag from Olivia, disappearing behind the kitchen door.

When she returned she said, "I've contacted the lab. We'll have the results by the end of the day. I'm nearly one hundred percent sure what they'll find, but I need the evidence for a court conviction. This will surely lead to a major legal battle."

Olivia turned toward Michael. "You seem awfully quiet. Aren't you even curious how I came by that EpiPen?"

Michael tapped his coffee cup with his forefinger. "I think I know how you got the pen, but why you kept it to yourself is puzzling."

Janis nodded. "After the fire last night Mike and I talked. I know. I know. On the one hand I never suspected you, but on the other hand? The facts and how you held back important clues would suggest you were involved.

Olivia looked back and forth from Michael's thoughtful gaze to Jets's intense stare. They'd obviously talked a great deal about her. She drew a deep breath. *Pillow talk?* Then her gut settled. *No*, she thought. *They're good friends. That's it.*

My instinct tells me so, and I don't want to keep treating Michael like Don, who was a scoundrel with women. Michael can show me who he is if he wants to, but I am not going to assume anything. It's not healthy for me.

Olivia cleared her throat. "The day after Marla died ..." She inhaled deeply. "It's still hard to say *Marla* and *died* in one breath. Anyway, that day Mayor Maguire led me to the crime scene for the second time. I kept behind the yellow tape the police left, but he didn't. When he was done sniffing he went farther into the woods, so I followed him.

"That was when I found the EpiPen. At first I didn't know what it was, but the Mayor nosed it as if he wanted me to pick it up. So I did."

"And?" Jets encouraged her to keep talking.

"I knew Marla had allergies when she was younger; I wasn't that surprised to read that the pen was for preventing anaphylactic shock. I mean, she used to wear one of those bracelets that said she was allergic to beestings and peanuts and something else. So I figured she'd dropped the pen. Then I saw it had not been used. It was still loaded and ready to inject."

Michael interjected, "So why didn't you hand over the EpiPen to Janis or at least mention it to me?"

"I thought you both figured I'd killed Marla. I didn't want to implicate myself further, so I pocketed the pen, waiting for a better time—when I was out of the suspect pool."

She continued, "I also decided then and there that I would find the person who murdered Marla. Then I could hand over the EpiPen. It seemed like a good idea at the time."

Michael shrugged. "So what I don't understand is why you didn't tell me any of this."

"Oh, that's simple. I thought you murdered Marla, or at

least I wasn't sure. At first you when were around a lot, it seemed a bit sketchy. I didn't trust you at all. I think it was the smoke in the chimney that first morning, and then the way you turned up so quickly after I found her body. It was like you were waiting to frame me for her death."

Michael shook his head. "I knew you didn't like me much at first, but I had no idea how deep your distrust ran. I did everything I could to explain to you about this place and Marla. I tried to be such a nice guy."

Olivia shrugged.

"By the way"—Michael leaned toward Olivia—"when did you, or did you ever, change your mind about me?"

Without any remorse, Olivia grinned. "I did change my mind. It wasn't anything you said, exactly. It happened when I found you hiding out in the constabulary office, pretending to be the suspect yourself."

"How did that help you trust me?"

"I figured a really diabolical person would never come up with such a silly plan. You seemed surprised to see me that morning. I guess you underestimated my need to find Marla's killer."

Janis stared at Michael, who looked away. "More coffee, anyone?"

All three laughed.

"All right," Jets said in her police voice. "Let's summarize what we know from this confession."

"It was not a confession!"

"Okay, it was more evidence. Can I say that? You brought more to the table that we can consider."

"That's much better," Olivia agreed.

Officer Jets continued, "On the one hand, we think Marla went into anaphylactic shock. I'm not certain what brought on the attack, but the medical facts tell us her heart stopped, which is common when people have severe allergies."

"What about the other hand?" Olivia teased. "Tell us about that."

Not understanding the joke, Jets added, "On the other hand, I also think someone was with her when she went into shock, and that someone took her EpiPen and threw it into the woods so that it could not be injected. It was the removal of the EpiPen that led directly to her death, not the allergic reaction."

Olivia's eyes clouded over. "Marla must have been so frightened those last few moments. I just feel awful for her."

Michael said in a somber voice, "She did not deserve to be treated like that. She was a good woman."

No one spoke.

Finally Olivia lifted her head. "I think I know who tossed her pen. In fact, I'm very certain I know."

Jets's eyes widened. "So do you want to tell us now or wait until I ask Mayor Maguire to exert his influence?"

"I want to tell you everything, but I'd like all of Marla's friends to be here when I do the telling."

"Like one of those mystery book finales? Are you pulling a Miss Marple?" Jets inquired as her eyebrow lifted.

"Oh no, Janis," laughed Michael. "Most certainly she's pulling a Nancy Drew. You wouldn't believe how good this woman is at discovering hidden closets and safe rooms."

Olivia blushed. "Well, you found most of the secret passages. You built them, after all, at least the originals." She enjoyed being teased by Michael and Janis. "So how about if I say I'm pulling a denouncement? Can that be arranged?"

Janis Jets stood. "Give me a couple of hours and I'll gather everyone here in the kitchen. We can set up a circle of chairs. I want everything revealed as quickly as possible. Once word gets out that we've found our suspect, the town will go crazy with alternative facts and supernatural causes."

Sadness reached up like a hand to grab at Olivia's heart. She'd have to tell everything now, and then it would be over. She wanted justice for Marla, but after they arrested the killer, she would have to move out of Lily Rock.

CHAPTER THIRTY

Overheard in Lily Rock

"You haven't lived in Lily Rock until you've helped a hot girl move and then never see her again."

Later that afternoon Michael held the passenger-side door as Olivia's boots slid to the pavement below. "I have something I want to say to you—later," he told her in a firm voice.

"You mean after our denunciation at the constabulary?"

"I can wait until then." His words acquiesced, but his jaw told a different story.

"You seem quite insistent on waiting."

"I know you plan to leave Lily Rock. You've made it abundantly clear. Before you dart out, just let me have my say. Could you do that for me?" He leaned forward, eyes pleading with hers.

Her gut turned with apprehension. "We can talk later. Right now we have some denouncing to do."

Michael nodded. He held the door as Olivia walked inside the constabulary. Janis Jets sat in her usual place behind her desk.

She smiled at Michael, then cast her gaze toward Olivia. "Don't look so grim, you two. This is the good part, when we arrest the bad guys."

"Did you contact everyone on my list?" Olivia asked Jets.

"I did. One said he'd be late, but the rest are already assembled in the back room. Hopefully this circle arrangement will make people feel comfortable."

"Good thinking," said Michael. "It will remind them of a recovery meeting instead of an interrogation. Everyone goes to some kind of recovery meeting in Lily Rock."

"Is that so?" Cayenne had told her about that one meeting but...*I'm not staying*, she reminded herself, *no use getting connected.*

Following Janis Jets down the hallway, Michael and Olivia entered the interrogation room. Voices stopped speaking as eyes turned to look at Olivia.

She shrugged off her discomfort. *I have the distinct impression everyone thinks I killed Marla. I know they were talking about me before we walked in.*

Four empty chairs were interspersed in the circle, which made it difficult for Olivia to decide where to sit. Sage shyly smiled at her first. Seeing Meadow and Sage holding hands, Olivia continued to look at the other faces in the circle. Arlo looked away before he leaned over to whisper into Cayenne's ear. Cayenne shook her head as if to say no.

Michael took one stride with his long legs to sit between Cayenne and Sage. Jets patted the empty seat next to her, so Olivia sat down.

The next moment a voice hailed the assembled group from the doorway. "Well, well, well, look who we have here. My favorite people all in one room." Dr. May smiled as he looked over the heads of those assembled. He sat in the remaining empty chair. Doc crossed his legs, presenting a casual attitude as he cast an expectant glance toward Officer Jets. "I'm sorry to be late. Have I missed anything?"

Jets cleared her throat. "You may wonder why I called you all together this late in the afternoon."

"Perhaps you want to start a new dinner group?" mentioned the doc, his finger scratching at his temple, a grin lurking at the corner of his mouth.

Olivia wondered why Doc presented such an easygoing attitude. Unable to decide what he was up to, she looked more closely at Sage.

Should I tell her what I know now, in the group? Is she ready?

"We've come to some conclusions about the death of our friend Skye Jones," Janis Jets said in her even voice.

"It was a tragic affair," admitted Doc May. He glanced over at Olivia. "I'm going to grieve a long time over her passing."

"On the one hand, I don't want to interfere with your grieving, Doc. But on the other hand, we have to get to the bottom of why she killed herself. Let's discuss." Jets waved her hand over the group to encourage them to speak.

What is she doing? Olivia wondered. *Is this going to be an informal conversation or a denouncement?*

"I am delighted that you've gathered this group to honor our friend Skye," the doctor began. Olivia felt her spine tingle. *I think the doc may take over this group if Janis doesn't make an effort to amp up the energy.* She felt Jets shift beside her in her seat. Tempted to steer the course of the conversation back to Marla's death herself, Olivia kept quiet. She sat further back in her chair.

She had to admit, Janis Jets was proving to be a far more interesting woman than Olivia had originally thought. *Let this play out,* she told herself. *Janis is the director. She can tell the doc to shut up. I am a small actor in a much larger drama.*

"I knew Skye Jones." The doctor produced a handkerchief from his back pocket. "You knew her nearly as long," he added, looking over to Meadow.

"I did know Skye even before I moved to Lily Rock." She glanced at her daughter. "I got to know her better after Sage was born."

Olivia waited, biting her lower lip.

"And Dr. May, just so you know, I told Sage everything last night."

"Everything?" The surprise in the doctor's voice brought Olivia's eyes up from her lap. "But I thought we'd agreed—" Gone was the cavalier persona of Dr. May. Deep lines formed on his brow, replacing his initially jovial countenance.

Meadow shot the doc a defiant look. "You've been warning me for years not to tell Sage the exact circumstances of her birth. Since the first day when you placed her into my arms you threatened me not to tell anyone that she was adopted. I kept my promise because I thought you'd take my baby back if I ever said anything against your wishes."

Sage looked at her mother, then Dr. May. "So why didn't you want me to know? What's the big problem with telling a child she's adopted? It's the twenty-first century. There are books in the library about how to navigate the conversation with children. There's nothing to be ashamed of, so what were you hiding?"

The doctor shrugged. He planted his leather shoes on the floor, shoving his back against the chair. "I thought we gathered here today to talk about our friend Skye. At least that's what you told me!" Doc May pointed a trembling finger at Officer Jets, his voice clipped and accusatory.

Doc May turned toward Sage. "I suppose it doesn't matter

now. But back then I was concerned that you would be taken from your mother since—"

Here it comes, thought Olivia. *Finally some truth.*

"—I didn't file the correct paperwork."

Before the information could sink in for everyone, Sage spoke. "Did you steal me from another woman?" She stood, glaring at the doc.

"Now, now," Jets interrupted. "Sit down, Sage. We'll get to the answers."

Sage sat back down, poised on the very edge of her chair. She pointed her finger at Jets. "You told me I'd find out about my father at this meeting. That's why I came!"

Instead of addressing Sage's accusation, Jets looked back at the doctor. "On the one hand, I appreciate that you felt compassion for Meadow and her new baby. But on the other hand? Like Sage, I wonder about the birth mother. What about her?"

Doc May's voice pleaded, "You don't understand. I delivered Sage three months early to a young woman who came to the free clinic where I worked. After the birth, she was exhausted and in need of rest. The mother was only sixteen years old, a baby herself. The early birth was the perfect excuse for me to take charge of a terrible situation. So I worked with Skye, my nurse practitioner, who had a list of women who wanted to adopt babies.

"Skye connected with Meadow and asked her to donate the adoption fee to my nonprofit corporation, the animal shelter. As soon as the money was put into the account we gave Meadow her new baby.

"Skye encouraged Meadow to move to Lily Rock. Meadow could tell people the baby was hers, and no one would question her. And my friend Skye agreed to help her with the small baby. Premature infants require special care. In my opinion I'd arrived at a perfect solution to a very difficult situation." The doctor smiled, as if to congratulate himself.

"What about the birth mother?" Olivia blurted out. "What did you tell her?"

"You told me she died giving birth," Meadow insisted, alarm showing on her face.

The doctor did not rise to the bait. Instead he scratched his chin. "Well, that part gets complicated. I know I told you the mother died. She actually returned to high school. I told her the baby died, just to put her mind at rest. That way no one would follow up on the details."

He turned to Meadow, his voice growing stern. "I did need to swear you to secrecy, though, just to make certain no one would question my decision and start digging around for paperwork."

Olivia glanced over at Michael to see how he was taking the news. He rested his hands on his knees and spoke. "Let me get this straight. You told Meadow the baby's mother died, and you told the baby's mother the baby died. Who made you God, anyway?"

Michael has a justice streak, she realized. *Funny I didn't notice before.*

Janis Jets's face remained calm. She asked, "Did anyone consult the baby's father about all of this?"

Doc May shook his head. "Probably some unfortunate high school renegade on the Indian reservation down the hill. Why would I subject a newborn infant to such a circumstance? I stand by my decision at the time."

He swept his hand toward Meadow and Sage. "Now you both have each other. It's my understanding that the baby's mother passed away a couple of years ago. But before that, she had another child; she most likely did not miss the first one at all. So all is well."

Olivia shuddered, then raised her voice. "All is not well. My friend Marla told you what she knew about the baby's father!"

"Now, now, darlin'," came the disingenuous voice of the doctor. "None of that silly nonsense. Marla didn't know a thing about baby Sage's father." The doc glanced around the circle of faces, waiting for someone to speak up on his behalf.

Janis Jets leaned forward to face Olivia. "So tell us what you know—that you think Marla knew—about Sage's parents."

The doctor's voice exploded. "There's no reason for Olivia to tell us anything. She's not from our town. We can't even trust her. She's psychologically unstable. What about that escape down the hill? If it hadn't been for the snakebite—"

Olivia closed her eyes to think. Did she need to help Jets or just remain quiet as the drama unfolded?

The doctor spoke loudly, pointing at Olivia's face. "It's you! We all know you killed Marla to inherit her house and her boyfriend. You're the only one who benefited from her death, so stop trying to say otherwise."

"That's enough," roared Michael.

A sly smile appeared at the corner of Janis Jets's mouth as everyone in the circle glared at her.

Arlo interrupted. "You told me and Cay to come to this meeting to talk about getting a permit for our medical marijuana shop."

Jets's face lit up with relief. "And it worked. You all came for different reasons, but I can assure you, everyone will leave with the truth."

Dr. May stood from his chair. "I am a medical professional. I'm not going to sit here and be accused of doing harm to one of my patients. I'll sue you." He pointed to Olivia. "No matter what Marla told you—and she did have some wild accusations—if you repeat what she told you, then you will have besmirched my character in front of these witnesses. You'd better keep your unsubstantiated opinions to yourself."

Olivia spoke quietly. "Nice try, Doc. I haven't said anything to anybody yet. And when I do speak up, just remember, you can't sue me for telling the truth, and it's not just an opinion; I have proof. Right here." Olivia reached into the back pocket of her jeans. She extracted a small metal object. "This is a thumb drive. Marla's extensive research about her own birth father, right here for anyone to read."

The doctor's face paled. He wobbled on his knees before sitting back down.

Olivia turned to face Sage. "Brace yourself."

Sage's knuckles grew white around Meadow's hand.

Olivia looked into the faces of everyone in the circle. She stopped when she reached Michael. He looked at her expectantly.

"For better or worse—Dr. May, you are Sage's birth father."

Casting his hand to his face, Doc flopped back farther into his metal chair.

The words hung in the room as everyone sat in stunned silence.

"But Olivia, how do you know that?" Michael asked quietly.

"Marla left me her research. She'd hidden it in a place she hoped no one would find—in plain sight. She handwrote and took photos of the information, storing them in cardboard boxes in her closet. There was no evidence on her hard drive, so that's why the police didn't pick up any clues about her investigation."

For a moment the group looked over at Cayenne, who

patted her open hands on the top of her head in excitement. "Actually, Marla did leave hard drive evidence. I was the one to erase everything. The doc told me to." Cayenne gestured at the old man. "He called me and told me to erase her computer before the police arrived."

"I did no such thing," the doctor mumbled. "You can't prove that I did."

"Oh yes, you did," Cayenne insisted in a deeper voice. "You told me Marla kept gossip on the computer about me and Arlo. You threatened me too. If I didn't wipe the hard drive, you would out Arlo for his illegal marijuana business."

Now Arlo turned to Cayenne. "So that's how you found out about my business."

Cayenne patted his hand. "I confronted you a few days later. Then you decided to come clean and ask for the town council's forgiveness."

"Which they will never give!" barked the doctor. "I made sure of that. I burned the place down so that you'll never get a dime from that illegal enterprise."

Stunned into silence, the group glared at Dr. May. Janis Jets took that moment to reach under her chair for her laptop. She flipped open the computer. "I'll add arson to my official indictment. You put the entire town of Lily Rock in danger with that fire. The judge won't care if it was your property. We may even throw in insurance fraud to strengthen our case. How about that, Doc?"

"I built the place, and I can burn it down. You have no jurisdiction over my property." The doctor's face turned red with anger.

"We'll see about that," Janis replied in a clipped voice. "But back to Sage. So the doc is your birth father. That must come as a surprise."

"I don't understand." Sage shook her head. She looked at Olivia, tears filling her eyes.

Olivia spoke gently. "Doc is your father. Marla found out that Doc was also her birth father. Marla had been looking for him since we met in high school. By the time she moved to Lily Rock she'd already begun extensive research online, including a background check of her own DNA."

Olivia continued to explain. "Marla discovered that she had a number of half siblings. She connected with them on Facebook. Then she hired a detective to fill in the blanks. It seems Dr. May worked in the Native American clinic down the hill. For years he volunteered his time, along with his assistant, Skye Jones."

The doctor interrupted her story again. "And a good thing some of us know the value of giving to others without being paid. Everyone at the clinic revered my name in those days. Just go and ask some of the mothers I helped along the way."

Olivia ignored him to continue. "It was a well-known fact that the government turned the other way when complaints were made about the doctor of the clinic. No one had any interest in the rights of Native Americans—especially women.

"It wasn't too long before women who were unable to conceive, who lived in more affluent neighborhoods, found Dr. May and his abundant source of babies."

Olivia swallowed past her dry throat. "He promised the women that they could avoid the paperwork and fees of legal adoption by going through him. He'd discreetly remove Native babies from their mothers to place them with families who desired children—for a fee, of course, deposited into a nonprofit the doc organized. His own shell corporation, the first animal clinic. That way the money could not be traced. In time Doc May didn't even try to cover up his practices. Pretty lucrative for him over the years."

The circle of faces stared at Olivia, her news stunning them to silence. She continued. "When Native women figured out what was going on and stopped going to Dr. May, he continued to see more affluent couples from Los Angeles. He used his own sperm to sell to women who wanted to have a family but were unable to conceive. Marla's mother was one of those women."

"So, I know about my father." Sage glared at the doctor. "But what about my biological mother? If he"—she pointed at the doc—"is my father, then who is my mother?"

Olivia faced Sage. She lowered her voice for this last bit of shocking information. "I have a feeling the relationship with your mother may not have been consensual. Your birth mother may have shown up at the clinic looking for birth control advice, and then—he raped her."

Dr. May stood, blustering another excuse. "I don't have to rape women. They want me. Always have. Even now!" He glared at Olivia, his eyes narrowing, looking snakelike as his words slithered toward her for a bite. "Don't forget, Little Bit," the doc's voice drawled, "even you tried it on with me. Remember the evening at the pub, how you sat and gazed into my eyes and then tried to kiss me when we walked down the stairs?"

Stunned at his obvious lie, Olivia felt her throat tighten. Instead of keeping silent she spoke, surprising herself. "I met you at the pub as a kindness. You stitched up my head for free. It was the least I could do. I guess I kind of felt sorry for you."

Olivia leaned back in her chair as the silence grew fuller. She focused her eyes straight ahead.

With her silence, the cunning of Officer Jets's plan became instantly apparent to Olivia. Glancing to her side, she saw Janis Jets point to her screen. The red dot for recording glowed. Olivia inhaled deeply. With enough pressure, the doctor would out himself as a rapist and a predator of women. His ego would require nothing less. And Janis? She'd have it all recorded in his own voice.

Taking advantage of the pause in conversation, Janis Jets spoke. "So then, Doc, am I to assume that Marla confronted you about being her father?"

Before the doctor could respond to her question, Michael interrupted. "How many women did you inseminate with your own sperm?" Olivia knew by the tone of his voice that he'd seen Jets pointing to her laptop. Michael helped, his question keeping the doc off balance.

Placing both hands on his knees, the Doc's jaw tightened. He rocked back and forth, perspiration forming on his brow. When he spoke his voice quavered. "Oh, there were several infertile women. Maybe dozens. No one has complained yet."

Disgust formed in Olivia's gut.

"You didn't answer my question about Marla. Did she confront you?" asked Jets again.

"You can't prove a thing." Doc crossed his arms above his thickening waist. "Plus," he added, "the obvious killer is Olivia."

"If what you say is true, and she killed Marla"—Michael glanced at Olivia with apology in his eyes—"if Olivia killed Marla," he repeated, "why did Skye Jones confess?"

"She didn't confess," stated Meadow, loud enough for all to hear.

Now the eyes of the group pivoted to Meadow.

"Say more, and speak up, please," insisted Jets, who typed into the laptop placed precariously on her lap.

"I know that Skye accepted responsibility for what she'd done to hurt Marla, but she did everything to please the doc." Meadow pointed to the doctor. "Skye loved Doc May since the first time she saw him, long before I moved to Lily Rock.

She'd tell me story after story about the people he would save. She worshipped him."

Meadow's voice grew stronger. "One day, after Marla had lived in Lily Rock for a while, Skye overheard a conversation. You know how she had the habit of eavesdropping? Marla threatened the doc. Skye took matters into her own hands. That very day Skye began a campaign to undermine Marla's health, hoping she'd move out of Lily Rock."

Meadow continued, "She realized how allergic Marla was to peanuts and bees and any number of plants. She knew just how to proceed with her plan. Pretending to help Marla with gardening, Skye planted marijuana in the corners of her herb garden. She borrowed the house key from Cayenne to work on the inside by filling the house with plant leaves and pollen. She rubbed pollen into the fabric of her clothing and pillow cases."

"Skye broke off flowers from the plants to crumble in her fingers and place in the back of all the kitchen drawers. She even distributed the flowers behind Marla's clothing in the closet. It only took a few days for Marla to develop symptoms."

"That's what Marla wrote me in her letter," Olivia said. "All of her symptoms, the sneezing, stuffy nose, rapid heartbeat, and dizziness must have come from being exposed to the marijuana pollen."

Olivia shook her head. *Poor Marla. She didn't realize what she was up against.*

Olivia caught Meadow's eye. "You put CBD drops in my tea those two nights."

"Yes, I did. Along with other herbs. I use this combination with everyone who needs more sleep. You're not the first. Just know that I only supplemented your tea to help Skye. The doctor told Skye to pick up the plants and the crushed flowers with the pollen from Marla's house before you or anyone else noticed them. I thought you needed some sleep after such an ordeal, so I helped both you and Skye at the same time."

Suspicion crossed Olivia's face. "That's why I discovered the uprooted plants in the garden."

"Skye didn't have time to cover the holes. I think she felt very guilty when she paused to think about what she'd done. It started to eat away at her, how she had protected the doctor for all those years. And then it must have been too much. She shot herself."

Meadow's eyes filled with tears. Sage leaned over to take her mother's hand in both of hers.

Before Olivia could settle back into her chair, her mind pinged. "But what about the EpiPen? Even if Marla collapsed into anaphylactic shock, why didn't she use the pen?"

Appearing asleep for the conversation, the doctor's eyes fluttered. He stood up as his chair clattered to the floor. "Epi-Pen? She must have forgotten to take it with her that day in the garden. I warned her!" Dr. May walked through the center of the circle toward the exit. He spoke loudly from the doorway. "I think I've had just about enough here. Since I am not responsible for any of this and you can't prove any of your ill-begotten suspicions, I'm going to my surgery."

Immediately on her feet, Janis Jets spoke. "Not so fast, Dr. May. We have Marla's EpiPen. The last person who saw her before her death flung the pen into the woods so that she would not be able to use it to save her own life. That person would be you!"

Doc sprinted toward the exit. For an old man he could be quite spry when he chose to be. Instead of chasing him, Jets nodded to Arlo, who put out his leg, sending the doc sprawling sideways onto the floor.

He scrambled to regain his footing, and Jets reached into

her back pocket. "Stop right there. Stand up and put your hands behind your back. Dr. May, I'm arresting you for the murder of Marla Osbourne. You have the right to remain silent."

As soon as Janis finished reading him his rights, she pulled the doctor's arms behind his back, clasping his wrists.

"Let's go," Michael ordered, shoving the doctor through the doorway, toward the jail cells.

"Let me go!" The doctor's repeated shouts resonated in the room as the rest of the circle sat in stunned silence.

Janis Jets was not through. She stood to her full height, using her most stern voice. "Just so you know, Dr. May was the last person to see Marla Osbourne alive. Olivia kept the evidence with his fingerprints a secret, so we were unable to officially arrest him before—but now we have his words recorded." She gestured to her computer.

"I suggest you all go home. And you, Meadow, thank your lucky stars that I'm not putting you behind bars for dosing Olivia and whoever else you've done that to. No more of that! Do you hear me? They haven't even tested the long-term effects of CBD use. Despite your self-satisfied understanding that you know best, you don't! There are laws."

Meadow looked sheepish. Sage placed her arm around her mother's shoulders. *They have each other,* Olivia admitted.

Only Olivia knew she had more information, absorbed from Marla's files. She wanted to relieve herself of what she knew, but it was not the time. Enough had been said. Looking at Sage's and Meadow's faces, Olivia felt certain she'd made the right decision to remain silent on the topic of Sage's mother, who, it turned out, was her own mother too. Half sisters—no wonder they had felt the kinship from the beginning.

Arlo and Cayenne stood first. Olivia watched Sage and

Meadow move toward the exit. Janis Jets gathered the computer as Olivia observed. *I'll remember all of you.*

As they began to chat between themselves, Olivia quietly exited down the hallway. With one more glance at the constabulary sign, she walked toward the road that led to Marla's house.

Olivia inhaled the scent of pine mingled with wood smoke. Her steps plodded softly on the boardwalk as her shoulders dropped with relief. Now that Marla's killer had been revealed she felt free to leave. Her mother's words drifted into her thoughts: "Take up your own life before it's too late."

Olivia stopped to catch her breath. She turned in a circle to take in the three-hundred-and-sixty-degree view of the forest, with Lily Rock standing above like a sentry to watch over the residents.

It took fifteen minutes for Olivia to pack her small suitcase. With a last glance at the great room, she closed the front door, leaving her keys under the mat. On her way to the car she told herself sternly, *I can't stay. I have to go.*

Carefully navigating the road out of town, Olivia passed underneath the *Welcome to Lily Rock* sign. She nodded toward the constabulary. The office looked empty in the early-evening dusk. Olivia passed by the doctor's office and the library next door. She drove past the grocery store, heading out of town.

Only when she accelerated past the outskirts of town did she remember Michael's last request. His pleading eyes. She knew then she would not give him that last word. No more men to waylay her journey. She'd promised her mother. *I left him the keys,* she thought. *He'll be happy being in charge of his great creation. At least up until the house is sold, I'll ask him to be the caretaker—assuming he's still speaking to me.*

Since arriving in Lily Rock she'd felt fate breathing heavily over her shoulder. Between her connection with Sage and then Michael, she had felt drawn into their world. She could have stayed. Hadn't Marla overlooked her own biological half sister to give Olivia her house, just to keep her in Lily Rock?

Yet the promise to her mother would not allow room for more entanglements. "Promise me you will get away from Don. You need to be yourself, on your own, before you get into another relationship," Mother had insisted, her frail hand grasping Olivia's.

In the end Olivia knew why Mona had insisted. She told Olivia her story days before her death. Mona had only been sixteen years old when Dr. May raped her. Once her young mother realized she was pregnant, she hid from her family in shame. Dr. May provided her a place to stay. Then when the baby was born early, and she was told the baby died, she consoled herself with alcohol.

Only months later she fell in with a handsome boy and she got pregnant again. He went away to college before she could tell him. She got sober and kept Olivia, raising the baby on her own.

Olivia steered into the first curve, which came up suddenly. She continued winding her way down the hill, one curve at a time thinking about Marla. *I didn't plan your memorial, old friend. I will when the time is right.*

"Goodbye, Lily Rock," she told the mountains. *Apparently I am the one who gets away. I'm not like the rest of you. I am me.*

EPILOGUE

"Can you get the phone?" Olivia Greer's boss hollered from the back room. Before she could pick up, a postal worker stood in front of her desk.

"You the new temp?" he asked, winking at her. He held out a paper for her to sign.

"I've been here for six months." Olivia scribbled her initials on the paper.

"I guess I haven't seen you before. My name is Mark."

Mark reached down to lift a heavy package, handing it to her across the desk. Olivia placed it on her desk. "This thing weighs a lot," she commented, grasping her desk scissors. The phone stopped ringing. "And it's addressed to me."

Mark watched her slit open the box. "I kinda wonder what's inside," he told her. "But I can go if you don't want me to know."

Olivia looked more closely at the return slip. She read, "Lily Rock, California."

"Where is Lily Rock? I've never heard of that place."

"It's about three hours from here, in the mountains," she told him, impatiently ripping at the box.

After running the scissors down the seam of the package, Olivia turned back the cardboard flaps. Beneath her fingers, the bubble wrap crackled. She reached into the box, putting both hands into the contents.

"What the—" Mark's face registered shock.

Olivia stared at the wood, smoothing her hand over the back of the instrument. She ran her thumb across the strings. "It's an autoharp," she explained, pulling away an envelope that was on top. She opened it and read the letter to herself:

Dear Olivia,

I hope you are doing well. Since you left, things have been pretty dull here in Lily Rock. You didn't stop to talk to me after the doc got arrested—I still have the keys to your house. Heard from your attorney that you want me to be the house caretaker —could we talk about that? Kind of presumptuous, don't you think, since you left me without a word.

After I got over being mad, I realized how much I miss having you around. So I decided to send you the autoharp. Sage said she gave it to you, and I took the liberty of refinishing it and putting on new strings. You'll have to tune the thing, since I haven't a clue what it's supposed to sound like.

The amphitheater is being framed, and we should have the venue completed and running by next Christmas.

So, Olivia, I hope the autoharp reminds you of your friends here in Lily Rock. I hope you will find your way back to us sooner than later. I just want you to know that the mayor and I are waiting for you. You can call, write, text, or just drive up the hill. Watch out for those curves in the road.

Your friend,

Michael

Olivia folded the note, slipping it in the drawer of her desk. "Don't you have another delivery to make?" she asked the overly attentive delivery guy.

He grinned sheepishly, walking toward the exit. Then he turned to wave.

"Olivia, can you come in here for a minute?" her boss yelled.

"I'll be right there."

She lifted the lid of the box to look inside again. The smell of fresh varnish filled her nostrils. "Hello, you beauty," she told the instrument. Using her desk scissors she carefully removed the address label from the outside of the box.

"I have something to show you," Olivia called to her boss. She walked into his office, holding up the instrument for him to see.

"What is that?" His face held surprise.

She explained, "An autoharp. My friend in Lily Rock gave it to me."

"Lily Rock? I've never heard of—"

"If you have a minute, I'll play for you." Olivia sat in a nearby chair, running her fingers over the strings. "This one is called 'Wildwood Mountain.' Ever heard of it?"

She inhaled, then her clear voice rose above the hum of the air conditioner. With the purity of a songbird, Olivia Greer sang. The voice of an angel filled the room as tears filled the eyes of her boss. Olivia sang as only she could, as her mother had taught her.

I'll call Sage tomorrow. It's been long enough. Maybe we can pick up where we left off, and one day, I'll return to Lily Rock.

Continue the series with *Influenced to Death*

Chapter One

On the way to their campsite, Sage greeted people while Olivia kept her eyes cast to the dirt pathway. Consumed with her own thoughts, she heard Sage yell from behind, "Olivia, your cell!"

Reaching into her back pocket, Olivia looked at her screen. Meadow McCloud. Why didn't she ping her daughter instead? Olivia tapped redial, and Meadow's voice filled her ear.

"Olivia, I'm glad you called me back. I have some difficult news."

Olivia froze in her spot, the toe of her boot digging into the dirt. Since the sun had gone down, her cell phone was the only light to illuminate her stricken face. "What is it, Meadow?" She struggled to keep the panic from her voice. What if something happened to Michael or M&M?

"It's your house, dear," answered Meadow.

Olivia took in one quick breath. Frequent fires made all Lily Rock residents anxious. Has the house burned down? Olivia had hefty fire insurance on her house. Michael had advised her to get a reliable policy as soon as she inherited the property.

"You will feel a lot more secure," he'd said, pushing a stray piece of hair from her face before quickly removing his hand.

Michael did not insist. She had to give him that.

"What's wrong with the house?" she asked Meadow, doing her best to sound calm.

"Oh my, I am so sorry to have to tell you this." Meadow's voice got slower, her words coming out one by one with a small pause in between.

I bet this is the voice she uses to tell children stories at the library, all soft and calm. Olivia's impatience got the better of her.

"Is the house on fire, Meadow?" she insisted. "Just tell me right out, okay?"

"Oh, no. Your house is not on fire. It's intact. I called about your renter. What was her name again?"

Olivia searched her brain. The renter paid on time, with an automatic deduction. Olivia arranged the lease over the phone in a hurry nearly a year ago, and so far she'd had no trouble. What's her name again?

"I think her name was Lana something. Let me think. I know! Her name is Lana de Carlos. Sorry, I forgot for a second. She pays with an automatic deposit."

"I understand a brief lapse in memory. In fact, I have an herb blend with Ginkgo—"

Olivia interrupted, "I'll talk to you about that later, Meadow. What happened to Lana?"

"Oh, right. Lana. That's why I called. Well, Olivia, it seems that one of our Lily Rock residents found her dead, right on the doorstep of your house, just a couple of hours ago."

Olivia squeezed the phone in her hand as her legs began to tremble. Another dead body at Marla's old house?

She felt Sage's arm around her shoulder. "What's the matter?" Glancing down at the screen, Sage hissed. "What does my mother want?" She took the phone from Olivia's shaking hand, holding it to her cheek.

"Mom, it's me. What's going on?" Sage listened and then said, "Olivia looks like she's seen a ghost. Tell me what I should do."

By the time Sage clicked the phone off, Olivia had sat in the dirt, her knees pulled to her chest. "It's happened again. Another dead body. What is wrong with me? Am I attracting all of this death for some reason?"

Sage leaned over to sit in the dirt next to Olivia. "Of course not. You weren't even in town when it happened. Not like last time." Both young women huddled together for a few minutes, letting the news sink in.

Swallowing down her emotions, Olivia stood up on wobbly legs and dusted off the seat of her pants. She considered her next words carefully. "Does this mean I have to return to Lily Rock?"

End of Sample
To continue reading Influenced to Death, pick up a copy at your favorite retailer.

ABOUT THE AUTHOR

Born and raised in Los Angeles, Bonnie Hardy is a former teacher, choir director, and preacher. She lives with her husband and two dogs in Southern California.

Bonnie has published in *Christian Century*, *Presence: an International Journal for Spiritual Direction*, and with Pilgrim Press.

When not planting flowers and baking cookies, she can be found at her computer plotting her next Lily Rock mystery.

You can follow Bonnie at
bonniehardywrites.com
and on Instagram @bonniehardywrites.

facebook.com/bonniehardywrites

instagram.com/bonniehardywrites

goodreads.com/bonniehardy

bookbub.com/authors/bonnie-hardy

amazon.com/author/bonniehardy